WORLD
SHIFTER

WORLD SHIFTER

ECLIPSE BOOK TWO

Lindsay French

Podium

WORLD
SHIFTER

CHAPTER ONE

A year ago, after I fought and won the hardest battle of my life, I longed in vain for the respite of peace.

So much changed after I killed the Prophet of the Valley, and not in the ways I hoped.

Screams ripped apart the usual quiet of the small village, echoing through the dirt streets and against stone houses peeking from the face of the hills. The wails of villagers converged with my disorientation from teleporting into a splitting headache. I traveled here the moment I received the alert of a demon attack, and yet I still arrived to guttural sobbing that told me all I needed to know.

The demon had already taken lives.

The cries of those left behind testified to yet another loss I could not prevent and shredded my heart with fury.

Enough.

My body bolted forward on instinct, seeking out the feel of the attacker's power, rushing toward the screams. My mind trailed behind, though, distant from the violence that flooded the Valley after the death of its tyrannical leader.

For a surreal moment as I ran past the blur of homes, the horizon that spread beyond the hills stole my attention. With the sky thin and blue, the Mountain of the Gods looked like clouds faintly frosting the distance. Nothing in this world was ever as it seemed. Freeing our people from a cruel reign didn't bring about peace. That called for a war of its own. One I had no idea how to fight, apart from tirelessly battling anyone who threatened my people.

So I traveled across the Valley, day after day, hour after hour, destroying the countless opportunistic threats that flooded our small piece of the world in the vacuum of power left behind.

"Eclipse!" A woman I didn't recognize shrieked my name. "She came! We're saved."

"This way!" A man pointed to the east. "Hurry."

I sensed a flicker of power, no more noticeable than the warmth of burning embers. Twisting, I skidded to a stop at the door of a home just as it slammed open against the outer wall.

The stocky man who jumped out swelled with power now, exuding so much that I was shocked I didn't recognize him. With the demon-hunting Prophet dead, all those who previously avoided the Valley mistakenly considered the area free game. After fighting so many enemies, I thought I'd come to know everyone worth remembering. My allies helped in the efforts as much as possible, but since only I mastered the manipulation of space-time, no one else traveled like I did, and so I'd been the one to face almost every demon.

Had he come from faraway lands? The Skia Hellig Peninsula carved low into the ocean, with the mountains serving as a natural barrier against the north. We were small compared to our neighbors who amassed territories and kingdoms much larger than any people in our isolated land. I feared even worse threats from beyond the mountains may sweep through not only the Valley, but all of Skia Hellig.

Wind drove a blade of dirt through the air and blasted me. I raised a shield, but the gust still shoved me back toward the house behind me. This man most certainly traveled into the peninsula. I would have heard about attacks like these before.

The demon sprang forward while I slid across the dirt. He whipped his sword above his head and wind swirled about the blade in a dark twist of dirt, like a tornado.

His tricks might have impressed me if I allowed them to. He didn't deserve an ounce of admiration after he hurt these people, though, and I didn't have time to waste fighting him. This needed to end fast.

Glowing tendrils of emerald-green power swirled about my hands and materialized into an energy bow. With a careful aim, I drew back like I held a real bowstring and shot an arrow of energy through the air. It pierced the cyclone surrounding the demon's blade right as the tip of his sword struck my shield. Shaping my power into weapons familiar to me and relying on muscle memory greatly enhanced my combat abilities.

My arrow skidded across his weapon and ripped open the meaty flesh of his palm. His power scattered in a hazy mist and a cloud of dust. The demon screamed as he jerked his hurt hand from the hilt of his sword, now holding the blade with only his left one.

I jerked the fool closer with my power and bashed his face against my shield. His body trembled with exertion as he shoved his forearms against the barrier to escape me.

"Who are you?" I shoved him back and rammed him against the shield again. Energy sparked from the impact. "What do you want with this village?"

When he didn't answer, I raised my energy bow once again and aimed an arrow directly at his throat. Blood trickled from his nose and made his round eyes look wild.

Rage filled me at his silence. Not only had this fool crossed into territory under my protection, but he'd interrupted an important battle. At this very moment, Flatlanders and the demons they'd contracted attacked our border, intent on taking back land they claimed the Prophet of the Valley once stole. Even though Piercey promised me he'd watch over Nash, and I knew our allies could manage without me, I absolutely hated leaving them.

Most days had been like this since I killed the Prophet. Eskel the Ruthless had lorded over his piece of Skia Hellig and brought terror to those who dared to defy him. There had been order in his cruelty, however. His death had ushered in the swift dissolution of that unjust but absolute authority.

For every person enjoying their newfound freedom, another in the Valley suffered the sudden loss of security, a burden that heaped upon my shoulders like I alone carried the weight of the Valley's fight for survival.

The desperation and anger erupted from me in a roar. "Tell me."

"I don't answer to you." Blood marred his scowling, broken lips.

"You do when I hold your life in my hands."

"You alone decide my fate? How are you any better than the Prophet, then?"

The energy coursing through my bow and arrow pulsed in time with the anger that quickened my heartbeat.

His nostrils twitched. "This village was safe before you came along and killed the Prophet, you know."

"No," I said. "It was safe until you showed up and killed an innocent person. Don't blame me for your sins."

"You know it wouldn't have happened if Eskel still reigned. You know that to keep the demons out, you'll have to become him. Silencing me with your bow will not change the truth."

I shifted my aim and shot the energy through the base of his ribs on his left side, then swiftly fired another through his thigh. He collapsed on the ground and reached for the arrows sizzling with fiery green energy. Blood oozed around the melted skin. His howls rang out as loud as the villagers' wailing.

Looming over him, I spoke in a low growl. "You think it's your silence I want?" I placed the heel of my boot against his sternum. "Let the people hear your screams. Let the Valley hear what happens to those who take innocent lives."

"You're . . . no . . . better . . ."

"I don't care what I am. You're banished from this Valley. Return and I'll kill you."

I covered his eyes with my hand, focusing on the code Piercey had created to tag and track our enemies. Part of me believed I should just kill him, but I already wielded so much power. I did not want the authority to unilaterally sentence anyone to death. If an enemy fell to my blade, I had no qualms, but I'd stopped this man while his heart still beat.

Perhaps Piercey had tangled too deeply in my mind when we connected last year.

"What are you doing?" The demon's voice trembled.

Without answering, I transported both of us to the coast, far away from the closest village, to a small shack that housed enough supplies for him to journey elsewhere.

"This is the only mercy I will ever show you." I held his stare. "Stay away from my people or you will die. If you even take one step into the Valley, I will immediately travel to you and crush you."

He trembled, pale from blood loss and fear. "It's really true. No one can have this much power. You stole it from the sun during the eclipse."

"I'm going to check on you. There is nowhere in this world far enough away from me for you to run. If you continue to hurt the innocent, I'll kill you."

By his wide eyes, I knew he believed me.

"Bandage your wounds before you die." I glared at him one final time before returning to the village.

I found where the villagers had gathered, and stopped beside their chief. A man lay unmoving with the scarlet stripe across his throat brightly contrasting the dust dulling the rest of his body. The family of the slain man knelt around his corpse and wept. Their cries would echo in my heart forever, like the others.

"I'm sorry," I said. "I was too late."

"It was me." The chief lowered his head. "I didn't raise the alarm in time."

"This should never have happened in the first place."

He turned to me, the low-hanging sun reflecting as red in his eyes. "You're not a god." Despite the grief etched into his tight expression, conviction burned in that stare. "You cannot expect to save us all."

I couldn't talk about this. With a stiff dip of my head, I said, "Please give my condolences to the family. I'm needed in battle."

"Be safe, Eclipse."

That name had once been uttered only as a curse or whispered in terror. It had once been rumors of the demon who slayed an entire village. For the first time, some spoke it for a different reason, with reverence instead of hate.

I wanted to ask him to call me by my name. I was Max the Sharpshooter, not the demon Eclipse. Only a sharpshooter could not make the people of this village feel safe again. They needed something more.

I fought against gods and Prophets alike for this Valley and for these people. If they needed me to be Eclipse, so be it.

Let Eclipse be the last word uttered by those who threatened my people.

My heart remained with the grieving family, torn with them, as I returned to the battlefield with my comrades.

I landed right beside Nash, drawn to him, as always. Sweat slunk down the side of his face and wet the collar of his tunic, his swords already swinging for the enemy as he charged with our fellow warriors. Piercey's power coated his twin blades in a red sheen, lending Nash energy just like when we'd first fought the Prophet's disciples last year.

I launched into a sprint for the Flatlanders, no longer needing a few seconds to adjust to my surroundings after teleporting. War pulsed in my heart and drove my body without thought.

I didn't have time to tell Nash about what happened at the village. Even if I had, it wasn't necessary. Our eyes met and I was certain he knew by the grief in mine that we had lost someone in that village, just as I knew from his solemn nod he wanted to assure me it only mattered that we helped those we could. That, as the chief said, I couldn't save everyone.

I refused to accept that. Didn't know how even if I wanted to.

I would take back this Valley for the innocent just as I'd taken back this world from the gods.

A Flatlander commander whirled her sword toward Nash. I aimed my energy bow at the enemy warrior when out of the corner of my eye, I noticed a familiar form. His image appeared like a flash and then vanished, but it looked just like Piercey watching me from the right. Except I knew my friend actually stood directly behind us as he always did when he guarded Nash, so that they could battle as one. Glancing behind myself, I found my friend in his usual spot with his palms raised toward Nash. Definitely not at the edge of the battlefield.

My mind must have been playing tricks on me.

It unsettled me as I released my first energy arrow and focused on the enemies rushing at us.

CHAPTER TWO

Wind gusted against my back and whipped the blond plaits of my hair to the side as I scattered energy arrows high into the air. Their arcing path burned green through the sky and then pelted the dozens of demons we battled. Over a year ago, the Flatlanders began secretly working with demons, just like the Prophet of the Valley, and unleashed them on our camp the night Leif almost died. Now, the Flatlander alliance of demons swelled into a small army, forcing us to recruit Piercey's graduates and seek out others with power to help us.

While many enemies tried attacking the Valley, such as the coastal and mountain Prophets, the Flatlanders alone persisted in returning to our lands. Each time, we fought until we regained any lost ground, no matter the cost. This unyielding approach deterred some invaders, though our spies frequently sent reports that talk of conquest never ceased. Theus, the Prophet of the Flatlands, remained unflinching in his obsession to twist the death of our Prophet into an opportunity to steal our villages for himself.

That, paired with the random demon attacks upon villages all over the Valley, overwhelmed and exhausted me without end. I missed the simplicity of battling alongside Wren and Leif for our village when protecting our entire region felt so impossible. They hated not being able to join me, but Piercey couldn't lend his power to everyone, and Nash absolutely refused to stay behind. Early on, he'd convinced Piercey to fight alongside him as they did once before, and there'd been no going back.

Nash refused to allow his lack of power to keep him from my side at the front lines of this war.

Though I fought the tactic at first, I eventually admitted its brilliance. Piercey and Nash worked so efficiently together that it seemed as if they shared a neural connection. They complemented one another well. Nash lacked power, and Piercey a warrior's constitution. Together, they made an incredible team.

My dear friend guarded Nash and strengthened each thrust of his blade instantly, as if Nash used the power himself. Glancing at Nash as he stabbed into the bicep of a demon, I feared that one day someone with power would seek retribution at a time when he didn't have one of us to protect him. These concerns, of course, never swayed him. I couldn't blame him for his stubbornness either. Nothing would stop me from fighting this war.

We no longer bothered arguing about it, not just because I wouldn't dishonor Nash by telling him not to battle, but also because during the rare times I did ask him to stay behind, he quickly reminded me that we'd killed the Prophet together. That he carried the guilt and responsibility as much as I did. My stubborn heart struggled to accept sharing that burden with him.

Despite my worries, I did love fighting at his side.

A demon hurled a wave of energy at us that I blocked with my shield. Nash, trusting me implicitly to defend against the attack, never hesitated, but instead rushed the man. With the strength of Piercey's power enhancing his attack, Nash slashed his blades across the demon's chest. I followed up with an arrow right into our enemy's heart.

The tightness in my muscles tried to slow me down as I fired an arrow at another target. Fatigue wove like vines between every strand of muscle in my body and strangled me from the inside out. Through training and war, I soared beyond limits previously unimaginable, and yet no matter how strong I became, I still eventually ran out of energy. I could finish this battle quicker by teleporting around the field to strike our enemies, if only that power didn't drain my energy so severely. My chronic sleep-deprivation only worsened this problem. I needed to reserve enough for emergency transport. That meant fighting the old-fashioned way, with sword against sword, or my arrows flying through the air.

Truthfully, the most effective war we fought right now was not the spilling of blood, but that of the political arena. We needed leadership in the Valley to protect our people and organize our war parties. Piercey somehow stayed optimistic about creating a better system of governance than the Prophets. I simply wanted to avoid another Eskel the Ruthless. We needed someone we trusted to take his place and we needed it soon, because right now, I stood in the vacuum of power.

The calls for me to lead as Prophet grew louder with each passing day, even though it made no sense for me to leave behind the battlefield to govern the Valley. I cringed each time the people called for Eclipse to reign.

Just because I'd wound up playing the guardian of our land didn't mean I needed to be appointed as some Prophet. I didn't have time for politics between training and war. I thought Piercey would have been a suitable candidate, except he always scoffed and reminded me that the people didn't cry out his name. For every enemy I'd made—and there were countless—I'd also gained steadfast followers.

The frustration churned inside of me as I fought. I didn't want to lead the Valley and, if these people actually knew me, they wouldn't want me to either. They'd understand I was just a warrior.

Instead, they only saw the myth of Eclipse.

I knocked a demon back with a kick to the chest and forced her further away with a flash of power. She threw two daggers at me as she flew backward, but Nash knocked them from the air with his swords. I gathered my energy bow. Shot the glowing arrow through the woman's left eye.

Blood spurted.

Careful to reserve my energy, I fought strategically with my comrades until the remaining demons retreated. Some of Piercey's graduates moved for the wounded, but I shook my head.

"Tag them and leave them. Their people will return for them."

We held our captives at the Sacred School in old classrooms redesigned as cells, but we struggled to find the manpower to deal with powerful demons. Either we killed the injured or released them, and I figured I'd killed enough people for one day. It wasn't honorable to kill a warrior who lacked the strength to stand anyway. Our people considered it cowardly, a sign that we feared our enemy's return so much that we needed to resort to finishing them off when the battle had already ended.

Piercey's people didn't know our customs. They came from all over the world to the Sacred School. Fortunately, they often accepted our ways rather than arguing.

Nash leaned against his knees and nodded. Neither one of us had slept in almost twenty-four hours.

"Are you hurt?" I asked.

"No. Just winded. You?"

"Same." The anguish of the villagers returned to my mind. "We lost one," I said, voice as hollow as my chest felt. I turned my eyes to the darkening sky.

"I could tell." Nash straightened and drew me to his side. "Let's go home. The others can manage the rest of this."

I nodded but didn't transport us yet. "If you could do it again, would you?"

Even though I didn't say it—that I feared killing the Prophet had been a mistake—Nash knew what I asked.

He didn't hesitate. "Yes."

Once the pain might have forced tears into my eyes, but I'd traveled long past the point of crying. I didn't even need to try to keep my voice strong. "I would, too. I just didn't know what it would cost to kill Dr. Henderson and the Prophet. I suppose that was mercy at the time, not seeing all the pain ahead."

Dr. Drake's knowing eyes stared back at me in my memory. She'd said she'd been here before. In my fury, I'd refused to listen to her in the slightest, thinking she'd evolved too far beyond the chaos of my vengeance to understand what I needed to do.

Perhaps it had not been disappointment so much as anticipatory grief she'd felt for me. Because she must have known what kind of war I'd unleashed upon the Valley. Upon myself and Nash.

I needed to leave it behind on the battlefield to embrace peace at home. The energy it took to teleport both of us back to the Sacred School left me heavy and weak. My arms trembled as I unstrapped my armor in our living room. Too exhausted to actually put it away, I let it fall to the ground. Nash did the same.

I looked at the bedroom, but then slid down the wall onto the ground, holding my side. My entire body ached and sharp pain gnawed at my ribs. In all the battles, I'd lost track of where the pain even came from. Too many hits to keep track of minor injuries. How long had it been since I'd gone a full day with no fighting?

Nash's eyes barely stayed open as he looked at me on the floor. I thought he might tell me that it was ridiculous to not simply walk into the bedroom, only he settled beside me and pulled me into his warmth.

I couldn't have taken another step.

"You know how a week ago we said we wouldn't make it without a break?" Nash's voice hummed low and quiet from fatigue. "We're past that point."

"I know."

"How close are others to learning to teleport?"

I shook my head, disheartened to even think about it. "No one, so far."

"Damn it."

Nash always traveled with me when I received an alert from a villager, unless he was already in battle. He shared my exhaustion.

"You should start staying home sometimes," I said. "At least one of us—"

"I'm not discussing this with you again." Nash opened his eyes only long enough to narrow them at me. "We fight together. If I'm not already in battle, I'm going with you."

"Elsie needs more time with you."

Guilt darkened his expression. I felt it, too. We needed time to truly start our life together.

"It could be years of this, Nash."

"I see her every day."

"Not quality time."

He clasped my hand and drew it to his chest. "Let's fight after we sleep."

I managed to smile. "You really want to sleep here?"

But he was already drifting off, mumbling slurred words. "Just rest . . ."

I loved the way he looked when he first fell asleep, when peace relaxed his expression and body, and he left himself vulnerable and unguarded. Left himself for only me. I drew upon enough strength to crane my neck and softly kiss his whiskered jaw.

Nash's palm slid over my side, his arm heavy. I wanted to cherish lying in his arms and soaking up his peace, only soon sleep would take us both. There was never enough time. Never. We lived at a sprint and wrestled for any moments alone like this.

Sleeping near one another would suffice. I dreamed of more, though. What could be if only we had the time.

Something needed to change. Like the village chief said, I was not a god. Maybe once we found leadership for the Valley and helped the people to become stronger on their own, we could step back from war long enough to really rest. Or even live. Imagine that.

I closed my eyes, struggling to fall asleep despite my exhaustion. I just felt so unsettled. It wasn't only the death in the village or the long stretch of battles without a break. No, it was that flicker I'd seen after teleporting back to my comrades.

"Something strange happened today," I said, not even sure if Nash was awake to hear me. "I told myself it was my eyes playing tricks on me. I'm not so sure." He was definitely asleep. His breathing deepened. "I felt his power . . . the man who looked like Piercey . . ."

My eyes slid closed.

I didn't know what it meant. Even though I wanted to brush off such a brief glimmer, I couldn't. I couldn't afford to ignore any threats.

CHAPTER THREE

When I killed the Prophet of the Valley, two of his disciples immediately vied for power. This had split the Prophet's loyalists between them, and forced their focus on each other, which left the most power hungry vulnerable. Despite my initial plans to kill them, I didn't need to raise a finger to handle either disciple. The Flatlanders and their demons took care of that, while the race for taking power overwhelmed the Valley.

Even though the turmoil left us without a leader, we bonded together to fashion the order we needed to survive. The village chiefs and elders turned to one another, along with great commanders and warriors who vowed their lives to the protection of the Valley. The problem in our world, though, was that it didn't take very many people with neural chips to cause chaos.

That created this exhausting situation where I policed the entire Valley. I needed someone else to learn to teleport.

So, even though ordinarily I carved out time between battles to either rest or train—considering I rarely managed a full night's sleep—today I chose, instead, to visit the students of the Sacred School.

Nash traveled in my place to a council meeting where the heads of the major villages in the Valley congregated to fight their own manner of battle— the political one that I wanted nothing to do with, but understood might end this chaotic war. I was happy to have an excuse not to attend. Even though I planned to periodically visit the students and help with their training, I'd been far too busy. I hadn't even met this new group that had started studying five months ago.

I joined Piercey and his students in one of the largest training rooms for our long overdue meeting. Thirty or so students gathered before me in three orderly rows.

The students whispered as I walked across the room behind Piercey. One girl whispered, "Eclipse."

I tightened my jaw. "My name is Max." When I stopped walking, they all straightened, like I'd suddenly issued the command to do so. "Max the Sharpshooter. Don't call me Eclipse within these walls."

"Yes, ma'am," one of the students shouted.

"I don't have time to waste, so I'm going to be direct." I glanced from one end of the row to the other. Growing up at this school, we always attended class with similarly aged students. Now Piercey recruited people of all ages from around the entire world. "If others can't learn how to teleport, then we're all screwed. We have warriors. We need travelers. That's why I'm here today, because you're failing at our most important task, and I need you to stop. Get better."

Piercey subtly shifted to look at me, but I ignored his silent chastisement.

"Raise your hand if you're studying teleportation," I said.

Every student lifted theirs, which surprised me, because I'd always learned to focus on my natural talents first, and I doubted all these people were gifted with time and space manipulation.

"Well, most of you are wasting your time," I said. "Who actually shows promise?" More than a dozen hands raised eagerly. "Yeah, put your hands down." I walked closer and scrutinized their faces for any sign of either confidence or the self-consciousness of someone with an unrealized talent. "If you actually have the potential to learn this, raise your hand back up."

The students all peered at one another until finally three lifted their hands. I ignored them and instead watched a younger student who looked like he mentally wrestled with a powerful demon.

"You." I pointed at him. "Why didn't you raise your hand?"

Shocked eyes met mine. "I, well, I suck."

"Obviously. You all suck. That's not what I asked. I asked if you had potential with teleportation. Raise your hand, kid. I can tell by the look on your face that you're debating whether you should, which means you should."

Beside me Piercey nodded a confirmation, and the teen lifted his hand while he averted his eyes.

"Anyone else?" I asked my friend.

"I'd say this is accurate for this skill. Although . . ." Piercey leveled his look at a man at the end of the line who proudly held both hands raised. "I'm not quite sure he should be lifting his hands so high."

I snorted and turned my attention back to the students. "I need someone to respond to emergency alerts from the villagers. I'm expending too much energy and spending too much time responding to every crisis. This is now a top priority, because it's distracting me from the larger war for this Valley." Their faces looked serious as I spoke. Good. "I know many of you are not from this Valley, but please know that anyone who helps us defend this land will always have a home with us. We will send you back to your own people well equipped for whatever you face there. For now, while you're our students, we need your help."

I eased back and surveyed the students one last time.

"Okay." I clapped. "Those of you who raised your hands, you start studying privately with the director in the evening. When I'm available, I will train you myself."

"Yes, ma'am," the four students said together. So strange to hear them call me that, because one of them was definitely much older than me.

"You can call me Sharpshooter, Max, anything but Eclipse or ma'am."

"What about Commander?" The overly confident thirty-something year old man asked.

Commander. I didn't mind that. "That will do."

Piercey smiled. "Alright, back to training. Max, I'll meet you outside."

I left for the courtyard to wait for Piercey. Warmth from the climate control and the aromatic scent of flowers fooled me into forgetting the Sacred School sat perched upon the tallest mountain peak in Skia Hellig. The soft, manicured grass and towering oak tree always filled my chest with comfort. As a child, this had been a haven for me and my old friend. When I returned from the afterlife, I reunited with my loved ones here. Between battles and training, we often played with Elsie on the soft lawn. A deep breath filled my chest and spread deep into my stomach as peace.

"If we hurry, we can catch the end of the council meeting." Piercey started talking to me before I even turned around to see him.

I ignored him and raised both brows. "Tell me about that one kid. He can do it, can't he? I can just feel it."

"I hope so. It worries me that no one has been remotely successful."

"This one reminds me of you with the lack of confidence but obvious talent."

"Thanks, I guess," he uttered with a chuckle.

"It will take time, but one day he's going to do it. What's his name?"

"Asmund."

"Asmund . . . I'll keep my eye on him." I sighed, thinking about the council meeting. "I guess we should go, huh?"

Piercey nodded. "One of the graduates reached out to me through our neural connection. The council is discussing Valley leadership today."

"Do they want that one guy? The badass commander who loves to give speeches?"

"Yeah, but there's also the politician."

I rubbed my arm, disappointed at the lack of contenders. "Neither one of them can lead this Valley. The commander, Markus, he's a great leader, but he's not gathering enough support. If he hasn't by now, he won't. The other cannot even wield a sword. No one will ever accept him."

"I know. We need someone who will not be mad with power, but also can stand up against the threats we face."

"We just have to keep searching," I said. "I'm nervous to look beyond the Valley because they won't be committed to our people the same way, but we're running out of candidates."

Piercey tilted his head and raised his brows in an annoyingly knowing look.

"Don't." I jabbed my finger at him.

"I didn't."

"You did. You gave me a look."

"You're giving me a look now."

I groaned and smacked my fist against my palm. "I cannot lead these people, Piercey."

"You already are. You're single-handedly protecting the villages. Just your name is enough to keep most threats out of the Valley. Who better than you? Max, you died for these people."

That heavy feeling hung in my chest again. "That's why I can't. How am I supposed to protect people if I'm busy playing politics?"

Piercey lifted his hand. "You don't have to play politics. You'd have a council. You just have to step up as the head."

"No." I shouted the word with my fists tightened at my sides like a child, but it didn't matter if I sounded juvenile. The talk of this tangled me with so much panic I wanted to run from the room. "I already have to worry about Elsie and Nash. You and the others. I saw what dying did to everyone. How could I ever go into battle knowing a whole Valley of people needs me to live?"

"Oh, Max." My friend's expression softened. "You don't realize that it's already happened, do you?"

The heaviness and the panic collided like an explosion of dread. I closed my eyes and refused to let the thoughts play through my mind. Refused to sacrifice any precious time to fear. "It just can't be me."

"Okay." Piercey softly clasped my arms. "Okay, I'm sorry. You are leading this Valley, though, so you need to find someone who can do this better than you. Until then, the people will reject whoever tries to take your place."

I crossed my arms and looked to the tree where Piercey and I used to sit. Back then, I begged him to escape with me, convinced we'd find everything we wanted somewhere away from this mountain. "I miss when our world was as small as this courtyard."

"You do not," Piercey said. "You hated it."

"I didn't know any better then."

"Whatever. Let's get out of here. We need to go size up those potential leaders." Piercey backed up a step. "Let me get my bag and then I'll be ready. Don't leave without me."

He jogged to the door and disappeared. Who knew when I mastered teleporting that I was really volunteering to taxi everyone around Skia Hellig. So wonderful.

Something flickered from the corner of my eye again. Before I could even question it, a man materialized beside me.

My heart stilled in my chest. Piercey's deep brown eyes looked into mine even though he just ran back inside.

"Max," he said.

Breath fled my lungs and the courtyard seemed to start slowly spinning. I stared at him, unable to breathe or think or feel.

Even as I grappled with the undeniable sight, I couldn't accept it as reality. His hair lay against his shoulders in long dreads while a full beard darkened his face. How the hell could that be when Piercey kept his hair buzzed and face shaved? He hadn't worn dreads since we were kids.

"I need your help." His serious eyes met mine. "I'm sorry for startling you."

The Piercey look-alike raised his hand, just like my friend always did, and though they shared the same voice, this man held an edge to his I didn't recognize. A look in his eye that didn't quite match up.

"You're in shock," he said. "It's like when you came back from the dead and didn't know how to soften it for your friends. There's really nothing I can do except show up."

If he didn't look and sound—feel—identical to my friend, I might have blasted him with enough power to incapacitate him. My instinct screamed *threat* because this was anything but normal.

A gasp ripped me from my stupor. I drew my energy bow and readied an arrow, aiming at the ground, because I couldn't bring myself to point it at Piercey.

"Explain." I clenched my teeth to cover how my voice wavered. Swallowed down the knot in my throat. "Right now."

"I don't have much time before your friend comes back. Come with me and we can talk."

"Come with you?" I shifted the bow slightly higher. "Hell no."

"Please. You're more powerful than I am. You can kick my ass."

"That doesn't mean it's a good idea to go with you."

"Max." This stranger who looked so much like Piercey reached his hand out to me. "I'm begging you."

It might have been my own arrogance in my abilities, or my stupidity, or my naivety, or the fact that I couldn't help trusting Piercey, but I shocked myself by grabbing his hand. Maybe I was just this desperate to break the cycle of fighting in the Valley that I foolishly hoped help arrived in the form of a friend. "You better not—"

A terrible ripping force spread throughout my body and cut off my words, threatening to pry my skin from my body. To shred each strand of muscle and separate each bead of blood. To rip me apart one cell at a time.

Right when I fully expected death to seize me, it all stopped.

I opened my eyes to bright sun and an endless field spreading out all around me. Stumbling back from this long-haired Piercey, I gasped for breath.

"I'm sorry," he said. "I didn't have time to warn you. I felt him coming. It would have been too shocking for him to see me."

I hardly heard what he said. "Where are we?"

"Before you panic, I want you to know that time is relative between each simulation. You won't lose any time back in the courtyard with Piercey. When I send you back, it'll be like you never left. There's no risk of missing any demon—"

"What the fuck are you talking about?" No matter how hard I breathed, air refused to reach my lungs. My mind couldn't process a single thing he said, especially not some Piercey diatribe about time relativity. "Tell me where we are."

He quieted for a moment. "We're in my world."

I leaned forward, feeling like a strong weight dragged me to the ground. "You mean—"

"Not your world."

My stomach lurched. I leaned against my knees, but just as quickly as the sickness came, it morphed into rage. I jolted back up and Piercey sprang backward, hands covering his face.

"Stay calm," he said. "I'll explain. I'm on your side."

"Then explain!"

"Okay. Okay. You know that the gods run experiments on other simulated realities."

My mind finally started to fill in the gaps. No, no, no. How many times would this happen to me? How many times could reality unravel before I lost my mind forever?

"You knew there were other worlds." His voice sounded as gentle as when my friend Piercey wanted to comfort me. "You just didn't know they were filled with your people." He smiled sympathetically. "It's us in every world, Max. They uploaded the same consciousness every time."

The truth of what he said resonated deeply within me, as undeniable as seeing Piercey's image in the courtyard, or even the flicker of him on the battlefield. I'd seen other versions of myself and Nash from our previous lives when Dr. Henderson reset our simulation. This wasn't new to me. Not the difference in hair and look, nor any of the subtle changes to our person.

I was looking at Piercey. A Piercey born in another world to another experiment. It made sense. If the gods wanted our worlds for the data, then they'd use controls. Why not use the same people in every experiment? I should have thought of this before.

My mind still could not grasp it.

I turned around, dizzy and overwhelmed. Knowing that we'd lived multiple lives in our world hurt badly enough. Now I knew that there were copies of me in other worlds. What did that even mean? Was the Max in this world still me? Or were we completely different people because we'd lived different lives in different worlds?

How had this Piercey learned to travel to my world when my Piercey couldn't even travel across the Sacred School? And how did he know so much about me?

I turned back to him, dizzy from questions. "I need to hear everything."

Just when I thought I was finally putting my world back together after Dr. Henderson, everything fell apart again.

CHAPTER FOUR

I'd learned in the white room while subjected to Dr. Henderson's cruel revelations that shock and disorientation hurt like physical pain. Staring at this stranger who looked and sounded exactly like my dear friend, Piercey—who literally shared a copy of his consciousness—flooded me with enough disbelief to choke on. It carved sharp chills down my spine.

"I know in my world," he said, "you need to see, or you'll just get frustrated. I know how you are."

"See what?" I asked.

He withdrew crude-looking binoculars from a side pouch on his tunic and passed them to me. Though we stood in an empty field, I noticed a small village to the east where smoke rose from dozens of homes, and what looked like training grounds to the west. If I squinted, I managed to make out the small forms of people milling about. I couldn't decipher many details from here, but the land looked vacant. If I had to guess, the village likely served to take care of whoever trained here.

I lifted the binoculars to see targets and dummies littering one area of the training ground while a large section provided space for sparring. Dozens of people trained now, not just with weapons, but with power. I let out an exasperated sigh. "I've seen this plenty—"

Long dark curls floated like a halo around a tall man's head as he hovered in the air. Corded arms glistened with sweat. A strong jaw closed tight in effort. Amber eyes shone with the sun.

Nash levitated in the field.

I dropped the binoculars and clutched my fist to the mouth.

The stranger behind me waited patiently for me to digest all these shocks.

"He has power?" I asked.

"We all do. Every single person in this world."

I'd only ever known one Nash. My Nash. In every life we'd lived, we'd found one another. This man was a stranger, though. He belonged to a different world, and if he'd ever met a version of me, he also belonged to a different Max. Panic thumped in my chest.

"That's the experiment here?" I picked the binoculars back up but didn't look through them again, too disoriented to see another version of Nash again. "The gods want to know what happens if everyone has a neural implant?"

"Yes. It's the counterpart to your world where only one percent received the quantum powers."

It was so surreal, not because it didn't make sense, but because the two worlds felt like double vision. My mind struggled to hold the two at once. I couldn't even find words for all the questions flooding my mind.

"Who are you?" I asked and faced him again. "How did you find my world?"

"My name is Elias." His voice, though soft, came out smoothly and matter-of-fact. "I'm a technology officer for one of the largest guilds in our world. My specialty brought me to you."

Despite the differences I latched onto to force myself to recognize that this man was not actually Piercey, the similarities overwhelmed me.

"That means a whole lot of nothing to me," I said. "Technology officer? For a guild? Does that mean you work on computers?"

"It's more than that. In your world, so few people have power that you're all forced into combat. The few who don't fight end up serving the strong. Here, we all can find our true path. We're all working to master our power and develop a much deeper knowledge of its potential than in your world. I know that Piercey is not much of a warrior but still had to learn how to fight. I've never trained in any style of combat."

I blinked. "You can't fight at all?"

"No. I use my neural implant to interface with technology and stretch the boundaries of what we currently know how to do. It's like when Piercey taught you how to hack into the afterlife."

Suspicion nipped at me, but I couldn't bring myself to feel distrusting of another version of my friend. "You really do know everything."

"I've dug deeply into these worlds of ours. I haven't gotten my hands on everything, but I broke into a great deal of data that's been compiled. There's a wealth of information about you since you're allowing the gods to watch over you."

It was strange for him to know so much about me, and yet, not at all when I'd connected to share all my experiences with Piercey in my world. "Tell me more about your guild and how your work with them led you to my world."

"It's complicated. Our guilds are so competitive. Originally, they started out as groups of people who joined together to focus on specific trades. Guilds grew into much more based on necessity. In your world, the few dominate the many. Not so here. At least, not so for individuals. When everyone wields power, more people can defend themselves, but more people can also fight. True power here comes from coalitions."

"Piercey would love that," I said.

"In theory, he would. In practice, it's problematic. The combined strength of larger guilds overpowers smaller ones. But it's not always about might here. Plenty of specialties and trades are just as important as combat. That's why it's guilds and not armies that have become such an integral component of our society. It's also why we push ourselves so hard to innovate."

I glanced over to where the man who looked just like Nash trained. "I take it that innovation led you to me. So, your world is run by these guilds?"

"In a way. We live in towns and cities. Kingdoms. Budding nation-states. But there's no government in the world that possesses more power than the guilds."

"Who rules the Valley in this world?"

Elias chuckled. "No one. There are more than a dozen guilds operating in the Valley."

"Are you at war like we are?"

"Mutually assured destruction can be a wonderful and terrible thing. All guilds in the Valley serve our kingdom. Some of us are locked in a feud, some not. It's not as simple as war."

This new world sounded better than mine, but first impressions could be deceiving. What did my counterpart do here? "Are we friends in your world? You and me?"

The look in his eyes, how his gaze shifted for a moment, made my stomach tense.

"Yeah," Elias said. "Close enough, at least."

Whatever that meant, I wasn't so sure I really wanted to find out. "Does she know I'm here?"

"No. She knows nothing about you. No one does."

The revelation startled me, and I couldn't quite say why. Not at first. Studying him, it finally came to me. In my world, Piercey worked within a team framework. He would never have traveled to another simulated reality without saying anything. In fact, my Piercey may not have been brave enough to go alone.

The differences between our worlds cultivated a Piercey truly distinct from the one I knew. Elias was different. I couldn't assume I should trust him.

"Why did you show yourself to me?" I asked.

The breeze toyed with his dreads and the long sleeves of his tunic. "You're the only one I know who has ever killed a god."

My hands remembered the effort of stabbing my blade through Dr. Henderson so well. I curled them as if I still held the sword.

Elias held my stare. "I have a god who needs to die."

This really wasn't my Piercey. Not at all.

"If you help me, I can help you with your war," he said. "The answers about how to live with this power of ours lie in my world. We need each other."

Dread climbed up my throat in a hot rush of bile. "Your supervisor is still corrupt."

"No." Elias shook his head. "It's not my supervisor." He walked closer and spoke in a quiet voice, like he was afraid someone was listening. "It's my guild."

CHAPTER FIVE

The notion of a guild proving as powerful as Dr. Henderson made me want to laugh at the same time it also brought a chill to me. I didn't know how to respond to what Elias had said. "Your guild is as powerful as a god?"

"Yes. They might as well be one."

"And you think I can take them down? Your entire guild?"

Despite the edge of sarcasm to my voice, he looked full of confidence when he said, "You don't need to take everyone down. If you cut the right strands in a web, you can weaken the entire thing. There are a few people at the top. One person, especially. Lote."

He meant it. He'd dragged me over from another world to kill the leaders of his own guild. Aghast, I scrunched my face at him. "I'm already fighting a war. I don't have time for another one."

"I told you I can help you with yours," he said.

"Then why can't you solve your own problems?"

"Because I don't have the help I need here. I told you I'm no fighter. Your war is different. You have warriors. They just need power. And I have something that could change everything for you."

He couldn't be saying what it sounded like he was saying. The skepticism on my face must have given away my thoughts because he suddenly grinned.

"I can make more of us." Elias spoke with his hands just like Piercey did when he was excited. "I can give people neural implants."

The possibilities spun wildly through my mind. Dizzyingly.

More than anything, we needed warriors with power.

Lifting the binoculars, I searched the training field for Nash once more and found him still levitating.

In my world, Nash was the best swordsman I'd ever met. Just thinking of pairing that with power made me giddy with excitement. He would be unstoppable. Together, we could fight so much more effectively than we did now when he had to rely upon someone else's power. Piercey would no longer need to wear down his soul with violence that broke him.

Leif and Wren would finally be able to fight with me again.

I ripped the binoculars back down and raised my voice excitedly. "We could bring peace to the Valley with more power."

"I told you." Elias smiled as he watched me. "It really is uncanny. You're so much like her."

"Same for you. You are different, though."

He had a faraway look for a moment. "Yeah. Just different enough to make it even more surreal."

Hope dared to bloom in my heart. "You really could give the neural implant to more people?"

"Easily," Elias said. "Everyone in my world has power. We can implant chips here. Since the experiment was to see what would happen if everyone had access to a chip, they ran it in the same way that they would in the real world. People receive the chip at age three when it is easier to help them learn to control it, but not so late that they lose the benefits of rapid growth in early development."

I watched Elias skeptically. "This most certainly gets abused. There must be kids who never get one or parents who are extorted."

He nodded. "We've had issues with this, but it actually is not very widespread because everyone joins a guild. You cannot survive in this world without one. No guild is going to allow any of their kids to go without an implant."

"Unless the guild wants to control their membership."

"Yes, only the competition with others is so fierce that you need all of your members to be incredibly powerful. The issue we've actually had is that children are given the implants too early, which can cause problems."

"Right." I thought back to stories I'd heard of babies losing control of their energy. "There's a subset of the population who really struggles to adjust to it as a baby."

"Truth is that everyone does. You're just used to it in your world. It's considered cruel here to give implants to an infant."

I chewed the inside of my cheek. "The Collective will figure out that we've given power to some in my world. They probably will figure out that you've brought me here."

"So, talk to Dr. Drake."

"No. I can't ask them for permission. They'll deny me. We must do it first. Then, I'll convince her to forgive me."

Elias nodded. "Okay. Sounds dangerous, though."

"The Collective and Dr. Henderson caused this chaos in my world. They need to let me fix it. We'll only give the implant to a few people. That won't skew the results of their experiment."

"This is why I wanted your help," Elias said. "No one else has ever made it out of our simulation except you. You aren't afraid to take action."

I watched this world's version of Nash through the binoculars again, still wracked with mild nausea from the strangeness, but also mesmerized. I absolutely needed to claim this power for him. Even though Nash never said it, I knew that it grated at him to rely upon Piercey's power to battle at my side. Nash was a true warrior. And if I could trust anyone to use their power for good, it was him. He'd fought beside me tirelessly this past year to defend the Valley.

It felt too good to be true and I feared that meant it must be.

"When can we do this?" I asked.

"Who are you planning to give implants to?"

"Nash, Leif, and Wren. They're the only ones I know for certain I can trust." I passed the binoculars to Elias. "They'll help your world as well. We repay our debts."

"I know you do, Max. I've seen enough to trust you. The power won't be easy for them to wield, though. It's hard to receive it as an adult and learn to use it. Dangerous, even. You know what power can do when you lose control of it. My people are experts in controlling power. They need to train here."

"You're sure about the time relativity thing you told me about?" I asked, understanding the reassurance he offered now that I calmed down. "That we're not losing time in our world when we're here?"

"Yes." He crossed his arms. "From what I can tell, the mechanic was built into the system to allow supervisors to travel worlds without losing time."

"Why would they need to do that when they can observe us from outside of the experiment?"

He watched me for several seconds. "Why do supervisors need access to avatars? I'm sure there's more going on than what the Collective told you. In fact, wouldn't you say they really didn't tell you anything?"

Dr. Drake had revealed far more information to me than the Collective did, but I suspected that she didn't know everything either. "Right. Dr. Henderson misused her avatar. What was their intended purpose?"

"Exactly," he said. "That's the question you need to ask the Collective."

"You don't know either?"

"Not yet. I'll continue investigating, though. This is still new for me. I only figured out how to travel worlds a few months ago, and that's how I discovered this trove of information."

When I began to ask my next question, Elias turned suddenly toward the training ground. I focused on instinct, sensing power growing by the second.

A man flew toward us. My Nash from a different world.

"Listen." Elias reached backward for me. "His name is Jaxon, and we're not supposed to be here."

"Seriously?" I moved away in frustration. "So why are we here, then?"

Elias winced in apology. My Piercey would never have been so careless. I didn't buy that this had been an accident. What was his agenda?

As the form drew closer, I made out the curve of Nash's high cheekbones and the deep nape of his neck where I loved to lay my head. Sweat glistened over it and along his collarbone. My hands nearly reached for him, to slide over his forearm and down to his palm.

Only this wasn't Nash. And I wasn't me, not in this world.

Jaxon landed and stumbled to a stop, staring at me with his amber eyes wide and truly shocked. "Ash." Hurt stained his voice. A shot of pain as deadly as an arrow stabbed into my heart.

His stare brimmed with so much history and emotion. We clearly knew each other in this world. The air felt so tense.

"I thought I felt you." Jaxon looked to Elias and then back to me. "You can't be seen here. Neither of you."

He sensed me even when I didn't use power?

"I'm sorry," I said.

Jaxon's eyes suddenly looked suspicious. It was like my own Nash looking at me, with his full head of curls longer than he had worn them this past year. Genuine pain flushed my chest to see this foreign look on him.

"You must have wanted me to find you," Jaxon said to me. "You didn't mask yourself like he did."

What the hell? Elias never told me to do that. I wasn't used to someone sensing me unless I accessed my power. It wasn't me who'd drawn Jaxon here but Elias, and I didn't like being fooled. The distrust Jaxon seemed to feel for me now latched onto me for the man who looked like Piercey, but apparently was nothing like him.

When I didn't speak, Jaxon walked forward slowly. His lips stiffened. His body strained as if he held himself back from a force that tried to suck him closer to me. "We made a promise."

I didn't know our history or anything about what this version of myself did. Clearly, something had happened between us, something significant enough for him to look like I'd just stabbed my sword through his gut.

"We're here because of our guild," Elias said. "This was the only way to discreetly reach out to you."

Anger gripped my gut as my stare shifted to the other man. Elias should have explained himself to me before throwing me into this situation. Why did he want to catch me off guard? What if I said the wrong thing?

Jaxon uttered a disgusted chuckle. "Your audacity astounds me. Using her, once again, to get to me." His hurt eyes turned back to me. "And you let him this time."

I opened my mouth, but nothing escaped. I couldn't think of a single thing that seemed safe to say.

The way he looked at me hollowed out my gut. It was betrayal, wasn't it? Jaxon felt betrayed.

"So, Ash," his deep voice said. "Will you keep our promise?" An awful beat of silence hung between us. "You don't even look concerned that I will. I suppose you knew I'd be too weak to do it. I'm still such a fool."

"Jaxon—" What had we promised to do?

"Whatever you two want, leave me out of it." Jaxon lifted into the air and turned to fly away when Elias's voice stopped him.

"You were right," Elias said. "That's what I came to tell you. I brought her because I knew you wouldn't talk to me otherwise. Don't blame her because she didn't know."

Jaxon glanced down at me.

"I didn't want to believe what you told me back then," Elias said. "I know the darkness within your guild. I thought I knew my own, too. It's worse than I could have imagined."

I wouldn't be played for a fool either. I glowered at Elias, struggling to hold the heat within me back so I didn't draw too much attention to myself. "You better start talking."

"I will," Elias said. "I promise."

When Jaxon spoke, I was surprised to find that he looked at me and not Elias. "There's no hope." His smile looked sad, but still appreciative. "Ashton will never turn on her people, even if that's what they deserve."

So, loyalties divided this world's version of Nash and me? We served warring guilds? That wasn't so different from my own world. Only, it seemed that in this life, we never found a way around that. Maybe Jaxon cared for his guild. It wasn't like Nash and the Prophet.

If this Ashton was truly like me, then I hurt even more for the two of them, because my singular focus on my people blinded me. I needed more information, but with so little said, it still was easy to piece together some very important details. Jaxon and Ashton had hurt each other here. They didn't expect to see each other again. They were, by the way he acted, true enemies.

There was more than just pain in his eyes, though, when he looked at me. "I won't kill you, Ash. I don't think you can kill me either. You would have long ago if you could. The promise was always a lie. But that doesn't mean I'll trust you. I made that mistake once."

Ashton and Jaxon once promised to kill one another. I couldn't imagine this happening in any world.

Jaxon tore his gaze from me and regarded Elias with a look. "I'm sorry you confirmed the truth about your mother, and that I was the one to break it to you. I still can't trust you either."

"At least hear me out," Elias said.

"No. The time for deals is long past. I wish you the best of luck."

"We could actually take them down. Don't be stubborn."

Jaxon only hesitated a moment before looking at me one last time. "Goodbye, Ash. Don't come back next time." The pain burned in his expression. What had I done to hurt him so badly? "You owe me that much."

When he flew away, he took my breath with him. Logically I knew this wasn't Nash and I'd done nothing to him, but damn did he look like the man I loved. I couldn't stand to see him like that.

I stepped closer to Elias, gripped by vengeance. "Why did you do that?"

Though he looked nervous, he didn't back away. "If I told you before, you wouldn't have talked to me. You're too loyal."

"What, Elias?"

He looked down in shame. "Ashton forgave me because I did it for our guild. You won't feel the same."

CHAPTER SIX

The offer to give neural implants to my people apparently was too good to be true. I couldn't trust Elias after he used me to force Jaxon into flying here without telling me his plan.

Elias stretched his hand out to me with his gaze pleading. "Let me take you back to your world. You've digested so much for one day."

Scowling, I smacked his hand away. "You brought me here as bait and didn't say a word about it. You deceived me."

"No, I just—"

"Let me be clear." I eased close to him with my voice low and my muscles tensed. "I will not be used. We don't know each other. You may look like my friend, but clearly, you're not him. Allies are earned and this is not how you earn that."

His expression sobered, and any attempt to dismiss what he'd done fell away. Instead, he nodded. "You're right. I should have told you the truth."

"So, tell me now. Don't force me to make assumptions."

"Jaxon's guild and mine are at war. Always have been. But because of Jaxon, I learned that my guild is not who I thought we were. I need help to make things right. There was no way I could talk to Jaxon at all without you—well, Ash. And that wasn't going to happen. It seemed easier this way."

Was the ploy so innocent as this being easier or was Elias trying to conceal the truth from me? "I want to know what you did."

Discomfort tensed his brow. "To even start that story requires telling you so many others."

"You just don't want to confess."

"Not really." He shook his head, voice sorrowful. "It cost me so much already. I can't ever escape it. It was nice to have you look at me again and not see everything between us."

"I'm not her." It must have really been bad, or at least posed awful consequences for him. I didn't want to pity him. Whatever he'd done, he'd brought it upon himself. I refused to let any compassion show, no matter how it tempted my weak heart. "If we're going to even consider allying together, we have to be honest."

"I know. Just . . ." Elias sighed deeply and finally straightened. "Can I tell you after I give your people the neural implant? Then you'll at least have some sense of connection to me. You'll have to give me a chance."

Was it so important to him to have my approval? I'd never considered whether my Piercey wanted this so badly, but thinking back, I did see how it tormented him if I felt angry with him. "You're insane if you think I'm going to allow you anywhere near my people when you're lying to me. No way I'm coming to kill the leaders of your guild either."

Elias drew back. "Max, you need those implants. You're killing yourself running around the Valley, fighting a war by yourself. We can help each other."

"I can't trust you."

"I'm not trying to deceive you. I'm just trying to become allies, not enemies. I'll explain everything. I swear. But there's things I need to show you first if you're going to understand. Go home, make your preparations, and when you return, I'll give you the full truth."

"And the neural implants."

"Yes."

When I'd suspected Flare before, it seemed clear to me that we weren't on the same side. Though I didn't trust Elias, I also didn't necessarily feel it was because we were enemies. Rather, he had an agenda that might not match my own. Or I wanted to believe that because he looked like my friend.

"You'll regret it if you try to fool me," I said.

"Trust me, I know that all too well." The sorrow returned to his voice, giving hint to a deep wound inflicted on the relationship between himself and my counterpart, Ashton.

"I'm still not saying yes. The neural implants come at a cost, one I'm not sure I can pay. I need to focus on my people, not destroy your guild."

"I'm on your side. Really. I want to help you and I need your help. What I did here is personal. I hurt Ashton and Jaxon because I wanted to protect them, and I ruined everything. Now I'm alone when I need them most."

That seemed genuine. "So why does it feel hard to trust you?"

"Because I'm not as good as the man you know. I'm not Piercey. In this world, I didn't become all you expect of me. You sense that in me."

"Why are you not as good?"

He cast his gaze to the horizon, quiet for several seconds. "I gave my loyalty to people who didn't deserve it, and I couldn't admit it to myself. Instead of confronting that truth, I twisted myself to fit a mold that didn't belong to me. I lost everything because of it. Once, I had it all." He watched me now. "I had it and I lost it because I lost myself along the way."

The wound ran deeper than I first guessed. Enough tension and hurt hung between us that, even though I knew nothing about this history, I didn't need to hear more to understand Ashton entertained a different relationship with Elias than I had with Piercey. The way he looked at me now, though meant for another woman, made it hard to breathe for the depth of his regret.

"I'm ready to go home," I said. This wasn't my world. I didn't belong here, and these people had a lifetime of problems of their own. At home, I could wrap my mind around everything I'd learned and plan with my people. "If I return, I expect answers. Otherwise, don't waste your time coming back for me."

He smiled. "You never mince your words."

I wouldn't entertain whatever he felt at the similarities between myself and Ashton. "Just so you know, I'm not hiding this from my people."

"I didn't expect you to."

"Openness and honesty don't seem as high on your list as mine."

Though he looked like he wanted to argue, he didn't. "I did what I did for Ashton and our people. It may not all have been right, but it wasn't without reason."

"If you didn't want me to be harsh, you shouldn't have ambushed me with a clone of Nash." Now I was the one extending my hand to him. "Come on. I have things to do. Even if I'm not losing time in my world, I only have so much energy, and I've been expending a great deal every day."

Elias took my hand, looking very much like Piercey again in that moment. He cared, even if we didn't really know each other yet. I felt that as we returned to my world.

I sat with Nash on one side of me and Piercey on the other, surrounded by dozens of leaders from the Valley who filled in the spots around the long table. Images of Elias and Jaxon bombarded me. Thoughts about everything I'd learned. The voices around me blurred into a buzz.

"You okay?" Nash whispered.

"I have something to tell you when this is over."

Concern knit his brows.

"It's okay. It's just . . ." What could I even say? I met his eyes. "It's a lot."

A man at the far end of the room beat his fists against the table and rose fast enough to knock over his chair. "No more! If we cannot agree, our enemies from beyond the Valley will take advantage of our weakness and plunder our villages." His long finger pointed at me now. "We've left the security of the Valley in one girl's hands. This is ludicrous."

The entire room fell utterly silent. Shock succumbed to fear. I never got used to seeing that. Ever since I killed the Prophet of the Valley, it took so little, even as little as simply entering the room, to see the quiet of fear still everyone.

I slowly rose with my arms at my sides, calm when I spoke. "Girl?"

The man gulped hard enough that his Adam's apple jerked in his throat. "I—"

"I'm not a child. You realize that, don't you?"

"Yes, of course."

I plastered a pleasant smile on my face and carried on in an even, smooth tone. "The situation is far from ideal. I, for one, would like to have a day off occasionally. But when I killed Eskel the Ruthless, I understood the responsibility I took on. Foolishly, though, I thought after a year we might have our shit together better than this."

"There it is," Nash muttered and hooked his elbows on the table.

I ignored him and leveled my glare at the man who spoke so rudely about me. It wasn't what he said but how he said it. "I want a leader for this Valley, and I want it now." I cast my demanding stare around the room at the gathering of chiefs, graduates, commanders, disciples, and even a select number of demons. "Can't one of you do the job? Who will stand up?"

Their silence made me want to scream. Finally, one older woman folded her weathered hands and cleared her throat, waiting patiently for everyone to look at her.

"I believe," she began, "that there is already one person standing."

A burning heartbeat. "I'm not the right person to lead the Valley."

That awful quiet captured the room again. Even the people who vied for ruler said nothing, likely afraid to position themselves as my opponent even though I didn't want the job.

"Why not?" she asked.

"I don't want it. I need to battle. And I'm too hotheaded." I shot my hand out to Piercey. "He's wise and patient. Don't you want someone like that?"

Enough murmurs of disagreement broke out that one of the chiefs winced and offered an apology to Piercey.

"Who would cross us with you in power?" a man asked.

I turned in shock at the baritone voice of the commander who ranked as one of the top contenders for ruler. Markus. He wanted to lead the Valley. Why would he say that? Why would he encourage me to take what he wanted?

Markus took his time standing and walked toward the center of the room, his demeanor and voice so easy that I immediately saw why so many people followed him. This man exuded all the political charisma I lacked.

"We're at war with ourselves and with the world." Markus gestured at me. "Who better to lead us through this war than Eclipse? The most powerful demon in Skia Hellig. Maybe in the world."

"What the hell?" I whispered under my breath.

"With a strong council behind her and two top disciples to lead at her side, we'll certainly claim this land as our own and make peace for our children."

Several clapped and I felt the room shrinking all around me, suffocating me.

"Let us guess," a woman I barely recognized said. "You would be at her side?"

Some chuckles broke out, and then Markus surprised me again by laughing as well. "Naturally." He held my eyes, directly across the table from me. "If the Prophet Eclipse would have me."

Heat flashed down my spine. I plastered my hands on the table and leaned forward. "I am no Prophet, and my name is not Eclipse." My voice boomed now. "I'm Max the Sharpshooter. The next person who calls me Eclipse is getting thrown through the wall."

Markus only smiled even though he lacked a neural implant and any hope of defending himself against me. "The only ones who can be trusted with power are the ones who never craved it to begin with. Will you truly turn us away when we need you?"

Everyone watched. Even Nash. I looked to Nash expecting to see him scoff at what this man said, expecting him to urge me to reject these ridiculous pleas, but Nash watched me intently instead.

Markus must have realized the futility in trying to seize power for himself, and understood that offering himself as my second created far more power than any other venture. It was not all for vanity, however. Markus was a mighty warrior. He'd proven himself in battle many times, especially over this past year. Though he did hunger for the power I wanted nothing to do with, I believed he wanted to take care of the Valley with it. His reasons were noble.

"Don't I have enough power as it is?" I looked down at my hands, unable to fend off the images of the life jerking from the bodies of the villagers I'd killed as a child.

The first woman to have spoken, the older woman, lifted her chin. "Who else do you trust our lives with?"

I clenched my teeth and nearly turned away, only that felt cowardly. Piercey stood now and calmly clasped his hands in front of himself. "I think it's best that we take a break to consider what we've heard."

Nice political speak for "Shut up, Max. Don't say another word." It took all my effort to keep from storming out of the room. Once a portion of the gathering had dispersed, I rushed outside straight for the woods at the back of the assembly hall.

Piercey and Nash ran after me.

"I'm not doing it," I said.

"Why are you so against it?" Piercey asked.

"I don't want it." I wheeled around as heat washed over my body. Energy burned at my fingertips. "How many times do I have to say it? Just because I killed someone doesn't mean I'm fit to lead."

Piercey caught my wrist. "What if you do it for a few years until we're stable?"

"Have I not sacrificed enough already?" I jerked away from him. "Day after day, I give all I have to this Valley and to these people. There is only one thing I've said I won't do, and still they harass me for it."

Nash hadn't said anything yet. His look stilled me.

"You do what you know is right," Nash said. "Just make sure you're trusting yourself as much as the rest of the Valley does. Eclipse is no longer a name of death but liberation."

I lowered my head, consumed by a wave of grief. "I faced the gods, and I stole our world from them. It terrifies me to wonder if I did the right thing. I don't know if I'm strong enough to keep making these kinds of decisions."

Nash worked close to me, his fingers trailing my arms, soft and soothing. "Look at me."

When I did, my world narrowed to only him, and the hum of his whisper.

"We fight together. I'll never leave you alone. We're strong enough for whatever comes next."

Saying nothing else, he firmly clasped the back of my neck to draw me against him and enclose me in the strength of his embrace. His quiet comfort eased my storming heart.

A frightening thought often drifted through my mind, no matter how many times I swatted it away. The peace I felt now allowed it to sneak up on me and catch me unaware, so it slipped through my defenses, and ravaged my heart. Perhaps, I so feared leading the Valley because I needed to do this, and I understood that my life would no longer be my own. After returning to this world from the afterlife and meeting Nash, I desperately wanted to live. I wanted more time in his arms like this. How could we ever move forward together if the Valley sucked all the life from me? I had nothing more to give.

"There's more," I said, feeling so weary. "I have something to tell you two."

CHAPTER SEVEN

The humble warmth of a summer day in our northern lands fell pleasantly over me and nearly fooled me into losing my sense of urgency. "It's an entirely different world," I said.

Nash's brows arched high and he leaned forward. "I could really fly?"

I slapped the back of my hand against his shoulder. "That's what stood out to you the most? Not that there are multiple other simulations populated with our consciousness? Multiple versions of you and me."

"I mean, yeah, but it's incredible that version of me can fly."

Sighing, I fell back on my heels and leveled my look at Piercey. He stared at the ground as he chewed on a fingernail, his expression speaking about as much as his silence.

Nash crossed his arms over his chest and studied me intently. "Did this other me also use twin blades?"

I honestly had no response. Of all the questions he could ask. "I don't know. I didn't see them."

"Must not. I'd never train without them."

Good point. Nash didn't even eat breakfast without his swords. "Don't you think—"

"I want to know how similar and how different we are," Nash said. "I started training with the swords when I was seven because my grandfather had been so skilled with the twin blades. It's one of the longest-lasting and most consistent parts of my life. Clearly, this version of me having power changed things."

True. "We know each other there, too, but that's also different. Something happened between us. We're enemies."

His shoulders straightened. "True enemies?"

"As true of enemies as the two of us could ever be. I . . ." The memory of the shocked and betrayed look in Jaxon's eyes gripped me. "I met him. Apparently, we promised to kill each other if we ever saw each other again, but he didn't want to."

"Damn." Nash pushed his curls back from his face.

"There's more, though. Elias said if we help him destroy his guild, he'll give neural implants to anyone I choose." I bit my lip and looked at Nash. "You'd have power."

A seriousness gripped him immediately. He looked down, deep in thought, and absently placed his hands on his swords. Determination flashed in his amber eyes as he met mine again. "Yes. Max, we must do this. With power I can help you protect the Valley." His voice lowered. "I can protect you."

My chest twisted. "Nash."

His hands came over my face and pushed into my hair. Nash searched my eyes, allowing me to glimpse how deeply he suffered at not being able to fight with me the way he wanted. "I will do anything for the power to give you what you need. Anything."

It killed me to see all the suffering he hid from me this year.

"Elias knows this because he knows Jaxon," Piercey said. "He knows Nash's desperation." He still stared at the same place on the ground. "His only condition was fighting his guild?"

Odd that Piercey already detached enough from the other version of himself to speak about him so separately. "Yes," I said, settling against Nash as he lowered his hands. "He sincerely needed help. He wouldn't tell me what he did, but it seemed like he used the connection between Ashton and Jaxon to hurt his guild. He alienated his allies."

"Do you really trust him to give the neural implants freely?" Piercey asked. "What if he alters them in some way?"

"I don't know. I don't really trust him," I said. "Then again, do you think you'd do that in any world?"

"He obviously betrayed you in some way in that world. We can't know how much of our personality and the decisions we make are shaped by our environment." Piercey finally lifted his gaze from the ground. "You can't assume anything about his nature just because we originated from the same seed of consciousness."

I knew he was right. "So you think he may do something to the neural implants to control or coerce us. Like hurt or even kill whoever had one."

"There's likely many things he could do," Piercey said.

Though I didn't trust Elias, I wanted to. Needed to.

"I will take this implant," Nash said. "It's worth the risk. It's worth everything. I refuse to watch Max get herself killed, and we all know if this continues, she will."

"Desperation is a powerful tool," Piercey said. "What better to hold over your head than what you need most?"

Nash's low, nearly inaudible grunt vibrated against my cheek. "I'll find a way."

"If I learn how to travel worlds, this might work," I said. "That way, if he tries anything, I can kill him. That'll keep him in line."

"Not everything can be solved by threat of murder," Piercey said.

Nash and I both looked at each other.

"It can solve an awful lot," Nash said.

My old friend groaned and leaned back against a tree. "We need to connect with him. That's the only way to know if he's telling the truth."

Brilliant. Would Elias do it? Probably not, considering he liked to hide things. So that meant I shouldn't trust him, right? It seemed like a clear indicator I shouldn't, and still I struggled to tame the temptation.

"That can be our condition." I clenched my hand into a fist. "He has to connect with one of us so we know everything about him."

Piercey nodded as if considering.

"We all need to meet him and talk," Nash said. "Connect with him. Do what you need. But you can tell a lot from looking into a man's eyes and asking him an honest question."

"We can't keep doing what we're doing forever." I rubbed my aching neck. "Nash is right that it will eventually kill me. I can't fight against the entire world. Nash, Leif, and Wren could help me protect this Valley and get control into the hands of leaders we can trust."

Nash held me tightly. "I can't fathom having the power to fight with you on my own."

"It changes everything," I said.

"Yes." Piercey's tone was serious and cold. "It does."

Tension wound my gut into knots. "We have to deal with this no matter what happens. Elias knows how to travel to our world. He's not going to just disappear."

Sticks snapped nearby. Nash and I pivoted, both of us pointing our swords in an offensive stance in the short time it took to face our intruder.

"Max the Sharpshooter." A coy smile met me.

Markus. The charismatic commander who didn't know when to shut his mouth.

He sauntered closer, as confident as ever. "I hope you didn't mind that I took the liberty of speaking to the people earlier."

The men eyed him quietly while I stepped closer to him. "I know what you're doing."

"Of course you do. It wasn't my intention to hide it. With me serving at your side, we could change this Valley forever."

"I already said no."

"Except you already are."

My nostrils flared. "The people deserve a real leader who knows what they're doing. I'm a warrior, not a ruler."

"Take time to consider it. I understand this is far from your comfort zone, but I know you didn't kill the Prophet and save the Valley just for us to fall into the hands of someone as bad, or even worse. We're wasting time when we could be trying to end this war."

Despite my intense distrust for this man who often wore far too charming of a smile, his eyes looked honest now. Nash spoke the truth earlier. A person could tell a lot about someone by looking into their eyes.

"Why not you?" I asked.

He smiled sadly. "You know why. It's you whom the people have chosen."

My heart started to beat harder beneath all this pressure when a bright light in the sky caught my eye.

Green bolts of lightning sparked above the assembly hall and branched out into dozens of jagged trails. They struck the ground, shaking the woods around us in a clash of branches and leaves.

The sensation of incredible power erupted.

Without saying anything to Nash or Piercey, I teleported directly in front of the building, my energy bow already drawn.

CHAPTER EIGHT

Remnants of green energy still sizzled in the air like heat lightning, and danced over the skin of five warriors. Behind them, a perfect black circle ate into the sky, now rapidly closing. The edges blurred and distorted until finally it dissolved to a mere pinprick. Then nothing.

I didn't recognize any of these people, nor their leather armor lined with thick orange stitching and embossed with the symbol of a sun. A short but broad man stood at the head of the group, staring past my energy arrow to my eyes.

No one spoke for the first few seconds. Village leaders fled into the meeting hall while the few with power lined up behind me. The warriors lacking neural implants stood at the ready in a perimeter around them. Nash ran around the building, continuing for me, but I raised my hand to stop him without looking in his direction. I didn't want to take my eyes off these guests of ours for a moment.

"Where did you come from?" I asked.

"I doubt you've heard of our land, though we've heard of you all the way across the world." The man who stared at me spoke coolly and subtly lifted the corner of his lip in a hard-to-detect smirk. "My name is Gael the Vanisher. I've looked forward to meeting you in person."

"I'm busy these days," I said. "So why don't we skip this part and get to the answers you know I want." I aimed directly at this left eye. "Now."

Neither the weapon nor the threat appeared to intimidate him in the least. The slight smirk remained in place. "I come from the Kingdom of Hezala, far south of this frigid land. My king would like a conference with you."

"How did you get here?"

"I traveled like you do. It's a power passed down in my village, though it differs from your own. I create a portal using my energy. I've never seen anyone travel the way you do."

Incredible and dangerous. "You've seen me travel?"

"I've watched you often this past year," Gael said. "I simply wasn't ready to introduce myself."

I ground my teeth down, incredibly annoyed with the slow drip of information. Patience had never been my strong point. Now that I was so overwhelmed with defending the Valley, I struggled to control my temper when someone wasted my time. Growling, I lowered my arms and let my energy bow vanish. Best to save every bit of strength I could. It was my most precious commodity these days. "Will you really make me keep asking questions?"

"We've heard many tales," Gael said. "I travel the world gathering information for my king, and he's taken a keen interest in you."

I noticed Piercey moving closer at this. He likely wanted to ask more about this man and the other travelers. Piercey previously discussed using my power to teleport around the world and gather information about kingdoms and rulers that we knew little about. He dreamed of a world map and a collection of interviews to help us understand the geopolitical condition of our world. Something I knew could help us defend our Valley, and something he believed could serve as a guide for the creation of a thriving kingdom or nation. We'd hoped the white room would have given us more information about our world, but we lacked the access the supervisor had. Knowledge about the peoples of our world came from word of mouth.

I'd been too busy defending the Valley, using all my energy to defeat bad actors, to travel around the globe with Piercey making maps or writing records. These strangers made me regret not finding the time. I knew nothing about them, their land, their people, or their king. I knew nothing about what they genuinely wanted. I only knew their power. And it was substantial.

Gael dipped his head. "I would like to formally invite you to speak with my king about a partnership to help us both prosper."

Why were these potential allies suddenly appearing? First Elias and now this group. "You seem powerful enough on your own. Take care of your own people."

"Your vicinity to the Sacred School is appealing. We come from a powerful lineage and have cultivated one of the best forces of Prophets and disciples in the world. Even so, the incredible security of the Sacred School is unmatched. There are powerful forces in our world, Eclipse. We need a safe place to train with villages close enough to travel to."

So they wanted to take over the Sacred School. It sounded like that to me, anyway. "We're overcrowded as it is."

Gael peeked behind himself at a woman standing slightly to his right. She nodded. "A meeting with our king does not have to take long," he said. "Please hear us out. We carefully guard our knowledge of traveling, but with the right partnership, we will share what we've learned. My kingdom is in danger, just like your Valley. Don't turn us away until you see what our part of the world is like and hear what we have to offer." He nodded at me. "Please. You need help. It's very clear to see. We do as well."

Piercey and Nash approached my side now, both studying the group.

"If you want to have a conversation with me, then earn my time." I eyed Gael. "Show me what your people can do. What you have to offer."

"Is this a challenge?"

"Yes. Follow me around the Valley and fight me. Can you track me?" I'd instinctively learned to do this with Flare. If he couldn't track after training, then he wasn't worth talking to.

"I can," Gael said.

"Good." I rolled my shoulders. "Do you accept?"

The woman he'd spoken to earlier caught his sleeve, but he shook her off. "I do."

Though I worried about Piercey questioning me, I knew Nash wouldn't. He'd trust me to handle the threat. Yet, to my surprise, Piercey said nothing, and, for the first time, I realized I'd earned more of his trust.

"Gael," the woman said quietly. I saw clear concern in her eyes. "Shouldn't you set ground rules?"

"Eclipse is honorable. There's no need for rules. We'll fight and learn about one another through battle."

That tempted me to like this guy. "Fine with me. Ready?" I asked.

"Yes."

No sooner had the words left his lips than I teleported to the sandy beach where I'd left the demon bleeding out the other day. I wasn't sure why I chose this place. Maybe it had become a habit since I always brought those I banished from the Valley to here. Or maybe I just wanted to show this man where he'd end up if he crossed me.

I grinned when the explosion of energy rocked the ground beneath my feet. The green bolts of lightning lit the air and branched out in a circle, slicing open my view of the cabin and replacing it with darkness. Gael stepped through and landed on the ground.

Without wasting time, I teleported behind him and drove my fist toward his kidney. His traveling took more time and expelled more energy than mine, so I wasn't surprised when he didn't try to utilize his portals. Instead, he jolted forward at an impressive speed, dodging my hit. His heel whipped around as he spun into a kick.

I teleported once again before the hit reached me. He proved able to follow me, but I wanted to see if he could keep up. How often could he portal? How quickly?

I waited around twenty seconds before the portal opened again. With the amount of energy he released, he would run out at some point.

"How far can you travel before having to rest?" I asked.

"Usually, I can craft around twelve portals a day. Sometimes more if I'm well rested. Most of our travelers can do four to six."

I respected his expertise in his skill. "Does the distance you travel matter?"

"No. Any portal takes the same amount of energy."

Nice. The distance mattered greatly to me. While I could travel more often than him, it required far more energy for me to travel across the world than it did for him. If he taught this method of teleportation to students at the Sacred School, we'd create an army of travelers ready to defend the Valley.

I was getting ahead of myself, though. These people were strangers from an unknown land. Trusting him simply because I respected his abilities made no sense, but I also did usually have good instincts about a person.

Breathing in deeply, I rapidly created my energy bow and lobbed three arrows at once. My speed impressed even me. I'd gotten much faster in the last few months.

Gael dragged his arm in an arc, creating a shield that swallowed my arrows entirely. A blast shot back at me, glowing green like the color of my weapon, in a repurposed ball of my own energy.

I smacked it away with my own power in a forceful, unseen wave.

"You're well trained," I said. "Disciplined."

"You're a rare talent. Not many people could harness your abilities after having their power sealed away."

I really despised this trend of strangers knowing so much about me. "Why did you speak up now?"

At first, he said nothing, perhaps considering whether to tell me the truth. "I sensed the most powerful portal I'd ever felt one day. There was no visible trace of the portal, only the sensation. I felt it several times before I managed to watch the travel take place. A man who looks just like your friend Piercey walked out from it."

My breath caught. He knew about Elias.

"I know his power works similarly to mine, but it's far more sophisticated," Gael said.

"He works very deeply within the nature of our world." I didn't know how to explain code, especially not without telling Gael more than I ought to. "I'm sure you know that I've met him."

"Yes. I sensed the portal open at the Sacred School and then your energy disappeared."

"You can feel me?"

"I can if I'm close enough," he said. "That's how I track you."

"Even when I'm not using my power?"

He nodded.

Wow. These people possessed knowledge that I lacked despite my training at the Sacred School. "So why did Elias speaking with me inspire you to finally come forward?"

"You changed our world once already," Gael said. "I don't know everything you did, but I know you killed the Prophet of the Valley, and that mysterious demon Flare. Whatever this strange man wants with you, I believe it will change the world again." He thumped his fist against his chest, voice rising in pitch. "I must fight for my kingdom. It's not simply the Sacred School or your power that I'm interested in. It's the future you're creating as well. I want my people to curry your favor."

I saw in him the same love for his kingdom that burned within me for this Valley, and I could not for a moment question its authenticity. But I was taken aback by this insinuation that I would do something to change the world again. I'd already defeated our god. What did I need to do other than fight for stability in the Valley? "How can you be so certain my favor will be worth anything to you?"

"Your people beg for you to lead them because they know what you're capable of. I see it as well. I want this partnership for my kingdom. I will give anything for it."

The pressure of so many people crying my name, a name I didn't even want—Eclipse—overcame me as I stared into this stranger's eyes. My voice rolled out quiet and strained with the exhaustion of holding our Valley together. "I'm just a warrior. I can't give you what you want."

"We both know that's not true. Not anymore. Whatever happened in this Valley didn't happen between a ruler and a warrior. You fought gods. The ripples of that battle continue to spread over our world to this day. It's drawn this powerful man who can portal in a way I've never seen. So, I am drawn as well. I know you don't want to stand at the center of so many people, but you're here."

The truth of it infuriated me. I did stand at the center, and so many people ripped at me in so many directions I thought my body might explode. "I'm tired."

Why did I say it to him? I didn't know him. He had no reason to care. It wasn't even smart to admit to a potential enemy. The words escaped like a deep groan, though, one I possessed no control over.

"It's like I said." He walked closer, voice quiet. "You need help, and we do, too."

I needed respite from this constant pressure. "There's still more of your abilities I need to see." I smirked, sensing the love of battle in him, thrilled to see what else he could do.

Gael's eyes opened wide and he slid his foot back as he drew his sword. "That power."

"I don't feel it."

"Only those most skilled with portals have been able to sense this."

"Max." The voice sounded like Piercey and yet my mind immediately registered it as Elias for the way he said it.

I pivoted to see him a few feet away from me.

"We have a major problem." Elias leaned against his knees and gasped for breath. "Say goodbye and come with me. Please."

I scowled, not liking that he expected my compliance. "Do *we* have a major problem or do *you*?"

Elias raised his voice. "*We*, Max. We do. There's no time."

"That doesn't give you an excuse to intrude on my conversations." I stabbed my finger against his chest. "Don't do it ever again. This is a private meeting. I may not want you to see who I'm with."

"Fine." He waved a hand at Gael. "I read about your people. I'm assuming you want some kind of treaty with Max's people. I promise that I'll return her in time."

Sweat dampened Elias's brow. Whatever happened, it had shook him up.

"I'll find you soon," I said to my new acquaintance. "You've earned my attention."

"I expect to finish our sparring match, then," Gael said.

I couldn't help smiling at that. "We definitely will." Looking back to Elias, I made my voice stern. "Piercey and Nash are coming this time."

"I've never let myself see him," Elias said. "I don't know how our human psyche would react to seeing another version of ourselves. I—"

I recognized a Piercey freak out when I saw one. These two at least shared this in common. "Quiet. There's company."

Elias closed his lips tightly.

"Nash is coming, then," I said.

"Fine."

"If you lie to me this time—"

"I know, Max. We need to hurry."

I jerked his arm toward me and teleported us back to Nash.

CHAPTER NINE

The shock hadn't subsided from Nash's expression since I appeared with Elias. I wasn't sure it ever would, honestly. I still couldn't wrap my mind around another version of Piercey. Now the three of us stared at each other like idiots. *Enough of this.*

"Say it already," I snapped.

Elias scratched the back of his neck. "The leaders of my guild know I figured out how to travel to other worlds."

Without thinking, I took one step toward him, perhaps to move close enough to punch him in his stupid face. "How could you let this happen?" I asked breathlessly.

"It was my energy reading," he said. "They saw the pattern, and data analysts tracked my movements."

"What does that even mean?" Nash demanded.

"The code. They saw what I did. It's only a matter of time before they figure out how to replicate it."

My thoughts careened out of control. Every single person in his world possessed power, whereas only one percent of mine did. If they wanted to take over our world, they could. Would his guild do that, though? What a foolish question. Someone out there always wanted to conquer others. It didn't require a majority of the population, only a small minority. Without a doubt, a group from Elias's world would certainly abuse ours.

"We need to stop my guild," Elias said. "Our world is gridlocked in this power struggle and fighting over resources. There's so much potential in your world. They'll seize it."

"So you're saying if I don't stop your guild, they'll take over my world. Your stupid war is now my war."

He held my stare despite fidgeting uncomfortably. "I'm sorry. If they come here and realize your people don't have power—"

"I don't believe this!" I shouted.

Nash wrapped his hand around Elias's shirt and ripped him closer. "You've placed us all in danger."

"I only meant to help," Elias said.

When Nash released him, the other man stumbled back several steps and dusted himself off.

"I should kill you," I said. "For all I know, you told them yourself."

"Why? That doesn't benefit me. We can figure out how to deal with my guild. They want to become more powerful. You have untapped resources here, so you have something to offer. They may even recruit your warriors to give them neural implants and bring them to my world. I doubt they'll want to simply cause destruction for no reason."

"How reassuring," Nash said.

"It's my world they want control over," Elias said. "I only wanted to get help for my people, not place your world in danger."

My hands curled into fists. "As if I didn't have enough demons and Prophets to fight. Do you know what it takes for powerful people to torment those who are weaker than them? An impulse. A bad day. The craving for a thrill."

Elias's jaw clenched as he lowered his gaze. "They know nothing except that this world exists, and that I can travel here. That's all. But if I refuse to take them, they'll try to force the knowledge from me. Lote will, at least. I don't trust him."

"Can they do that?" I asked.

"Not always. There's supposed to be a willingness to connect, but people in my world train in coercion."

"They would torture you," Nash said. "I know how it is to serve what you hate and feel you have no other choice."

I nearly touched my finger to the scarring weaving down his spine.

Nash looked to me now. "If his rulers are that ruthless, then we're compelled to consider his cause. Wouldn't we do anything to free our people?"

"Not place other innocent lives in harm's way," I said.

"I'm sorry," Elias said, his voice broken. "Time won't pass if you leave your world, though. Come fight with me in my world. Put a stop to this before it threatens yours further."

"I've never turned my back on a fight before," I said. "No matter the odds, I've always believed in fighting until the end. It's finally too much." It felt like my insides collapsed into a bottomless pit. "I travel all over this Valley battling whatever threat suddenly appears, while trying to win coordinated war efforts on all fronts. People just ask for more. They're pulling on me to be their leader." I clutched my chest, exhausted in a way I'd never felt. "I cannot save another world or another Valley when my own is falling apart."

"Max . . ." Elias spoke with such tenderness that I forgot we didn't really know each other. "What I've learned from the version of you in my world is that sometimes when you are so focused on one thing, you can't see anything else, including what you need most. I meant what I said before. The answers you need are in my world. If you won't fight for me and my people, then step away from this chaos here long enough to find a better way."

"It's not that I won't fight for you, Elias. I wish I could." The weight of the Valley bore down on me, trying to send me to my knees, but I refused to yield. I remained standing, strong and determined. "I only have so much to give."

Nash laced his fingers with mine, drawing my attention. "This isn't working. What we're doing is not sustainable. We've been saying that."

"I know, but running off to another world is not the answer."

"Why not?" Nash asked. "He has neural implants. Better yet, his people know how to properly use them. Their entire world is dedicated to mastering its potential. Stepping back might be just what you need."

"I can't walk away."

"You're not," Nash said. "Nothing will happen while you're gone. Maybe you could manage a full night of sleep over there." Nash pinched my chin, lifting my face to his, as he looked deeply into my eyes. "Trust me. I'm the one saying this. We should not walk away from this battle. You want to help those people and they can also help us. I need this power to fight with you."

I squeezed his hand and had that sinking feeling that I couldn't deny what he said.

"You're too close to it," Nash said gently. "You need to step back."

When I looked over at Elias, I noticed that he watched Nash with a strange expression. Beneath the gratitude and relief, a subtle but undeniable heaviness lurked. A sorrow. What happened between Ashton and Elias in that other world?

"If I do this, I want the neural implants first," I said. "For Nash, Leif, and Wren."

"Absolutely." Elias nodded.

"And I want help training them."

"Anything."

"What am I signing up for, exactly?" I asked. "Do you have some kind of plan?"

Elias nodded. "If we kill our most corrupt leader, Lote, it'll end a great deal of the dysfunction in my guild. While my leaders struggle with the fallout, the other guilds will seize the opportunity to fight. We just need to spark their war and force them out of their stalemate. Give the advantage to the other side. Other guilds will step in to create balance when our peace is disrupted."

"Sounds dangerous," Nash said.

"If Max kills Lote, I can take care of the rest," Elias said. "Someone has to stop him and my guild."

"Wait." I tilted my head. "Why did you make me hurry and leave Gael if time doesn't progress without you in your world?"

When Elias didn't respond, the realization thudded as a headache in my temples. "What did you do?"

Elias winced. "I told her we'd only come this once. I needed to talk to you to know if you'd help, so I'd know how to handle her."

"Who, Elias?"

"You have to understand how deep her loyalty runs. It's like having one of them here. One of the guild leaders. She will never turn her back on our people."

Beside me, Nash twisted in a circle, looking around. "Where is she?"

Elias shook his head. "I didn't want her to hear us or for anyone to see her. I've hidden her—"

"Hey!" I shouted. "Come out!"

"I'm not sure you should see each other," Elias said.

I raised my fist at him. "Bring her here or I swear I will knock every single tooth out of your mouth."

"Threats won't make me put you or her in harm's way," Elias said.

"Harm's way?" I asked.

"Damn it." Elias reached for my hand. "If I take you, then you have to stay hidden and quiet. Close your eyes and don't look. I'm not sure how this works. Better yet, you should do the traveling. Right now, I only know how to go between worlds. I'd have to take us to mine first."

"Where?" I asked.

"The cabin you showed me."

Grabbing onto both men, I immediately brought us to the closest tree line. "Get her to meet you out here so I can hear," I said.

"Oh," Elias groaned. "That won't be a problem."

Before I could ask why, I heard a door slam and the sound of stomping. Elias rushed from the tree line and stopped twenty feet away.

"You said five minutes," the woman yelled.

The voice seized my heart in my chest and refused to allow it to beat. Nash clasped a tree in front of him as we both watched the strikingly familiar form appear.

Elias made me promise not to look, but that wasn't possible. Someone who looked exactly like me rushed away from the cabin for Elias, fiery with anger.

I stared into a mirror, only the reflection acted independently of me, refusing to do as I willed. I saw my own eyes flashing with rage, bright in the sun's light—eyes that belonged to another version of myself.

A wave of nausea swept over me.

"This isn't good for you, Eli." The woman who looked and sounded like me slammed her fist into her palm. Ashton. My counterpart. "First you hide all of this, and then you take off from me once we're here."

"It's complicated." He lifted his hands. "Why can't you trust me for once?"

"Really? I wonder why."

"Stop holding that over my head," Elias said. "It was for your own good. You told me you agreed—"

"You still went behind my back and made a fool of me with Jaxon. And don't pretend this has anything to do with us. I'm speaking purely about guild business. You've been acting weird for months now. Since when do you keep everything a secret from me?"

After a beat of quiet, Elias chuckled low. "I don't know, Ash. Since when?"

Ashton drew back. Turning her face away, she spoke quieter. "I've seen this world. I can report back and buy you a few days. That's all, though. I want answers, too."

"I know." Elias sighed deeply. "I promise, I'll explain everything soon."

The way they spoke to one another, argued with one another, answered so many of my questions about them.

"It's really you," Nash whispered.

"Yeah. It messed with my head, too, when I saw your version."

"Are you okay?" he asked.

Strangely, yes. She looked at Elias in a way that reminded me that we were different people. I'd never looked at Piercey like that. This identical woman was not me, and my brain instinctively understood that to be true.

In their world, Nash and I—Jaxon and Ashton—remained enemies, true enemies. And this version of Piercey and myself had been much more than friends at some point. Their life differed greatly from ours.

But many things remained the same. I recognized immediately in Ashton that she served her people as fervently as I did my own, and the thought of those two purposes clashing flooded me with apprehension.

I couldn't deny what I saw as I looked at her. This woman was ferocious. So was I. And we wanted different things.

Many times in my life, I'd felt as if I fought against myself. Now I feared that it might literally come true. If Elias wanted to war against his guild, it meant warring against Ashton. It meant battling against another version of myself. I needed to do what Elias failed to do and convince Ashton to join our side.

I was not an enemy anyone would want to have.

CHAPTER TEN

Almost two years ago now, I lived here in Leif's home with his family, only a few doors down from Wren. Since that time, my circle had grown to include Nash and Piercey, and little Elsie. Sitting with those most dear to me in Leif's house today, I wondered how we might look in another year or two. It was for that future we fought for the Valley, and now against this threat from another world.

"Here's the plan," I said. "We'll get neural implants from Elias's world and learn about our enemy there. Back home, we'll have our allies investigate Gael and his kingdom." I frowned at Leif when his expression soured. "Before you say I'm being too trusting, I only want to learn about them."

Leif balked. "You once promised not to trust Nash. Now look at the two of you."

"Here I was thinking we were past this," Nash said with a sly smile. "Are you still thinking of killing me?"

"The threat remains forever," Leif said. "If you ever hurt Max, I'll rip your throat out and feed it to you. It went something like that, right?"

The two men laughed while I only rolled my eyes.

"Come on," I said. "Get serious."

"We've been serious for a year," Leif said. "Maybe that's the problem. I say we hold off on the plan, get drunk, and spar until we can't stand up straight."

As much as I wanted to entertain the idea and joke with them, seeing another version of me and knowing we faced an all-new threat had shaken me too much. Nash must have noticed because he sighed and took my hand.

"We can save the drinking for after we get neural implants," Nash said. "It'll be more fun after that anyway."

I needed to calm down. I breathed out deeply. "Sorry. I'm on edge. Have been for months now."

"That's why we need to consider this partnership with Gael." Wren gave Leif a pointed expression. "Max needs help."

"Once we have neural implants, she won't need anyone else." Leif puffed his chest out and thumped it hard. "Only us."

"They can portal," Wren said. "Maybe they'll teach us."

As the two bickered, I shifted my gaze to Piercey. He looked out the window without speaking. "Hey," I whispered. "You okay?"

"I'm bothered that time doesn't progress when you leave our world." He turned his pensive face toward me. "The supervisors only deal with one world and one experiment. The Collective wouldn't have made a mechanic they didn't plan to use. So who did they make the time relativity for?"

I swallowed uncomfortably loud, a shaky feeling coming over me. Even though I didn't fully grasp the implications, I knew he was right. This might have been more serious than a more powerful world discovering us and potentially invading. "Time passes in our world for Elias, though. Just not his. It's only relative when we belong to that world."

"So whoever they built this for must be connected to multiple worlds."

"You think the gods are traveling between our worlds?"

"They must be." Piercey looked out the window again and chewed his thumbnail absently. "Why?"

His question reverberated through my mind. The Collective hadn't told me everything. What secrets did they hold back? When I'd pursued Flare before killing her, the woman accused the Collective of experimenting on her as well. Watching her devolve. I really didn't know what they were capable of.

"Piercey." My voice fell. "I've been so focused on holding this Valley together that I let myself get complacent with the gods. I think I messed up."

Without taking his eyes off the window, he reached out and squeezed my hand once. "We're only human, Max."

That didn't help us, though.

With Elias back in our world preparing a plan to sneak us into his kingdom without his guild noticing, we continued our preparations in the Valley. The worry of him leading us into a trap loomed over me. While Elias wasn't as honest as Piercey, I believed that he cared just as much, and wouldn't betray us like that. But did he deserve that belief? I felt like Elias made his choices not out of malice or the desire to deceive, but to help the people he loved. My people were too good of allies to pass up. Elias wouldn't throw us away by handing us over to his guild. Or at least, he wouldn't turn over someone who looked exactly like the woman he obviously loved.

If he did, I'd just have to kill him and his guild leaders. We needed those neural implants.

Our world would not stop and wait for Elias to return, though, so I refused to allow the worry to slow me down or distract me. Scouts on the southern border of the Valley reported sightings of coastal warriors this morning. For months, we had clashed with such war parties in short-lived battles. I didn't understand why they kept returning every few months. Each time, we fought and held our territory. They retreated once they faced too many casualties. It seemed pointless, but they must have had a plan.

Nash thought they tested our abilities, whereas Leif was convinced they aimed to distract us. I wondered if they just wanted in on the fun of wasting my damn time.

When I teleported our group to our uninvited coastal neighbors, I dropped us directly where the scouts reported they camped. We landed in the center of seven tents circling a large fire. I didn't want to deal with such nuisances any longer.

"Eclipse." A commander I vaguely recognized rose to his feet from his place at the fire and grinned as if we were old friends. "You didn't wait for us this time. I expected to meet on the battlefield. Excuse me for not being prepared for you."

"I'm short on time these days," I said. "Who keeps sending your people? My friend Piercey has spoken with several chiefs from your area. They all deny any involvement. I hear it's a few rogue commanders playing around in our lands."

"Commanders like me?"

"Like you." I narrowed my eyes.

"You want to know why. I've heard things as well. That you've been asking questions."

"So stop avoiding them."

"No, I don't think so. Why talk when we can battle?" He unsheathed his sword and the other warriors followed suit, leaving their tents to surround us. I scanned each of them and counted sixteen. I really needed to know which, if any, had power.

"You've become a pest," I said.

Was that the point? It may not have been that they simply wanted to be a distraction. They wanted to wear me out. What if they were working with the Flatlanders to weaken me by forcing me to fight so many battles? It might have been the same for the demon attacks.

I growled and fired my energy arrow directly between the commander's eyes. As expected, it lodged in a shield formed of power and disappeared. My eyes shifted to the right. A warrior near one of the tents emitted the energy.

My group moved like we shared a body. While I turned on the one with power, Nash charged the commander, Leif lunged for one on the right, and Wren slashed her sword toward a close enemy. The battle erupted quickly. Piercey stood in the center of us all and surrounded our friends with shields.

Swords clashed around me as I used my energy to mercilessly tear at the body of the one with power, anticipating a great resistance from him, only to have my attack easily penetrate his defenses.

I regretted it immediately.

His chest caved in and blood rushed from his eyes, ears, and nose. It felt like killing a helpless child. I'd prepared a powerful strike thinking he would make for a challenge. In seconds, I pulverized his bones into a fine powder, so his body fell like a sack of flour onto the ground. I flinched in shock at the sound.

An enemy warrior turned away from the battle and threw up on the ground, leaving her vulnerable to Wren's thrust of her blade.

Damn, that had been way more brutal than I meant for it to be. Why send someone so weak?

I searched out more power, but even as the warriors struggled to break through Piercey's shields to attack my comrades, no one emitted even a blip of energy.

They only brought one person with power? What a foolish decision.

Nash's twin swords sliced open a man's gut. Pulsing intestines spilled out in a gush of black blood.

Pathetic.

The commander stared at me as his warriors quickly fell to our blades.

"Stop." I lifted my arms and cried out as I flung all the remaining warriors across the ground. I'd missed many of the moves my friends made, but I counted three dead already, and several severely wounded.

"Do you care nothing for the lives of these warriors?" I pointed an accusing finger at the commander. "How can you be so careless?"

By his haughty, taunting sneer, I knew he truly felt nothing about the blood pooling on the ground, or the warrior clutching her torn side, or another holding closed the tattered edges of his splayed hand. Such senseless death and violence. I resented him for forcing me to choose this. I would not apologize, though. If I didn't fight, they'd take this Valley for themselves. I hadn't warred against the Prophet for my people to fall into the hands of another tyrant.

"Our lives mean nothing," the commander said. "Nothing compared to our great purpose."

The ground trembled. A wall of earth sprang up, blocking us from the commander and those warriors closest to him. I reared back and blasted a hole in the makeshift barrier with a forceful wave of power. But he and three other warriors jumped onto their horses to flee.

I could stop them. Surely, they knew this. Except at least one person, if not more, concealed their power. This unknown risk endangered my friends.

Better to ask our scouts to track them to allow our spies to investigate further.

Sadly, they'd abandoned their wounded on the ground. "That commander is a priority now," I said to Piercey. "Put as many graduates on him as it takes to get answers. They're up to something."

"What about them?" Wren asked quietly. At least four still lived. I listened for their heartbeats and discovered that one who appeared dead actually had a faint pulse.

I didn't like taking captives after what I went through with my people. We didn't have the capacity to hold very many anyway, but we needed to talk to these survivors. "They'll come with us. Piercey, will you heal them?"

"Of course."

I looked around at each of the warriors, my anger swelling more with each passing moment. Whoever these stray war parties attacking on the coastal boundary worked for, they had no hope of taking over the Valley. Clearly, they didn't come here to win any battles. Just to take from me. To wound me. To slow me down and exhaust me.

Wheeling around, I shouted at everyone, at everything. At the entire world. "I'm sick of this!" Then, looking at my friends, I managed to barely lower my voice. "I want a meeting with Gael's leaders *now*."

CHAPTER ELEVEN

Nash was so right.

I knelt on the grass of the courtyard at the Sacred School where Elsie played while Nash and I relaxed after training. This was exactly what I needed.

After my shouting episode, he insisted that we finally take a much-needed break. Flowers budded on the tree in front of me in white petals with a soft yellow center. They scented the air with their sweetness. Elsie plucked one and lifted it into the sunlight, her cheeks round and her eyes dazzling. Her little hand wrapped around Nash's pant leg as she gave it a tug and lifted the flower to him.

Those eyes of his. The sun glowed deep within them as he smiled down at his daughter, leaned forward, and let her place the flower behind his ear so the barely unfurled petals nestled into his curls. Sweat still dampened his collarbone from training, but he looked so gentle with her that his hands looked only capable of tenderness when they knew war so well.

For years when my power was sealed, I yearned to unlock it to fight for my people and free them from the grasp of the Prophet. Back then, I wanted nothing more than to return home with Leif, Arn, and Rune, to sleep with the peace of knowing that I could protect my family. I wanted to wake in the morning to train with Wren, and feel certain that each day we fought for a better future. Having this power I now wielded, freeing my people from the Prophet, returning to the home I'd shared with Leif to see peace . . . These dreams dominated my heart once.

Then I met Nash and Elsie.

Before, I'd wanted the power to win wars for my people. I now wanted something new, something I didn't even know to dream about in the old days.

The heaviness of guilt bore down on me. I longed to turn off the neural connection that allowed the villagers to alert me to demon attacks, and take these coming days to travel with Nash and Elsie to the sea. To lose ourselves to the crystalline waters and the towering cliffs guarding the sea. I wanted to forget about the power I fought so hard to regain, abandon the fight for peace, and leave my village behind for days of bliss with my new family.

I wanted our own home.

We needed to return to work soon. Elsie deserved more than that. *Needed* more than that. So did we.

Even though I knew that we deserved happiness and a life of our own, the desire to abandon my responsibility here, even for a few days, burned painfully.

Nash picked Elsie up and set her on his lap, while giving me that look that said it all. We couldn't give up on fighting for more time for us. We made a promise to each other when we decided to be together, and now we let the war in the Valley explode between us.

Elsie pulled the flower from his ear and placed it against mine. "Pretty Maxy."

"Hey," Nash said. "That's my flower."

"It's our flower, Daddy. We all share."

He chuckled and kissed her temple. "That's right, baby."

"Watch this." Elsie sprinted away toward the big tree in the center of the courtyard where her bag of belongings waited. That and the two sticks she grabbed.

I sank back against the firmness of Nash's chest, trying to quiet the mess of guilt and longing tormenting my mind.

Elsie wheeled around and slashed both sticks down. Stomping one foot forward, she let out a cry and jabbed one makeshift sword while raising the other in a convincing, albeit clumsy, guard.

"Wow," I said and clapped, truly mesmerized by the determination in her eyes. "You've been training."

"Every single day, Maxy. Just like Daddy." She screamed in a mock war cry. "See that?"

"Yes," I said.

"Maxy, I'm gonna be in a show, you know." Elsie bobbed up and down, pumping her sticks in the air. "All the kids are. I'll fight with my swords. Will you come see?"

"Of course, sweet girl."

With a burst of excitement, Elsie kicked, spun, and launched into a series of swings. Her coordination at the young age of five surprised me.

"Maybe we should take her to battle," I whispered.

Nash pinched my side. "I can't even joke about it."

"Because you know she'll be charging in one day. Look at her."

"Please. I'm hoping to have at least ten years before I have to worry about it. Maybe twenty."

"Twenty?" I cackled. "Are you insane? You'll be lucky if you make it ten years before she's trying to get to the front lines."

"I love her courage, but I'd rather her be a coward. I want her to stay home and safe forever."

"Don't let your fear hold her back," I said.

Nash nodded, looking serious now. "I know."

My head rolled back against him. "Thank you for making me come back before meeting with Gael. I wouldn't have made it without this."

When Nash lifted my chin to meet his eyes, the weight alleviated me for a few seconds and allowed for my world to shrink down to only this courtyard.

"It's not your fault we're at war," he said. "We always have been." His thumb traced along my jaw. "Don't let your guilt kill you."

"How do I say no to people who need my help?"

"I don't know. That's why we're meeting with Gael. So the Valley has more than just you to look to. Even if you make an agreement, you still have to be willing to let someone else take care of the people."

I chewed the inside of my lip while watching Elsie play. "It's hard to step back. I feel responsible for the turmoil. I know you're trying to tell me I'm not, but I did make certain decisions, and those decisions had consequences."

"Listen." Nash lifted my face to his again. "I stayed at your side for every step of that journey. This is not all on you."

My lips melted against his. With the three of us together in the courtyard, all finally felt right. "I don't know what's going to happen with Elias's world," I said. "The gods will figure out I've traveled there, and they may get mad, especially after we give you an implant. Is this truly what you want?"

"Absolutely." The muscles in his jaw knotted. "You remember what it was like when your power was locked away inside of you. Imagine how it feels to have none. It kills me that I can't fight the way you need me to."

"You never said until recently."

"But you knew."

I nodded, my chest tightening. "Of course I knew."

"I want that implant. I don't want anything to hold me back ever again. If that power can help me make a peaceful home for you and Elsie and everyone we love, then I'll do anything to get it."

"The gods—"

"Make them listen, Max. Dr. Drake cares about you. Win this battle."

I closed my eyes. "Alright. We just have to make this work. We need more people with power we can trust. It bothers me a little, though. Deciding who gets power and who doesn't."

"Don't get caught up in it. We're in a crisis and this is part of the solution. You can beat yourself up about it later."

I chuckled. "Fair enough. Our enemies aren't wasting their time on right and wrong."

"Now no more talk about anything serious." His fingers stroked my arm. "Rest."

I settled back again and closed my eyes against the warmth of the sun shining through the glass top of the climate-controlled courtyard.

It felt like I drew in my first breath in days.

CHAPTER TWELVE

Chiseled pillars climbed the four corners of the meeting hall where we joined Gael, his king, and a group of advisors around a massive table. Exquisite paintings stretched across the domed ceiling with ribbons of gold weaving together the images, catching the glow of electric torches in a way that resembled natural light. I knew nothing about art. Absolutely nothing. Right now, as I stared up at the image of an adorable and incredibly chubby baby holding a scroll in one hand, I realized I had zero idea of what it meant. Apart from books at the Sacred School, I never encountered any architecture like this before. But it sparked my curiosity.

I had never been too proud to admit my shortcomings. Well, perhaps that was too generous. I wasn't too proud to admit obvious shortcomings after realizing it would be embarrassing not to. Sitting at the table with Gael's people in their main hall, I simply had to acknowledge the downfall of my tendency to focus so singularly on the safety of my people. They needed my devotion. However, if I never broadened my horizons, how could I grow into who they truly needed me to be? I knew so little of the world. This hall proved that to me.

Piercey gazed with an awestruck look at the paintings hanging from the walls. Leif seemed equally entranced with the bountiful food filling the table. He lifted a piece of watermelon to his nose and sniffed. This fruit didn't grow in our frigid northern climate, but it did grow bountifully in my childhood village. I loved eating it back in those days. When he bit into it, his eyes widened to round orbs.

"The juice," Leif said.

Nash reached for a hunk of his own and appeared to swallow it without chewing. "Woah."

Both men popped in a few more pieces before seeming to remember their manners and reluctantly sitting back. Wren sat the furthest away from me and gazed up at the flowing and gauzy veils that stretched over the table.

I needed to travel more, not just to fight demons, but to experience the rest of the world. Gael's land differed so much from my own, and his people mastered powers that no one in Skia Hellig even knew about. I'd been so fixated on the Valley that I neglected to ever consider the benefit of learning from other lands. Piercey had tried to convince me to care about this sooner.

"Thank you for coming." Gael's leader, King Tyroin, dipped his head in my direction. "I feared that you may not be amenable to meeting with us."

"The reputation of my stubbornness has crossed the ocean," I said.

The king at first looked hesitant to smile until I did so first. "You're an impressive leader, Max the Sharpshooter. I can only assume that your steadfastness and conviction enabled you to not only set your people free of the tyrant Eskel, but also to protect your precious Valley from falling into the hands of another."

This guy was way too nice. Piercey ate up the skill of King Tyroin's diplomacy, but Leif narrowed his eyes to slits. I fell somewhere between the two of them, wanting to believe his authenticity, but worried that eloquence may paint over a much uglier picture.

"I can see a few things about you as well, Your Highness," I said. "You rule a large kingdom and manage a great number of people. I'm sure that it requires as much grace and tact as it does strength."

While I would not call him traditionally handsome, he flashed such a charming smile that it almost transformed his appearance entirely. "Warriors never trust politicians," the king said. "I can't blame you for understanding that our tongue is the same as your sword."

Nash glanced at me, the concern clear in his eyes. Though I knew about Nash's past and that he had acted as a spy when he served the Prophet of the Valley, that time of his life never felt quite real. I'd heard plenty of stories by now of his success with the Flatlanders, so he understood the warfare of politicians much better than I did. Nash, too, wielded his charm and charisma to control a situation and gain the advantage. Even if this king was genuine, he possessed the skills to manipulate. I needed to confer with my friends before saying very much at this meeting.

"Your Highness." I breathed in deeply and met his eyes. "I'm going to be honest with you because you clearly already know that I'm a much better warrior than diplomat. It's hard for me to trust you."

"As it should be," he said.

"It must be hard for you to trust me as well."

He seemed to consider this and sat back, looking to Gael. When he returned his attention to me, he spoke in a quieter and more casual voice. "I'm a skeptic. It's true. Gael came around to you before I did. We've watched you, Max, and you are very consistent in your traits. You will do anything for your people and that one fact rules every moment of your life. While I cannot claim to trust very many people in their relationships with me, I can trust their nature. A liar will lie. A loving parent will care for their child. The protector of her people will protect."

Man, I hardly resisted being pulled into his good nature. I felt enthralled as I sat beneath the beautiful dome ceiling and smelled the freshness of the sliced fruit. "Just say it, Your Highness," I said.

"Whether or not I can trust you, I can trust your behavior. You will never put your people in harm's way. If we make a treaty, you will honor it. You will not bring the wrath of a powerful kingdom down upon your people."

Accurate. Was I too predictable? "So why should I trust your treaty?"

"Because you can kill me at any time."

I blinked at his words, quickly shifting my eyes to his guards and finally to Gael. These were powerful people. Could I really? Did he overestimate me?

The king sat forward. "I'm not trying to be overly dramatic by saying that. I just feel it's true. You could travel to me any time you want to, and I believe you have the skills to ultimately kill me if you so choose. My warriors may strike you dead after. It's difficult to say whether you'd survive the effort. But breaking a treaty with you, betraying your people, these are things which I genuinely believe place my life in jeopardy. It is an inopportune time for me to die."

A laugh escaped, one I quickly swallowed down. "Inopportune?"

"We have no suitable leader to take my place and we are facing many dangers. Not only do I want to live because I value my life, but I cannot abandon my people here without someone to take my place. You and I share something in common. Our people depend upon us, and they are in danger."

My heart wanted so badly to trust what he said. It made sense to me. Why would he send warriors halfway around the world to pick a fight with presumably one of the most powerful people in the world? Especially someone like me who was so dedicated to my people? He could have a motive, such as taking over the Valley. But why would he want the Valley?

We looked into him, and he'd never made any move to acquire new lands. He contented himself with taking care of the kingdom he already possessed rather than try to expand it, especially to a land halfway around the world.

I looked to Wren now, because while I trusted Piercey's mind and Nash's heart and Leif's loyalty, it was her wisdom that gave me peace when I felt uncertain. Wren didn't claim to have answers very often, but when she did, I trusted her implicitly. She never spoke unless she was certain.

She held my gaze for several seconds and then she nodded. No more needed to be said. Wren trusted them enough to at least continue this conversation.

"Let's talk actual logistics." I settled my hands on my lap. "Then I'd like to speak with my people."

"I want to hear from everyone." I crossed my arms, keeping my voice low in case anyone listened. The king provided us with a small room off the hall, but I didn't trust his people not to spy on us.

Piercey sighed dreamily. "Well, as I'm sure you know, I'm in love. I want to move here immediately and become a member of this society. Think of the time I'd have for science. I imagine there's so much time for science here."

Leif rolled his eyes. "You've been so easily seduced. I admit they have a few things going for them. Their riches, for one."

"Watermelon, for another," Piercey added with an edge of sarcasm to his voice.

"We don't know them, though," Leif grumbled. "We have no reason to trust them. They want to come to our home. They want to learn our skills. What else might they want?"

"To teach us theirs," I added.

Wren tugged Leif back against the wall beside her, silently telling him to calm down. "He's right," Wren said. "They may want something we aren't willing to give. However, no one survives alone. We're stronger for our families, our neighbors, and our village. Our people. Our Valley is changing and it's as important to find our allies as it is to identify our enemies. Consider Nash. What if we'd followed Leif's paranoia? He'd likely be dead."

Nash shrugged. "She's right. Alliances are important and Leif is obviously a terrible judge of character." The sly smile on Nash's face earned a threateningly raised fist from the other man. "They also have plenty to offer, from their wealth to their skills."

"But," I said.

"But . . ." Nash sank onto a bench. "Their king knows how to work a conversation."

"Doesn't mean it's a bad thing," I said.

"You've made up your mind already." Leif groaned. "Why even ask what we think?"

I sighed. "I haven't. I'm sorry."

"When you want something, you try to force it, girl." Leif clasped my shoulder. "You may well be right. You have been in the past."

My brow cocked. "You mean when you yelled at me for falling for Nash?"

"Particulars don't matter," Leif said.

"So, what do you think?" I looked at Nash. I really couldn't imagine him ever acting deceitfully, but he'd been a good spy. I never forgot his charm from when I first met him. Though Nash had been interested in me from the start, that wasn't the only reason he started talking to me. He'd wanted me to fight with him and had been very convincing. So, his opinion of the king mattered a great deal to me. Nash wouldn't mistrust as a rule like Leif, but he might see through the charm better than me.

"I'm not sure, to be honest." Nash considered his words a few seconds more before speaking. "Good leaders are sometimes good manipulators. They use their skills to inspire and influence rather than control or trick. But it's hard to say what he is without learning more about him."

"Here's what we do know," Piercey said. "He's agreed to help defend the Valley while his people train at the Sacred School, and teach our students how to portal. That's exactly what we need."

"Exactly," Leif said. "He's giving us a deal we cannot resist."

"Isn't this what just made you suspicious of Elias?" I asked Piercey, making him glance away.

"See. It's dangerous," Leif said.

"It's hope." Piercey spoke with renewed confidence. "Gael gave us no reason to mistrust him whereas Elias already deceived Max. We cannot afford to pass this up. Max is killing herself out there. Do we even have a choice?"

"We always have a choice," Nash said. "We have to, or we're primed to be taken advantage of."

"True," Wren said. "We can't accept a partnership out of desperation, just like the neural implants. If we do get those, though, it does offer us defense against this king and his people if they are up to no good."

"We need a termination clause." Piercey stalked back and forth. "Both sides need the ability to cancel the agreement if our relations become tense, our interests no longer align, or we suspect foul play."

While they continued to talk, I replayed the conversation in my mind. "You know it isn't the king I trust. It's Gael. He's honorable, and I only needed to spar with him for a few minutes to see that he's one of the most powerful people I've met. We need to spend more time with them and see how their people conduct themselves to really know."

Piercey nodded. "So the next stage of negotiations would be to invite some of them back to the Valley."

"Yes. But we need to get to Elias's world," I said. "Once we return, we'll be busy with the new neural implants."

"I can take care of this next step," Piercey said.

"So, what do you think, everyone?" I looked at each person one final time. "Should we take the next step?"

Leif rubbed his chin. "We won't be making any promises?"

"No promises," Nash said. "I think it would be premature."

"Agreed," Wren said.

"It's settled." I knocked my fist against my palm. "We'll continue getting to know each other."

I couldn't race across the Valley, warring every day of my life forever. Allies like Gael and King Tyroin, and greater power through Elias's neural implants, gave us hope for a long-term solution. Both carried with them their own threat, however.

I closed my eyes. Too many problems. Nash told me I needed to let others help take care of the Valley and he was right. It wasn't possible for me to do this alone. My whole life, I'd fought tirelessly beside my fellow warriors. I needed to do the same now with the political affairs and the defense of the Valley.

"Thank you, everyone, for coming here with me," I said. "I need each of you."

Wren drew me into a hug that warmed the deepest reaches of my core. Leif kissed my temple.

"Let's go start our next journey and get the neural implants." Nash laced his fingers with mine. "I know it's not what we expected and it's far more dangerous than we'd like, but it might be just the answer we've been looking for. Maybe we'll return home to allies we desperately need."

"I don't know. I really don't." I squeezed him around his waist and looked out the window. "I'm ready for the three of you to have power, though."

Desperately ready.

CHAPTER THIRTEEN

When Elias returned to take us back to his world, Nash and I met with him in our apartment back at the Sacred School to lay out our demands for working with him, even though we didn't actually seem to have much of a choice. His people surely planned to act on their knowledge of our world.

Elias looked at me warily. "So that's your condition? I have to connect with one of you and share everything?"

"Yes," I said. "We need to know if we can trust you. There's no waiting until one of us gets a neural implant to learn about what happened with you and Ashton. If you don't want to tell everyone, fine. You will tell one person everything, though."

"I understand why you want me to do that."

"It's not just because we don't trust you. We need to know more about your guild and your world. This improves our odds of helping you."

He watched me now, looking pensive.

"You don't want to do it," I said. "You'd rather keep your secrets than give us the best shot at beating your guild." My voice rose with every word. "You—"

"Max." Nash nudged me and made a face like he was trying to clue me in on something, but I had no idea what he wanted to tell me.

Across from me, Elias lowered his head slightly, gaze falling.

The same heavy sorrow overcame him as when he watched Nash and me in the woods. Oh.

"Connecting with someone is not something to take lightly," Elias said in a quiet voice. "It's very intimate. You'll be peering into a world that could have been, or maybe almost was."

The discomfort filling Elias since this conversation began now shifted to me.

"How long did it last?" Nash asked, the only one apparently ready to directly broach the subject.

Elias glanced furtively between Nash and me. "One year the first time. We ended things and got back together. That time was three years."

"Three years?" Surprise squeaked into my voice. Elias had been with Ashton much longer than Nash and I. Connecting with him meant experiencing a life that this other version of myself and Piercey shared together. I didn't want to live through that. I didn't want to see Piercey that way, or really face the way Ashton saw him, at least at one time. Most of all, I didn't want to confront how I broke his heart by never choosing him.

But to make Piercey live through that seemed far crueler. Much too intimate.

"I can do it," Nash said. "Connect with me."

Elias's brows knit together. "You'll experience Ashton and me together. You won't become enraged and strangle me, will you?"

Nash laughed, but not without the heaviness of the task. "As long as it's not my Max, I suppose I can let you live."

"You can't." I said it gently, understanding now how Nash's limitations this past year had pained him. "Only those with power can connect."

His eyes closed. "Damn it. I don't know what I was thinking."

"That you want to save me from this." I squeezed his hand but he felt stiff and unsettled, burdened by not being able to fight with me in the ways he wanted.

Soon, that all changed. I needed to make this work.

"I wasn't thinking either," Elias said. "I'm not accustomed to this lack of power."

I nearly winced at what he said, but Nash didn't allow any emotion to betray his expression. Instead, he turned his attention to me. "I know you don't want to do this, but you must not want anyone else to experience those memories either."

Never. That Elias even possessed them made me want to run from the room in discomfort. Ashton chose a life with him, though. In another life, I chose one with Nash. "We should leave it up to Piercey. This is his counterpart and his vision of what could have been. I trust him with the story of Elias and Ashton as long as I don't have to think about it again."

"I do have another idea," Elias said.

A sinking feeling weighed down my stomach. Elias's proposals always ended up stressful.

"You're identical to Ashton," he said. "Your code must be the same. If you can travel through your life—"

I straightened. "I could travel through hers."

"You'd see less than through a connection," Elias said.

It felt like a hot needle poked into my chest. Ashton and I shared a soul, but we'd lived different lives on different planets with different people. Her life was not mine to take.

Would that even work regardless?

"We still need to know if we can trust you." I clasped my knees. "This is the price of our neural implants. Nothing comes without a sacrifice. If Nash, Wren, and Leif are to fight with power alongside me, then this is what we must do. I can't risk anything happening to them. I'll talk with Piercey and one of us will do it." I met Elias's eyes for the first time since this conversation started. "If you're willing."

"If this is the only way to show you that you can trust me, then I'll do it."

It sounded as if more may come after that, words he didn't want to say, or that he wanted to say to Ashton, not me. That he'd do anything for me. For her.

Elias clearly still harbored deep feelings for Ashton.

We eased into Piercey and Elias seeing each other. Now as they sat across from one another, they both gawked, dumbfounded at interacting with another version of themselves.

"It's no different than a twin in a certain sense," Piercey said. "Two copies that share the same DNA."

"Clone feels creepier." Elias wove his fingers together atop the table. "Identical seeds of consciousness even more surreal."

Soon their conversation shifted to shooting theories at one another rapid-fire enough to make my head hurt.

"Look." I pushed myself to my feet. "You two won't be satisfied until you've hypothesized about this for years. We don't have the time. I'm going to give you privacy to make up your minds about connecting, but you better stay focused on our mission or I'll knock both your heads together."

Piercey leaned in and spoke quietly, as if I couldn't hear him clearly, which I obviously could. "Is she as scary in your world?"

"Scarier," Elias whispered. "This one is nicer."

"I'm standing right here," I said.

"Nicer, really?" Piercey looked deep in thought for several seconds. "I wonder why."

Great, more theorizing.

"I believe it's the time she spent living in the village," Elias said. "Especially being an aunt to Rune and now having Elsie. She's more mature and considerate, which makes her feel nicer."

"I'm just as scary." I lightly slapped the back of both their heads. "My threat is real."

The emotion in Piercey seemed to shift as he looked at me. "Max, I know you said to do this, but are you sure?"

I could see the difference between Piercey and Elias now, not just because of their hair, but because of the way they looked at me. Piercey held all our memories in his eyes, memories I knew. I didn't recognize what I saw in Elias's.

"Our world is at stake again," I said. "I trust you. When I connected with you, it's not like I lived through every memory anyway. In a certain sense, I just knew you. Truly knew you." It was more intimate than that, but I needed to distance myself from the idea of these two connecting. One nod at Piercey and I hardened my voice enough to signal not to question me about the decision. "This is up to you now."

When I left the two of them alone, I paced the hallway, taking the time to be alone and not busy when that hardly ever happened anymore. I expected them to take longer, but after only twenty minutes, they approached me.

Piercey must have decided against it. Surely he needed more time than this to make up his mind and prepare himself for it.

When my oldest friend in the world saw me, he smiled warmly. "It worked."

Fear, rather than relief, struck me. Did he see me differently?

But his smile didn't dim and he looked just like my same Piercey. "You don't need to worry anymore."

"We can trust him?" I asked.

Piercey's gaze was full of memories that he possessed and I knew nothing about. "Yes. He's made tough decisions and he has his regrets, but he's not going to hurt our world. He really does want us to help each other."

"Thank you, Piercey." My heart ached as I thought about him seeing that other life. "Are you okay?"

He nodded, looking thoughtful. "I really am."

Though I didn't want to, I tried imagining the life he'd just seen. In a strange and entirely unexpected way, I didn't mind Piercey peering into a world where we'd loved one another as much as I expected. If he had escaped the Sacred School with me, we might have been together here. I knew how it felt to be in love and to want someone so badly I couldn't survive without him. While I couldn't give Piercey my heart here, he'd received it in another world, and now both versions of himself had some kind of closure.

We said our farewells to Piercey and began to walk back to the apartment to meet with the others.

"Has he moved on?" I asked Elias without facing him. "I can't bear to ask him and risk hurting him."

Elias nodded. "He has peace. He's moving on, especially recently."

I gasped and twisted to him. "What does that mean? A lady?"

"You need to talk to your friend about this. I'm just letting you know that you don't need to worry."

Who could it be? I hadn't noticed any hints of interest in a woman.

After hesitating for a few moments, I asked another question that bothered me. "What about you?"

The pain I saw answered my question. "It's easier for Piercey than it is for me."

"Would you switch places? Make it so it never happened?"

"No." Elias spoke confidently and without hesitation. "Never. It was worth the suffering."

The assurance stilled my breathing. "Does she know how you feel?"

"She does. It seems no matter the world, we aren't meant for each other. Maybe one day I'll find my peace like Piercey."

"I'm sorry."

"That's not something to apologize for. You don't owe anyone your love, in this life or any other."

It touched a sore place inside for the guilt I carried over not being able to make Piercey happy. Knowing he found peace helped me put that away.

Once everyone gathered back together, we all locked arms and prepared to travel to Elias's world. There we'd seize the power we needed, and we wouldn't return without a solution for the guild that threatened our world.

CHAPTER FOURTEEN

Elias's world defied all of my expectations.

Paved streets painted the city in dark gray stripes, rough enough on the skin to break it from a minor swipe. Brick buildings crowded out my view of the Mountain of the Gods, leaving only the distant peak creeping over the twelve-to-fifteen-story buildings. A trolley system followed a long rail down the left side of the main road. It looked like something out of a book at the Sacred School.

We arrived in a rural location in the woods to ensure no one sensed us coming, and then we disguised ourselves before traveling into the city. A thick robe swished about my ankles, the head covering hot with the summer warmth. Elias dressed us like members of a remote, small guild that covered their entire bodies due to how their power specialty created a significant skin sensitivity. Our outfits did draw attention because of the rarity of their guild members in the city, but Elias said that he carried a reputation for making connections around the world. If his guild questioned him, we were to say we came to the city to study, and he needed information about our technique to master his ability to shift worlds.

His guild, after all, demanded answers about what Elias hid. He told us he still possessed enough of their trust to buy time by saying he needed to study more, but that time rapidly dwindled.

First, we planned to get the neural implants, and then Elias needed my help handling a meeting with the corrupt leader of his guild, Lote. Though the guild officially offered more time to Elias, Lote insisted on hearing from him. Impersonating Ashton would allow me to meet Lote and study him, and for us to better control the meeting when we didn't know what Ashton would do.

"Amazing that they don't need horses." Wren slowed to watch a motorized carriage carrying a family down the road. Most of the people I saw walked or rode horses, but several types of vehicles milled about the town, some as simple as a seat atop four wheels that they powered with their energy.

On the way into the city, we passed multiple routes of train tracks. Leif had grumbled when he watched one of the "massive beasts" cut through the city, while Nash looked on with excitement. The two men surely remembered our time on top of one in vastly different lights.

We walked down the streets together in stunned silence, apart from the occasional mutter of surprise.

"You said your world needs resources." I leaned toward Elias. "Is that why you still ride horses?"

"Yes. We're making progress with technology to improve mining and production, but there's steep competition between kingdoms and guilds. Some hoard these resources and dominate our mines to keep others from advancing. We're gridlocked. No guild wants to help the other, so we've sabotaged our own advancement. The conditions you see here in the cities are far superior to smaller villages and rural areas. Guilds take on special projects in the cities to improve conditions and master new inventions. It's a competition, really."

I nodded as I looked up at the tall buildings. Their world progressed much faster than ours. I didn't smell the stink that often accompanied such a populated area, meaning not only did they drive automobiles, but the use of plumbing also must have been widespread. "This is incredible."

On the right, we passed a building where I glimpsed children lined up in rows through the window, each of them holding small flames in their palms. "Is that a school?" I asked.

"Yes. All children go to school in the city. Our Sacred School is extremely hard to get into. It's prestigious. In a way, every community has its own Sacred School. We each receive a basic education in utilizing our powers and the essential elements of learning, like history. Around the age of ten, once our talents begin to show, every student chooses a discipline to specialize in."

"Discipline?"

"Combat, technology, medicine, infrastructure, connections, and inventions."

"Connections like how we connect?"

"It's a complex field," Elias said. "Think politics, psychology, and communications rolled into one. People who study this are experts at connecting, which runs much deeper than your use of it. Bringing our consciousness together in any form creates dynamic opportunities. It's one of our most versatile disciplines, and its applications vary from interrogation to community leadership."

I shook my head. "Crazy. At least some of the disciplines make sense to me, though. You chose technology. I would be in combat."

"Each discipline has major categories of study as well. Combat, for example, breaks down into dozens of main forms, as I'm sure you can imagine."

"What's the difference between inventions and technology?" I asked.

"Inventions focus upon thinking outside of the box to develop uses for our powers that we haven't yet considered, or improving underdeveloped technologies. While there is overlap with technology, traditionally, a person in technology will not be inventing, but mastering and utilizing their technology."

"You found a new use of power, though," I said.

"It's one reason I got away with keeping it a secret. It's not every day that new powers are discovered, especially by someone in technology rather than invention. We have millions of skills that we've developed as a civilization. It's the one thing the guilds can work together on—sharing knowledge of our neural implants. We record everything having to do with our power in a digital library that all of Skia Hellig and our neighbors beyond the peninsula can access."

Wren took my elbow. "Max, we could take this information to our world."

"I can help you do that," Elias said. "We have ways to share and store information. I can send files back with you to take to the Sacred School."

Nash and Leif continued walking without joining the conversation. Both men seemed captivated by the sights around them. I smiled while watching them and realized that once they received their neural implants, they'd experience something even more shocking than this sight.

What would it have been like to grow up with everyone having power? Again, I could not help but think that this world turned out better than mine. Sure, they had their problems, but this city amazed me. It would take hundreds and hundreds of years for my people to reach this level because war consumed the time and energy of those of us with power. We failed to explore a fraction of the uses of the neural implant that these people had discovered.

"We have so much to learn." I crossed my arms. "Our people need this. They must not be plagued by as much sickness. It's cleaner than our cities."

Elias looked happier than I'd seen him. "Our world can offer you so much. If my guild manages to find a way to travel to yours, it would be a disaster, but if we can keep it between us, think of what we can do."

"You think the gods will allow that?" I hadn't thought Nash was listening until he spoke. "It's only a matter of time before they check in with you, Max. What will they say about us mixing up their experiments?"

Chills snaked down my spine. Us even seeing this affected their experiment. I'd considered the gods and worried about this, but I'd gotten so caught up in the excitement of this city that I'd forgotten about them since arriving.

The question quieted the group. What if the gods did decide to shut down our worlds? They'd agreed to let us live in peace, but they didn't want us altering their experiments. They wanted their data. Could I really trust that they'd allow us to live if we defied their will?

Nash slowed to join me. "Dr. Drake will advocate for you. Don't worry. I'm just saying that we need to think carefully about what we do here and what we bring to our world. We need to be discreet."

"He's right." Elias stopped at one of the buildings. "We should carefully consider all actions we take."

"Is this it?" Butterflies tickled my stomach. Could this really be happening?

"It is. Are you ready?" His eyes moved from Nash, to Wren, and finally to Leif.

Nash didn't hesitate. "Yes."

Wren and Leif glanced at one another before nodding.

"Good," Elias said. "My friend won't ask questions or look at your face. He's discreet. But for any social setting, it's important to know about our practice called composure. It means to regulate how much of our power we allow others to feel at any given time."

I didn't often hide my power anymore, but I knew how to do this well enough.

"Consider it the same as your voice," Elias said. "Your tone and volume, as much as your words, will speak during negotiations or discussions. It's polite to remain neutral, which is your most comfortable place of rest. However, some choose to always conceal their power until they're ready to use it. While this can cause suspicions, it is considered socially acceptable."

"What does Ashton do?" I asked. "In case my face is seen."

Elias grinned and rubbed the bottom half of his face. "Ashton does as she pleases in the moment. She's known for getting a little loud with her energy readings when it suits her. It's not like her to overly moderate her resting state. So, when she does choose to carefully control her composure, it is very significant and telling."

"That sounds about right," Leif said.

I elbowed him. "So, I can follow my instincts on that."

Elias's lightheartedness dissolved. "Maybe I should have connected with you, too. You need this information."

By the conflicting look on his face, I knew it truly pained him to think about entirely exposing himself to me—his life, his memories, his spirit. The ways he failed Ashton.

"Let's save that for if we really need it," I said. "Right now, I think we're fine."

Now that Piercey possessed the knowledge, I could connect with him to receive it. Elias wouldn't have to endure the process. For now, I'd keep that to myself. He looked too thankful for what I'd said for me to bring it up again. The way Elias hid truths from me led me to focus on his differences with Piercey, but this sheepishness reminded me of my friend. It softened my heart.

"We'll go inside, then," Elias said. "Just follow my lead and let me do the talking."

Soon, we'd take power for my dearest friends. Hope rooted in my heart.

CHAPTER FIFTEEN

Elias's associate scrutinized us as we stood in a small room lined with chairs and little else. It smelled sterile and reminded me of the all-white room that I hated so much as a child.

"Thanks for helping us," Elias spoke quietly like it was only to him. "I'll pay you back in kind, I promise."

"Just don't tell me anything you don't need to unless I specifically ask," his friend said. "I don't want to know."

"That's fair. I get it."

I watched the man as he spoke, trying to judge whether I trusted him.

"So, the three of you want implants." Thick fingers scratched into his fluffy beard. "The procedure won't take long, but you'll need time to recover. It's best to sleep for a few hours while your body adjusts. I'll bring you back one at a time, and when you're done we'll let you rest in one of the dark rooms. Sometimes people experience a headache. Otherwise, with rest, you should be fine."

"What will it be like?" I glanced at Nash's tall form hidden beneath the robes with a nervous feeling in my stomach.

We needed this, but I remembered how difficult it had been in my childhood to control my power. Children learned so quickly. Their minds were primed for growth and transformation. While adults brought discipline and understanding to their practice, much of the power of neural implants best came through instinct because they were so integrated with our bodies. Piercey possessed an affinity for purposefully controlling his power and utilizing study to enhance his abilities, whereas I naturally picked up skills faster. But even for someone analytical like him, in childhood his power had been as unbridled as a wild horse. It was how we'd both ended up in the Sacred School.

These worries didn't even take into consideration my questions about the risks of the procedure. I'd been born with my power. It was like a switch the gods flipped in my code. How did it really affect adults who received fresh power?

"We actually implant it through a needle in the center of the eye so that there's no need for surgery." Elias spoke slowly even though he acted like there was no cause for concern, because he likely noticed my anxiety considering how well he knew Ashton. "It's a tiny device that integrates with the neural pathways in your brain and then begins to grow. It takes a few days for it to fully mature, but you'll notice some powers immediately. That's why we have people sleep at first. The process is unique for each person."

"Have you ever implanted one in an adult before?" Wren asked.

At least someone else had the sense to ask questions. The way Leif shifted and crossed his arms told me he didn't want to wait, but his presence felt as still as in battle when he studied an opponent. The man never backed down once he wanted something, and he wanted to fight with me without limitation. Despite not being able to see his face beneath the head covering, I imagined his expression well enough.

Nash was determined.

"Yes," Elias's friend said. "I worked with a few people who didn't get implants as children. It's rare, but we study people like this. I know one woman personally whose mother wouldn't let her get one when she was little. She hid her away and her village didn't even know about her. A sad, abusive situation. We gave her the implant when she was discovered at the age of nineteen."

"How did it go?" I asked.

"It's a challenge. Adults sometimes adjust to it very well. Sometimes not. We don't see as many impulsive displays of power or as many losing control. But it can take longer to master the basics. It's like trying to learn a new language as an adult. You can study and dissect the language, but you're never going to keep up with a young mind that has more neural connections."

By the look on my friends' faces, I knew they weren't following at all. This man wouldn't know that they lacked the kind of education every child in this world received.

"It's strange to see three of you without one," the man said.

"It was a religious situation for them," Elias said. "They came from a very small community that strayed off into a very niche sect. None of them have implants. They wanted to remain natural, as the gods created them."

The man snorted.

"Well, should we get started, then?" The man clapped his hands together and looked from one waiting patient to the other. "I assure you that it's safe."

"I'm done waiting," Leif said. "Take me first."

I grinned at his eagerness. Wren nodded to indicate that she was fine with it while Nash merely looked impatient. But I appreciated Leif going first so that I could talk with Nash.

"Can it be removed?" I asked.

"No," Elias's friend said. "I have no idea how to go about removing it from your neurology once it becomes a part of you. Only decide to do this if you're sure."

Leif groaned. "Yes, yes. We're sure, my boy. Let's get on with it."

I chuckled and then grabbed my dear friend in a hug. "Be safe."

"You know I will be. Don't let your mind run wild." Despite trying to wave off my worries, his burly arm wrapped around me, and he hugged me tight. "All will be fine, girl. We're hungry for battle and this is the best meal we've had yet. No one will stand in our way."

When I pulled back, I pressed my forearm to his chest. He clasped it.

"My flesh," I said.

"My blood."

Then he messed up my hair beneath the covering and pushed me back. "Go dote on Nash and smother him with your worries. I will not waste another moment before getting my hands on this power. Our sparring matches will now be a sight to behold."

"Yeah." I smiled, set at ease by his confidence. "I'm looking forward to it."

One squeeze to my shoulder and then Leif followed the man.

"Leave your head covering on," the stranger said. "I'll only need to remove the veil from your eyes."

I heard their voices fade as they disappeared down the hallway.

I looked at Elias. "You're sure we can trust him?"

"He's good. Absolutely."

"Okay. Wren . . ." I gripped her hands. "You know you don't have to do this, right? Leif getting power is such a help on its own."

"I want to," Wren said. "I've watched you race around the Valley for a year trying to hold us all together by yourself. Now when we travel with you, we can truly help. And maybe I'll learn to portal."

"I just hope you know how much you've already done for me. You guys have pulled me through this year. You pulled me through the fight with the Prophet and—"

"I know, Max." Wren took my face in her hands, her voice soothing. "It's okay. You're not pressuring us. This is our decision. Be at peace." Her head shifted to Nash. "I think he's the one you're really wanting to talk to. Go. I'll sit with Elias."

With Elias's friend gone, Nash drew the face covering down, giving me that look. The one that said he knew me far too well.

"I don't know what's wrong with me," I said, twisting my thumb. "I'm so nervous."

"Nothing is wrong with you." He pulled my covering down as well and tucked away the stray strands of my hair. "You know how much suffering this power can bring, even though you also know its great potential." Nash drew me beneath his arm and walked with me to the other side of the room. "You carry too much responsibility. Let us take care of ourselves."

"You're right."

He hooked my chin and lifted my face to him. "Seriously, Sharpshooter. We've got this."

When I first fell for Nash, every look felt tantalizing. That excitement never left, but something deeper grew day by day beneath the surface. We made the rest of the world stop while we looked into each other's eyes, the connection between us stronger each time. It quieted all within me and around me, no matter the chaos we faced. As much as I loved the fire of his look, I loved the peace that grew with each day even more.

The tips of my fingers softly trailed the side of his face. "You're sure you're ready?"

"No doubts. This power is for you and Elsie. I'll stop at nothing to gain and master it." His large, familiar hands smoothed up my sides until he held me firmly. "There's no need to fear for me. It's our destiny to battle alongside each other."

"Do you even believe in destiny?"

"Only when it's about you. We always find our way to each other and we always fight together. This power fulfills that bond. I know it's right. Some things not even the gods can change."

No matter how much my anxiety flared up now, his assurance made it impossible to doubt him.

"Let me take care of you for once." His whisper tickled my ear. A tender touch trailed my back.

"You always take care of me."

"Not in the way you need it most. I need to fight, Max."

I drew back enough to look into his amber eyes again. "Please know I love you just like this. You don't need to change."

A sly smile crawled up his face. "You just don't want me to start beating you at things."

"I'll still win."

He cocked a brow. "Keep telling yourself that."

We both laughed and settled against one another. Nash was right. I needed him to get this power, not just for the Valley, but for me. I felt like we were waiting to start our life together because I'd been so busy. It was silly to get nervous like this.

Hardly twenty minutes passed when the man called for Wren to join him. Though she insisted that I not worry, I hugged her long enough to force her to peel my arms away. Such a life-altering procedure shouldn't be so short.

"When we go home, I'm learning how to portal." Nash grinned with ambition lighting his eyes. "No, I'll learn to travel the way you do. The way no one else can."

I noticed Elias watching us, though he didn't look jealous or wistful, but rather quietly curious. Maybe he wanted to understand what Ashton and Jaxon shared, and where he fit into that.

"Elias," I said. "Why do you think I travel so differently from others?"

Possessing Piercey's mind and the knowledge of this world, I expected Elias may find answers my old friend never could.

"Something seemed to happen whenever you lost control during the eclipse in your childhood," Elias said. "I also think that your world being reset played a role. It's just my instinct, but the fact that no one in my world has figured out how to travel like that is telling. For you to instinctively pry open space-time like that is wild."

"You figured out how to do something no one else did," I said to him.

"After intense and obsessive studying and trial and error."

True. "So there's something about our past lives."

"I'm not sure what, but it's possible." Elias pulled a chair beneath his legs to recline. "Trust me. I've been thinking about it."

I rubbed my palms together and looked toward where I last saw Wren. "You think everything is going okay?"

"They're fine," Nash said and laced his fingers with mine.

Soon that stranger came for Nash, and I really didn't want to let him go. Wild scenarios ran rampant through my mind.

"Do you want to come?" Nash asked.

I shook my head. "If I watch him shove a big needle in your eye, I might just punch the guy."

He laughed loudly. "I'll see you soon. When I do, I'll be more the person I know I can be. I'm meant to fight alongside you, not hide behind someone else's power."

I saw it clearly. He was meant for this. The gods had it all wrong. Nash, the man who had trained so diligently as to become the best swordsman I knew, certainly needed to wield this power I'd been born with.

"I love you," I said.

Nash kissed me softly. "I love you, too."

"Next time I see you, you better have an impressive power."

He winked. "You know I'd never disappoint you."

I held my breath and watched Nash leave the room.

The greatest and most terrible part of loving him was knowing I couldn't live without him.

CHAPTER SIXTEEN

Waiting for Nash's procedure to end, I sat across from Elias and tried to keep from tapping my foot with the same pace of my heartbeat. I knew he'd be fine, but my body refused to listen to reason.

Elias simpered at me. "It's okay to be nervous. Ashton always is with things like this."

I breathed out sharply through my nose. "Not okay. I ran into battle with that man. How can I let this scare me?"

"You can protect him in battle. This is something you know nothing about."

The truth of it only unnerved me. "Let's just talk out our plan. I need a distraction."

"I hope you know I am honestly sorry about my guild. I never meant to put your world in danger. You shouldn't be forced to fight for us under the threat of world invasion."

"What's new?" I asked.

He raised a brow. "Max."

"Look, Elias, we can't do anything about it now. We have too much going on to dwell on regrets. Let's really look at the threat and figure this out."

"Well, our first step is to get you all ready. Then, we need to recruit allies. You're the only one who can get Jaxon on our side." He gave me that pleading look again and I already knew what he planned to say. "Did you decide whether to try living through Ashton's life?"

"I don't know. It doesn't seem right to break into her life. Talk me through this plan of yours and how that's going to change your Valley. Convince me that it's actually worth it to do what you want me to do, and that Ashton will be better for it in the end. Let's say we do take down your guild. What then? I'm sure you can see from my world that it's not smart to kill your leaders with no alternative."

Elias smirked. "I can definitely see that. Piercey saw it, too. He warned you."

"You're right." When Piercey and I reunited after Nash and I nearly died, he told me that swooping in to save the day wasn't always the answer. If only I'd listened back then, not because I regretted killing the Prophet, but because we might have contained the fallout better if I'd not been so bullheaded. "He understands that the people in the Valley should pave their own way, or they'll never be successful. I just didn't really get it before."

"You saw something Piercey didn't, as well." Elias shrugged. "You saw that the Prophet needed to die, no matter the cost. It's something I've come to see in my own world, especially after observing yours."

Despite Elias's certainty, I questioned the effectiveness of wounding or destroying a major guild in a world gridlocked by competition.

"When we remove my guild from power, we won't dismantle them entirely. They'll still serve as a check to the other guilds. My hope, though, is that others will see what we did, and try to hold the other guilds accountable."

"That's a naive hope, Elias. Your Piercey side is showing."

He chuckled. "I suppose I'm very much in your situation where I know we need a change of power, but I don't know how to replace it."

"Your people are well educated and powerful. They've been trained since birth. I'm not sure you need me to come in and kill gods as much as you need to get your world to start fighting back."

Elias snapped his fingers. "It takes a spark. Besides, my guild needs to go. My world has problems, but it works well enough having different guilds to balance each other out and keep any one from becoming too powerful. Most of the guilds don't want to take over the Valley. Mine is different. They do. I can't let them."

"Why do they want to take over?" I asked.

"It's all about the resources. Take the Silver Moon Guild. They control critical mines that we need. It's inhibiting our innovation."

"It can't all be for resources," I said. "This guild war is for that?"

"Think of it as a door that takes multiple keys to unlock and each guild holds a different key. Our guild is quite powerful, but they're running out of resources, and they can't acquire them. It's not like we're the only ones playing dirty. We're just doing it the best."

"Once they get these resources, they'll be able to produce what they need to gain advantages over other guilds."

"It's more than that," Elias said. "They'll improve the quality of life for their people and our technology. Remember that people choose which guild they want to join. We aren't born into guilds. At least, we aren't supposed to be. If my guild becomes known for cutting-edge innovation and for becoming more powerful than the others, then the best of the best will join us. We'll be stealing recruits from others without actually having to recruit."

"It's a win in every sense of the word."

He nodded.

"What is it that you really want me to do?" I asked. "Why do I need Ashton's memories so badly?"

"I want you to impersonate Ashton in order to convince Jaxon and his allies to join the fight so we can take down all the corrupt leaders in my guild. Specifically, I need to get to Lote. He's incredibly careful about who he lets near him. He's paranoid, but he trusts Ashton more than he trusts anyone else in the world."

I considered this. "That's how I'll kill him."

"It's your best chance. You need to get him alone. He's very good at empowering others, so if there's anyone around, he'll increase their strength tenfold and overwhelm you."

"Do you think I can beat him as I am?"

Elias nodded. "You could beat him on your own, but it might nearly kill you. Together, we can do it."

"I thought you weren't a fighter."

"I'm not, but I can make the fight harder for him. I have my ways. I've helped Ashton before."

He looked sad every time he said her name.

"There must be something keeping her connected to this guild beyond her devotion," I said. "I would never blindly serve people who hurt others. If they were manipulating me, I'd eventually start to see it."

"Your dad betrayed you in your world. That changed you. Ashton has never been betrayed like that before. She trusts the people she loves."

I'd never thought about how that experience must have impacted me in less obvious ways. "Ashton and our dad couldn't have had a good relationship."

"No, they didn't. It wasn't the same, though. He obsessed over his own power, not hers. He never spent time with her. It left her longing for family, and now that she's found it, you know how hard it'll be for her to let go."

I ached for her after hearing that. I couldn't imagine needing to turn on my people. "If we get Jaxon on our side, then what?"

"He's clever and has plenty of plans for how to fight against our guild. All he needs is some inside help. He can tell his guild when to strike, too."

"Aren't you worried about his guild taking over?"

"I planned for that, too. I will stop them."

"Hm," I said. "That sounds suspicious. Are you going to destroy them, too?"

"The Silver Moon Guild will be so focused on mine that they won't see me coming. They have so many resources at their disposal. The Valley is angry with them for hoarding them, but they're the only ones capable of dealing with my guild's military expertise. My skills will make it simple for me to hack into their systems and redistribute some of that wealth while they're busy killing my guild."

"I never knew Piercey had such a conniving side."

Elias smirked. "I'm capable of more than you'd think, Max. I'm doing this to put more power into the hands of the people. They know what to do with it. They're just stuck between two guilds that have become too powerful."

"It'll only happen again."

"Maybe," he said. "Maybe not."

"You need to get people from both guilds to agree to work together or you'll be at war when it ends."

"I don't know how to get them to do that," Elias said.

"Someone will. Delegate. I hear that's what I need to learn to do."

We both chuckled and it felt a little like talking with a friend, rather than an impersonator who'd forced me into his world and placed my own in danger.

"That's why I really think you need to learn how to travel through Ashton's past on your own." Elias sounded animated like Piercey usually did when talking about something that intrigued him. "Ashton refused to tell me anything about her time with Jaxon after what I did, and I know that they talked about how to make peace between the guilds. I need the information she has."

"Can't you explain why to her? I just don't understand why she's completely refusing to help you. I'm worried about wasting time trying to travel through her life when it may not be possible."

"I've tried talking to her. It's a dead end. This is the waste of time."

I tensed at his impatient tone. "You're not always easy to trust, Elias. It isn't a waste of time for me to ask questions for myself. I won't blindly follow you around."

"Fine. Fair. I'm sorry. It's just that if I knew how to defeat the guild right now, then I'd tell you how to do it. I'm missing pieces."

"What if trying to travel through her past doesn't work?"

"I don't see why it wouldn't work," Elias said. "The gods uploaded your consciousness to these worlds. There shouldn't be any difference at all apart from your lived experiences. Theoretically, because you are identical, you should be able to travel through her timeline. The only thing to hold you back is finding the entry point."

I sighed with a great deal of discomfort in the pit of my stomach. "I don't know. When I travel through time, I'm remembering. I can't remember a life I never lived."

"What about when you'd slip?"

"Well . . . I guess it was different. When I slipped, sometimes I did remember, but often there was some kind of trigger. I'd just suddenly fall through time."

"If it was like a flashback, then you were remembering at some level. It could be that a scent reminded you of that time or a feeling."

"Wait." I lifted my hand. "I lived multiple lives in my world from when Dr. Henderson reset the simulation. Why can't I travel through those previous lives?"

"It makes sense to me," Elias said. "When she reset it, she wiped it. You can't travel to a time that's been erased from your world. It's worth trying to live through Ashton's life. You need information, and I'd rather avoid connecting with you, too."

Honestly, I desperately wanted to avoid it, too. Connecting with Piercey, one of my closest friends in the world, almost proved too much. I would rather live through the life of another version of me than to connect with Elias. Thanks to Piercey connecting with Elias, I knew that we could trust there wasn't anything terrible Elias was holding back. I really didn't want that level of intimacy with him, or to peer into his experiences with Ashton.

"We have time while they recover, Max. Let's try. It will help you know how to interact with Lote when we meet in a few hours."

"If I travel back through Ashton's life successfully, should I target the time where she was with Jaxon?" I asked. "I can try to rely on my emotions to pull me back to when they first met." I certainly remembered the feeling of falling in love with Nash well, the way I fought it, and how incredible it felt to finally give in.

"Yes," Elias said. "Before that, we told each other everything."

"What about after she and Jaxon split up?"

"Not as important because even though things were strained, we did talk. But if you can, yes. What I need the most, though, is what she saw behind enemy lines. She fought with the other guild at one point when our kingdom was under attack."

Was it right to travel through Ashton's life as though it belonged to me? I didn't need to wonder about that. Of course, it wasn't. I needed information, though. I didn't have time to sit around worrying about ethical quandaries. I needed to defeat this guild before they invaded my world, and if Ashton insisted on defending them mindlessly, then she'd created her own fate. I wouldn't go easy on myself, not even in another life.

After I learned from Ashton's life, I'd better know how to kill Lote. Part of me wanted to just charge in and blast the hell out of his guild.

I should remember, though, that this world grew up on power. Every individual devoted their life to mastering it. Their people had advanced beyond what I could imagine because they all worked on it together, rather than a small percentage of people like in my world.

Once I heard that Nash had successfully received the implant and now slept in recovery, my nerves calmed. I worked with Elias the same way Piercey and I used to when I wanted to learn to master my control of time. We hoped that together with my instinct for travel and Elias's skill of breaking into the code of this world, we'd find our way into her life.

Elias wore a pair of goggles while we worked, toggling things in the air I couldn't see. I quickly learned that traveling through my life in my world did not work here, but I also wasn't able to travel through Ashton's. Though we shared the same consciousness, the gods must have created a way to differentiate us.

"That's it." Elias pinched something unseen to me and then dragged it down. "I can see you in the code. You're designated not only by your personal identification, but your world."

"So, it won't work?"

"I think it can. If you try traveling while I work on the code, we should be able to splice you into Ashton's life."

That seemed like a long shot to me. "I'm not sure how to do that."

"You don't do anything differently. Imagine that you're Ashton and try to travel back to when you first started working with Jaxon. I'll do the rest."

Closing my eyes, I sank into the feeling of first meeting Nash, imagining instead that it was Jaxon. Elias exclaimed in surprise, and then I felt myself slipping. Slipping far away.

"No . . . way . . ." I managed the words as the feel of the chair beneath me faded.

I often felt as if I stood in two bodies while slipping, my soul drifting somewhere between. It happened now, but also with my own personhood. For the first few seconds, I still sensed myself. I was Max looking through the eyes of Ashton. Quickly, though, my awareness of myself drifted as I fell fully into Ashton's past. I looked around at the verdant grass of the field and the strangers surrounding her, wondering who they were until their names began to fill my mind, and my love for them sparked in my heart. Rapidly, I became her. I became her so fully that my last fleeting moments as Max carried with them the fear that I'd never find my way back to my true self, to the Max who loved the Valley in my world and wanted to make a life with Nash.

This thread to my true self dipped into the river of Ashton's life, and no longer did I feel anything of my old life.

The canvas of the tents whipped with the wind as I gathered with my closest comrades, prepared for a battle that might change everything.

"I can't do this," I said.

"Ash." My friend let his head fall back as a frustrated groan slipped out his mouth. "I'll go crazy if I hear you complain one more time."

"We don't need them, Ralphy." The four coastal kingdoms united to try claiming dozens of villages along our Valley's border. They were powerful, and it required all the Valley kingdoms working together to rebuff their attempts. Our guild and the Silver Moon Guild agreed to partner together and share resources for this effort. I didn't trust a competing guild to work with us, especially not them.

"Right," my friend said. "We only need your sword and your thirst for battle."

"Obviously. I don't want to work with anyone from another guild when it's unnecessary, but if we're forced to ally with others, why them? Why our worst enemies? Why—"

"Because they're the best."

"We're the best," I said.

"Other than us. You know they're good. Put away your pride and think of our kingdom."

That ignited my fury like nothing else. "Don't act like I'm not doing that. You think this is good for the Valley? Pretending that we can work together only confuses the people who want to see our feud end. We need to actually resolve our issues, not ignore them."

"So, you'd make peace?" Ralphy asked.

"I'd love to make peace." I pursed my lips. "As long as they're willing to admit what pieces of shit they are."

My friend laughed. "You're a child."

"You feel the same. You just don't say it."

"Really, though. If the leaders came in today saying the feud was over, what would you do?"

"Easy," I said. "I'd welcome our new brothers and sisters, provided they actually intended to behave themselves. The problem is I don't trust them. They're going to use this situation to soften our resolve and fool some of us into trusting them. They'll try to plant dissent or wait for the perfect moment to strike."

Ralphy scoffed. "Paranoid."

"Realistic."

When he looked at me this time, he fell quiet long enough that I realized he really was worried. "Ash, this is a significant threat. All our guilds want to see our kingdom survive. Sure, we want different people in power and that doesn't benefit everyone. But any guild here taking power won't wipe anyone off the face of the Earth. These coastal guys want to destroy us and steal our resources. They literally want to kill every last one of us."

I winced. "I know."

"We can't take chances. We have to work together."

"It's a simplistic claim that is going to get some of our people killed, Ralph. Just because we all must fight our common enemy doesn't mean we should stand side by side. It will only make it easier for them to stab us in the back."

"Well . . ." Ralph sighed. "I guess watch your back, because we already have our assignments."

I grabbed his arm, horrified that he'd concealed this news. "Who? Who are we stuck with?"

His grimace told me all I needed to know. I wouldn't like this.

I stared at the enemy guild members who we would spend the next few days training with in preparation for entering the battlefield. Despite my arguments against working with them, I did see the wisdom of it. We practiced many battle strategies. This one, breaking into groups based on combat specialty, should be effective against this particular enemy. Our group of similar warriors increased from six exceptionally lethal warriors to eleven by pairing with the Silver Moon Guild.

I just couldn't believe they'd dared to give me a Silver Moon partner. We always paired with one member of our team in case we needed to branch out, but for the first time, that member wasn't one of my comrades. I stared at the mop of curly dark hair atop my so-called partner's head. He dared to smile at me, like we were friends. Or worse, like I was a joke.

I only narrowed my eyes in response. The stupid bastard chuckled appreciatively.

I'd teach that asshole not to underestimate me. And if he wasn't, if he just thought that I was someone to smile at, then he was in for a rude awakening.

"We're going to be working together for a few months, at least." Our group leader, an older but ferocious woman, seemed to give me an extra hard look. "Be on your best behavior. Get to know one another."

"Just don't get too cozy," I said.

The curly-haired fool crossed his arms, still not having the decency to look serious. I'd run into this guy before. Name was Jaxon and he was the hotshot of all hotshots. In his mind, at least. He could also fly. I'd never actually met another person in the flesh who'd mastered it at his level, and he let that get to his head. I did hate how that skill level gave me a thrum of excitement. I also hated how tense his gaze made me feel. What did he think he was looking at?

"How should we get to know each other?" Jaxon wandered a step closer.

"Don't fucking think about it."

"Think about what?"

I wrinkled my nose and glanced down his face, frowning at his easy half grin. "That. You think you're charming or cute or something. You're obnoxious and I already can't stand you."

"Ouch." He rubbed his chest. "My poor heart."

He was mocking me. Didn't look hurt in the slightest. I'd fix that for him.

I folded my arms over my chest. "We're gonna kill some coastal warriors over the next few months and then never see each other again. I don't need to know you to kill people in your general vicinity."

"We're fighting together."

"I fight alone," I said.

"Do you? I've seen you before. You're a team player."

"Not for this team."

"Man, you're going to be really fun."

Maybe it wasn't fair to be so antagonistic. I just didn't want to let that smile convince me for one moment that we could be friends. I'd lost actual friends to these people. This wasn't a bloodless feud between our guilds. Maybe we all wanted to fight for the Valley, but they were still my enemies.

Something told me that I shouldn't have to work this hard, be this mean, to keep someone as my enemy. That maybe I could let up. Only another part of me understood the danger of such thinking when Jax looked at me with his amused smirk.

Joining together was so foolish.

CHAPTER SEVENTEEN

Plunging headlong into the river of Ashton's life felt like I peeled the flesh from her bones and dug my way into the pit of her soul. I owed her every apology I could ever utter. But she was me, wasn't she? And yet she wasn't. How deep did our connection run? If I had the ability to travel through her life, if we were connected enough for that to work, did it mean I had the right?

I knew the answer. Because I knew that if she wanted my life, I'd give it to her willingly, but I'd want her to ask for it.

"What if we tell her the truth?" I rubbed the ache from my temples. "What makes you so certain that you can trust me but not her?"

Elias let his head fall against the wall and ran his hand over his face. "Because you trust Piercey, but she no longer trusts me. She can't let herself trust me. We've drifted too far apart. Coming back together would only hurt us."

Ashton made decisions in her life that had pushed her away from the people whom I held the closest to me. I didn't want to believe that in any life I'd do that. Thinking about the distance between her and Jaxon and Elias reignited my own fear about losing the people I loved. Everyone rested in the other room, safely. I needed to remember that and not allow the worry to cloud my thoughts again.

"I think you're underestimating her," I said.

"You know how stubborn you can be."

"I love my people. She must love you, Elias." My heart softened. "That's it, isn't it? She loves you. That's why she's pushing you away."

Confusion came over his face. Of course. I'd been here with Piercey, but we'd moved past it, because I didn't give him too much of myself. More than I wanted to give.

"Elias, if she gets close to you, it hurts you. As much as it hurts right now, being in her life without being with her obviously kills you. So she's letting you walk further from her. It doesn't mean she doesn't trust you."

This man was too hurt to see clearly. I practically heard his heart begging the question. Why not him? Why never him? No matter how much he loved her and no matter what he sacrificed, why was it never him in any world?

He visibly tensed, the embarrassment he must have felt at his weakness apparent in his reddened cheeks. "She's strong enough to handle that."

"No, she's not. You're her weakness. Her people are. I would not be able to stand breaking Piercey."

Elias looked at me now, and that life that he and Piercey had shared with one another seemed alive in him. The knowing look drilled fear into my heart. "Not if you didn't know."

Piercey wouldn't want Elias spilling secrets. Why had he said it? Had he not learned the self-discipline my friend had? Or was he so hurt that he couldn't help himself? I didn't care for a bitter version of Piercey, though I couldn't help pitying him.

"Sorry." Elias pinched the bridge of his nose. "You've done nothing wrong. You're not obligated to fall in love with someone and you've been a true friend to Piercey."

"You mistake me for her."

"I guess so. I didn't mean to lash out."

Elias shared the softness of Piercey's heart.

"One day," I said, "maybe you'll realize that while Ashton isn't in love with you, her love is just as deep and just as true."

"Don't. I'm not ready for that. Our life here is different, okay? I had her. She gave me her heart and I knew what it was to be with her. I ruined it. I ruined it before it even started because I knew she didn't feel the same way about me. I thought if I loved her enough, she would love me, too."

"Elias . . ."

"We never shared what you and Nash do. That's the worst part about all this. I realize that even after years with Ashton, I never actually held her heart."

I swallowed hard. "Do you see why I don't want to go peering into her life? Tricking Jaxon? This has consequences."

"There are consequences to not fighting this war. Ashton would do it to you. She'd enter your life and use it to save her people in a heartbeat."

What did it really matter if Ashton never knew? I shouldn't have been copied and dispersed over the worlds anyway. "Let's just get ready to meet with Lote. I want to be back by the time everyone wakes up."

Lote's office looked like it belonged to a man who spent too much time decorating when he supposedly helped run one of the most successful guilds in Skia Hellig. His cobblestoned walls stretched high up to the tall ceiling. Paintings, some reaching from ceiling to floor, adorned the room, along with shelves packed with books. The largest desk I'd ever seen dominated the room on the other side of the seating area where Elias and I both sat on separate leather couches. The furniture was so huge, it felt like I'd sink into it and never find my way out.

Fortunately, living through only a piece of Ashton's life helped me to impersonate her easily. With us sharing the same consciousness, it all came very naturally. She always worried about Elias and would see this meeting as a chance to help him. She'd also be afraid for him that it wouldn't go well. Protective skepticism. I needed to convey that conflicting emotion of not entirely trusting Elias but wanting to hide that from Lote.

Lote reclined in an impressive leather chair with his ankles crossed on the glass table between us. Bronze tattoos crawled up his fingers like thorny vines and wrapped around his wrists. His long auburn hair lay over one shoulder. "It's time, don't you think?" Hazel eyes drilled Elias.

My comrade appeared unfazed. "You said two weeks. I thought we were meeting just to talk."

"The guild said two weeks. I never agreed to that."

Tense.

Lote crossed his fingers over his midsection. "Your time has run out. It's that simple. We have no more patience to offer you, Elias. The only reason that we're speaking today instead of throwing you into a cell to await your trial is because Ashton swore to us that it'll all be worth it in the end." Lote pointed a long, thorny finger at him. "I remember a time when I would have trusted you with anything. You've squandered my trust with this stunt."

Elias didn't appear remotely nervous. I'd seen Piercey get this way, but not often with someone threatening his life. "Do you know why I needed privacy?" Anger tinted his voice, something I was not used to hearing in Piercey. It shook me. "It's because of you."

Lote's eyes narrowed.

"Elias," I said with warning.

"You've become greedy, and you've started reaching too far," Elias said. "You've opened us up to extortion and—"

"You don't know what you're saying," Lote said.

"I do. Don't worry, I haven't told anyone. I see now that it's dangerous to open your mouth around here these days."

Lote shifted forward. "What the—"

"You wanted to get at the Silver Moon Guild so badly that you've made us vulnerable," Elias snarled. "You've been secretly working with operatives for years. If I told you and Ashton what I was doing in this other world, you couldn't have resisted getting involved, and the operatives you're working with would have reported to you. Because they have been for a long time."

This silenced Lote.

"So, you want to yell at me for keeping secrets?" Elias asked. "I had to until I settled everything, because Ashton cannot help trying to save me and you cannot help your greed."

"I should crush your fucking head." Lote's tone did not change, nor did his expression expose his anger. The threat, spoken with such calm, chilled me.

"I suppose you can," Elias said, "if you don't want to know the secrets stored inside."

Lote uttered a low, throaty chuckle. "You're brave now, Elias. Brave and stupid. What's happened to you?"

"What happened is that I have discovered a power no one else has, and it opened worlds to me that you cannot imagine. My horizons have been broadened, Lote. I can see beyond you now."

The way that Lote quieted reminded me of a snake waiting to strike.

"So, are you going to come clean?" Lote asked.

"My official instructions from our guild—"

"You know that's not how this works."

"It's the way it's supposed to work," Elias said. "You are not our king. I'm gathering sensitive information, and I can't risk it landing in the wrong hands. I'll have everything ready within the allotted time." He stood up, signaling an end to the meeting, when I doubted anyone ever ended meetings with Lote. He seemed the type to decide when the conversation was over. "If my directives have changed, then send along the official word to me."

"You've gone insane," Lote said.

"I should get back to work so I'm not late on the report."

"I can compel you to talk."

Elias didn't hesitate. "So compel me. Or would that take official guild action that you seem reluctant to pursue?"

"You were right to run away, Elias. Leave before I lose my patience for your disrespect."

The other man dipped his head slightly. "Of course, sir."

Lote's eyes narrowed. The leader watched as Elias exited to the hallway. Then he sank back into his chair, kicking his feet back onto the table. "What a disaster. I've never seen such stubbornness in him before."

I needed to calm down and speak to him properly. Ashton saw Lote as a mentor. She thought that she owed him something and had no idea what a bastard he was or how little he cared about her.

"I knew he wouldn't say anything," Lote said. "What did you find out from him?"

"Is what he has to say as important as what he chooses to hide?" I asked. "I've seen enough to make assumptions about his misdirection."

"Explain."

Ashton would want to see the glow of his approval and hope to garner favor with him to earn patience for Elias. I needed to pretend to be hungry for his approval. "I don't think he wants to tell us about the other world at all. He's not just buying time."

"You don't think he was trying to come up with a strategic advantage at first? To increase his standing with the guild? Truthfully, his refusal to speak makes me wonder if he's already working with another guild. A year ago, I would never have been able to imagine saying that about him."

I needed to navigate this carefully. "No, I'm confident he's not betraying us for another guild. Elias is convinced that our guild will enter the other worlds and take their resources for ourselves." It might have been a mistake to say it, but Elias seemed certain they planned this, so I wasn't giving our enemy ideas.

Lote tapped his fingers on his armrest. "He really believes this is our plan?"

"Yes. I'm certain he believes that. Here we have so many guilds to contend with whereas over there we don't have any of our usual enemies."

"We may have new, unknown enemies. They could be more powerful."

I didn't want to disclose to him how helpless we would be against him and his people. "It's an opportunity, though. Something new. Would we pass that up?"

By the way he eyed me, I thought that he attempted to gauge my willingness to engage in his plan.

"Well," Lote said. "You did say before that he took you to a remote area in the world and you didn't sense even an inkling of power. I don't think they have the kind of power we have. No matter where you go in our world, you feel it. It sounds like an opportunity to me."

Dangerous and hard to control alarm stormed through me. I struggled to keep myself in check. "It's not our world, Lote. What business do we have there?"

"Don't be naive. If they don't have power or if they don't have as many people with power, then their resources won't be overly mined or controlled by others. Think of what we could do with more at our disposal."

"You think they'll let us come from another world and plunder their resources?"

"Do they even have a use for them?" he asked. "We can trade. If they lack power or as much power as us, there's plenty to offer them."

"What about Silver Moon?" I asked. "They'll want in, too. If we start traveling worlds, they're going to figure it out and learn to replicate. It's a matter of time. The war we have will spread to the other world."

"If the Silver Moon cannot be trusted not to invade and war in other worlds, then is that our fault? This is even more reason for us to gain control now."

This was not a trustworthy man. Gael's people wanted to strike a mutually beneficial deal with mine. I was quickly learning the power of allyship. Lote was not a man who had allies, though. He had underlings.

I considered carefully before saying the next part. "It's our fault if war spreads to their world. Imagine how devastating it may be to their world. Here, we want to protect our resources and our people. We work incredibly hard not to let our fighting hurt our kingdom. It's only natural that we won't share the same respect for another world. This is opening the door to horrors we cannot imagine."

"You're being dramatic," Lote said. "We're not going to destroy their world."

"An imbalance of power inevitably leads to violence when unchecked. I don't trust the kingdoms of our world to responsibly negotiate with a less powerful world when we cannot negotiate here. It'll be war and the people of that world will be dehumanized. We'll become invaders. Destroyers. It'll be genocide."

"Genocide?"

I almost lost control of my tone. "I have no doubt."

"You're reading too many books." The hunger for power emanated from Lote. I sensed his need to dominate my every thought. "Where's your trust in our guild?"

"My trust tells me that we'll be responsible and leave their world alone. Let's deal with our own land first. We need to fix our problems in our kingdom, not create new problems in new kingdoms."

Lote waved his hand at me. "You always have wise words. I'll consider this, though our leadership is very set already on working out an agreement with this other world. Elias is right that we plan to do this. He's just wrong to stand against it."

I couldn't let that happen. Multiple guilds or multiple kingdoms fighting over resources, or even land, in our world would be disastrous. I had to put a stop to this.

"What if Elias continues to refuse?" I asked.

"We'll force him to connect, then."

I struggled to hide the fear creeping over me this time.

Lote leveled his look at me. "Elias has been making terrible decisions. If he wants to remain a member of this guild, then he'll follow our leadership like everyone else. We can't give him any more grace. If we take this beyond our guild to the kingdom level, then he'll be imprisoned if he refuses to aid us. We are still managing conflicts over our borders. We need every advantage. He's a traitor if he refuses to help our kingdom. The questioning is to show him how serious we are. He won't let it go beyond that. Elias might be feeling rebellious, but he's no traitor."

A traitor. That was it, then. Lote had certainly made up his mind.

Elias told the truth when he called Lote a dangerous man. I didn't need to know him well or long to see what had been apparent about the Prophet and Dr. Henderson. Lote needed to lose his power. How the hell did Ashton not see that?

"I'll talk to him," I said. "He's going through something. He's probably a little scared about the power he uncovered."

"Then go. Convince him." The threat didn't need to be stated because I heard it loud and clear.

"I will. Just give me time. I want to watch him a little more, do some investigating. Help ease him into it."

"I'm willing to give you some time. Just don't take too long."

"Thank you, Lote. I trust you that we'll be responsible with this new world."

"I've never let you down before, Ashton. I won't start now."

I sincerely doubted that.

CHAPTER EIGHTEEN

We returned from meeting with Lote while everyone still slept, and I waited anxiously for Nash to wake up. If the implant worked properly, Nash would possess the same power I had. I knew too well that power served as a curse as often as a gift.

Maybe I feared that this major change may alter our life too much.

When the door opened and his broad form filled my view, I half expected him to look different, even knowing that wasn't rational. Seeing his same lighthearted smile settled my nerves.

Nash and I stepped into a recovery room away from the others. As much as I wanted to check on Leif and Wren, I needed this moment with just him. I needed it to be just us for once.

"How does it feel?" I held my breath after asking the question.

He tightened his hands into fists, staring at them intently. "I feel this strange sensation running beneath my skin."

Excitement bubbled up in me. "It's the power. Try to let it out."

"I don't know what will happen if I do."

"I'm not the best at containing power, but I can contain yours. This is fresh. Go ahead."

"You're sure?" he asked.

"Yes. Do it already."

Nash's face tensed in a rare look of worry, but he still smirked anyway, both eager and uncertain. A smokey, light blue haze wafted from his hand. Seeing him wield power stunned me.

"You see that?" Nash shouted.

I laughed and gripped his wrist. "Yes." Carefully, I placed my hand above it, testing the heat emanating from it. "Look at that. You're a natural."

"How do you know?"

"It's not easy to draw out meaningful power on your first try. You can use this energy in battle. You just need to learn how to propel it or gather it into a better form, like an arrow, or a ball."

I sensed the energy slowly dissipate while the blue sank back into his palm.

Nash touched his hand. "This is incredible."

Pride and joy burst within me. I jumped up to grab him around his neck and squeezed while I squealed. "You have power!"

"I know." He didn't sound exhilarated like I did, but rather somber. The emotion ran much deeper than that for him. He clutched me firmly. "I will fight with you."

I never knew how much it had hurt him to lack the power to fight the way I did. To protect me and fight with me on his own. How must he have felt every day this past year? Especially when I left him behind to fight?

Nash eased me back against the wall and opened my mouth with his, tilting his head to kiss me properly. My insides pooled in my stomach.

His eyes opened wide midkiss and he gasped. "Did you feel that?"

"What?"

"This explosion of intensity."

I naturally heightened my senses at times, often without realizing it, so the feel and taste and smell of him magnified. "Sometimes, yeah. Many times."

Nash pushed his fingers into my hair and pulled my head back, gazing down my face. "You've been holding out on me, Sharpshooter."

A giggle spilled from my lips as he melted his mouth against mine and roamed the soft of my tongue with his own, his kiss like electricity. His hands dug into the contours of my body, working me closer and closer to him. A pulse of power sparked from his palms and rushed through my body. I ripped back, startled.

"Did I hurt you?"

Vibration buzzed against my skin and buried itself in my bones. I struggled to draw in a breath. "I wouldn't say it hurt."

He smiled. "Yeah?"

"I think . . ." My fingers stole down the side of his whiskered cheek. With his curls falling over his amber eyes and the raw emotion of his power awakening, he looked as handsome as ever. An aching want buried in my core. "I think we should save this for later."

He nodded, eyes intent on my mouth. His gaze skittered down my body. "We should." He kissed along my jaw and murmured. "We should . . . But it's always later . . ."

The longing for a life left unlived clawed into me until I wilted in his embrace.

"Everything changes now, Max." Nash held my weight for me. "I swear to you that every day of my life, I'll hone this power and fight for a peaceful home for us."

A year of blood and battles, sleepless nights and desperate chases across the Valley. A year of wanting more. The vines of exhaustion never relented, insistently ripping me apart in my depths. Nash loosened them with the rumble of his voice, the promise of his words, the strength of his arms.

"You're tired." He lowered to a chair, bringing me with him, holding me as I allowed my eyes to close. "This is our fight, not just yours. I'll learn how to wield this power faster than anyone ever has so you don't have to wait for me any longer."

"I've wanted to run away sometimes." The confession burst from me before I could catch it. "To find some quiet with you and Elsie where nothing matters except for us."

"It'll be okay. Everything is okay now."

I rested against him and let myself believe his vow without question.

"I think mine is broken." Leif punched his fist through the air like it might force his power to shoot out. "Come on!"

The three of them all recovered well from the procedure and gathered in the waiting area.

"You're overthinking," Nash said.

"You aren't thinking enough," Wren corrected.

"Everyone taps into their power in a different way," I said. "Leif, you need to be patient. You're locking yourself up by trying to force it."

"I've heard that before." Leif's lip twitched into a frown. "Arn thinks himself funny when I'm stuck in the outhouse. This is a battle I've faced before. One I always win."

"For the love of the gods," Wren muttered.

He crouched and lifted his fists in the air. "Come out!"

"I can't tell if he's actually about to take a shit." Nash snickered.

Seeing normal amid completely unbelievable—all three of them having power now—reduced my previous anxiety entirely.

We'd be just fine, wouldn't we?

"Don't force anything," I said to all three. "You're eager, but this will take time. Elias and Piercey both said they'd help you with your abilities."

Wren raised one brow at me. "What about you? Not willing to help?"

I flashed a skeptical smile because she knew I was an awful, impatient teacher. "I'll beat your ass down when you're ready to fight."

"Now I really have to get this power working," Leif said. "I can't allow a challenge to go unanswered."

Nash lifted his palm as a small, glowing ball of energy popped over one finger at a time.

"Are you serious?" Leif growled and pounded the air with his fists. "Where is my power!"

Wren placed a hand to her stomach.

"You feel it?" I asked.

"It's like water trickling through my body."

"Mine is like fire," I said. "I should have expected yours to be more peaceful and in control."

She looped her arm through mine, quiet as she watched the two men.

Yeah, it really would be fine.

A sense of urgency broke through the calm, and suddenly I felt as though I slipped. I met Nash's eyes just as the world was ripped away from me.

In a chilling sense of déjà vu, I lifted my face to the pale ceiling of the all-white room.

White crashed all around me and swept me back to the days of meeting Dr. Henderson. Though I immediately met the kind eyes of Dr. Drake, I still expected to see the old supervisor of my world lurking behind her.

The disappointment and disbelief etched into her face tightened my stomach into a hard ball.

"What were you thinking?" Dr. Drake asked.

I breathed in slowly. I needed to stay calm, collected, and most of all, confident. "You know what I was thinking. You understand it, too."

"Max. You entered another world and took implants for people who weren't born with them. The Collective will not be happy."

"Do they know yet?"

"Not yet," she said. "The supervisor of this world contacted me because she knew that I was working with you."

I blinked. "So she knows we came from another world?"

"She monitors new neural implants. It didn't take long for her to figure out that you're from another world. You're marked in the system."

Dr. Drake knew things that she'd never told me. That didn't surprise me really. I just had never thought about it.

"You knew that it was our same consciousness populating all these worlds," I said.

"What good would it have done for me to tell you?"

"You see what I've been through and what I've accomplished. Don't coddle me and don't underestimate me."

"Okay." She sighed. "That's fair."

"How many other worlds are there? Tell me the truth."

"Well . . ." A look of shame came over Dr. Drake. "Each experiment runs on four worlds. We have ten cohorts of worlds, all with different people. So that the Collective can compare data between the group of controls."

"Controls. You mean us. Human beings."

"Yes."

"Why does it always get worse?" The anger edged into my voice, even though I knew that Dr. Drake didn't agree with the Collective and cared about what happened to me. Standing here in this white room, saying things like *we*, I barely separated her from the rest of the Collective, or even from Dr. Henderson.

Dr. Drake looked frightened for me. "I have no idea what the Collective will do about you sneaking into this world and taking powers for your people. It can't happen again."

"It's not going to. I needed help. You see the fallout of what Dr. Henderson did to our world." I straightened my shoulders. "I'm not a child, so I won't pretend to be ashamed of my actions or act like I didn't understand the implications of what we did. I won't act like I didn't know how the gods would feel. I did what was best for my people. We all did."

"It's just, if you'd come to me first—"

"Would my friends have this power if I had come to you?"

Dr. Drake looked away. Answer enough.

"The only advantage I have is that you guys are not constantly monitoring me in real time," I said. "I'm sure that'll change now. You've learned your lesson that I can cause more problems than you thought. That is on you, though. I escaped my simulation once before."

"You scare me sometimes." Dr. Drake pulled her sleeves over her hands, fidgeting. "I don't know how to keep you from doing things that the Collective will not accept."

"Then explain to me why it matters. Really. My world cannot be considered a valid source of data any longer. You guys promised to let us live in peace and stop experimenting on us. So don't interfere. Let us do what we want and simply observe."

She sighed. "Still, that doesn't mean that they want to let you start mixing worlds and borrowing technology and advancements. They want to salvage what data they can."

"It's their own fault for making it possible to cross worlds."

"They aren't going to be happy about this. I can tell you right now that this time relativity component will be changed. They certainly are not going to want you spending days on end, years even, in another world without losing time in your own world."

"Why?" I asked.

"The data, Max. It's all about the data."

"The data on what? Why do you need more data than you already have? Giving the implants to one percent of the world does not work."

"They knew it wouldn't. The point is to have different control groups to compare so that we can learn about how people behave with the implants and prepare for all scenarios."

My nostrils flared. "This is my life, not their experiment. They failed us so they don't get to trap us in our world when we learned how to travel ourselves."

"You're right that you deserve to live life to the fullest. I'm explaining their mind frame. There are limitations, Max. I can't change the Collective."

"They shouldn't stunt our advancements. We should be encouraged to reach the heights of our innovation. Isn't there value in that data? Sure, it may not be what you wanted originally. But can you not find a way to start your study anew? A case study. Or a qualitative study."

She paused. "You've been talking to Piercey."

"Hell yes, I have. My world is a mess. Elias has answers that can help us. I'm not giving everyone in the world powers, only a few trusted comrades."

"Where will it end, though?" she asked. "Their world knows how to shift between worlds. Yours will figure it out now that you've seen as much as you have. Should only the people you love and trust get the power?"

"For now. We have no better way of vetting people. It's all fallen on top of my shoulders. So yeah, my people and I, we're the ones deciding."

"You better find another way soon. That's all I'm saying. Introducing power to people who previously lacked it changes everything. If the wrong person got their hands on this ability, think of what they could do with it."

I closed my eyes. "I know. I understand the problems with what we're doing. We're desperate, though. Dr. Henderson orchestrated so many power plays and enabled some of the worst people in Skia Hellig to pursue their ambitions unchecked."

She carefully placed her hand on my shoulder. "I'm going to do what I can with the Collective."

"Are you afraid that they'll remove me from this world? Or shut us down?"

"It's too late for that. The fallout of you breaking into the afterlife and Dr. Henderson being removed has rippled beyond the Collective. It's not widespread knowledge, but enough eyes are on you that they can't just kill you or destroy your world."

"So why are you scared?"

"The Collective has time on their hands," she said. "An abundance of intelligence, wisdom, and power. I want to believe that they'll do right by you, but look at the mistakes they've made. If you keep causing problems, I worry about how that will affect you once you've reached the Kethios, whether in the afterlife or in the rest of society."

I needed to think about the next few years, not a future I couldn't wrap my mind around. "That's a problem for another day."

"What if they take away your power?"

"They said they couldn't."

"Your instructors sealed your power once," she said. "It's possible. This time, you may not get it back."

I didn't consider this long. "If they want to steal away the power of the person who is safeguarding an entire region, then that will be a very sad day for them. I'm not hurting my world. I'm just hurting the Collective's agenda. Take care of this for me. Apparently, they have plenty of other worlds they can watch."

"You know that I'm on your side, don't you? It's why I care about you being in danger with the Collective."

"I know that you care, and I know you think that the safest thing for me to do is to keep the Collective happy with me. What you don't realize is that if I wait for permission from people, then I'll never escape the limitations they put on me. My world is in peril and it's up to us to fix it. I can't rely on the Collective for that."

Her shoulders lowered. "I understand. I just want you to be safe."

"You know what I really think? There's more going on here than they're saying. There's a reason they let Dr. Henderson stay in control of my world after she devolved. I don't believe they had no idea. There's a reason they let me come back and kill her. And there's a reason they continue to allow me to defy them. More than that, there's a reason that time is synchronized across worlds for people inside the simulation."

Dr. Drake looked just as troubled.

"Who did they intend to walk between worlds?" I asked. "What do they want?"

"I don't know," she said.

"You need to find out. They created this mechanic for a reason."

She bit her lip. "You may have to ask them yourself. If I intervene too much on your behalf, they may think I'm too emotionally invested to work with you. I'll find out what I can, but please consider talking to them. I'm sure that as soon as they realize what you've done, they'll want to meet with you."

"You know, I'm sure they will. And I don't really feel like waiting around for them to call. I want to see them now."

"Max . . ."

"I'd rather approach them."

The first time I placed my hand against the window holding back the waters of the Collective last year, I had no reason to believe I would ever return to my home world. At the time, I felt entirely at their mercy. Since then, I came to understand that the Collective needed me. It was why they allowed me to return to my world and why they let me stay there after I killed Dr. Henderson. I may not have understood what they wanted with me, only that I had more power than what had first appeared.

They waited for me to speak first. For a being that existed beyond the traditional sense of time, it seemed awfully manipulative. They didn't need time to process or think for as long as I did.

"I don't plan to explain myself," I said. "You know what I did and you're smart enough to know why I did it."

"We are smart enough to also see that you are not remorseful in the slightest."

"I'm as remorseful as you are for leaving us in my world with no power after Dr. Henderson made such a terrible mess."

A moment of hesitation. For me, no doubt.

"You're committed to your people and will do what you feel is best for them, no matter the trouble it places you in," the Collective said. "Taking power must have been worth it to you to anger us. It touches us that you have some sort of faith in us after all that has happened. You believed that we would not end your life, and we're happy you feel that way."

"Are you really?" Could the Collective lie? What a dumb question. Of course they could. I just wasn't sure how often they chose to do so.

"Yes, because we do care about the people in the worlds we created." Their voices blended in perfect harmony, a song of an untold number of souls. "In fact, it's important to us that we do all we can to help you flourish, especially given the mistakes we've made."

"I'm not sure you see them as mistakes," I said. "You're allowing experiments to continue in other control groups. That doesn't sound like remorse."

"We've told you before that having created this problem in the first place, we should at least reap the benefits of the experiments."

A smile curled my lips. "If you could go back, would you actually do anything differently?"

"No."

I appreciated that they answered quickly and didn't pretend like they needed time to think about it. They wanted me to trust them. They knew that I wouldn't believe any supposed regret or a false show of uncertainty. "Then I truly have no reason to regret my actions."

"We suppose not. It's problematic for us, though. We cannot have you operating with no rules."

"I have rules. I do what's best for my people." I stepped forward, studying the light rippling through the clear water. If I looked close enough, I could detect a rhythm. "You can predict what I might do knowing that about me. You shouldn't try to interfere. We have a deal. You observe me. That needs to be enough for you."

"You're abusing the mechanics of your world."

I steeled myself. "So are you."

"We're shutting down the synchronization of time," the Collective said.

"No." I punched the wall of water, busting the skin of my knuckles open. The water barely rippled beyond the red smear of my blood. "I need time to deal with the threat in Elias's world."

"Control yourself, Max."

"You control yourself. You're punishing me when it'll cost innocent people in the Valley their lives. It is your temper, not mine, that causes the most damage."

My blood faded from the glass until I no longer saw it.

"This isn't vengeance," the Collective said more gently. "You'll age more than the others in your world, and it's difficult to say how that will affect you. It isn't safe to allow corruptions to nature to continue, no matter the consequences for your people."

Sounded like an excuse to me. "How am I supposed to fight the war for my Valley and Elias's guild at the same time?"

"Follow the order of nature, Max. Do that, and we'll look the other way for your recent indiscretions. We will not overlook you sharing neural implants with others or sharing resources across worlds, especially not technology or people."

My fist ached. I tightened it, grounding myself with the pain. "You've created your own nature. I'm sure you can handle whatever problems my world shifting might cause. I'm dealing with a dangerous situation. A guild wants to enter my world. I need time to stay still in my world when I'm gone."

"No, absolutely not. The world is not meant to work this way. You've brought your friends in on this, too. You're threatening the stability of two worlds. We will not yield on this matter."

I swallowed hard. "Will you block our ability to travel worlds?"

"We don't know if we necessarily can without altering the conditions of your experiment. You've used your power to do this. You did not use your power to freeze time in your world. That was our doing."

"Why?" I leaned forward. "Why did you build this into our worlds? Who has been traveling between our worlds?"

"We needed it as a mechanic in case, just like how we have the ability to have avatars."

"And why do you have those?"

"We wanted all methods of observation to be available," the Collective said. "Supervisors require the ability to enter the world as one of you and gather that kind of qualitative research."

These sounded like half-truths. That may have been the Collective's preferred way of lying, not to outright weave together lies, but to paint an incomplete or skewed picture.

"Is there any other reason why you made that mechanic?" I asked.

"We told you the truth. Clearly, you won't believe us."

I settled my forehead against the window.

"Will there ever be peace between us, Max?"

"I don't know," I said. "I'm angry."

"You're tired as well. We hear it in your voice. It's why you needed Nash, Leif, and Wren to take power."

"I need just a little bit of mercy," I said.

"We know." The Collective's voice sounded as smooth as honey now. "We don't blame you for what you did, but it worries us for what you'll do in the future."

"I'm not going to let anyone else from my world receive a neural implant. This was a onetime thing."

"Will you travel to the other worlds?"

"I don't know." Maybe I should have lied, but I truly didn't want to. I was tired of the lies, the half-truths, the hidden mysteries they refused to unveil. "What do you really want with me?"

"We want to watch what you do."

"It's more than that."

"Max, go home. Don't simply care for your people but live your life. We offered you another chance to live for a reason. Don't let it waste away."

The longing for quiet days with Nash and Elsie tightened my throat. "Why are you letting me get away with this? I think you should. I believe in my argument. I just don't trust your motives."

"We would also find it hard to trust in your situation. Though you refuse to believe us, we care about you. We want you to live."

I hated not knowing what they really wanted.

The pressures of two worlds squeezed my skull in a dull ache. How could I fight wars in two worlds at the same time?

Dr. Drake whisked me away to the white room in the midst of hope, the joy of my people gaining power, and returned me with the burden of an impossible problem. The demon attacks, Flatlander raids, and coastal skirmishes would not wait for me to kill Lote in Elias's world.

The worries spun my stomach into knots, so I physically flinched when Leif slapped my back after I returned.

"You won't believe it, girl," he boasted. "I felt the power."

"You did?" I swallowed down my anxiety and forced myself to smile.

"I did. I couldn't draw it out, but I felt it inside of me, like this other being that now dwells alongside my spirit."

"What about you?" I looked at Wren.

"I think I'm picking it up quickly."

I didn't need to question Nash about the same. I could tell by the sharp determination in his eyes, the confidence in his form, that he had excelled while I was away. "Are you ready to fight?" I asked instead.

"Absolutely," Nash said.

"No," Elias said. "None of you are ready to fight with your powers yet."

Nash lifted his twin blades and stared intently at the one on his right and then left. A subtle flutter, like a breeze, unfurled from the swords. He thrust them both forward, piercing the air far faster than ever before. Undeniable power.

"Holy shit," I said. "You can already wield it."

"I've spent time with you while you trained." Nash nodded. "I'm prepared. I may not be ready to fight with my full potential, but I won't waste time. We battle side by side now."

As much as I wanted quiet days alone with him, the thought of using our powers together and learning how to draw it out of ourselves exhilarated me. I grinned and nodded.

"There's going to be plenty of battles for us to fight very soon," I said.

"Agreed, unfortunately," Elias said.

My people needed me back in my world and I couldn't waste any time here.

"The gods aren't happy." I settled my hands on my hips. "We've escaped the worst consequences, but time will now pass in our world when we're here."

Leif unleashed a string of curses and twisted in a circle, scratching at his beard. Nash lowered his head.

"We need to go home," I said.

"But—" Elias drew back, looking shocked.

"Our world isn't prepared for us to disappear," I said. "We need to get back home and prepare. Can you get us home without raising too much suspicion?"

Elias groaned. "I can take you home and bring you back again. It'll be hard, but I can do it at least one more time. First though—"

"What now?" I asked. "Really, Elias?"

Elias clasped his hands together like he was pleading. "Live through more of Ashton's life so we can plan. It doesn't take you that long to live through one or two memories. Try again before you go home."

"Time is passing in my world. What if there's an attack?"

"I'll make sure you're awake after thirty minutes. Okay? Surely, for thirty minutes your people will be okay."

I couldn't assume that. More than likely, though, we could squeeze in a small amount of time. "Thirty minutes. Use your power to wake me up if I'm still out."

CHAPTER TWENTY

My first few weeks working with the Silver Moon Guild and with Jaxon as my partner tempted me to think of these rival warriors as more than they were—our enemies. I stayed strong, though, in my commitment to protect myself from my own weakness.

As the coastal kingdom ramped up their war against us, we gathered for the largest battle of my life. I'd primarily witnessed such events in mock wars, held annually as training to mobilize our forces in the event of a large-scale attack by enemy kingdoms. Never in real combat, however.

I had fought against plenty of surprise attacks and ambushes during our dispute with the southern kingdom over the last month, but for the first time our armies faced one another head-on. We confronted our enemy on their war path to one of our cities.

I was ready for this battle.

Even if I didn't feel quite ready to fight with Jax as my partner.

The dissonance of serving the same kingdom with our rival guild muddied my mind. In the end, we'd die by each other's sides if it meant protecting our people. How could we be so loyal to one another as compatriots and yet enemies as members of our guilds?

Our competition fractured our kingdom. Competition that soured into an outright blood feud. I feared that with time, the zeal of our feud might overcome our loyalty to our kingdom. Our souls would not survive such a day.

As much as I resented fighting alongside the Silver Moon Guild, this battle-field forced me to acknowledge my childishness for complaining that first week. I didn't like having to collaborate, but I recognized the necessity now. The four coastal kingdoms temporarily worked together several times in the past to challenge our borders, but they never formally united until now.

It was unprecedented. Shocking. Deadly.

I looked to my side where Jax stood tall, showing no signs of fear. He appeared entirely born for battle, from the hunger in his eyes to his large form. He was a war machine. I felt the same way. My natural talent for wielding my powers in combat stoked plenty of jealousy within my guild. Maybe Jax wasn't such a bad partner after all. I wouldn't confess that to him and would probably deny it to myself as soon as the high of battle wore off, but the thought seemed obvious to me in this moment.

As quiet blanketed the battlefield like a prelude to our war, my mind stilled.

Our army moved first, charging forward together, no longer opposing members of warring guilds, but determined warriors of one united kingdom. The lines between us no longer existed, and the conflict that seemed so deeply entrenched, so impossible to forget even minutes before, faded like a distant dream.

The sharp screeches of steel blades sang out, punctuated by the first screams of the injured. I drove forward with Jax and the rest of our group, immediately cutting off the hand of an enemy warrior in my second strike. No one in my group used energy weapons. Usually, most warriors preferred this. Despite their strength and versatility, they required energy. Instead, I preferred to strengthen, shield, and power my physical weapons.

As I swung my blade, the field darkened. Navy storm clouds of power rolled through the sky above us. Our enemy already vied for dominance of the airspace.

Battles of this size posed logistical problems because the collision of so much power threatened the safety of our region and the destruction of the natural resources we all desired. In school, we'd studied battles from the last few decades that resulted in unintended mass casualties, or the ruin of scarce resources. In a chilling example, one battle that took place a full one-hour ride from the nearby village reduced every structure there to rubble from a surge of collective power.

When we fought, our power collided, and even grew as one, boiling over the top. Halting the power of warring armies was like subduing a massive avalanche. So we couldn't throw all that we had at one another or reach our full potential. When using power in war, we focused as much on control and strategically holding back as on overpowering the enemy.

That was why we were divided into crews. Warriors on the ground, like my team, used our power individually, only combining temporarily if a strategic opportunity presented itself. We engaged in targeted combat against individuals within a close vicinity. Those in aerial support hid in the woods and united like one body to gather their individual energy into one massive and deadly pool. They didn't target individuals but groups, or even entire divisions.

The defenders protected our entire force and looked over as many individuals as possible. They banded together to shield groups or strengthen lone warriors.

We all worked in unison, the warriors, the defenders, the aerial support, and the commanders. Trusting one another.

So I ignored the threat that swirled above me and darkened the sky in a navy film of power. If our defenders lost their hold on that immense energy, it would crush all of us beneath it in a second, no matter how great our power. I could do absolutely nothing about this, and so I banished the threat from my mind. It crept in at times, especially when bolts of power cracked like lightning. But I needed to focus only upon my battle.

My group trampled slain bodies underfoot to break through the enemy line.

"Now," I shouted. I darted to the side, slashing my blade and unleashing a wave of power from its edge. The burst of energy sliced through a calf, sending the leg spinning through the air. My attack continued and collided with the glint of an energy shield.

Another blade caught mine, the edges clashing with a sharp cry, powered by our energy. I pivoted on my heel and used the energy coursing around my blade to drive it unnaturally fast into the kidney of a nearby warrior.

Jax fought with equal speed and precision, his sword cutting through the back of a warrior as he skidded to a stop beside me. I dragged a deep breath into my burning lungs, trying not to grin. This wasn't for fun. People were dying. Rarely did we get to face such an enormous battle that tested our limits like this, though.

A group of warriors locked their eyes on us, perhaps seeing all their fallen comrades around us. We didn't wait for them. We charged.

Jax flew into the air, spinning rapidly, spreading bolts of power down in a perimeter around us. Usually, warriors did not attack with so many at once. His power of flight gave him a unique and fascinating advantage. I'd never actually fought with someone who could fly before.

My heart thudded in my chest, and it wasn't entirely from the battle. He fought so beautifully. I saw the discipline behind each move, the testament to rigorous and passionate training.

The warriors we encountered now differed from those before. Faster. Stronger. More brutal.

A man with a blade the size of both my legs combined and muscled arms about the same thickness reared back, eyes locked on me.

He lunged. I dodged. We danced around one another until the mighty swing of his blade whizzed within inches of my left forearm. This time when he reared back, I faced him head-on. I caught the strike of his blade with my own, pouring my energy into my weapon.

My body strained beneath the unwavering steel and the incredible power of the attack. Jax noticed, tried to sidestep a warrior pursuing him, but had to deflect a strike.

I couldn't defend against this attack. Any moment, the blade was going to snap mine in half and cut through my chest. An instant kill.

Releasing all my energy, I shot to the side. The massive sword thudded into the ground so hard that the earth swallowed it up. The man hefted it free with ease. Dodging out of the way was only a temporary solution. He wasn't winded in the slightest. He'd let me evade because he likely had hundreds of those same attacks left in him. I wouldn't win in a power or endurance competition with this beast.

Instead, I drew the energy from my body out of every pore, so tiny droplets of power glazed my body. The man charged for me. This attack depended upon the flexibility of the form my power took, so I didn't channel it into a weapon or even attempt to prepare a shield. Instead, I fell completely into my instinct, trusting my reflexes.

This would never work for people like Elias who grew their power through dedicated study. I was an instinct fighter, and I needed to give myself over to those instincts and to the speed of my subconscious mind, which worked far faster than the part of me that needed to think and dissect.

The man nailed me with a hit so powerful that it clapped like thunder and shook the ground. Only it didn't hit. The beads of my power converged on the blade on all sides, each exerting a forward force so the weapon stopped inches from my face. The remaining beads darted out to cover him like flies on a rotting carcass.

My enemy cried out in alarm and jumped backward, blindly swinging his massive blade.

Beads popped against his skin in tiny explosions. Thousands of bloody pinpricks littered his body.

I drew my energy back to me in the form of a long, sharp spear. Hurled it at his throat. He chopped the spear in half, failing to realize I had only thrown it as a distraction.

A quarter of the beads hadn't exploded against him, but gathered into a knife at the base of his skull. He drove his own head into the energy blade as he jumped back to avoid my spear.

I breathed in heavily, drawing as much of my energy back to myself as I could. It wasn't accurate to call my power a finite source, like a pitcher of water. Rather, I thought of it as a waterfall breaking through a cave wall. Only so much water poured at once, but a flood always waited to spring out.

Sometimes, I could break the hole in that wall open further. I focused on resting to replenish my energy as I turned to see Jax's sword midswing through the enemy's neck. In an instant, he held a severed head as the body crashed to the ground.

Jax dropped the head, staring at me. He looked as shocked as everyone else who'd ever seen me use the strategy of the beads. While I didn't create that attack, I didn't know anyone else in the Valley who had mastered it well enough to use it in battle.

"What the hell was that?" Jax asked.

I smirked, unable to help it. We could teach each other a few things. I couldn't deny how incredible it was to fight with him, nor the sting of disappointment that we fought on opposite sides of the feud between our guilds.

We did, though. And nothing else mattered. Jax was my enemy.

One day, my blade might cross his.

The battle stretched on for seven days as warriors swarmed the area to stop the march to our city. In the end, we fended them off, but I expected they'd return with a vengeance.

For now, it earned us a few days' rest in the city we battled to protect.

Elias met our group there, worried about me after hearing about the massive battle. The time apart and the stress of the past few weeks softened the tension between us. I'd never wanted there to be any in the first place. We'd broken up nearly a year ago and sworn to stay friends, so why couldn't we put it behind us?

"It's inconceivable that we should have to join forces in any way, shape, or form," Elias said with a bitter note to his voice. "How did we let this happen?"

"Even your greatest enemy becomes your ally when outsiders try to steal your home." Jaxon stretched his arm across his chest. "Don't worry. As soon as we've dealt with this threat, we'll go back to kicking each other's asses."

"Yeah right." I leaned against my knees. "I'm going to kick your ass. There's no 'each other's asses' in this scenario."

"Try." Jaxon shifted to the side. "Come for me right now and show me what you can do."

Elias guffawed and turned away as if he could not stomach the sight of Jaxon fooling around, but it only made me want to kick his ass even more.

I swiftly slammed my boot forward. He dodged, of course. But I'd erected shields on either side of him.

Instead of slamming into them like I hoped he would, he pushed off one with a shimmering zap of energy that sent him flying past me at an angle. With horror, I realized that he aimed for my own ass. Presumably to kick it. How had he anticipated the wall? Did he possess such fine detection abilities that he sensed it, though he couldn't see it?

Didn't matter. I'd look like a fool if I let him reach me.

I funneled my energy against his chest. He blocked this, but it gave me time to reposition. I dove for the ground and swung my leg for its target. Jaxon leapt into the air and hovered there.

There was no denying how good that move was. Pushing off the ground with a blast from each hand, I flipped and slammed into him. Though I didn't connect with the ass I wanted to kick, it did allow me to grab him around his waist so he couldn't fly too high.

A laugh bellowed from Jaxon as he ripped my arms away from him. We both landed on our feet—my palms raised to him and his fists to me. The sound of his laughter snapped me out of the daze of our skirmish. We weren't friends, and enemies didn't laugh together.

I shifted my eyes away from his easy smile and nodded at Elias. "The only good thing about working with them is learning for our future fights."

Jax looked skeptical as he sauntered closer, quirking his brow at me. "I don't buy your act, Ash. You're having fun."

"I'm having fun imagining the day I rip your head from your shoulders."

Damn, that sounded like we were having fun, didn't it?

"You think I'm joking," I said. "I'm not."

"Sure," Jax said.

Elias eyed the two of us and it made me feel even more like I needed to set the record straight. Ensure everyone here knew where we stood.

I shrugged. "I'll confess that your warriors fight admirably, and that you're more deserving enemies than I originally thought."

"Your praise means everything to me." The sarcastic tease of Jax's voice grated at me.

Instead of responding, I rolled my eyes and walked away to keep my space.

The day passed slowly as I rested and sharpened my blades for the next battle. Eventually, Elias found me, letting me know he planned to leave in the morning to return home.

"You'll be safe?" he asked.

I sat up on the bed to face him fully. "You know I will."

"It's hard to leave you here when I know you'll be in danger."

He always worried when I battled.

"You have to trust me," I said.

He nodded. Forced a smile. "I do. Your group is skilled. I feel better knowing you're fighting alongside the best warriors." I realized I was pursing my lips when Elias chuckled. "You really can't let yourself warm up to them, can you?"

"You know that I let people in too deep. I can't give them any room in my life, or it'll be too hard to go back to being enemies."

A look of understanding passed over him. "You don't want to feel any loyalties to an opposing guild." Elias sat down beside me, leaving enough space for me to remember a time when nothing separated us. "You commit too deeply."

That sounded loaded and I supposed it was. For all the years I'd spent with Elias, I knew for most of them that we shouldn't have been together, but I couldn't walk away from the relationship. It felt like abandoning him. In a way, it felt like abandoning myself, because he was so much a part of my life.

The pain of loving Elias cut into my heart like thorns. I genuinely cared for him and always had. I'd learned to love him. Had sought out and discovered every beautiful thing about him. He was like a wine that I grew to appreciate and adore. But we weren't right for each other, and I realized I should never have trained myself to enjoy his taste. Loving Elias robbed me of him.

He reached across the space between us to settle his hand over mine, likely feeling the hurt churning in the empty space like I did.

I missed him so badly that I would do anything to have him back—even teach myself to crave him again. That wasn't how love should work, though. I should long for him, not make myself accept him.

He'd always felt the absence of my heat for him.

I had to let go of this part of our relationship so we could both move forward.

A jolt of grief slammed my heart against my ribs, ripping me free from the currents of Ashton's life. I awoke back in my own body.

My heart ached from a lifetime of experiences that didn't belong to me.

"Are you okay?" Nash asked, helping me to a sitting position.

Elias reached for me as well, and I viscerally remembered his hand sliding over Ashton's. Her heart had been so broken. His, too. I almost told him to keep his distance, wanting to avoid the sadness twining him together with Ashton. Except her memories showed me the futility of pushing people away.

"I'm fine," I said. "It's jarring, that's all."

"What did you get?" Elias watched me eagerly. "Anything we can use?"

"Nothing for you. It's useful for me, though. I think I need to go further. Ashton is still really closed off to Jaxon in the memories I lived through." It felt like a betrayal to share anything of Ashton's with Elias. If she wanted him to have it, then she would have given it to him. "Let's get to my world and we can talk more."

CHAPTER TWENTY-ONE

Fortunately, we lost only an hour of time in our world after the gods destroyed the mechanic we needed most.

We now sat with Gael and a group of his warriors in a conference room at the Sacred School. I couldn't ignore the threat in Elias's world, and I only knew of one hope for protecting the Valley while I dealt with Lote.

"You're saying you want to go forward with the partnership?" Gael asked with a note of surprise.

"You've had a year to watch us and decide whether to trust us," I said. "I'm confident you've had the time you need to decide. In ideal circumstances, we'd like more time as well." It scared me to trust Gael with this information because it showed a vulnerability. When I'd met Nash and struggled with deciding to trust him, I chose to follow my gut. Now I needed to do the same with Gael. "We're dealing with a threat that will temporarily take our attention off the Valley."

Gael and several of his warriors exchanged glances. "Something we should be worried about?" he asked.

Instinctively, I wanted to lie and dismiss his concerns. That wasn't fair, though. We were about to build a partnership. "It concerns all of us if we fail. I can't share everything right now. It's not that I want to hide anything, just that we have to be careful to not create more conflict for ourselves than we already have."

Gael drummed his fingers on the table, looking lost in thought. "You have dealings with the gods that no one else in the world has. I suppose that is a blessing and a curse that comes with the Sacred School.

We already considered that you'd have some limitations imposed by them."

Piercey leaned forward at that. "I promise you that we want to tell you what we can. Angering the gods will benefit no one, however."

"We understand," Gael said. "Don't think it means we're happy about it or we're not going to press for answers."

Fair. They couldn't allow us to live in secrecy with no questions asked. The gods made for a convenient excuse. We really couldn't tell them about Elias's world, though. Not without sharing so many more secrets that came with it.

"If I fail, we may face a terrible enemy, like nothing we've encountered before." I hoped that Gael detected the sincerity in my voice. "If we can't stop them and they attack, it'll take us all to defeat them. I've dedicated myself to protecting the Valley. To do that, I have to leave to fight this new battle." Just saying this made me sweat. I detached myself, not ready to feel the fear of stepping away.

"You can't tell us where you're going?" Gael asked.

I shook my head. "I'm sorry. I can't."

"Will you warn us if you fail?"

"Absolutely."

Gael sat back and looked to the woman on his right, the two of them speaking quietly. "As our partnership grows, we'd like for you to share more. For now, we'll respect these limitations."

"Thank you," I said.

"How soon do you need to leave?"

"As soon as possible. I need your help patrolling because you can portal when no one else can."

"We've agreed to this," Gael said. "That's fine. If you need increased support for a brief time, we can work that out. I'm sure that you'll do your part when you return."

"If you take care of the Valley while I'm gone, I'll be personally indebted to you, even beyond the limits of our partnership." I didn't try in the slightest to hide that emotion from my voice. Gael needed to see my desperation to understand that I really meant what I said. "I never forget when someone shows kindness to my people."

He spoke more quietly now. "I imagine that you don't, Eclipse. Why don't we wait to bring our students to the Sacred School until you return? In the meantime, our trained warriors will make preparations here for the young and help patrol the Valley."

Heat climbed my throat. I still didn't feel comfortable leaving the Valley, but this helped.

I couldn't believe I invited strangers into our Valley and entrusted them with security. Then again, did this bring us closer to a secure Valley? I didn't know how to lead us out of the darkness of chaos. Surely we needed connections beyond our small piece of the world to do that.

I swatted away the temptation to remind Gael of what I'd do if he crossed me. Sitting back in my chair, I closed my eyes for a moment and calmed myself. One day, I should learn when to stop fighting.

We needed to return to Elias's world soon, before they tried to force answers out of him, but first I needed to secure the safety of the Valley.

Gael asked for a few days to transport his force through the portals to the Valley due to the limitations on how many knew how to portal. He planned to bring nearly two hundred warriors to help patrol the Valley and set up training grounds at the Sacred School. As many students and family members intended to follow when we returned from Elias's world.

And while I needed to help Piercey as he rushed around the school to prepare for this influx of people, a spike in demon attacks and coastal skirmishes stole most of my time. I carved out an hour to train with Nash on using his power while Elsie played. Now we rested on the bench, both incredibly tired after the very long day.

The increase in attacks worried me.

"It's because Gael's people are coming," I whispered quietly to Nash while Elsie played in the courtyard. "This proves that the attacks aren't random. They're watching us and they're coordinating. Their spies know."

"So they're distracting us during a transition?" Nash asked.

"That and testing us, maybe? I just keep thinking about those warriors we ran into not long ago. Remember the ones who hid their power? They even let some of their own people die."

"Yeah." Nash furrowed his brows. "I remember."

"Ever since then, I've been playing back demon fights in my head, and feeling like some of them were holding back. I don't know. I may be paranoid. I know there's a lot of people wanting to use our power vacuum to their advantage. I just think more of this chaos may be orchestrated than we realized."

Nash wiped a smudge of dried blood from my neck that I had missed when I washed up. "I'm still angry you left without me."

"Elsie's here and we're going to be gone for who knows how long."

"You're exhausted. You only slept three hours."

I nestled against him. "I'll just have to nap on you."

"I'm serious, Max. We're about to travel back to Elias's world and take on his guild. You can't go into it completely worn down."

"You need to be with Elsie and work on your power. I'm fine."

Nash growled, his body stiffening. "I've been patient for a year while you've been running around the Valley killing yourself. I'm ready to fight with you."

I stopped myself from speaking because Nash wouldn't relent. Forget that his powers were brand-new, he promised to fight beside me, and he meant that. It hurt him that I left him behind, just like when I tried to go confront Dr. Henderson in the all-white room without him.

After a beat of quiet, I wound my fingers through his and let my heavy eyes close. "Back when my power was sealed away, I still slipped. The past was so powerful, it stole me away even from the instructor's curse. I remember sometimes I'd lie in bed and try so hard to feel my body and stay put." I slid my arms around his waist. "When I hold on to you, I always feel myself. I never slip away."

The tension clung to Nash's body until he uttered a quiet sigh. "I know. You don't feel alone anymore, and you don't want me to think you do."

"I want you to understand how powerful you are already."

We looked at one another with the light filtering through the dome of the courtyard, dimmed by the snow dusting the glass. "One day you won't need to reassure me of that, because I'll actually be powerful enough for you to need me."

"Nash—"

"Don't soften it. Don't tell me it's okay and I don't need power. I don't care about any of that. I care about watching you destroy yourself while you travel around this Valley. No words or sentiments matter. Until you can sleep through the night in our bed, I am not content. My power will grow in battle. I need to fight."

A fiery desperation flooded me, the kind that arose amid a fight, to deny everything he said and force him to accept himself, love himself, the way I did. Wasn't that insulting, though? If I couldn't fight a battle, would I want someone telling me it was okay? Nash hadn't been born with power, but he'd been born to wield it, because he carried the drive to fight the most powerful of enemies. We'd set something right in this world by getting him a neural implant.

"Fine," I said. "I'll stop arguing with you and let you feel how you feel on one condition."

Surprise filled his eyes. I never backed down on this fight. "What?"

"You accept that to me, you're everything I need, and you always have been."

Nash wanted to fight that, too. I saw it burning in his golden-brown eyes. He nodded, though, and drew me back against himself. "Okay. Now rest and don't fight battles that don't need to be won."

I smiled to myself, the weight of exhaustion, the weight of a Valley, falling off onto him. This feeling never lasted, but I cherished the brief moments of peace. "I'm sorry," I whispered. "You've said that same thing to me so many times before, and I'll need you to say it to me so many times in the future."

Elsie ran to us suddenly and smacked her hands against my knees. "I did it, Maxy. I did the perfect jump. Did you see?"

"Yes," I lied. "It really was perfect."

Elsie clapped her hands. "I'm good with my swords now. I'll do real good during the show. You can still come, right?"

"Of course. I can't wait." I looked over to two practice swords lying on the ground, an upgrade from the sticks she'd ripped off a branch in the courtyard and stripped of their bark. "I see you're prepared."

"Daddy said he'd go, too." She lifted her face toward him. "Right?"

"Of course," he said.

With her attention back on me, she wrapped her arms around my neck. "He said you guys will sit right up front and you'll watch me the whole time. He said you'll clap, too." She gasped in a loud breath, somehow speaking before she'd even finished inhaling, so excited that she couldn't take the time to properly draw air into her lungs. "There's candy, too. Mommy is making candies. Have you had her candies, Maxy? Chocolate ones. The berry ones, too."

I nodded along with her.

Elsie quieted suddenly. "Maxy?"

"Yes?"

"Can you have another name, too?"

The innocence in her eyes made my heart pound with that desire—that need—to run away from all this stress and take them someplace quiet.

I piqued my brows. "Another name?"

"Yeah, like Ba has two names. Mommy and Daddy have two names, too." Nash chuckled. "What's my other name?"

"Well . . ." Elsie thought for a moment. "Maxy calls you Nash."

"Very good."

"That's not my name for Daddy, though. I want a name for Maxy. My name for her."

It felt like water trickled through my chest and pooled in my heart. "Do you?"

"What are you thinking?" Nash asked.

"Well . . ." Elsie scrunched her nose adorably as she thought. "There's Mommy and Ba." She made a humming noise and then bobbed into Nash's arms. Her body twisted so she could grab my shirt. "So, Daddy and Ma!"

My world and all its chaos stopped existing. My voice quivered despite how I tried to keep it steady. "Ma?"

"Is it good?" Elsie lowered her head bashfully.

"I love it." I stole her from Nash into a big hug, clutching her tightly to me. Did Elsie see me the way she saw her parents? Had I become more to her than Maxy? Did she need me the way she needed them? What did that mean for us and the fact that I was gone so much? What if I completely ruined her? What—

"Max." Nash drew me close, holding me as I held Elsie. "Breathe."

Panic consumed me.

"Ma," Elsie said, testing the new name. She tilted her head back and tapped her chin. "Ma. Ma. Ma. I think I like it. I might call you Maxy, too."

"Call me whatever you want," I said.

"Like how you call me sweet girl and baby and cutie and Elsie and Elsie-girl?"

I smiled. "Yes."

"And baby girl and stinky girl. And . . ."

This felt like such a moment, and yet it came out of nowhere right before we needed to leave. Maybe I was doing this all wrong. Although, if Elsie wanted to call me Ma, then I must have done something right. I'd won over the sweetest girl in the world.

The past year taught me I couldn't allow my joy to slip away. Fear and grief no longer stole me through time and forced me to relive my past, but I often acted trapped there anyway. I replayed the past on instinct. What if I freed myself entirely from the clutches of my past?

Closing my eyes, I nestled my head against Nash's chest again, tightening my arms around Elsie. Gently, I whispered, "You're my sweet girl. No matter how old you get, I'll protect you with everything I have."

"I'll protect you, too, Ma. And Daddy. Oh, and Mommy! And Ba!"

I laughed and nodded, my eyes wet when I opened them. "I bet you'll do great."

"Uncle Leif, too. Uncle Arn. Aunt Wren. Rune for sure. He definitely needs me to watch out for him. Uncle Piercey."

Elsie continued to rattle off all the people she needed to guard, including each of her sixteen dollies that lived between three houses—with her mom, with us at the Sacred School, and at Leif's house when we visited the village.

Could I blame myself for wanting to sink into this life? Before, I thought I'd die beneath the eclipse and lose my chance at having a family.

As deeply as my devotion to this Valley ran, what I felt for this one girl eclipsed all that I had loved for the last decade of my life. It was this child, with amber eyes that shone like her father's, a smile that reflected his own, and unbridled joy bursting from her, that I wanted to protect more than anyone. Even more than Nash, because I held his heart in my hands right now. He would die a thousand deaths for Elsie. When had that become true for me, too? And if I'd die a thousand deaths, why shouldn't I live a thousand lives? Lives full of joy and peace.

My people still needed me, though. How could I shift between two worlds I loved? Between my people and this family.

I felt so guilty. So inadequate and ill-prepared.

If Elsie were in my shoes, though, I'd want her to live her life. I'd want her to do more than protect people. I needed to live a life worthy of her, the kind I wanted for her.

I refused to flounder beneath anxiety and guilt any longer. But damn it, I had no idea how to free myself of these burdens. The questions pounded my head until Elsie jolted me awake by hopping, and I realized I'd fallen asleep against Nash.

Late that night after I traveled to check in on warriors waging a long battle against Flatlanders, I found the door to Elsie's room open. Nash leaned against her bedside with his long legs stretched out, watching her as she slept.

I knelt and rested against him, eyes on her as well. "You need more time together."

"I know." I recognized that pain in his voice. "I feel like I'm missing her life."

"You aren't."

"She looks older. I think she's having a growth spurt." He pulled the blankets higher over her and then drew her hand into his while she slept. "One day I'm going to come home and she won't be little anymore."

"I don't think it'll just happen one day."

He smiled, but it looked sad. "I know in my heart that I'm doing the right thing. She needs us to make this Valley safe for her. I just don't know how doing the right thing feels so terrible."

I almost told him that he needed to stay home more, only we'd already argued about this once today. Last year when I tried to convince him to turn back from the Mountain of the Gods, he asked me what kind of father could do that.

I hadn't just chosen Nash, but Elsie as well, and I left our budding life on pause to save the Valley. I couldn't walk away from my duty to my people, but I couldn't abandon a family I never thought I'd get to have.

At some point, we fell asleep there at Elsie's bedside, unable to bring ourselves to leave her when we already missed so much time with her. I only realized that we'd both fallen asleep when I awoke from the sensation of alarm.

Another demon attack.

Nash wouldn't be happy if I left without waking him, but he'd also feel bad about staying behind. Torn on what to do, I nudged him before I traveled, having just enough time to whisper against his ear. "I'll be home soon."

We didn't have time for him to find someone to watch Elsie. This time, I had to leave him.

So I vanished. Vanished from a life I wanted desperately to live with the two people who had become most dear to me.

CHAPTER TWENTY-TWO

The rage at facing my second demon attack in less than twelve hours poured through me like lava. I should have been home with Elsie and Nash. Instead, I faced off with a demon woman I didn't recognize. These fools needed to realize that I wasn't going to ever miss their attack and I always put them down. Did any of them really believe they would finally be the one to best me? It didn't make sense unless someone wanted to wear me out.

"Who sent you?" I curled my lips in a snarl.

The demon answered with a bellowing roar and her palms aimed at me, nails sharp like claws.

The gust of wind hit me first, immediately followed by razor-sharp points as thin as needles. They shot through the air like hundreds of translucent daggers that faintly picked up a trail of dirt around the thin edges. I erected my shield in time, but the points cut through the wall behind me and poked tiny holes in every inch from the floor up to the ceiling. One managed to pierce my shield and slice through my forearm in a flash of pain.

Not long ago I fought another demon gifted with wind attacks. Were they connected?

I couldn't give her time to weaponize the very air around me and create a wave of razors. Darting forward, I drew my energy blade along the ground, scattering dust as I swiped up along her torso. She dodged, but the dust I'd thrown into the air coated her next attack.

With a powerful blast of wind, she volleyed four massive discs of air at me, the dirt swirling through their middle. These were so sharp and large that I worried they'd penetrate my shield, considering one of her daggers broke through already. I didn't simply brace for the attack, but slammed the shield into the discs of air and followed up with a powerful swing of my energy blade.

Two of the discs slammed against my shield and exploded back toward the demon. But the other two sliced through and landed against my sword midswing.

Gritting my teeth, I pushed all my power into cutting through the discs. The energy of her attack hit me like an actual explosion, the kind used to blow up cliffsides to make way for the trains. One disc snapped in half and burst through the building behind me on either side. But the other dug into my sword, refusing to give. And then the blade snapped.

The demon stared into my eyes through the dusty air, looking ravenous with hunger for power and the yearning to put down the great demon Eclipse.

I teleported behind her, energy sword ready against her throat. She was too vicious to try saving.

Only the wind shoved my blade enough for a sliver of air to appear between her slender throat and my sword. She twisted toward me, hands searching for my stomach, the air between us already whipping into a frenzy.

I teleported again, and this time my sword drove deeply into her gut.

She was still twisted the opposite way, looking for me, when the other end of the energy blade burst through her back in a flash of red power and black blood.

I hated unfair advantages. Teleporting felt cheap to me, and I cursed myself for relying on it. But I was too tired to spend time fighting her.

"Your power is incredible," I said as she sank to her knees.

The demon collapsed onto her stomach, unable to stop the blood gushing from her wide wound. "Someone . . . will get you . . . one of these days."

Probably true. I possessed no illusion about invincibility. I wielded a great power, sure. Gael and his people couldn't travel as often as I did, and it took longer for their portals to open. So my teleportation still proved more advantageous. Someone would figure out how to counteract it one day, though. Inevitably, I'd find someone stronger than me, smarter than me, perhaps just luckier than me. Even then, I would only want to grow beyond them.

The demon twitched below me. I didn't want to kill her. I never wanted to kill anyone. The thought felt useless and far too little, far too late as she trembled in a heap, choking on her own blood. With a swift slash of my blade, I ended her misery.

The villagers tried to talk to me, hug me, thank me. Invite me in for something to drink or to wash up. Turning their kindness away felt terrible, but I barely found the stamina to even politely decline. I needed to go home.

With the little energy remaining to me, I returned to the room where Elsie still curled up sleeping and Nash sat awake, waiting for me.

"You're okay," he said. I knew he considered saying more. He hadn't wanted to stay behind, even though he needed to watch Elsie. He wanted to help me, even though his power wasn't great enough yet to take on that demon. He wanted to ease the burden I'd been left to carry.

"Soon," I said, too tired to manage much more. "I promise."

If what I said confused him, he didn't show it. Nash pushed to his feet and placed his hand against my back. "Soon," he agreed.

I smiled, hoping he understood. Soon, neither of us would have to feel this way. With his power growing and our alliances taking shape, we could all fight together. I couldn't imagine being able to truly step back from any of these fights, but I knew I needed help. Without it, I would fail Nash and Elsie, and I refused to do that.

Nash lifted me into his arms. The relief immediately relaxed my body, just like floating in the water. I closed my eyes, wanting to stay like this longer, despite the fact that it took less than a minute for him to carry me across the apartment to the bedroom. When he settled me down, I gripped his shirt, eyes still closed. He slid me over to stretch out beside me and held me close. Though I knew that he hurt as well, he held it back from me, taking care of it himself. I wanted to ease his own burden, if only I had the strength.

For the first time in a year, I felt that if I let go, I would slip away. The shakiness inside of me returned. I didn't want to leave the Valley and go to Elias's world. What if someone hurt my people while I was away? If I couldn't step back to fight in his world, how could I ever figure out how to be with a family?

"Sleep," Nash whispered, just like he had in the cave the first time he'd held me. "Sleep; I won't let go."

I found myself lost between the two worlds, between my dreams and my reality. My thoughts flittered over fantasies of a future where we tucked Elsie in every night. And just as quickly I imagined demons storming our villages the moment I left for Elias's world. His guild joining them. My people, my family, left broken in the stampede of warring threats against this Valley.

Maybe I shouldn't have killed the Prophet without taking his place. I'd left an opportunity here for anyone to seize and now I lived out the consequences.

I hadn't killed him to help myself, though. I wanted to save my people from his cruelty. Did doing that mean I no longer deserved to live my own life? I never meant to fall in love with Nash and dare to dream of a home and family of my own. Still, I knew I not only had every right to seize life for my family, but every responsibility.

I just couldn't get my heart to believe it.

It felt selfish to wish for peace when others suffered, not only because I played a role in the destabilization of the Valley, but because I wanted to help take care of them. Having a family felt like turning my back on the people. This was who I was—the person who protected and took care of my people.

It's who I'd been since Leif welcomed me into his home. Who I'd been at the Sacred School. Who I'd been when my father awakened the flame inside me and failed me so badly that I knew, fucking knew, that I'd never be him. From the first day that my father broke my heart and left me to clutch the shattered pieces alone, I'd known that I would be the one who'd hold others together.

So who did I choose to care for when I failed to help everyone? My family or my Valley?

There was no answer because it wasn't the right question to ask.

Nash and Elsie deserved to be the center of my world. Our family deserved peace, just like the Valley did.

Once, I'd retaken the power inside of me that the gods had sealed away. What if I retook more of my power? If I retook what my father destroyed. If instead of saving the Valley, I raised up a generation of warriors to do so. So long as I killed myself protecting everyone else, I hindered others from using their own victories and losses to grow strong. I needed to give others the chance to become powerful.

"Nash."

He rolled his head toward me, eyes looking bleary with sleep. "You okay?"

I worked my arm around him. "I'm sorry."

"For what?"

"For not giving you all of me. For giving to everyone else what should be ours."

"Max . . . You give me so much."

"I'm holding us back." The realization cracked through my chest, first in a shot of pain, but then in soothing warmth. The kind of healing that hurt and felt good at the same time. "This whole time, I've weakened us, not saved us."

Nash likely didn't at all understand what I meant. I needed to hear myself say it, to make it real and make it mine. To ensure that I didn't bury it away.

I didn't know how to let the Valley shift from my center to its proper place, but I needed to learn. And I needed to learn now because I would leave for Elias's world soon, like it or not.

CHAPTER TWENTY-THREE

We completed much of the preparations needed to safely leave for Elias's world to battle Lote. Today, Piercey worked on connecting Gael and his warriors with the neural interface so they could receive alerts about demon attacks like I did. Leaving during the increased attacks bothered me, as did not knowing the cause. What choice did I have, though? I couldn't allow Lote into my world.

The worry plagued me as I rushed through the Sacred School on the way to see Elsie's performance. I meant to arrive sooner, only Piercey needed help testing the alarm system. I finally reached the courtyard and breathed in the fresh air, ready to hear Elsie squeal my name. I bit my lip and looked at the place where she normally kept her wooden swords, finding them gone. She'd already left.

Nash must have already taken her to the apartment to get ready. Elsie was probably so excited to get there. Cutting through the courtyard, I decided to go straight to the show, because I was sure Elsie would be there soon enough.

The tingle of warning struck me like lightning and turned my legs to lead. One of the villages called for help. What the hell was happening? How could I possibly be dealing with another demon attack?

I would miss Elsie's show if I left. My breath started to come in short spurts, my eyes trained on the door leading to her. She'd worked her ass off for this and I would miss it?

If I sent a message to Piercey, Gael could travel and fight the demon. What if the demons were too powerful, though? I couldn't sit there watching Elsie play with swords while children were slaughtered in the streets. I needed to travel there, assess the situation, and decide whether to leave it in Gael's hands.

When I departed for Elias's world, I wouldn't be able to do this. I'd truly be leaving my people.

Dread churned in my depths.

For the first time, leaving felt real. I couldn't do this. I couldn't abandon the Valley with someone I barely knew. My hands shook and my thoughts spun wildly out of my control. My breath came too fast to stop, no matter how I tried.

What was I doing? Abandoning my people for another world in some of the worst days since I killed the Prophet?

I clasped the armrest of the nearby bench, bowing forward. Now wasn't the time for this. I needed to reach out to Piercey, travel to the village, and try to get back in time for Elsie. The sensation of falling nearly swept me away.

I clung to my world, desperate to concentrate hard enough to communicate with Piercey through the neural link, but for the first time in over a year, my world slipped through my fingers anyway.

I managed to hold on to my surroundings long enough to feel my body smack against the ground, and then I was gone, traveling into a past I lost control of.

The Prophet and Dr. Henderson couldn't hurt my people again. That fact rolled through my mind as I lay there with Nash, breathing in the night air in the days after we had killed them.

"Death isn't hanging over you anymore. You can live." Nash's breath warmed the side of my face.

"It's so hard," I whispered. "I feel like I can't stop."

"You know, Max"—Nash tangled his fingers in my hair—"battles create warriors, but the greatest commanders create peace from war. It would be a shame for you to never heal just because you're strong enough to keep fighting forever."

I'd never felt such freedom. Not even the looming war for control of the Valley hampered the thrill of a life with Nash.

What if we lost this? What if I lost what I finally dared to take for myself?

CHAPTER TWENTY-FOUR

I shoved myself off the ground so fast that dizziness knocked the world into a spin, and I fell back onto my hands. What if I slipped again? How much time did I miss?

My stomach rolled with waves of nausea as I tried to travel. For the first few attempts, nothing happened, and then finally I forced myself through the space separating me from the innocent villagers. People cried out for help, unanswered for the first time.

The acrid scent of smoke burned my sinuses and blotted out my vision. The small village housed only a few dozen people, and it sounded like all of them were screaming. Stumbling forward, I searched for the feel of the demon, desperate to figure out who attacked this poor village.

How many people had died while I slipped through the past?

A massive surge of power cast the smoke back against me.

Half a dozen men and women charged at me, all teeming with energy.

Of all the days. I aimed my energy bow and shot arrow after arrow, feeling like I spiraled out of control. "Who are you people?" At any moment, I might slip away again. I thought I had moved past this, but the fear suffocated me. These demons inundated me with an onslaught of attacks while Piercey helped Gael and his people transition here.

I remembered Elsie's excited voice, shouting about her show.

"Fuck!" I screamed it so loud that my throat ached.

My arrows tore through a man's arm and shredded his bicep.

I couldn't miss this. Elsie was so excited for me to come, and I missed everything all the time. That sweet girl never complained no matter how much she missed us. Her mother always reminded her that her daddy and I fought to keep her safe. Meaningless words to a five-year-old climbing onto a stage and seeing the seat beside her father empty. Nothing mattered except that I wasn't there. And I wasn't just Maxy anymore. I was Ma.

"Where the hell are you all coming from?" I roared. "Answer me."

I sprinted toward an enemy, teleported, and ripped his chest wide open with my blade. Spinning, I moved so fast that I didn't need to travel. I stabbed my sword through another's throat.

Blood burst over my hands and glistened in the sunlight.

Three more ran for me like blind, panicked fools.

With my energy bow back in hand, I shot one through the chest. Another managed to cast the arrow away, so I rushed him, using my palm to throw a ball of energy against him.

He slammed back against the building, twitching.

That left one staring at me now. The courage fled his eyes, but he didn't run. He walked toward me, sword raised, shield ready. Was he really connected with the skilled woman I had defeated the night before or was this all random?

I shot forward so fast that he might have thought I'd teleported, and I wrapped my hands around the collar of his shirt. With a strength far beyond my own, I ripped him off his feet into the air and shook him.

"Answer—"

Right when I started to question him, a tall man cut through the haze of smoke with his sword dancing for me.

No time to chat. I sliced a small dagger of energy across the throat of the man I held and dropped him. Turned just in time to drive my energy blade for the new demon. His physical sword clashed with mine as the ground beneath me began to shake.

"Who are you?" I asked.

With a cry, he forced my blade away and spun to cut for my throat. I blocked and hurled a forceful wave of energy at him.

"Answer me," I said.

Power erupted around the village, none of it emanating from this man. More demons lurked about.

The rage and adrenaline temporarily made me feel wild with power, but that came at a cost, because now it felt like every ounce had been spent. My weakness from the past few days and the lack of sleep compounded with the effects of slipping through time, so my legs wobbled just from standing. This was dangerous. I'd lived like I could endure any amount of suffering, and it finally caught up with me. Why did I always do this?

The demon rushed me with an onslaught of attacks, fast and strong. I could beat him, if only I could grasp a hold of my power. It leaked out from me like water falling between my fingers.

My hands felt numb. Was it happening again? Was I about to slip?

I unleashed a cry and sprang back with my energy bow materializing in my hands. Shot five arrows rapidly. Instead of drilling them into his body, I sent them flying around him in a circle. The surprise caught him off guard and gave me enough time to detonate the arrows.

The explosions crashed into him from all sides.

I didn't wait to see the damage I inflicted. With my arrows triple nocked, I aimed for where I heard his heart beating. Then I tried to teleport to him, skipping to a stop only three feet away.

Every inch of my body tingled. I'd overdone it in my weakened state, and struggled to travel. With a shot of energy, I cleared away the smoke surrounding the demon when lightheadedness and dizziness threw me off-balance. I stumbled.

Elsie waited for me and there was something wrong with me. My body burned, not with power, but with panic. If I slipped now, this demon would wreak havoc on this village.

The demon's severed hand dangled by a thread. The explosion had ripped bloody and burned holes all over his shirt and pants. Blood dribbled from his nose and both sides of his mouth. The three energy arrows protruded from his chest, not deep enough to pierce his heart, but enough to hurt him.

I raised my bow unsteadily. He raked in a rattling breath and let his injured arm fall to retrieve his weapon. The amputated hand bounced against his leg.

A massive surge of energy physically shook the town and throbbed in my chest like it had hit me there. What the hell was that? I drew my arrow back as a sense of awareness scratched at me.

A demon spun through the air like a human spear, hurling himself directly for me. I pivoted to aim the arrow at him, but it merely bounced off his body.

Bracing myself, I struggled to gather the energy for a strong enough shield when a form slammed into the spinning demon and sent him careening out of control.

Gael caught himself midair, hovered for a few seconds, and then landed on the ground, hard.

He'd come. Why hadn't I called out to him for help like I'd planned? Stupid. Careless. Between slipping and the panic of another demon attack when I needed to watch Elsie's show, I hadn't been thinking rationally. I'd mindlessly jumped into battle, ready to fight. Just like always. As helpless against my compulsive battling as my slips through time.

I had to start thinking again. This was like slipping without traveling through time.

Gael cut a look to me, seeming to take note of my appearance. "Are you injured?"

"No. I'm just . . ."

"Exhausted. Your energy feels strange. Return home and we'll take care of this."

I didn't even realize anyone had come with him. Turning around, I noticed two warriors behind us, scanning the perimeter, and caught a glimpse of others in the smoke, spreading throughout the village.

That surge of energy came from his portal. "I can't. I don't have enough strength."

The man Gael had knocked to the ground rose and stumbled toward us. The strength of his own attack had thrown him down hard enough that the left side of his body was scraped from head to toe.

Gael didn't move. A sheen of energy crackled against his skin, his eyes trained on the enemy. Chunks of the earth dislodged and wavered in the air between us. The sparking sheen around Gael intensified until it glowed like the sun. That same power sparked against the massive chunks of ground floating in the air.

They slammed into the demon and buried him in a pile of dirt. The sparks danced along the pile until I sensed the last of the demon's energy die out. Gael lifted his hand, forcing the demon's body up through the air and threw him down between us. Shit. I hoped Gael never crossed us.

My attention fell to the demon. The rage at this attack coming on the heels of the others fueled me now. "Talk."

Blood pooled at the nape of his neck. "Your arrogance astounds me. You think you can fend us off forever. We're only getting started."

"What do you want?" I asked.

"Everything." He bared his bloody teeth. "This world is broken and hopeless. We need to tame it and make it into something worthy of the gods."

"Only a fool lives for gods who care nothing for them." I planted my boot against his bloodied throat to keep him down. Using my power on someone weakened so greatly never felt right. "I know you're connected with the other demon attacks. Who is sending you?"

"You aren't as cruel as them. No one will ever talk to you until—"

"As them? Who are you talking about?"

He uttered a mocking laugh. "If I tell you, will you take me out to the cabin like you do for the others?"

A tremble started in my numb fingers and spread up my arms. "You've talked to the ones I let live." What had I done? I'd left them alive to connect or even return to whoever sent them.

He gasped as my boot pressed against his throat.

"Eclipse . . ." the demon said. "I expected you . . . to be more ruthless."

My nostrils flared. "That's not my name."

Blood dripped from the side of his face from where it had scraped against the ground. "I'm never going to speak . . . So kill me now . . ."

"I won't kill you, but you're not going to the cabin either."

Gael walked closer. "My men say they can handle this village without any problem from here."

"We need to ask about casualties," I said.

"Only two."

Only two. Fortunate considering the number of demons here, but those were two innocent people. If I hadn't slipped, they'd be alive. Anguish gripped my chest.

"I'll take you home," Gael said. "They're fine here."

How could I leave this mourning village behind while the flames still burned? This was my test, though. If I couldn't leave now, how would I go to Elias's world while time continued unpaused here? Elsie waited for me, and Gael needed me.

"Okay," I conceded quietly and clasped his arm. "I'm glad you came."

Gael opened the portal in an explosion of power that nudged me back a step. Impressed, I watched him for several seconds, before finally nodding at the demon on the ground. "He's coming with us."

CHAPTER TWENTY-FIVE

Frazzled and more tired than I ever remembered feeling, I opened the door to where families and children gathered in one of the larger classrooms.

Tears flooded my eyes as I saw Elsie sitting beside Nash with the training swords lying on her lap. I stepped forward and caught Nash's eyes as he turned around. The relief on his face looked palpable when he saw me. Surely he'd been worried sick about me.

He closed his eyes for a moment and breathed out slowly before whispering something to Elsie and slipping into the aisle. I tensed, thinking she'd turn around to see me, but her attention remained glued to the little boy dancing at the front of the room. Elsie knew the lineup by heart, which meant I did as well, because she recited it so often.

The dancing boy came second to last, three performances after Elsie. I had missed her sword fighting.

Grief battered my bruised spirit mercilessly.

Nash caught my hands and stepped into the hall with me. "What happened?"

"Another attack."

His eyes scanned me, searching for injury. "How bad is it?"

"I'm not hurt."

"You're sure?"

I let my head fall against him, feeling too weak to stand. "I slipped, Nash."

His hold on me tightened. "Okay. Come on. Come sit."

"I missed it," I whispered, unable to hold back the tears.

"It's okay."

"It's not." When he started to lead me to the door, I pulled back. "There's no reason for me to go in there. Let her finish her show. It'll only cause a commotion."

I hung out near the back while Nash returned to his daughter. When the crowd dispersed at the end, Elsie looked all around, her eyes settling on me. She released her dad's hand and sprinted to me.

"Ma!" Elsie ran into my legs and clutched me. "Where were you?"

When I knelt, I realized that she wasn't angry, but relieved. Frightened. Guilt pounded hot in my temples. "I tried to make it. I promise."

"I watched for you."

"I'm so sorry, baby. I'm so sorry."

Her eyes filled with tears. Her face puckered. I knew she was seconds away from full-blown sobbing, so I carried her out into the hallway and away from the crowd.

She buried her face against me and cried hard.

"I thought you were never coming back," Elsie wailed.

She knew I would never miss this performance, so she'd assumed the worst, no matter what anyone told her. My heart broke as I thought back to days I hadn't been around to witness, after I'd died and gone to the afterlife, when Elsie thought she had lost me forever.

I struggled to swallow down the sobs making my throat ache as she cried far harder than her little body seemed capable of.

Nash joined us, drawing me back against him, and my tears broke free.

Thinking about Elsie learning I died last year horrified me so much I usually refused to think about it. It haunted me now. That fear would live with her forever. She'd always worry that the past would repeat itself. But she was so little she probably didn't even know she felt that way.

I turned my face against Nash's chest to silence my tears.

"I can help you now." His voice sounded resolute despite the pain creeping around the edges. "I'll learn faster."

I wilted in his arms, lacking the strength to tell him how much training it took to wield power like I did.

Battle always brought with it victory and defeat. I'd tasted success and failure more times than I could count. But this failure, the pain and disappointment that replaced the sparkle in Elsie's eyes with tears, was my greatest yet.

Once Elsie calmed down, her mother took her to get ready for dinner, while I paced the hallway.

"Max—" Nash took my arm in his hand.

I pulled away, unable to stay in one place.

"It's not your fault," he said as I sought out the closest door to the outside. I stormed through the outer doors of the Sacred School into the white wasteland of the mountaintop.

The cold numbed me to the core.

"It's not safe to be out here without a coat, Max." Nash followed me.

"I've devoted myself to this Valley, and in one night I failed it and Elsie."

Nash took me in his arms again, holding tight when I tried pulling away. I couldn't deny his warmth in this bitter cold, but I didn't deserve his comfort.

A scream I was too tired to unleash grew inside of me. "I killed Flare and the Prophet, and now I can't put the broken pieces back together. It's killing me."

"I know."

"I can't let it hurt Elsie, too. I didn't just choose you. I chose her. I love her." I wiped my face, realizing I was yelling, but unable to stop.

Nash slid my hair back from my face and forced me to meet his eyes. "I'm the one who is failing her. I'm her father."

"I'm her Ma."

The words silenced us both, maybe the reckoning for each of us that we'd come too far for Elsie to be just his anymore.

Hot tears flooded my eyes and blurred his face. "She asked me to be her Ma and I said yes." She was getting taller, smarter, older. Becoming her own person. And I was missing it.

"Okay." Nash wiped my face, nodding. Voice quiet. "Okay, you're right."

"She needs me. I let her down. It doesn't matter that I couldn't help slipping. I let myself get to that point. I can't afford to fall in battle. I can't get so beat down that I regress to losing myself in the past. This is my power to control, my life to live, my responsibility to be alive and well for Elsie."

I might have kept yelling, except Nash's warm lips closed over mine, and I accepted them desperately.

"It's true," he said. "We can't keep doing this. We'll fix this. We. It's my responsibility, too."

"If I'm ever going to be the Ma I know I can be, I have to start taking care of myself. I can't die on her again."

Pain as deep as the Valley opened in his eyes.

"I can't die and miss our life," I said.

I was torn in two with the Valley ripping at me on one end and the family I so desperately wanted on the other. Gael and his men fought demons as we spoke. I could train others to protect the Valley. I couldn't call on anyone else to love my family.

If I didn't learn how to step away from the Valley, I'd lose everything.

"It's time to go to Elias's world." I wiped my face. "I'll use this battle to become who I need to be, and I don't want to wait any longer to do it."

The strengths and truths I needed were scattered in worlds unknown to me, where pieces of myself grew without me, waiting for me to find them and put our worlds together.

When I returned home from Elias's world, I'd make sure to come back as the person I needed to be, just like when I'd returned from the afterlife to kill Flare and the Prophet of the Valley.

That night, I tossed and turned in bed, but I clung to my determination. In the morning when we woke up, ready to travel, I watched Nash getting ready, and knew I needed to do one more thing.

"Nash."

He sheathed a hidden dagger and pulled his pant leg down before turning to face me. "What?"

It hurt me to even say it because I knew how he'd react. "I need to go to Elias's world on my own this time."

Nash's jaw slowly fell slack. "You can't be serious."

"I—"

We didn't fight often. It wasn't at all like my bickering with Leif or the arguments with Piercey back when we fundamentally disagreed about how to handle the Valley. It felt more like a tug-of-war between Nash's heart and mine. This, though, defied a simple disagreement.

"I can't believe you're even trying this," Nash said. "How has anything we've talked about lately made you think that's what you need to do?"

"Our plans changed. Time will pass in our world while we're away, the demon attacks are increasing, we're investigating the connections, and do I really need to go on? We need everyone focused on the Valley. We have to put our feelings aside and do what's best. You should train here with Piercey and continue our work while I'm gone."

I adored Nash's fighting spirit, his ferocity in battle, his insatiable hunger for improvement. No one trained more diligently than he did. I might have first fallen for him as a warrior before I did as a man, dazzled by the flash of his twin swords and the seemingly choreographed dance of his fighting. Right now, though, I wished he was less of a warrior so he could see that I was right this time. He needed to stay home.

Nash looked ready for the fight, unfortunately. His voice sharpened. "You can't be over there by yourself without anyone to back you up other than Elias, who, sorry to say, obviously has his own motives. It's not our world he puts first. And you're not the you he'll put first either."

I paused at that. "I know it feels like shit to stay behind, but I need you to do this for me. I can't really trust this Valley to anyone but you and Piercey. You are needed here. Elsie needs you here."

"A man does not stay home from a battle."

"He does when his daughter and the woman he loves need him to."

Nash's nostrils flared as he turned away and picked up his tunic from the bed. "Max," he growled low under his breath and gruffly pulled the shirt over his head.

Before his clothes fell to cover him completely, I touched my fingers to his back, feeling along the script of Eskel's name. Winning against Nash was no simple matter, not in an argument or a battle. Stubbornness and strength alone didn't give him the endurance to stand up to the Prophet, however. A little girl he loved deeply, did.

"I need you at my side," I said quietly, my fingers drifting down the smoothness of his skin, my touch sliding from the tightness of his back around to his stomach. I rested my face between his shoulder blades. "I always need you there. I just need you here even more this one time. I'm not strong enough yet to leave behind the people we love without you here to take care of them."

I felt the tension unwinding from his body. "The day you died, and Flare delivered your lifeless body to us, it broke me knowing that I hadn't been with you. I hadn't fought for you." He gripped my hands against himself. "After you returned to me, I vowed to never leave you alone in battle again."

"You aren't, Nash. We're fighting in two worlds at the same time, together. It's not fair to ask you to do what I'm not ready to do. I'm asking you to let me go when I'm struggling to let go of everyone else. You're better at this than me, though."

He spoke in a throaty grumble. "I'm tired of you trying to save everyone from their pain by taking it on for them. I don't want you fighting alone."

"It's different this time. I swear. We don't have time to fight these battles one at a time."

Nash faced me once more, muscles tight again and jaw bunched. "I'll consider it on one condition. Elias has to bring you back in three days, no matter what is happening."

I didn't need to think long before nodding. "I think that's smart."

"I'm not saying I'll do this. Just if I do, no starting a war over there. You can set up for one, but you are not fighting it by yourself. I absolutely will not forgive you if you do. I can't watch you leave without that commitment."

"I promise." How had I never truly understood Nash's difficulty in seeing me live under constant threat? He carried the stress of it so well, kept it to himself so much that I never really saw it before. I slid my hands up his chest to rest over his heart, not wanting anything between us. I couldn't get close enough. "You stay safe, too."

He bent to press his forehead against mine, looping his arms around me. "I'll find out who's attacking our Valley. You figure out how to defeat this guild."

His confidence soothed my heart as much as his closeness did. Damn it, I really didn't want to leave him. We fought for time alone like this. We were always busy, all the time, and there was always someone's life at stake. Everyone's life at stake. The urgency filling me never abated and I knew that I needed to walk out the door to get to Elias's world. I needed Nash, though. Needed only him without the Valley creeping in all around us.

Our eyes met and there was no walking out that door just yet. Nash hoisted me from the floor and settled me on the bed, taking his time looking down my face. His fingers wound through mine, and he drew my hands above my head on the bed, holding them tightly.

"You don't get to die again," he said sternly.

Hot tears gathered in my eyes. My voice sounded small. "Okay."

His lips tickled my cheek. "We have a long life to live."

I could only nod, unable to speak. Every speck of my soul yearned for this, for him, and for us together. Strong hands roamed down my arms and over my body, our kiss deep enough for us to get lost in one another's souls. I thought by now we would have lost the surprise of discovering one another, but being together meant uncovering bottomless depths we wanted desperately, and could never fully explore.

"I accidentally learned something," he whispered against my lips.

A tingle licked my side and then branched into dozens of trails, like the lightest touch of Nash's fingers. I gasped, clasping his shoulders. "That is not what you're supposed to be training for!"

He laughed low, his grin as sly as when we'd first met. "I told you it was an accident."

"Liar."

"Fine." The buzz of his mouth on me made me question if he'd used his power again or if he always felt that incredible. "I'll never do it again."

Longing bound us together and cast away a world intent on encroaching upon us. We discarded our weapons that distracted us and the clothes that hid us from one another. Nothing comforted me more than his skin melding with mine and his body burying me against the bed. Our souls opened to one another and war no longer existed. Nor cold, nor fear, nor heartache. I was fully his and he was fully mine. Only we existed for this time.

"I'll come home," I promised when I lost myself so deeply in him, I felt like I was dreaming.

I promised him the rest without words, but with a connection that didn't need such things. I promised to come home, alive, and ready to fight for the life we deserved to live.

CHAPTER TWENTY-SIX

I convinced everyone to let me go alone with Elias to his world so they could continue to work here. It was far from ideal, but the complications required flexibility. Elias's guild wanted to break into our world, and the gods had destroyed our unique advantage of time relativity.

Before leaving, I wanted to talk with everyone together to make sure we were on the same page, and check in with Gael and his warriors. We gathered a group that included my chief and half a dozen other important leaders in the Valley.

I let Piercey do the talking this time as he explained my upcoming absence.

"Whoever is staging the demon attacks wants to wear us down," I said after Piercey finished. "Specifically me. That's why they're spreading them so far out all over the Valley, so only I can respond."

"My people will put a stop to them," Gael said. "Together, we can respond to two dozen demon attacks a day."

"You'll exhaust yourselves," I said. "Trust me. If your people patrol one week on and one week off, how many can you stop?"

"Half that, then."

I breathed in deeply. "You're also training your people and mine."

He shifted and sighed. "I suppose realistically on a long-term basis we can only handle a few a day. That should be plenty, though."

"Unless they wage all-out war."

"Then we pause training and focus on this. We're allies now. If you fall, our efforts here fail."

I'd made up my mind to trust him and I'd have to do just that. "I thank you for that."

"We have spies working to get to the bottom of these attacks." One of the military leaders of a major village spoke up now. "You should not worry about your absence, Eclipse. We will all continue our efforts while you handle your important matters. Our new allies will protect us."

His words brought a smile to my face even though I felt so anxious about leaving. It was short-lived, though, because of what I intended to discuss next.

"We're currently holding several captives at the Sacred School," I said. "They aren't giving us any information. A few are from a small battle at the border and another from the most recent demon attack. I have an associate who can force information from those with power."

The table fell noticeably quiet.

"He can connect, like Piercey and I do, so that we use our powers to share our memories and experiences. Only, he knows how to do this without their willingness. It's not a pleasant experience."

Piercey lowered his gaze to the table, and I didn't need a connection to feel his emotions. He didn't agree at all. I knew he wouldn't. He'd once begged me not to kill the Prophet moments after the bastard almost strangled him to death. I needed his unyielding morality to guide me when my own unyielding commitment to the Valley blinded me.

The surprise came from Leif. "There's no honor in stealing another's soul."

I couldn't disagree. This wasn't something I ever wanted to do, and couldn't believe I was even considering it. We were at war, though. "They killed a child." Pain etched in my voice. I hadn't let myself think about it since I'd heard the news. "He was three years old."

Beside me, Nash closed his hands into fists on top of the table, looking ready to charge into battle even though he had no one to fight in this room. Everyone reacted to the news. No one felt like a stranger anymore when we all fought so hard to protect each other.

"I don't think it's right to do," I said. "I'm not willing to let them kill more children, though. They took advantage of the fact that I released demons on the coast with the tracking system. We didn't catch any suspicious activity, but we're too busy to monitor them properly. Some graduates are looking into the demons we're tracking now to see who they're talking to. But we have little information so far and even less time."

"Some would not hesitate to steal the information," Gael said in measured words. "It encourages me that it's a dilemma for you. This is not something I need to consider long, personally. You lived under the iron rule of the Prophet for so long that you carry a keen sense of injustice, and you haven't had to make the kind of decisions you are now. Having power is quite different from not having it. I've been in a position of power long enough to tell you that in a war, you must follow rules, but those rules will not be fair, or good."

"We need to decide together," I said. "And we need to think carefully, because whatever we do sets a precedent for the future."

"We vote," Piercey said, always ready to take every opportunity to start a culture of voting in a land where such ideas were very foreign.

"I recommend that you do establish formal rules, whatever you decide," Gael said. "Our king is an admirable ruler in this regard. We are happy to advise on the subject."

"Thank you, Gael," I said. "Can you all discuss this while I'm gone? If we haven't made progress with our investigation, then we'll need to move forward with whatever we choose. My friend also cannot interrogate them for us. The gods limit us. We need to learn how to do this ourselves."

Everyone agreed on the discussions, even Piercey, despite his visible distress.

"We'll need to continue our talks of leadership," my chief said. "It's as important as the demon attacks. We'll be seen as weak until we unite under one head."

I felt the eyes on me like I did at all these meetings. "For the past year, I've struggled to find the time to sleep because I've been fighting and fighting and fighting," I said. "I'm starting to see a future where our Valley protects itself. Still, I feel like I'm too busy fighting to also take on leadership." They all waited patiently, watching me. "I didn't understand before that proper leadership means no longer fighting all the battles myself."

The chief looked proud as she nodded. "There's a reason leaders are not battling in the mud every day, young one."

"That's where I love to be. At least, it's where I did love to be. I'm needed in other places now. Other battles." I looked up at Nash. "I don't want to be the leader of the Valley, but I don't want to spend the rest of my life so busy fighting that I can never sleep. I don't know what will happen, but we all need to make changes. Myself included."

Nash nodded at me, the agreement clear.

We talked logistics, with Wren discussing our strategy for the border, and Gael providing an overview of their plans for handling security threats in my absence. When we finished, I stopped Gael on our way out the door.

"You remember what we talked about?" I asked.

When Gael first approached me with the offer for a partnership, he told me that he chose now to act because he sensed the energy from a man who looked like Piercey. I hadn't told him more since that day, and I wasn't ready to share very much, but offering trust mattered in a partnership.

He stepped closer, nodding.

"You were right about the world changing," I said. "I really do want to tell you more. I can't yet."

"Then it has to do with the one who looks like Piercey."

I didn't respond, but wasn't that response enough?

Gael folded his arms. "I understand there's more at stake than any of us know. I'm choosing to trust you this time. Just prove to me when you return that you are serious about this being a partnership."

"I look forward to having the chance to do that. Please, take good care of everyone while I'm gone."

"I will. I honor my commitments."

"I do, too," I said.

"Then this will work out well for us."

Smiling, I lifted my arm to him, and he clasped my forearm. I didn't need to explain that this was the custom of my people when he'd been watching us for a year. "Okay," I said. "Be careful."

"You, too."

When we parted ways, I met up with Leif and Wren.

"I know you don't like that I'm going alone," I said. "I promise I'll be home in three days and that I'll be smart. You do the same. Don't try to use your powers in battle yet. You aren't ready."

"We know," Leif said. "We'll continue to train. Deal with that guild and come home to fight our war here."

"It feels wrong leaving the Valley."

"You have to."

I hugged them both goodbye before I moved on to Piercey.

"Have you worked out the alarm system for Gael and the warriors?" I asked.

"Yes. We want to do one more test, but it's working well." Piercey lowered the notebook he'd been reading through and looked at me. "Changing plans like this is risky."

"You should close up this deal with Gael and his king and train our friends."

"I'll do what needs to be done so that we're prepared to fight alongside you next time."

I slid my arm around Piercey's side in a brief hug. "Thanks for always being here."

He squeezed my shoulder. "You're always there for me, too."

Meeting Elias and learning about his relationship with Ashton renewed my guilt for ever hurting Piercey. I wouldn't change it because I loved Nash, and I didn't believe that I would make Piercey happy when I didn't want to be with him. It was just hard to shake feeling bad for causing him any pain.

"Piercey," I said quietly before leaving. "I've been thinking about how I haven't given myself time to make a life for myself. It's been one battle after the next, even before I killed the Prophet. It feels like you've done that, too."

He thought for several seconds before speaking. "I'm in a good place right now. I've been finding myself. We'll talk soon. Maybe help each other figure out how to make room for ourselves in all this chaos."

The guilt dimmed and I smiled, my heart warm. "I'd love that."

"Bye, Max. Three days. Don't be late."

"I won't be."

My last stop was always the hardest every time. Nash decided to spend the afternoon with Elsie because both of them would miss me while I was gone, and she really hadn't had enough time with him.

When I hugged her goodbye, she clung to me without letting go.

"How many sleeps, Ma?"

"Two or three, sweet girl."

She leaned back to look into my eyes. "Then you'll come home?"

"Then I'll come home."

I reached for Nash, still holding Elsie.

"When I get home, we're going to spend time together." I met his eyes and then hers, still heartbroken over missing her performance. "I promise that I'll fight for that time as hard as I fight for the Valley."

"That's real hard," Elsie said.

Nash kissed my lips even though Elsie covered her eyes and made a gagging noise. He whispered quietly against my ear so only I could hear.

"You can do this."

It was what I needed to hear most, and somehow, he always knew that.

CHAPTER TWENTY-SEVEN

Leaving my world—my family—to travel with Elias ripped my chest wide open.

So much could happen in only a few days.

But I left the Valley in capable hands, and that's what mattered most.

As I walked beside Elias in his home city, I imagined being born in this world instead. I wore my hair in a bun that Ashton often sported, in case anyone saw me. Elias asked her to take a few days to train in the countryside and not contact anyone. At first, she refused, but Elias begged her and promised to tell her everything, so she begrudgingly agreed. Their bond and commitment ran deep beyond the strain in their relationship.

I tilted my head back to see all the way up Elias's tall apartment building, and I marveled at all his people had accomplished. This looked straight out of a book at the Sacred School. After climbing the stairs, we walked into an undecorated, small apartment. Apart from a couch and a small stove, it looked more like an office. A desk wrapped around the far side of the room, covered in books, papers, and gadgets I didn't recognize. I glimpsed a tidy bed through the open door to another room.

"Is it safe here?" I asked, plopping onto his couch.

"Yes. I make sure no one can spy on me. I even have defense systems so no one can monitor our energy levels. It's one of the safest places in this world."

His skills as an information officer were useful. I wouldn't understand entirely, so I didn't bother asking him to explain. All I needed to know was that what I could do in war, he could do with technology. Defend, attack, infiltrate.

"I don't want to waste a single minute while I'm here." A constant burn rolled through my stomach. "It's too hard being away from my people. Let's get into Ashton's memories, gather the information, and figure out how to recruit Jax so we can kill Lote."

Elias scratched his chin. "Do you think you can control where you land better than last time, since you've done it a few times?"

"I know there must come a point when she starts to soften to him. I remember how that felt with Nash. Maybe if I think about that, I can get close."

"Good thinking."

I fell back on the couch and covered my eyes with my arm. "Let's do this."

Our group trained and fought together diligently over the past three months. We spent a hundred days stitched together like we'd never been enemies in the first place. Every shared laugh and beer wound us closer to each other. I worked so hard not to care about the warriors from the other guild, but how could I not?

A fire flickered at the center of our group. Jax sat across from me as usual, like he knew I'd never allow him closer than that even though we were partners. He drew near only in battle or in training. The steel edges of our blades sparking together was the closest I let him come.

Thinking about it left me feeling exposed as I met his eyes across the flames. His look set my insides aflame, hotter than the campfire. I spent a long time telling myself I didn't notice how wonderful he looked, and an even longer time excusing how long my gaze lingered on him when he wasn't watching.

Jax was beautiful and his smile dangerously charming. At some point, I accepted my inability to ignore that, but I still felt infuriated with myself.

I fled the campfire for a momentary reprieve to refill my mug of beer, only to knock into Jax when I turned around. His form cast a shadow over me.

"Sorry," he said.

"It's fine." I sidestepped to leave.

"Ash."

Why did my heart throb so badly to hear him say my name? "What?"

"I . . ." He hesitated and then offered that smile of his, the one that both irritated and melted me. His face looked handsome in the red glow of torchlight. "I enjoyed fighting with you today."

I nodded, unable to find my voice.

The deeper look worried me that he might say something else, so I started to walk backward. "You, too," I managed.

I spun around. It was so obvious I was avoiding him. How embarrassing.

The beer helped me forget. We drank late into the night, later than we should have. Others returned to camp, but our group stayed up, caught up in stories and a camaraderie difficult to escape.

We laughed hard enough that a warrior from another tent threw a rock at our fire.

I leaned back on my hands, more settled than earlier. It was nice to forget about the war and the feud between our guilds. To forget I didn't want to enjoy looking at Jax across the fire. To just be people felt refreshing.

A loud thud interrupted our laughter.

My heart seized when I twisted around. One of the Silver Moon warriors lay face down by his tent, his mug beside him in a spreading pool of beer.

I jumped to my feet before my mind caught up with what I saw.

"Ambush!" my friend Ralph shouted. "Wake up! Ambush!"

I reached for my sword before remembering I had left it in my tent. No matter. I erected an energy blade and searched the quiet darkness. Whoever approached concealed their energy.

Jax rushed to my side, and together we crept close to a nearby tent for cover.

Everything fell silent as we searched for any sign of our enemy.

On the moonless fall night, our only light emanated from the torches and campfire we left burning longer than normal.

My heart filled in the silence, thudding steadily. Pain dug into me for the man who died even though he wasn't one of my own. This was the power of fighting alongside one another for so many days. I couldn't avoid the connection of blood and the high of battle. The unity of drinking by the fire.

Or of being so close. Jax's body warmed mine in the cold of the night.

The enemy knew where we were, so they already had an advantage. I saw no reason to leave cover to run around searching for them. Better to listen and feel. To watch for an opportunity to arise.

With my senses sharpened, I heard a blade piercing the air and flying in our direction. Jax must have heard it, too, because at the same time, we both slashed our energy blades to knock it away into the darkness.

Jax flew in the direction of the blade far faster than I remembered ever seeing him move. It was dangerous because they may have been trying to draw one of us out. Instead of following in a direct path, I sprinted to the side and tracked Jax's barely visible form in the darkness.

There.

Beyond the black wall of the camp, I detected footsteps. Since we fought together for long enough, I trusted Jax to recognize my power and to evade my offensive maneuvers. I gathered a massive ball of energy and threw it toward the sound.

The stillness and quiet of camp erupted into the clash of warfare in only moments. The attacks and counterattacks popped up all over camp at the same time. Where moments ago, the enemy hid with their power carefully concealed, they now swarmed us from all directions.

I shot as many blasts as I could muster in Jax's area, focusing on the enemies I now sensed, while I ran forward. He moved much faster than me when he flew, but he relied on the cover I provided from a distance while I caught up. We made a wonderful team. Something I wouldn't even try to deny.

As I ran, groups of our aerial fighters emitted a bright wave of power that swept over the camp. Light yellows and oranges poured between every tent like water and then swelled into a fog of power that consumed our entire camp. The fog offered protection, but Jax darted beyond the reach of the defensive mechanism.

I burst out of the swirling fog and made out his dark form whipping through the air. A dozen enemy soldiers swarmed the wooded hillside where Jax flew, deftly dodging every attack, raining down strikes of his own.

The sky brightened with powerful blasts of power slamming into the fog over the camp. They didn't penetrate the defense of our guilds, but over time they would weaken it and the warriors who had erected it. We needed to hurry.

What a cheap move to attack in the night.

With power sparking all over the sky and ground like fireworks, I discerned flashes of my surroundings like the sun blinked on and off. Jax dove through the air and smashed into a warrior who lobbed attacks against the defensive fog.

A few more minutes, and I expected our aerial warriors to surprise our enemy with the second phase of their defense. While neither of our guilds invented the fog tactic, it wasn't used widely in our area, and I doubted these warriors understood what they were fighting against. Each attack did weaken the integrity of the defensive fog, but our warriors did not allow the power to simply escape. They collected it in an arduous process called recapture.

We didn't use it often because it often went terribly wrong, terribly fast. This was urgent, though. We'd been caught unprepared by an enemy who clearly strategically planned this ambush. We needed a surprise to win.

I sped up as I ran for a line of enemy warriors. They defended their own aerial fighters, a group of roughly ten gathered beneath a powerful dome shield.

The warriors targeted an area of the fog to break into. One enemy warrior ran straight into it with his sword extended, only to get thrown onto the ground.

The fog relied upon self-identification using our energy signals. Through our neural implants, we could subtly adjust our energy output to create a signature, one as difficult to detect as carefully hidden code. The defenders controlling the fog monitored all energy signals to allow us into the fog, or to not harm us—a fallible, imperfect practice.

This was one reason it was so difficult to wield.

I trusted my comrades implicitly and spent no time worrying about their failure, despite the extreme consequences.

The warriors converged on me as I neared them. Four continued fighting to break into the fog while three targeted me. Another three focused on Jax in the air, and the final four shifted between the two of us.

We really needed someone to back us up. Why hadn't anyone else left the fog? Obviously, they wanted to remain behind its protection, and it was smart to keep a sizable force within its defensive barrier. But we couldn't leave all the fighting to the aerial team. I hoped that others left to battle like us, and were simply fighting other groups.

I released a signal with my power to alert my group that we needed help.

Taking on three warriors and defending against another four who alternated between Jax and me wouldn't work if I attacked blindly. We were so exposed out here. The other warriors who focused on other tasks might notice an opportunity and strike unexpectedly.

Jax chose a great approach in taking to the air, allowing him to retreat when he needed to reapproach. I was stuck on the ground, really wishing that I had learned such an incredible skill.

The best strategy was for me to distract and manage attacks whenever possible. If more joined us, then we could face them in an all-out battle.

I continued sprinting, fueling myself with my power so my feet barely touched the ground, and each step carried me much further than I could from my own strength. I leapt far across the ground.

Beams of energy shot into the grass after me, missing as I dodged.

I left a trail of my own power like a toxic gas that permeated the air. The warriors staggered back from it. Seeing my strategy, they darted to cut off my path, but I excelled at this. My mentor, Lote, called me a speedy little devil. As soon as I saw them shift to block me, I twisted and shot toward the fog.

Above me, Jax only narrowly avoided a hit. As I dove back into the camp, I lobbed energy at his attacker to give him time to recover.

My first attack didn't inflict much damage, but it reduced the number of warriors assaulting the fog on this side.

From within the safety of camp, I pelted the enemy with bullets of energy, blind to whether any of them actually hit, apart from hearing a few cries. I stayed rapid and unpredictable to keep the advantage of surprise and force their focus to remain on me.

They might have expected that I would remain in the safety of the fog. I could do some damage here. But after they adjusted to my long-range attacks, I wouldn't be as effective.

My sense of pride as a warrior pushed me to pursue the three who previously targeted me.

I leapt forward, running faster than before, and dragged two energy blades at my side.

One blade made contact, ripping open the bowels of one warrior.

The other was deflected.

I rolled off my shoulder, feigned right, and then twisted to run left. They were figuring out my speed and their inability to predict my next direction. And seeing as how they possessed the numbers to cover so many directions, they very effectively boxed me in by doing so.

It didn't matter. I anticipated an attack where I landed and erected a shield around me. A sword slammed against it at the same time that a beam of energy hit. The shield erupted, smacking the swordsman square in the face.

He stumbled back, grasping his bloodied mouth.

I needed to return to the fog, but they wouldn't let that happen so easily. Jax flew over my head and fired in a circle around me, pushing the enemy back.

I leapt back to the cover of our defensive fog when Jax drew close enough for me to notice the blood running down his arm. I'd missed the injury and that wasn't acceptable. I couldn't leave my partner helpless.

Rage filled me that no one had yet joined us. What were they doing? The ambush hadn't begun long ago, and, considering that most people couldn't run as fast as me or fly like Jax had, maybe they needed more time to arrive. It irked me, though, that others failed to move as fast as us. Maybe that was one reason they had paired Jax and me together. We were fast and took risks. The kind of warriors who fled the protective fog to take on twenty warriors alone.

We were crazy, weren't we? Stubborn, perhaps. Maybe just arrogant.

Jax sure was.

I knew that when I left the protection for the third time that I would not return unharmed after our enemies had enjoyed so much time to observe me by now. I braced myself as I ran north and emerged further from the group.

Silencing my power, I disappeared into the woods. This close, someone might track my heartbeat and my steps. But I took the chance as I stalked quietly through the trees and identified my target.

The man never saw the attack coming. I used such a small amount of energy that the cacophony of power swallowed it up.

That gave away my location, but I rather liked the cover of trees.

This time, as warriors pursued me in the woods, I raced further away from the fog to force them to divide their forces. It was risky to move so far away from my group, but I firmly believed that risks paid off. I also knew that Jax flying overhead offered as much protection as the fog. We had to trust each other if we wanted to defeat these warriors.

I expected half a dozen warriors to pursue me, which I considered manageable given my speed and the trees surrounding me. The rush of footsteps following me took me completely by surprise.

I sensed the swell of energy and dodged. A blast of green energy consumed an entire group of trees inches in front of me. In seconds, the power vaporized them completely.

Shit.

They'd combined their powers, and they were all coming after me, weren't they? All of them except for the aerial fighters.

Smart move. Taking care of the pesky lone warrior allowed them to focus their attention on their true target.

What if I forced them to pursue me deeper in the woods?

I darted backward, losing myself in the darkness of the trees. I relied upon the sound of the wind and my sensitive hearing to navigate through the maze. While I no longer saw Jax, I felt him pursuing me, likely above the tops of the trees.

The warriors followed me. I wanted to rejoice that they fell into my plan, except this meant that the forces attacking us boasted such large numbers that they could afford for a dozen warriors to break away from camp.

Trees all around me vaporized. I sensed the attack before it came and evaded, but it was getting too close for comfort. That and destroying my convenient obstacle course.

Finally, the prick of familiar energy soothed me. Others from my group pursued those following me. I stopped running, plenty far from the camp, and turned toward my enemy.

The warriors bombarded the forest with blasts of their energy. I darted past one enemy warrior, my sword clashing with hers. But I didn't stop. Didn't slow down. I couldn't afford to.

I spied three of our comrades attacking the enemy forces with Jax now in combat on the ground.

They outnumbered us still, but I trusted our combined forces.

Together, we fought as hard as in every battle. Sword against sword, energy against energy, will against will.

Blood splattered my feet as my energy sword broke the guard of a sword-wielding warrior and sliced open his shoulder and the inside of his neck. Three suddenly turned on me, like they silently communicated this.

I struggled to fend off their assaults, but refused to despair. I kicked one back, hefted my shield to defend against the slash of a sword, and unleashed a powerful wave of energy to force them back.

One enemy closest to me wheeled away from his opponent, grappling for me, taking me by surprise. It left him open to an attack that my comrade didn't allow to skim past his sword. But the warrior sacrificed himself to catch me off guard, forcing my focus off the three warriors I defended against. Forcing me to choose where to leave myself open.

Jax shot out in front of me. A fist meant for me rammed so hard into his gut that the surrounding trees shook from its impact. Flashes of power erupted from the enemy's hand against Jax.

Why did he do it? It was meant for me.

"Jax!"

I stabbed past him and tore open our enemy's side.

A hit like Jax took could have literally ripped his guts open, though he managed to absorb the blow well enough to only slide across the ground. Jax's meaty hand wrapped around the man's face as he roared, palm burning bright and red with energy. He ripped his opponent's wound open with both hands, shoved his fist inside, and blasted his organs with energy.

Woah. That attack.

Jax's knees buckled, and he caught himself on the leafy floor, gasping in a breath. He was hurt.

I shot another wave of energy to keep everyone away from him and tugged him to his feet.

He leaned against my shoulder, clasped my wrist, and funneled his energy into me. The heat of his power poured down my arm, crawling beneath my skin, ready to erupt from every pore.

Using our combined energy, I unleashed all our strength into a single oppo-nent. She countered with a shield, but the radius of the attack surrounded her, and her barrier dissolved.

The skin melted from her bones and hung loose as she dropped in a heap.

The battle continued and there was no room for weakness or a break. A sword skimmed my thigh. A blast of energy burst through my shield and hit me hard in the gut. I faltered, gasping from the onslaught.

After all this fighting, five of us and eight of them remained.

We needed to escape back to camp.

"Go," I shouted and shoved my closest comrade in the direction of the fog. We made a mad dash through the woods, our enemies chasing after us. Jax burst into the air, shooting energy behind us to cover our escape.

The energy fog glowed not far ahead, but the aerial fighters who still worked behind their shield cast a cloud of energy over us.

This would instantly kill us if we didn't escape.

"Faster!"

We rushed for the fog, not even attempting to defend against an aerial attack like that.

My muscles burned and tore as my legs brought me within one leap of the fog, but none of my comrades kept up with me. Craning my neck, I saw that everyone was close behind, except for one. She wasn't going to make it.

Bolts of power shot down from the cloud just as my foot hit the energy fog. I skidded to a stop as two comrades beside me rushed in. Jax dove through the air for our straggling warrior, but he wouldn't make it in time. I brought my hands together and hit our struggling friend with a wall of energy, sending her back-ward. Bolts of power bit into the ground where she'd been standing. The ground quaked. Pain flared up from my feet and shot through my body, the shocks of the enormous bolts of energy spreading along the ground and into me.

My comrades dragged me into the energy fog. I collapsed, my body seized in a tremor from the power. I screamed through gritted teeth as a ray of power burst through my side in an explosion of the worst pain of my life. All the power that coursed into my body had gathered there and escaped.

My hands clasped the tattered edges of my bloody side.

CHAPTER TWENTY-EIGHT

curled, clutching the wound closed, oblivious to its seriousness, whether deadly or merely a flesh wound. I only knew it hurt so badly I couldn't think.

Hands grabbed at me. I managed to gasp in a breath as Ralph pulled me up against himself. Jax landed in front of me and fell onto his knees, plastering his hands against mine over the wound.

"How bad is it?" Jax asked.

"Where's . . ." I couldn't form the words. I replayed the image of my comrade's body flying back through the air after I had hit her. Sure, it saved her from the bolt that would have roasted her body like a chicken over the flames, and sure, she was from the Silver Moon Guild. But we were supposed to help each other, and I'd definitely hurt her.

Jax slipped to the right, so I saw her lying safely within the energy fog. He must have picked her up and carried her in.

I pulled my hand away covered in blood.

Ralph pressed down hard on the wound and I almost bashed the back of my head against his jaw. It hurt so insanely bad.

Tendrils of his healing power flowed through me. He wasn't skilled enough to heal me fully, especially considering the exhaustion from the fight, but he slowed the blood loss.

"I'm not an expert, but I don't feel anything too serious," he said. "I think it's mostly flesh. The exit wound is the size of my fist, though. You may have internal damage that I'm not sensing."

If we didn't fight, then we'd die.

I pressed my blood-soaked fist against the ground and started to push up. Jax caught my shoulders, forcing me down.

"Don't move," he said.

"We have to keep going."

"We need to get you bandaged." Jax ripped off a thick strip of his tunic and helped Ralph tightly bandage my side. Pain screamed from the wound as they tied it.

The enemy warriors left alive relentlessly attacked the fog dome. The color surrounding us looked duller than earlier, something that happened as the quality decreased.

"They'll be in here soon enough," Ralph said.

I refused to lie here doing nothing. "If you want to help me, then get me closer to the edge of the fog. I'm going to shoot those bastards in the face."

The pain tried to consume my thoughts, but I wouldn't give in. Jax slid his arm around me to help me up, his hand stained with blood from a wound to his arm.

Together, we traveled to the edge of the fog and attacked the people trying to break in. They easily evaded our strikes, but it did slow them down.

I didn't like being stuck behind this fog when I caused more damage beyond it. Worse, with every shred of energy I became weaker and weaker.

A ghastly shriek, like a hundred children crying out, erupted into the night.

The enemy warriors fell back from the fog. It screamed like it was dying.

I focused on releasing the signal to let our aerial warriors know not to target me. As the fog sank lower, barely covering the tops of the tents, acrid smoke washed out from its base. Yellow tinted the rush of dying fog. It raced out into the woods, sweeping over the warriors.

Their screams joined with that of the fog, its gas burning their skin and singeing their clothes. Soon they erected shields, but the smoke lingered and ate at their defenses.

"Abandon camp."

The order flooded the fog, carried and amplified by every tendril of power.

Jax and I looked at one another. We knew what to do. Disappear into the night like we were never here. Abandon everything. It was a loss, one that would save everyone's lives.

The logistics of abandoning a camp during an attack were not exactly simple. The aerial team kept their defenses up while we escaped, but that left them isolated and trapped. So we fled in waves and remained hidden in order to help them.

It was dangerous and we would lose some warriors in the process. If they thought we needed to abandon camp, though, then that meant the alternative was for everyone to die or be captured.

Jax's eyes fell to my stomach.

I didn't wait for him to ask. I didn't want him to coddle me. "I can still move."

"You're sure? We need to strategize if not."

"I'm telling you I can. We're in the first wave to leave anyway. Let's go. I want to find a place to offer support when the second wave flees."

He nodded.

I grabbed Ralph's hand. "Be careful."

He clasped my cheek, worry bright in his eyes. "You, too. You won't have a healer."

"I'll be okay."

We couldn't wait any longer. I remembered the powerful hit that Jax took to his stomach for me. How much longer would he manage? His movements lacked their usual precision. He covered it well, but he was hurting.

I stopped by the warrior I had hit with my power before we left. "How bad is it?"

She shook her head. "I'm okay. You saved my life."

I smiled, not sure that I'd directly saved the life of a Silver Moon Guild member before. Of course, in battle we supported each other and undoubtedly all saved each other with our efforts. This was new ground. So was fleeing with an enemy guild member turned partner.

Jax and I left the dying fog of camp together. He ran beside me, pulling me along, lifting me over branches. I stumbled my way through the woods, wracked with agony, but I didn't stop.

I hated abandoning camp even more than the possibility of defeat, because at least in loss, we finished the battle. When Lote had created our plans for fleeing camp, I told him that no warrior would accept it. He insisted that our lives were our kingdom's greatest resource and the most important thing to the guild leadership. I understood the necessity.

I just resented not being strong enough to take down these enemies.

As Jax and I escaped into the smokey debris of the collapsed fog defense, I witnessed the magnitude of the enemy's force for the first time. The warriors we had fought were only the first wave. I sensed more surrounding the perimeter, waiting to join the reinforcements.

What cowards. I'd make the coastal kingdom pay for ambushing us in the middle of the night. How did they get this close anyway?

I faltered as we stole into the woods and caught myself on a tree. Jax drew me against himself so fast that my feet lifted off the ground. He didn't slow down, but held me as he ran. I managed to get my feet underneath me and continue with him, not wanting him dragging me around like a child.

"I'll be fine," I said.

"We can't slow down."

He breathed harder than he normally did while running. Begrudgingly, I allowed him to keep hold of me. My ankles started to itch from the smoke irritation. It attacked us as well, which meant that the defenders no longer sought out our energy readings to protect us from the remnants of their attack. I only hoped it wasn't because they'd all been killed.

The sensation of energy as solid as a mountain beamed in the distance ahead of us. Hundreds of enemies. Several strayed closer to us, maybe patrolling the woods.

"Wait!" My body bowed as I pulled away from Jax and gathered my power into a sword. Three warriors moved in our direction. We'd been spotted or sensed.

Jax and I let them come to us this time. We didn't need to communicate it to each other.

I parried a hit and tried to kick, except my foot completely missed when the enemy dodged. Pain ripped at my side, my weakness a weight that dragged me toward the ground.

Fresh blood dribbled down my side. The wound Ralphy worked so hard to close tore open from the combat. Jax charged two warriors and forced the attention onto himself.

Panic scratched at me. It wasn't just this immediate danger right here. The enemy surrounded us. All of us. What if no one escaped?

We didn't have the strength to fight these people off, especially not me. I'd have to swallow my pride and let Jax help me. The only way to evade these three would be for him to carry me while he flew away. Did he have the energy to do it?

I couldn't even communicate the plan with him, though, because I was breathless from the fight and the blood loss. I swung with all my might only for my attack to be easily knocked away. My knees buckled and I crashed to the ground.

Forget honor. I gathered energy in one hand and, from the ground, thrust my blade with the other. When the warrior shifted to defend herself, I abandoned the attacks and launched myself toward Jax with my remaining power.

A blade broke my partner's energy sword in half and cut through the edge of his chest. He threw a dagger of energy at his opponent, but the warrior swatted it away.

"Jaxon!" I skidded across the ground on my knees and erected a shield with my energy, screaming as the blood pumped from my wound. An ax sank into the shield, trembled, and then dislodged. It nearly snapped my shield in half.

Jax's body sagged as he struck clumsily with his sword. A boot slammed into his wounded chest and hurled him to the ground.

My fear exploded inside of me and powered a blast of energy that enveloped his attacker. The enemy fell back from the force. I pushed more of my strength into the attack, reaching into my depths until I broke through his defenses and sent him flying back onto his ass.

"Can you stand?" I struggled unsteadily to my feet. Any second, I might collapse.

Jax's voice came out strained. He rose beside me. "Yes. Thank you."

"I couldn't let someone else kill you, could I?"

I heard his sly grin in the tone of his voice, despite the pain lingering there as well. "That honor is saved for you alone."

This damn man was rubbing off on me. What was I doing teasing him when we were both bleeding to death and running for our lives?

"Can you fly?" I asked.

The three warriors, now back on their feet, attacked at once in a coordinated effort.

Jaxon caught me around my waist and shot into the air. Pressure gripped my gut. Branches and limbs snapped against our bodies. It hurt like hell, but within seconds we flew above the tree line.

I couldn't draw in breath. Agony screamed from my wounds and strangled my lungs.

Jax suddenly fell lower in the air and then caught himself. His hot blood soaked my back.

"Hang on," he said.

He tried to reposition his arms, but no matter how he held me, it hurt horribly. Finally, he twisted backward so I was lying on top of him. He flew with his back to the ground.

I gasped in a weak breath, digging my nails into my forearm to keep quiet. The world spun, not just because of his flying, but because of the blood and pain and the dizziness.

"Can you . . . make it . . . ?" I asked.

"Yeah." His voice sounded as strained as mine. We flew slower with every passing minute, but we didn't fall.

Jax and I couldn't provide cover to our retreating comrades like this. Protocol said to keep running if severely injured, but our fellow warriors still fought for their lives back there.

Tears burned my eyes. "Jax," I said. "The next wave."

"We can't."

That was it. He said nothing else. I wasn't sure that I even had a say in it because I could hardly talk, and I couldn't exactly climb off him to plummet to my death.

I tried to speak again but my voice came out only as a groan.

My heavy eyes slid closed.

"Hang on, Ash." Hearing him say my name soothed me.

The trees blurred beneath us as we disappeared into the dark of the night sky. I missed the summer when the midnight sun never left us. These days, the nights had grown longer and longer. Soon came the horrible cold. Deadly cold. Too cold to war. That wouldn't stop any of us, but it would likely slow down the fight for territory until spring.

I wanted to tell Jax sorry that I couldn't help and that I literally weighed him down. His breathing turned ragged against the back of my head, his flight incredibly slow. His hard chest pressed against my back, straining from the effort of carrying us both away. I figured that he probably never carried someone around while flying, especially not while wounded and exhausted from a late-night ambush.

We cleared the woods and passed over a narrow stretch of field between the trees. Jax slowly lowered toward the ground until we landed with a thud. Not a crash landing, but not exactly graceful. We both moaned as we rolled onto our sides, his arm still around me.

I couldn't move. I doubted he could either. His heavy arm was limp.

If we could rest for only a few moments . . .

No. Jax bled still and needed bandages. Blood soaked through my own as well. We needed to find shelter.

I started to crawl out from under his arm but collapsed on my back. I looked over to see his body covered in sweat. Dark blood stained his chest and his left arm. His eyes just barely opened.

"We can't stop," I said.

Together, we shoved ourselves to our feet and clung to one another as we stumbled toward the next line of trees. We were far enough away that I no longer felt anyone's energy.

We needed water and bandages. Medicine. Things we lacked.

Jax and I stumbled along together, holding trees for support, until he pointed out a little creek.

We chose a spot where the trees grew in a bundle, offering us protection. It felt like we were slowly dying.

Jax and I both dropped down next to the stream and drank desperately.

"Okay," Jax said. "Okay. Let me see your side." He rolled me to him.

His body pressed against mine and his heavy breath washed over my temple. So near to me. In all the chaos, I forgot who we were, what he stood for, and who he served. The temporary loss of this reality faded. We were once again Ashton and Jaxon, enemies from the two most powerful guilds in the Valley.

I shoved him back, panicked I'd let him close to me, refusing to allow myself to be so weak as to rely on him. "Take care of yourself. You're hurt."

"Stop it." He grunted as he pried my soaked bandage from my wound. "Why are you being annoying?"

"I don't want your help."

"You know what, we're going to fight. Right now." He mercifully lifted off me in a pathetic attempt to stand, only making it to his knees. "Get your sword ready."

I choked on my own laugh, too breathless to let it out. "Look at yourself. You'll pass out."

"Look at you. I've put up with you long enough. If you can't even let me help you—" He lowered his head, breath catching. "Shit. If you . . . can't let me bandage your wounds, then we just need to fight it out."

I took it too far this time. I'd let myself panic from the feel of him against me. That was all. Not that I wanted to admit that to him. "You really want to fight me?" I asked.

"You clearly want to, so yeah, let's fight."

Sweat peppered his temples. I felt my own wetting the small of my back. My laugh bubbled up again and, in my exhaustion, I gave in. The sound came out winded and more than a little pathetic. Practically a whimper. But I couldn't hold it back.

Jax watched me for several seconds before a tired grin crawled on his face and he laughed quietly as well.

"Fine," I said. "I concede." Gasping at the pain from moving, I dropped my hands from my wound to let him help me. "We have to take care of you soon, though."

He studied my side. "It's not good, Ash."

"Yeah." I rolled my head to the side and glanced down his body to search out any injuries I'd missed. "Do you think that punch damaged any organs?"

"I think I'm just bruised from it."

Jax ripped away more of his tunic, leaving a swath of his stomach bare. We were all used to the cold here, but we didn't have blankets. He was going to be *freezing. Gooseflesh prickled his skin already. The contours of his hips and abdomen caught my gaze for longer than it should have.*

I closed my eyes while he rebandaged my wound, not needing to find a way to distract myself from him for long because it hurt horribly.

"If you help me, we can close my wounds without bandages," Jax said.

"Sorry. I'm not good at this."

"You can't be good at everything. It's fine. Just focus on strengthening what I'm doing. I can get us both to stop bleeding at least."

I felt his eyes on me. Glancing over, I met his gaze, my face so close to his. He didn't seem so bad. In fact, he never had, and that always scared me. I so easily fell into unyielding loyalty for my friends. If I let him into my heart at all, then I'd struggle to keep him as my enemy. He might not have had the same qualms about me. His easy attitude made me suspicious.

Jax held pressure on my wound while I did so to his chest.

"You lost a lot of blood," he said.

I nodded, trying to hide how shaky I felt. "What about you?"

"I didn't lose as much. It just looks nasty."

"Probably feels nasty, too."

He managed a weary smile, and I was too exhausted, too hurt, to draw my defenses up against him. It was hard to keep him and the others in his guild from encroaching upon my heart when we fought and bled together on the battlefield. It was especially hard to keep him out. He made it seem so harmless to pretend we weren't enemies. I reminded myself I couldn't be his friend, that I should remain cold to him, only the worry in his eyes as he looked at me seemed so genuine, it disoriented me.

I closed my eyes, wanting to drift to sleep and escape from him.

"Hey . . ." His voice roused me from the verge of sleep minutes later.

I murmured.

His voice was soft, and the smile absent from his face. The seriousness of his eyes took me by surprise, as serious as in battle. "You sure you're okay?"

"I'm fine."

"You didn't look okay. You were groaning in your sleep."

I glanced down at the blood soaking my bandage. "We should sleep."

After staring for a few more seconds, he nodded. "Just wake me up if you start to feel bad. I can try more healing."

Jax had reached the limit of his abilities. No way I'd ask him that.

"Thanks," I said.

He hesitated. "You, too."

For the span of only a heartbeat, I met his eyes, unable to keep myself from seeing how beautiful they looked with his dark whiskers making the gold in them pop. My heart pinched and I turned my head away.

Helping each other with our wounds was as close as we could get.

Absolutely under no circumstances could I allow myself to feel anything, no matter how infectious his smile, or how convincingly deep his gaze. This man devoted his life to a guild that threatened the existence of my own. It was not that he simply belonged to them. His conviction and loyalty matched my own. We were enemies. The truest form of enemies.

So why did I always have to remind myself of this simple fact?

"You fight better . . ." My voice started to fade. "Than anyone I know . . ."

His fingers still touched my hand and I felt them move ever so slightly, caressing my skin.

CHAPTER TWENTY-NINE

T he more I saw of Ashton's life, the worse I felt peering into her past without her permission, especially given that Elias expected updates. I refused to tell him any details and promised only to share with him what helped us protect my world from his guild and defeat their corruption in this one. So far, I gained little, because I only saw Ashton just starting to open up to Jaxon.

I knew so well where her story led next, though. They were as drawn together as Nash and me, in a bond that defied time and the boundaries between worlds. My heart ached thinking that their story didn't end the same as ours, and that while I started a life with Nash, Ashton continued hers alone. While I yearned for more time with Nash this past year, seeing another version of ourselves made me so thankful for our love that I was desperate to return home to him. Desperate to promise that nothing would ever get between us because I'd seen a world where we were torn apart.

At the same time, submerging myself in the life of another version of myself opened my eyes in other ways not so obvious. It was easier to recognize my poor decisions in Ashton's life or recognize my untapped potential. The same was true of this world. Being here, learning more through Ashton's eyes, served as a mirror to my world.

The lack of unity robbed this Valley of peace, just like in my world, only for different reasons. While the guilds were afraid to join together and lose power, in my world, we lacked someone willing to take power, or even just able to take power for themselves.

Thoughts I didn't want to consider stirred inside of me. I knew that soon I needed to face them and stop running away from the growing certainty inside of me. I wasn't ready to peer into a future that scared me.

Looking into Ashton's past felt safer.

"You really don't have anything yet?" Elias asked.

"No. It's not easy to travel around someone else's life. I don't have her memories. I'm trying to find a time when she felt close to him."

Elias groaned, and hearing his frustration broke the last of my self-control for my own. "I'm the one who should groan at you."

He sat back, audacious enough to look surprised.

"You don't get to be annoyed," I said. "I'm meddling in someone else's life, and now I have to impersonate her with your deranged leader. There's the potential for so many problems, especially if I go through with your crazy plan to try recruiting Jaxon. You realize that if Ashton and Jaxon meet again, she might try to kill him, right? He's going to be so confused and devastated."

"It's the only way."

I thought back to Ashton's memories of fighting at Jax's side. "I think we should be honest with them. They're good people."

"You haven't seen what I have. Keep watching Ashton and you will. Things are different here. In your world, Nash held no loyalty for the Prophet because he basically enslaved him. Jaxon is loyal to his guild. Ashton also completed her training at the Sacred School and chose her guild. These two grew up with their guilds. I'm telling you that it is way too risky."

"You and Piercey do have one thing in common. You always imagine the worst-case scenario."

"And you never imagine something bad enough," Elias said. "That's how you and Ashton get caught up in messes that Piercey and I have to clean up."

I drew back. "Who asked you to clean them up? I've been cleaning up your mess."

Elias heaved a sigh of frustration and ran his hands through his locks. "Look, at the end of the day, you got power for your friends. Be happy for that."

Annoyed with Elias, I closed my eyes before continuing. "You know what, let's just get the meeting with Lote over with. I hope you planned something better than just pissing him off. We've toyed with Ashton's life long enough for one day."

Elias mumbled to himself as he prepared to leave.

As we left his apartment and traveled down the paved sidewalk, small between the tall buildings, I thought through Elias's plan so far. He wanted to keep Ashton in the dark and secretly recruit Jaxon to fight with me while

I pretended to be her. We'd assassinate Lote and set the fall of his guild into motion. The pieces did not add up for me. Ashton needed to be a part of this battle. I'd felt how she saw Elias and I knew she'd never betray him. Surely she cared about whatever turned Elias against his own people.

I wanted to see the rest of what had happened between Ashton and Jaxon and witness what Elias did to betray her. I needed to know more than that, though. That was all that Elias wanted me to see. What was he hiding? I needed to peer through more of Ashton's life to see what had happened after she and Jaxon separated. Elias connected with Piercey, but Piercey didn't know Ashton. He could have missed the implications of something Elias did. I would understand now that I'd lived through so many moments of her life.

"You promised to tell me the truth." I spoke quietly as we walked. "You said when we returned to your world, after you gave my friends the implant, you would fess up because we wouldn't be able to just get mad and abandon you."

"You'll see soon enough what I did."

"Why are you being cowardly? Tell me yourself."

Elias stopped walking and faced me. "The truth is that my own guild killed my parents and Ashton continued to serve them."

Shock gripped me as I remembered Elias telling Jaxon that he'd been right about what the guild did to his parents.

"Elias—"

"They learned the truth about Lote's corruption, and when they tried to stop him, Lote killed them. He framed the Silver Moon Guild, but it wasn't them. So don't talk to me again about how we need to be honest with Ashton, or how I'm being cowardly for not wanting to tell you. This has torn my life apart."

"I'm sorry." My heart beat wildly at the raw emotion on his face.

"I just . . . I think you should see it all for yourself. It's better that way since you don't really believe me."

"I never said I don't believe you."

"You're suspicious." He started to walk again, carrying an air of darkness that I'd never witnessed in Piercey.

How could Ashton continue to serve the guild after learning about the murder of Elias's parents? She would never do that. But then, she had. I needed to travel again and see this for myself. To get in her mind and understand what she was thinking. Was she trying to protect him? If standing against the guild had killed his parents, Ashton may have wanted to secretly rebel without Elias.

I'd never understood why he didn't want to tell me the truth until now. I also didn't want to tell my story about my father using me to kill my village. Compassion melted my resentment over Elias dragging me into the crisis in his world when I had one of my own.

I caught his wrist, my expression soft. "I really am sorry."

Lote did not rise from the seat he sat in previously, but stared at Elias when we entered.

"I prefer that we do not wait," Lote said. "I need your decision today."

I took my place on the couch, but Elias remained standing by the door.

"Well," Elias said. "I've come to realize that the power to shift worlds should have never been discovered. It's dangerous and has the potential to end entire worlds. I thought that we could use it to learn and grow. Then, after you demanded to know about what I was doing, I realized what I'd done. No one can ever travel like I have. It needs to die with me."

I closed my eyes and lowered my head, imagining that Ashton would have been overwhelmed with fear at his statement.

Lote clasped the armrests of his chair and took his time standing to his feet. He stared down at Elias for a long while before speaking. "It's not up to you whether you share."

"Lote—" I started.

"This is not up for discussion. Ashton, you'll bring him back here tomorrow evening once I've had time to assemble a team for the questioning. If he doesn't show, then you'll both be placed under arrest. This is a matter of kingdom security. He is hiding information, and we need to know why."

"You'll arrest us?" I asked.

Lote looked at me for several seconds and then at Elias. "I already sought out the warrant from the court. According to our laws, you have a full day to decide whether to share with us. If you refuse, then we will force the connection."

"The leaders approved of this?" Elias asked. "What happened to the two weeks?"

"I told them I no longer trust you. My word is all it takes."

Only one day? Elias and I needed more than one day to deal with Lote's threat to my world.

"Ashton, the court allows for a guardian to supervise him. I trust you to watch over him in the meantime and keep him out of trouble. If he is not here at this time tomorrow, he'll be arrested. If he tries to flee, we'll have grounds to kill him."

Knowing what Lote had done to Elias's parents and having been exposed to corrupt leaders before, the manipulation seemed obvious to me. He didn't trust Ashton. He'd send spies to watch us. This was a ruse to keep his hold over her.

"It's okay, Ashton," Elias said. "I knew what would happen if I refused. This is not your fight. It's mine."

I genuinely hurt for him. My fists wanted to curl tight and slam into Lote's face. If I met his eyes, he might see it in me, so I averted my gaze, pretending to be too upset.

"Leave now," Lote said. "There's nothing more we can say. I hope that you'll change your mind before we're forced to question you through an involuntary connection."

"You don't belong in other worlds, Lote." Elias's resignation to his fate dulled his voice. "Leave this alone."

CHAPTER THIRTY

This is bad," I said. Elias sat down on the couch beside me, quiet and unresponsive. "Why are you not panicking?"

"I knew it would come to this. I've been preparing for it for a long time. We have to work fast. After they take me for questioning, I'll end up imprisoned. I should take you home first. We don't have as long as I thought."

"So, in the next day we're supposed to defeat your guild?"

He settled his head in his hands. "I don't want you to get stuck here. I need to take you home. If we can get Jax to join hands with us, then he'll help me break out. I have faith in him. Then I can return to your world to get you and your allies."

"I should spend this time learning how to travel worlds."

Elias tilted his head to see me, still resting it against his palms. "It's very dangerous. I practiced for months before I actually tried. It's a technical process for me, not something I sense. I'm not sure how to teach you."

"Instead of spending more time living through Ashton's life, we should assemble warriors to help you. It's time to come clean."

"No." Elias patted the back of the couch. "Take a few hours to learn more about Jax and then go to him. Only him."

"Why only him?"

"I can't trust anyone else from his guild. Ash trusted him and he told me the truth about my parents. I mean, he didn't know for sure it was true. He only confirmed that his guild didn't do it and that he suspected Lote. I know that if you ask him to help and you truly mean it, he will. I'm not a fighter, Max. I can't help kill Lote in the way that Jax can."

I leaned back against the couch. "I'll kill Lote before I leave."

"He's hard to take down."

"Listen, I'll travel through time again to prepare to talk to Jax, and I'll tell you information about what he planned. I'm not promising anything else, though. We'll decide this evening."

Elias sniffled. "Thank you, Max. You could have killed me for dragging you into this. I don't know what I'd do if you weren't here."

I let out a very long sigh.

"I want to show you what Lote did to my parents as well." He walked to his desk and picked up a pair of goggles. "After you finish traveling through Ashton's life, look through these. You'll find everything you need to know about what he did. You should understand the enemy we're facing."

The night Jax and I escaped the assault on our camp damaged the shield I'd erected between the two of us and I no longer knew how to protect myself. We survived our fitful sleep and painstakingly traveled to the closest city where we received healing treatments.

Since then, every day, every moment, assaulted that shield between us the same way the warriors had attacked the defensive fog. We spent too much time together, faced too much danger at each other's sides. It wasn't only the times we'd protected each other or saved each other that threatened to wear down my heart. It was also moments like tonight, when the moonlight glowed against his smooth skin, and his amber eyes found me in the dim light.

"Can't sleep again?" he asked.

"No."

He rolled onto his side. I grew so used to sleeping near everyone in our group that I didn't think about it anymore with anyone except for Jax.

Every single time he placed his cot beside mine, my stomach fluttered the entire night. I didn't want to admit the truth to myself, so I didn't. It whispered to me, though, in the heat in my cheeks and the drift of my gaze.

"Try going for a walk again," he said. "That worked last time."

"Why aren't you asleep?"

"I had a feeling you'd be up again. I noticed that when you're quiet at dinner, you end up with insomnia."

He'd learned that about me? I tried to hide when I felt anxious and I thought I did well with it, but I supposed I was more withdrawn than I realized.

In the past, I would have lashed out at him for seeing me and knowing me, for the intimacy of the time we spent together softening my heart to him. It seemed pointless today.

"Maybe I'll try that."

Jax pushed himself up and offered his hand to me. "I'll go with you."

"I'm okay. You should sleep."

He clasped my hand anyway and tugged me up. "I could use a walk, too. You mind?"

My hand was still in his, my body warm from his nearness. I shook my head, afraid that if I said anything, I'd give myself away.

Only it didn't take long for me to do just that. That night as we walked, we talked for hours without realizing how much time had passed. After that, no matter how hard I tried, I craved more of him, desperate to know him. The weeks passed, and soon there was nothing left guarding my heart from his. I'd seen his character in battle, and I'd become charmed by his surprising vision to bring peace to the guilds.

One day as we walked through the woods on our own again, Jax started talking of this future he wished to see. "We fight well together, and I don't just mean us. Our guilds. We're incredible alone but look at what happens when we unite. Take you and me. It doesn't matter where we come from or who we fight for. When we let ourselves forget, we're unstoppable."

"What are you trying to say?" Discomfort filled me because I didn't want to give myself the hope of ever being more than enemies.

"If we can make peace, so can our guilds. And they should. Imagine our potential if we work together and combine resources." It was something he said often with a dreamy quality to his voice. He dared not lose hold of this vision. "It's hard to overcome bad blood, and I think that's the main obstacle holding back our progress. Our guilds can work together, though. We're doing it right now."

He never talked like this around the others, so it felt like a secret only the two of us shared. Actually, I couldn't believe I was entertaining the idea.

"I'm not sure people can move past everything that's happened," I said.

"Maybe the next generation can unite if we pave the way."

"It's just that this hasn't been a bloodless war."

Jax hesitated. "Something happened to you personally."

"Not to me. To Elias. His parents were killed."

He nodded, speaking carefully. "You think my guild killed his parents."

"It's pretty well-known."

Jax took my hand, stilling my breathing. "I swear on my life that we didn't kill his parents."

"Then who did?"

"I just know it wasn't us. I've heard our leaders talk about them."

I didn't want to discuss this. I ripped my hand away, reminded again that we were not truly allies. Our time together seduced me into forgetting that we entered this war as enemies, and we'd return to enemies when it ended.

"Ash," Jax said.

"We shouldn't talk about this. We shouldn't talk about anything. This is why it's a mistake to pretend we're friends."

I started to walk away, but he caught my arms and turned me toward him, settling me back against a nearby tree. "We've been through too much for you to storm off like that. You know me. You know I wouldn't support having people murdered. We're all in the same kingdom."

Jax stood so close to me. The heat of his body burned against me like an inferno. Irrational anger stormed through my heart.

"You've been getting in my head," I said.

"You're not this childish. Why do you insist on pushing me away?"

"Because there's no world in which we can be friends, Jax. It's never going to happen. It doesn't matter who you are and who I am. It matters who we serve. Our people are enemies."

"Our people are this kingdom."

"You know that's not how it actually works."

I breathed so hard that it made my body brush his. He quieted, glancing down my face.

"I'm not going to play the game where we pretend to hate each other," he said. The touch on my arms turned tender as his palms smoothed up to my shoulders. "I don't hate you and I know you don't hate me."

I couldn't breathe. Not with him so close.

"I don't know if we can stitch our kingdom back together, Ash. But can't we at least overcome the wounds between our guilds? Why can't the two of us follow our hearts and find the narrow path that we can walk together?"

"There is no path."

"So what if we forget just this once?" Jax asked.

Forget and give in to what I'd been fighting. I didn't need him to say it when I read the want written all over his face and etched into his body.

"You want to live forever wondering?" he asked.

My eyes closed as the wondering took hold of me. Wondering how his hands would feel on my body. Wondering how his lips would taste. Wondering how we could make each other feel.

"Wondering is better than knowing," I said. "Once we know, we'll remember, and it'll be worse."

Jax leaned back and I felt so cold without his warmth. "Do you think if we were from the same guild things could be different?"

I swallowed hard, afraid to let myself think about it. "I think if the war between our guilds can hardly keep us apart, then surely in any other kind of life, nothing could hold us back."

"Then it seems so sad to give up without any kind of fight."

The earthy scent of his flesh filled my senses, stilling me so that his nearness worked through me.

I never understood people making stupid decisions about love before. I never understood not being able to deny an impulse or to walk away from a bad situation. In mere moments, Jax had undone a lifetime of what I believed to be my own restraint and showed me convincingly that I was not as strong as I thought.

"Tell me to walk away . . ." His breath tickled my ear when he leaned in. "And I will."

I begged the words to leave my lips, but the temptation of stealing a few more seconds of this incredible sensation turned into more time than I intended to give us. And I was staring into his eyes, no longer breathing, no longer moving or thinking. Something dragged my body toward him. It was this power he held over me, pulling on me. His lips looked soft and beautiful.

I'd never experienced a physical draw so hard to escape.

"I . . ." My voice failed me as his eyes carefully—as carefully as he wielded his swords in battle—raked down my face to my mouth.

"It's okay," he said.

"Is it?"

Embarrassment flooded me. I couldn't deny any of this. He told me he'd walk away, and I hadn't said anything or left. We both knew without a doubt that we wanted each other now, and I'd never escape this moment, no matter how hard I tried. I'd always remember it.

Truthfully, I desperately wanted never to forget.

Oh, damn it.

A pained look filled his eyes and then he sighed as he eased back, giving me the space I silently demanded. Only I didn't mean the demand. I hated it. The loss ripped through me as more and more space opened between us.

I caught the back of his neck with a desperate grip and lifted myself up to him, unsteady on my toes. His arms wrapped around my waist.

"It's not okay," I said. And despite my words, I plucked his bottom lip with mine, releasing it slowly.

The shield between us broke irreparably. Jax's body pressed mine against the tree, so he consumed my entire world. He raked his hands down my body without the slightest hint of shyness. Desperate, ravenous energy possessed him as he kissed me deeply.

My hands dug into his shoulders, my tongue gliding along his.

My guild may consider this a betrayal. Reality crashed over me and I ripped away from him with a gasp. What was I doing? Jax slid his hand through his hair, forehead settled against the tree while I backed away. I looked once at the shadows sinking against his chest and then forced my body in the opposite direction.

The next day, he sidled up beside me. "Do you want to talk about it?" he asked.

"No. Never. We should never admit that it happened."

He snorted and it made me want to punch him.

"Are you really laughing right now?" I asked.

"It's a little ridiculous," Jax said. "It did happen. You want to be in denial about it but that's not going to solve anything."

"It's already solved. We're not doing it again, and we're forgetting it happened."

"You can't forget." Jax worked closer to me, bringing me dangerously close to the sweet heat of his. The way his body eclipsed mine made me crave more. What had gotten into me? "It's going to happen again. Already is."

Cocky asshole. I pushed him back a step and jerked my hand away before I lingered or made the mistake of discovering more of him to struggle to forget.

He was right. I never forgot and it did happen again.

Jax's talk of peace sparked hope in me and tugged me back to him every time I tried to escape. Eventually, one day, I lost the strength to fight against the wonderful way I felt with him.

Then came the dangerous dreams of a world in which our guilds overcame the differences between them as well. We both were influential in our organizations. What if we pushed them back to one another?

Both of us knew it wouldn't be so simple as convincing guild leaders to try it. Our guilds had hurt each other and stolen from one another. As I'd always said, it wasn't a bloodless feud. So, we started planning. Could we mount political pressure for our leaders to share resources? That drove most of their fighting. We each needed resources the others hoarded, and this starved our innovation. If the people of the kingdom demanded collaboration over competition and backstabbing, then our guilds may one day unite.

I actually started to think it might happen until my delusions came crashing down around me.

After six months of battling the coastal kingdoms, we were gifted with a weeklong break in a city we stopped in frequently. Both of our guilds were housed in the same complex where commanders and guild leadership worked together on war strategy while the rest of the warriors took a much-needed rest.

Jax and I had come long past wondering and flew beyond guilty nights in the woods. We planned for the future.

Until halfway through the stay, when the door to Jax's room opened without anyone knocking, and a voice I knew so well tethered me in place.

"Ashton." The sound of Lote's rage twisted my stomach in knots.

Jax and I pulled back from our kiss to stare at each other wide-eyed. There was no hiding, no denying, no covering up the truth. My hands were buried in his curls and his hidden beneath my shirt, my knees straddling him.

Lote fell silent and I knew what that meant.

My heart began to pound out of control. The rapid-fire thoughts shooting through my head flooded my face with heat. How did he find us? Why did he even come looking? What the hell was I thinking putting myself in this position in the first place? Nothing could ever be more humiliating than to be found compromised like a couple of teenagers.

I ripped my hands from Jax and fell off his lap. When I turned, I looked directly into the shocked and burning eyes of one of the most respected leaders of my guild.

Lote's lips curled when he spoke. "I'm glad to see you two have taken this partnership between our guilds to heart."

Every word hit like an individual punch to my gut. Tears of humiliation bit my eyes. Jax stood to his feet, taking my arm to help me up. But his touch burned like the fire, in a terrible way this time. I withdrew, only embarrassing myself further.

"Can I speak with you alone, Ashton?" Lote asked. "It's about guild business."

I winced and walked forward, refusing to turn to look at Jax. My stomach churned as I followed silently after Lote through a maze of halls and what felt like an eternity of time.

When we entered his temporary office space, he pivoted sharply on his heel. Gone was the silence and the shock. "What the hell was that?"

I couldn't breathe. "I—"

"You can't explain. There is no explanation for what I just saw. Of all people, I never expected—"

"I know." I shouted it to overcome his voice. "You asked me a question so let me answer."

He slammed his palm against the wall, but I didn't let it rattle me. I'd been caught off guard and hit while unarmed. Now, though, I needed to rebound and compose myself.

"He's our enemy, woman!"

"He's Jaxon." I breathed in deeply, the fire that burned in my cheeks spreading into my heart. Yes, I never thought I would do this either. That didn't mean it was a terrible mistake. "You wanted us to fight together, bleed together, serve this Valley together. You expected us to work as a team. I never would have gotten to know him as a man if you hadn't insisted on us putting aside our differences."

"It's my fault you're in bed with our enemy?"

"No, it's your fault I had the chance to see who he really is. Jaxon is not my enemy."

If anything surprised Lote all night, it was this. While he'd been angry before, now worry crept into his voice. "Do you hear yourself? Jaxon is one of the most powerful warriors in the Silver Moon Guild. He has personally overseen missions that hurt us."

"Just like I did to his guild. It doesn't mean that Jaxon and I are at odds. It's our guilds that are at odds."

"And you swore your heart and soul, your life, to your guilds. That means that you cannot be together. You cannot give any of yourself to him when you gave it to your guild first."

I stepped closer, never one to allow him to intimidate me, or to pretend that just because he mentored me, just because I owed so much to him, I didn't have a voice in this relationship. If he taught me anything, it was that I should never surrender my power to someone else. "I can and I have. Jaxon is a good man. There's a way for our guilds to make peace. I see it now, because we made peace."

Lote listened without interrupting and then without warning he barked out a laugh, one that continued, and swelled, and reverberated off the stone walls. He leaned forward and gasped in a breath. "You're serious, aren't you? Our guilds can make peace because you found it in yourself to fuck our enemy?"

"I care for him."

"Perfect. I'm so thrilled to hear it is more than just a nice time for you. You realize this compromises us? What if he's a spy? Even if he isn't, they could use him to get to you or to us. You can't trust yourself not to be manipulated because no one can be on guard every second of their life."

Undeniably true considering Lote caught me off guard today.

What was he even doing here when he was supposed to be at war halfway across the coast? "Fine. I admit that's a problem. It doesn't change the fact that this war between our guilds has been hurting us and maybe it doesn't have to."

"You're acting like a silly girl. I'm embarrassed for you."

Claws of pain tore into my chest. I sucked in a breath, struggling to keep my emotions from blowing up again. "When have I taken anything for myself?"

"Don't start that. You aren't a martyr."

"I'm serious. What have I done that is just for me? You lean on me because I'm consistent and I'm dedicated. That's why you're so shocked. Open your mind for one moment and consider what I'm saying."

"We've tried peace, Ashton. We're not fools. They aren't willing to compromise, and we can't either, not for what they want. None of their demands are reasonable. No matter what, you and Jaxon are enemies, unless you plan to betray our guild."

I dug my nails into my arms, holding them crossed over me. "I didn't plan for this to happen. I never meant to fall for him."

Lote groaned. "No, Ashton."

Why did I say that? I hadn't fallen for Jaxon. We had feelings for each other and were enjoying each other's company. I'd finally convinced myself to open up to him. Surely I didn't really mean to say I fell for him, right?

Shoulders loose now, Lote walked to his chair, fell into it, and then indicated with his hand for me to sit as well.

"This is worse than I thought," he said.

"I didn't mean it like that."

He rolled his eyes and grabbed a drink off the nearby table, muttering to himself. "Of course you didn't."

"I haven't given away any compromising information. I've been with him every second of the day so I know that he hasn't been reporting on me or anything."

"You've given away that one of our top officers can be swayed into bed with an enemy. That you can be made a fool of."

Power plumed in my chest and nearly unleashed on him. Lote watched me for several seconds with warning in his eyes. Losing control of my temper only hurt my case and made me seem out of control. I closed my eyes for several seconds to calm myself down.

"That's unfair," I said.

"It doesn't matter. That'll be their assessment. I'm sure you share such a special connection. Doesn't matter. This is war."

"Why is it war? Because what we're fighting right now along the border, that's an actual war. So why should we be fighting a guild that serves the same kingdom?"

"We don't serve the same kingdom," Lote said. "We serve the vision of two utterly different lands. Given the chance, they'll take us in a direction we can't stand for."

"Any direction where we aren't in sole control of the Valley is one you won't accept."

Lote's frown deepened. "A few months with this man and you're already buying into his lies."

"I'm quick to fight. Too quick. But even I can see it's time for peace with Silver Moon."

"None of this matters. You need to gather your belongings. You're going home."

I jumped out of my chair, voice raising without my control. "No, I can't do that. I am not leaving our people here to fight without me."

"You did this to yourself and to them. I cannot possibly let you stay after this. I won't discuss it."

"Lote—"

"Ashton, this is a direct order. Pack your things and go home. You and that man are finished, unless you want to turn in a letter of resignation."

A letter of resignation might as well have been a death warrant, because living in this Valley alone and unaffiliated promised as much. Someone as high up in the guild as me wouldn't make it a day by myself. I'd be a target for literally every guild in the Valley. Even in all of Skia Hellig.

"I know that I shouldn't have engaged with him while we're away at war, not when we're from opposing guilds," I said. "I should have worked it out with our leadership first. Sending me home, though—"

"You're delusional, Ashton. Or just way more naive than I ever thought possible. No one in this guild will ever let you be with him in any way and under any circumstances."

"I can only shed my blood with him."

"Yes," Lote said. "You can only bleed with him because unless someone is bleeding, there is no reason for us to ever have anything to do with those people."

What more could we possibly say? I wheeled around and left without being dismissed, because fuck him. Fuck him for not trusting me at least a little after all that we'd been through and all that I'd done. I slammed the door shut and stomped down the hall with hot tears burning my eyes. My power beat at my chest in sync with my heart, desperate to escape.

I was rushing so fast and was so distracted by my rage that I almost didn't see Elias until I nearly ran into him. I skidded to a stop.

"Ash," he said.

"What . . . What are you doing here?"

Then I saw it all. I saw everything in his eyes like a written confession. I knew him too well not to.

The realization tore me in two. My stomach tangled in knots and my heart shredded. "It was you," I whispered.

"Let's talk." The desperation in his voice would have softened me any other time.

"Oh, you do not want to talk to me." I shoved past him and continued for my room.

He was foolish enough to pursue. "Ash—"

I turned as fast as lightning, my body glowing with power, nearly rushing out of control. "Not now."

He gaped at me, hurt and sorrow heavy on his strained face.

He said nothing else as I walked away.

CHAPTER THIRTY-ONE

I didn't turn around when Elias entered the room.

"Lote asked me to take you home."

"And make sure I stay put," I finished for him.

"Yes."

My hands curled tightly around my blanket. "I don't want to talk to you. I know you think I'll cave and you can explain yourself and try to make me see your reasoning. Today is not the day."

"I understand."

Normally, Elias compulsively obsessed over smoothing over any conflict with me. I expected him to walk closer, to speak in that sheepish voice, to tell me he loved me. Instead, he left me alone to finish getting ready, and I almost felt bad.

The day passed in the silence that I demanded. I stared out the window, hating that I hadn't said goodbye to Jaxon, and that I wouldn't join everyone in battle. What if something happened while I was gone? We were all a team. This was life and death. We needed each other. The regret and grief killed me.

I refused to stay home. I wanted to at least watch from a distance and try to secretly help. Elias wouldn't be babysitting me for weeks. Lote wouldn't assign me anything important to do because he was angry with me. I'd have a chance to return.

The day passed in slow motion. I felt Elias's torment at not having the chance to make amends. I wasn't trying to exact revenge. It just hurt too badly to speak, and I didn't trust myself not to yell.

Finally, when darkness descended over our carriage, I pried myself away from the window to face him. "I'm ready."

"Are you sure?"

I nodded, not wanting to say anything more than necessary.

"I know how it looks," Elias said. "I hope that you trust me enough to realize it isn't that."

It was all so raw. I'd never been so humiliated in all of my life. I worked incredibly hard to make it to this point and I couldn't lose my integrity because of a sex scandal. It wasn't that to me. It was so much more. But that was how everyone would see it. Something dirty, shameful, filled with lust. Jaxon meant far more than that to me.

"I know you have your justifications," I said.

"I can't tell you everything right now."

My hands tightened into fists at this. "Excuse me?"

"I can't."

"I looked the other way over the last year with your weird secrets, but I'm not this time. I know that you told Lote about me and Jax and where to find us. This might completely ruin my standing with the guild."

Elias tried to take my hand, but I shoved him away.

"Your standing will not be hurt," he said. "You're well respected even beyond the Valley. The guild needs you. It's going to be bad right now, but it'll be forgotten one day. Everyone makes mistakes. Everyone lets their heart go soft for someone at some point."

"I got caught with our enemy, Elias."

He glanced away, clearly uncomfortable with the situation. "I can't expect you to understand or forgive me or to accept the limits of what I can and cannot say," Elias said. "The only thing I can do is give you as much of the truth as possible. It's what I owe you."

"So talk, and if I do rage at you, shut your mouth because you deserve it."

Elias gripped his hands on his lap and nodded, stoic. "Lote was never going to allow you to be with Jaxon. It wasn't going to happen, and you know that. Eventually, he'd catch you. By then it'd hurt even more."

"I honestly expected better excuses from you. You didn't even try to talk to me about my relationship with Jax. Why not tell me this instead of having Lote show up while I was with him?"

Elias grimaced. "I have reasons, Ash. It needed to happen this way to protect you both."

"Wow. Really."

"Lote will never allow Jax anywhere near you again. I'll help you find a way to say your goodbyes. In the meantime, you need to go home and stay there."

I kicked my feet up and looked out the window, my chest as heavy as if a boulder were crushing it. "What hurts the most is that you can't even tell me the truth. When did we stop trusting each other?"

"It's not like that."

"I would have trusted you with anything."

"That's why you told me about Jax, then."

I chewed my cheek at that. "I didn't see a reason to hurt you. I can have a private love life."

"I'm trying to fix things and make sure you don't end up in a worse situation than this."

"Elias . . ." The tears came without permission, and I didn't try to stop them. I just gave in, ready to quit. "How can I ever forget this? I won't."

"I know."

The resignation of his voice made me turn to look at him. Why would he do this to us? He hadn't just hurt me but himself. He wanted to repair our relationship, not burn it to the ground.

"You have to let him go, though," Elias said. "At least while things are the way they are. You will both be safe if you do. That has to be enough for now."

"What are you holding back from me?"

"Don't try to make me tell you. I will once it's safe."

"I don't need you to protect me," I said.

He grabbed my hand fast enough that I didn't have time to think better of it and push him away again. Looking deeply into my eyes, he pleaded with me. "I cannot lose you to this."

My words were choked in my tight throat.

"If you've ever trusted me at all, then trust me now," Elias said. "I hurt you and I will live with that forever. But I'm doing something important, and I can't stop now. I can't. When this is over, you'll be okay, and maybe you can find him again."

"You think this is just about him?" A sob swelled in my throat. "You're my best friend. You betrayed me."

Elias drew his shoulders back, his eyes looking hollowed out. I didn't even recognize him.

"What happened to you?" I asked.

He released my hand. "I'm going to make things right."

"You think I can't forgive you for this, but I can. I can forgive you for just about anything, Elias. You know what I won't forgive you for? Shutting me out and getting yourself killed without giving me the chance to help you."

"Do you know how many nights I waited up wondering if you'd make it home?"

I couldn't answer. Couldn't even imagine. "You never said anything."

"It's always been you defending the Valley, upholding the honor of our guild, fighting day in and day out. I've never been able to save you from your pain. I've only bandaged your wounds. So let me, for once in our life, be the one to fight. I don't expect your forgiveness or understanding about what I did. I just want you to let me be the one to fight for once."

"We can do it together."

"No. We can't. Trust me."

"What does that mean?" I asked.

Elias settled back against his seat, eyes on the window. "I told Lote that Jax planned to infiltrate our guild through his relationships with our warriors. The time battling together provided the perfect opportunity for him to earn everyone's trust."

"That's not true."

"It doesn't matter," Elias said. "Lote is paranoid. He doesn't even need evidence. The mere suggestion is enough that he will never allow Jax to show his face near any of us again. He'll be working on getting him moved away from all of our people."

"Why would you do that? Jax actually wants to help us find peace. He's willing to put his life on the line for it. He's the reason I softened my heart to it in the first place."

Elias's voice sounded monotonous. "The further Jax is from our guild and anyone in it, the safer he will be. He was going to get himself killed. Get you killed."

"By who?"

He breathed out slowly and never answered.

"I want my Elias back," I said.

"Me too, Ash."

In that moment, I wanted to hate him because he'd derailed everything. None of this would have happened if he hadn't sent Lote to me and lied to him about Jax. What Elias and I shared was stronger than even hate, though. He meant so much to me for so long, and I believed in him so deeply that I couldn't hate him, even now. In fact, I was afraid for him.

It felt like I was peeling my own skin off because of how badly it hurt, but I reached across the seat and I slid my hand over his.

We sat that way for a long while before I spoke one final time. "Don't let our past destroy you. There's nothing you need to prove or fix."

But I didn't think he was capable of actually hearing me.

I thought before that our rival guild would be the ones to get close to us and use us. Never had it occurred to me that it would be my people. That it would be Elias.

Even though I couldn't stand to suspect it, I wondered if he'd done this for another reason. Perhaps it hurt too badly to see Jax and me together.

I should never have brought this pain upon any of us. Now Jax would only suffer.

After Elias left, I didn't reach out to him, and he didn't reach out to me for months. I hadn't been able to see Jax again, but I had written to him, telling him I was sorry, and that we couldn't see each other again. It felt like a slap in the face to send it to him, but it was better than saying nothing.

I never thought it possible to truly forgive Elias for what he did to me and Jax. With time, I came to see that I'd been foolish to think anything could come of Jax and I pursuing a relationship or trying to push the guilds to have peace. Lote would have always believed that Jax was a spy. Worse, though, after reexamining my conversations with Jax, I realized that the peace plan wasn't as peaceful as it seemed. He'd never actually said that uniting might require a war or the destruction of our current guild structures, but he implied it.

And then through our spies, Lote uncovered Jax's involvement in assassination plots on our leadership, not only in the past, but after returning from the war.

I saw the futility of a life with Jax then. Our guilds would have used us and one of us would have died. Maybe both of us.

Months passed before I allowed Elias back into my life. We met for tea in his apartment to try and find a way past everything.

"What happened to us?" I asked.

Elias's eyes brimmed with sorrow. "I got greedy thinking we'd work out and now there's too much between us for us to ever go back."

"Don't talk like that."

"It's not what you wanted," Elias said. "You convinced yourself that since you loved me so much as your best friend that you may love me even more if we were together. I let you delude yourself because I wanted it so badly. Look at us now."

I bit my lip, not wanting to say anything to hurt him, but also unable to hide the truth when we knew so much about each other. "That's not why we're like this."

"You said you forgave me," Elias said.

"Forgiveness and trust aren't the same thing." Pain hardened like a knot in my throat. "I don't want it to be like this. Tell me how to pull through it." Reaching for him, I hesitated, seeing the hurt and want both mingling in his eyes. Then I slid my hand over his cheek despite thinking better of it. Could I do it? I made myself love him once before. Could I do it again? "If I fight hard enough, I can make the last year go away. We can go back to how we were."

He trailed my hand, voice thick. "Ash . . . We were done before you met him. We'd been done."

"Then I want to turn back time to when we were only friends and make these choices that pulled us apart."

"Not me." The smile looked wistful. His thumb rubbed the back of my hand and then he released me. "I would give it up for you, but for me? No matter what I've lost, loving you was worth it. I never want to live a life without knowing how it was to hold you as you slept or to be the one who dried your tears."

"Elias—"

"Ash, you aren't responsible for how I feel. We entered into a relationship and we both played a part in it falling apart. Let go of your guilt for not being in love with me."

"I do love you, Eli. I'll always love you."

"You love me the way you love a childhood friend. You love with the confused love of a woman who gave herself to a man she never actually wanted. You don't love me the way you love him."

It felt like he'd hit me with a jolt of power. I never said that I loved Jax. Hadn't even thought it. Did I need to, though? What else, other than love, haunted a person for more than a year and made a heart ache so horribly? What else felt as gripping as real power, simply from the sight of him, from the brush of his skin? This was love. Not the kind that I shared with Elias. Maybe not even as deep yet, because it never got to grow. But I did love Jax. It started as a spark in battle and grew into a wildfire. Those embers burned stubbornly.

"It's my job to fix what I broke. You didn't have the chance to figure things out for yourself because I got in the middle of it." He wiped my cheek with his knuckles, hesitating, savoring the touch.

"It's already right. Jax and I shouldn't be together."

"I cannot accept how I made it impossible for you to look at me."

I bit my lip. "It's not because of what you did. It's because of what I did. I let that man get into my heart. How could I do that?"

"He's not a bad man, Ash."

"He tried to kill our leaders."

"Wouldn't you do the same to his guild?" Elias asked.

"Hell yes."

"So how can you blame him?"

"Whose side are you on?"

Elias laughed. "Our guilds are the same, Ashton. We choose ours because it's ours, not because it's better or right. If we learn to coexist, then we won't have this issue. Jaxon realized we needed one final war to get us to that point. Still, he isn't the problem. You aren't the problem. It's the pointlessness of this blood feud."

"I don't know how you can say that. The Silver Moon are the reason your parents are dead." My voice chilled until it turned to ice. "They stole everything from us."

Elias didn't respond to that, when normally mention of it riled him up.

"Did something happen?" I asked. "Why are you defending that guild and Jaxon?"

He smiled sadly. "We'll talk more later. I've been having a hard time, that's all."

I overcame the stain on my name from Lote and a select number of leaders discovering my relationship with Jax. I even started to feel happy again most days.

Then I felt the warmth of Jax's power nearby. I'd gone to the market, and he must have followed me here to this neutral territory.

At first, I pretended not to see him, stricken by an onslaught of all the feelings I tried to run from. Hope and defeat mixed into one because I knew we'd never be together. I had to forget about him and stop doing this to myself.

But for all the time that passed and all the time that came, I couldn't forget this man or that feeling he gave me deep in my chest. The fluttering, warm, sticky sensation I didn't feel with anyone else.

We hadn't known each other long or even well. We hadn't discovered nearly enough of each other. So why was he so deep in my heart? Why couldn't I forget about him?

It hurt to think about this, but as much as I loved Elias and as close as I still felt to him, I never struggled to let go of him like this.

Finally, Jax slid into my view, and I feared losing my sensibilities again.

"Ash," he said quietly, looking at me over a crate of apples.

"We can't do this," I said.

"Just a few minutes."

"Absolutely not." I looked around to make sure no one was listening.

When he followed, I groaned and fled to an alley.

"What?" I asked, whipping around to face him. I nearly ran into him. Everything rushed back to me, every touch and kiss, how I'd tried to deny him and failed miserably in the end. The humiliation of being caught.

"We have to talk," Jax said. "It's been too long."

"I meant what I said in my letter. We can't see each other again."

How did he look stunned when it was so clear that this was our only option?

"We made a mistake, and we need to move on," I said.

"We didn't."

I steeled myself against the pain lacing his words and my own resonating with his. Both of us fell helpless against the same waves in the same sea. "Jax, are you going to betray your guild?"

"It doesn't have to be this black-and-white."

"I'm not going to betray mine. I'm not going to leave them either."

He breathed out slowly, silent as he looked away, and then finally met my eyes with his emotions cooling. "Don't let what Elias did ruin our chance at exploring a future. We get to make this choice, Ash. I can't keep doing this. I miss you."

"We already made our choice a long time ago. You're a threat to my guild."

He laughed bitterly. "I can't believe you're acting like this."

"What do you think our life will look like? What Elias did simply reminded us of reality. We are enemies, Jax. Enemies."

He reached for me, and I tried to force myself to step away, except I couldn't. My feet were frozen in place. My body paralyzed. I couldn't even draw in breath as his large hands smoothed up my arms to my shoulders and then drew me against his broad chest. This had fooled me in the past. Feeling this good with him made me forget the impossibility of a life with him.

"I can't love someone who won't fight alongside me." I uttered the lie against the soft of his neck, desperately wanting to melt my lips against his skin instead. Breathing him in intoxicated me. My hands ached to crawl up his tight chest. "I should never have made you think I could."

"I don't believe you."

I let myself dig my fingers into his shoulder blades and rested my face against his chest. "How can I, Jax? Our values don't align as much as you think if we can't fight on the same side."

"We need to bring our people to the same side."

"We'll only become pawns and either we'll betray each other, or we'll betray our guild. I won't do that."

Jax's voice lowered. "So you'll preemptively betray me."

"It isn't a betrayal to say no to a life together when we made no promises." I swallowed down the painful lump in my throat. He risked his life seeing me like this. Lote wanted him dead. I needed to stop him from seeking me out again. "It might break our hearts, but it isn't a betrayal. It's a choice and one that is best made from a sound mind before we hurt each other too badly."

I pushed him away from me and made my voice sound cold.

"We can never see each other again, Jax. From here on out, we're enemies." I nudged him back. "Go."

It looked like he would argue with me, but finally his shoulders fell, and he turned away, voice sorrowful. "This is a mistake."

"Jax."

He turned with a vague hope softening the sorrow, like maybe I changed my mind.

I steeled myself, certain that I should put an end to this once and for all. "If I ever see you again, I'll kill you."

The attack hit him like the most swift and lethal blow—the blood pouring before he felt the damage. Several seconds passed where nothing changed except for an endless sorrow in his eyes, and then came the tightening of his jaw, the flicker of betrayal and hurt and anger.

"It's a promise we should make to one another," I said.

"You don't mean that."

Tears fell down my cheeks. Pain suffocated me so I spoke without breathing. "Jaxon, I swear to you on everything I am. If you show your face again, you are dead."

"Why? Because I refuse to stop fighting for our kingdom?"

"Because if I let you live, someone in my guild dies. You proved that."

This time he said nothing for several seconds. "I mean so little to you?"

My throat felt like it was on fire. "It doesn't matter what you mean to me. None of that matters."

"Only that we're enemies."

"Yes!" I tried so hard not to sob but it broke free. "You're my enemy. You're the enemy of my people and I cannot let you hurt them, not when I swore to protect them and uphold them. I cannot betray the people who loved me every day of my life."

The pain in his eyes looked as severe as if I had actually killed him, or at least tried to do so. "If you meant it, you'd kill me now. You don't want to have to face me again because you'll melt. You want to hide," he said.

"Promise me, too. If you care about me at all, then you'll match what I give you, because I already cannot bear it. Come at me with all you have."

"That is so twisted, Ashton."

"I don't care," I said. "If you ever loved me, then you'll say it."

He fell completely silent, staring at me. I struggled for breath. Right when I was sure he'd walk away, the emotion fled his face.

"I promise," Jax said.

Those two words hurt far worse than any wound before.

"Good." I choked the word out, unable to hide how badly it hurt me as well. "Now leave."

The pain I knew ravaged him was locked away too deeply for me to see. Jax looked unmoved. Unfeeling.

"If we ever see each other again . . ." My voice died out.

Jax's bright eyes looked dull. "It means death."

CHAPTER THIRTY-TWO

My Valley and the Valley in Elias's world both lacked unity for completely distinct reasons. Seeing it through Ashton's eyes gave me confidence that if the guilds actually came together under the leadership of the kingdom, life here would be so much better for their people. Instead, they bickered along faction lines within the kingdom, serving the leaders of their guilds instead. What did that mean for my world?

How could my Valley find unity?

Many times when I closed my eyes, I saw that older woman looking at me and saying that I was the only person she saw standing after I asked who would stand up to lead the Valley. I saw how desperately the guilds in this world needed to join together and how much better everyone's life would be. Maybe I didn't understand the power of unifying my Valley, not just for my people, but for myself.

It just scared me so badly to think of answering the call of those people looking to me, begging me to become their next leader.

The question of how to solve our problems haunted me when I woke from traveling through Ashton's life, no longer so much because I didn't know the answer, but because I did. The fallout of Elias's betrayal stoked my own tensions, leaving my insides cold and my body stiff. Fear about the safety of the people I loved and served combined with my resentment for leaving them to help this foolish man. It astounded me that Elias had actually acted on his delusional plans and hurt her like that.

Ashton never wanted to turn on Jaxon. Elias not only doomed any hope of their future together, but pitted them against one another by telling Lote that Jax intended to infiltrate the guild. I wasn't sure I could forgive Elias for that. Just like Ashton couldn't.

"You saw." Tears coated Elias's eyes.

"I saw. You left her alone. You took everything from her and then you shut her out from your life, too. No one knows better than I do how much she's lost."

"Please understand. I knew they'd kill Jaxon just like they killed my parents and that they might just kill Ash, too. Jax is way too dangerous to let near our guild, especially with his ideas of revolution. Add on the fact that he told me his guild didn't kill my parents."

"So you broke them apart to keep them safe from Lote. To keep Jax away from the guild. Lote couldn't let someone who knew the truth be close to Ashton when her support is so important."

"Yes, and even beyond that it was too dangerous."

Looking at Elias now, I couldn't believe that Ashton didn't see through him or Lote, or that she didn't realize Jaxon likely never made any assassination plot. I didn't believe that for a second. However, I looked through Ashton's eyes long enough to understand that Ashton couldn't see Elias the way I did, because I knew his counterpart so well. And I saw how far Elias had fallen from who he should have been. Ashton felt devastated, humiliated, and confused. She thought she could trust these two men who meant so much to her.

On the other hand, I knew Elias's lies too well. As much as I sympathized with Ashton's lack of information, it disappointed me to see her cast Jaxon aside the way she did.

"You should never have intervened like you did." I didn't spare Elias from my judgment when Ashton never held him accountable. "Facing impossible challenges is what helps me to become more than I know myself to be capable of. Ash's love for Jax would have changed your Valley. She would have united the guilds."

"It's not as simple as killing someone like in your world. This is a dangerous place."

"If I have to hear one more of your rationalizations, I'll lose my mind. I'm not going to lie to Jaxon for you."

Elias's eyes widened. "Do you want to protect your world from my people? Do you want to help my people gain freedom like yours did from the Prophet?"

"I could never do that to Nash in any world, no matter what name he goes by. Jaxon or Nash, it doesn't matter. I'm not lying to him, especially after witnessing what you put him through."

"We have to do something," Elias said. "We need him."

"You know who you need? You need Ashton."

"Well, Ashton refuses to help me."

Living through Ashton's memories didn't reveal as much of the information that Elias wanted, but it taught me plenty. I didn't believe Ashton refused to help him. I needed no evidence, no time to think. I knew Ashton now. And I knew with certainty that Ashton would never refuse to help Elias. As devoted as she was to her people, she was just as devoted to this one single person. Something else must have happened. Something more. Piercey had connected with Elias but didn't notice anything strange, and yet, I sensed that none of us had the full story.

Maybe Elias knew how to selectively share when connecting. Shouldn't he have been more panicked about Lote threatening to force connection onto him?

A cold chill swept over me.

Elias had been deceiving me this entire time, hadn't he?

"There's something you don't know," I said.

He straightened. "What?"

"Ashton saw Jax again."

Elias leaned forward, jaw dropping. "Are you serious?"

"Yes. She wanted to see him one more time, so she asked him to meet with her. I need to travel again to see what happened. It could be important."

Would Elias see through my lies?

No. He was too excited about this new development. Quickly, he pulled a pillow behind me. "Hurry. While there's still time."

I needed to find my way to a moment in which Ashton sought the truth and was denied it. I knew how Elias acted when he wanted to withhold information. If I just focused on that, maybe I could land in the right time.

"First, let me see the information on your parents. I need a moment's rest before I travel again."

I always spent the anniversary of the death of Elias's parents with him, but for the first time, he didn't invite me to sit beside him at their gravesite to read their favorite poetry.

The day was always a hard one for him, so I didn't want to ask him about it for a few weeks, to give him time to sort through the grief he always felt this time of year. When I tried to get in touch with him, he avoided me.

So I had no choice except to use my key to his house to enter and drag him out.

"Elias," I called out, not wanting to startle him. He'd become more paranoid about security over the last few years, and obsessively upgraded the equipment in his house to make sure no one could spy on him.

When he didn't respond, I walked into the bedroom of the small apartment and found him sitting on the bed, facing the window, an open book face down beside him.

"You haven't been answering," I said.

"I don't want to talk, Ashton. It has nothing to do with you. I just need time."

His back remained to me. So unlike him. Subtly over the past few years, Elias transformed, and I missed how drastic the changes were. Instead, it hit me all at once today. His shoulders were hunched, his body lax, his voice gruff and monotone. He looked like someone had sucked his personality out of his body and left him shriveled.

Pity and empathy twinged my gut in equal measures. I didn't like seeing him like this.

"Elias, tell me what's going on with you. For a while, I thought you acted like this because of us and because you weren't comfortable around me yet. Or that you were worried about the war. Clearly, it is much more than that."

My anger faded with each step I took closer until I placed my hand on his back. He stiffened at my touch but didn't push me away.

"Talk to me," I said.

"I can't."

"Elias." I sat beside him now and leaned closer, trying and failing to get him to look at me. "What happened?" On occasion, Elias did get moody, usually if his feelings were hurt or if he couldn't solve conflict in some area of his life. Never did it come without cause and never this extreme. "Lote is concerned."

Stiffly, Elias twisted his neck, a subtle flame of anger barely warming his cold eyes. "Concerned."

I blinked, on the verge of panic at his strange behavior. "You know that I'm on your side. I'm here for you. Let me help you."

A smile completely devoid of any warmth or happiness lifted his lips without showing in his eyes. "I know that you'll always choose me, Ash, whether it's what you truly want or not."

"What's that supposed to mean?"

"It means that I can see now that we were never going to work out. You saw that, too. So why haven't you accepted it? I finally have. You need to also."

"Accepting that we cannot be together doesn't mean that I'm not here for you."

He took my hand gently. "We'll always be dear to each other, but this has to stop. You have to stop giving up pieces of yourself for me."

"I love you." The words burst from my mouth before I could appreciate the implication and I winced. "You're my best friend."

Elias understood what I meant, though. Not for a second had there been any confusion or hope. That made him look even more sad to me. "You're mine, too, Ash. That's why I'm telling you no. No, you don't get to take on this problem."

The anger returned and I sat back, not sure why I suddenly wanted to yell. "That's not how friendship works. I gave you space. We should be here to help each other. Don't abandon me just because I won't be with you."

Everything stilled. My heart, my breath, the very air around us.

After a few seconds, Elias looked down. "I didn't mean to make you feel that way. I promise that's not what I'm doing."

"So, what are you doing? Ruining your standing in the guild? We worked so hard to get to where we are. You had the favor of all of our leaders. You were the darling Elias. They loved you and trusted you."

A bitter laugh wrenched from his lips, and he jerked away from me back toward the window, hiding whatever it was he didn't want me to see. "Go, Ash. This is my fight. Not yours. Not anyone else's. Sometimes people need to do things alone. It doesn't mean that we aren't there for each other. We just cannot live as the same person, sucking the life from each other."

"I suck the life from you?"

"That's not what I meant."

"You know what, Elias. You can say this has nothing to do with me, but you're wrong. They see us as a package. No matter how far you try to push me away, they expect me to figure you out and get you on board. Shutting me out doesn't do you any favors, and it certainly does me no favors."

I thought he would respond. I waited, hoping that what I said would break through the steel he'd erected between us. Elias didn't, though. He stared in silence. And I had nothing left I could say.

Instead of fighting a battle with a man who refused to engage, I pushed myself off the bed and swiftly left the room.

How was it that we overcame ending the life we'd led together and moved past him sending Lote to find me, only for this to push us apart? Whatever this was. I worked so hard to be the person he needed me to be. He'd said he didn't want me to do that. But did that mean he should cut me off completely?

Something happened and I had to find out what. It had made him angry with the guild and bitter with the leaders. He obviously felt like they never actually cared about him. So what made him feel this way?

For months after that, I watched Elias to find any clues about his crisis. I didn't want to ask around and put the spotlight on him, but I quietly investigated the situation without raising alarm about his strange behavior. Time passed and Elias began to act more like his old self, though he remained distant. I wasn't the only one who noticed, and it worsened his relationship with the guild. Fortunately, given his stellar reputation, leaders stayed patient with him. I wondered how long that might last.

I hadn't figured out anything at all and almost gave up on the endeavor altogether, until one day I noticed that Elias hadn't come home in days. A few days prior, I left his favorite snack at his apartment and discovered it untouched, something he'd never do, no matter how awful he might feel.

Panicking wouldn't help me to find him, and since he'd not been on the best terms with Lote, I didn't want to recruit anyone to help me look for him. First, I searched the cabin in the woods that only we knew about, hoping to find him hiding out there. But it looked like it had been empty for weeks. Fortunately, at some point while I searched the city for him, he came home safely.

I never figured out what he was hiding, and he refused to tell me.

Awareness of my own body in the present shattered Ashton's past and threw me back into myself.

Elias's white ceiling reminded me of the all-white room and the disconcerting sensation of confusion and lies I'd always wrestled with there.

He launched into questions, desperate to know if Ash and Jax met, and what came of it. His voice sounded like a buzz to me.

"You never told her." The whisper barely left my lips.

"What did they say?" he asked, not hearing me.

I jumped up off the couch, forcing Elias to nearly fall off the coffee table he sat on.

"There never was a meeting," I said. "I made it up."

If I'd given him time to feel shocked, I was certain he would have stared for a long time with his mouth hanging, thinking straightforward Max never would deceive him. That I, like Ashton, always came out swinging. I offered him no time for shock.

"Ashton never turned on your guild because you never told her." I felt breathless as the pieces fell into place. "You didn't want to tell me you hid the truth from her because you knew that I wouldn't help you."

"I did tell her. You must not have traveled—"

"No." Power ripped through me as my voice lowered to a deadly threat. "I warned you not to lie to me."

Elias looked up at the ceiling, biting down the fear I saw flash over him. "You know I did the right thing. You've been in my position before. This is what happens when there's no one opening their eyes to the truth. I'm forced to become something we both hate." His voice rose. "I knew you'd hate me just like she does. So no, I couldn't tell you. I need you. I need to believe that even if she'd abandon me, you wouldn't, because whatever happened in your world made you strong enough to fight any battle."

"You're a martyr, aren't you? Poor Elias, forced to sacrifice himself because no one can do the dirty work."

"I'm still Piercey. In my position, he'd do the same thing. So, take a second to try understanding your friend, because I know you wouldn't be so quick to turn on him."

"You are not Piercey," I said. "Don't you dare pretend you are. I won't be manipulated by you. I'm sorry for what you went through here, but it twisted you. You can't even see how far off the path you are."

He pinched the bridge of his nose and huffed out a breath. "I just needed help, Max. You know how desperate you can get when you need help."

He looked so pathetic to me at that moment that I struggled to keep my temper from flaring. "You should have been honest from the start. Instead, you coerced me through lies and misdirection. I thought I could trust you because you connected with Piercey. We were foolish to believe that meant anything."

I learned Elias's guilty look the first day I met him, and I'd seen it too many times since then to miss it. He kept his posture strong, but his eyes had that glassy, dismal look to them. "I'm trained to resist interrogation. I know how to hold back when connecting. It's hard and imperfect but I know how to do it. I just needed you to think I didn't so you would trust me."

How could he be so conniving?

"Every step of the way you've deceived me," I said. "You ambushed me with Jax the first time I came here without telling me anything at all about what had happened between us. You refused to tell me what you did to Ashton and Jax or anything about your guild. Now I find out that what you did to prove your trustworthiness also was an act of deception."

"Tell me what your first instinct is now that you know," he said.

"To tell her, like you should have."

"Exactly."

I cocked my head. "Come clean to her."

"She won't be able to stay out of this fight."

"Good. You need her, you idiot. You don't need me. If you had talked to her in the first place, you wouldn't have had to pluck another her from another world. Or make me live through her life like some kind of voyeur. You should have fought this war together from the start. Why don't you trust her? You're so convinced that she'll never betray her guild when I'm confident that she will never support what they're doing."

Elias shook his head. "It never had anything to do with that. I can't risk her life."

The words stole my ability to speak, until enough time passed for them to fully digest. "But you can risk my entire world."

"I didn't know—"

"That's a load of shit. You never considered that they'd find out what you were doing and come to my world?"

Elias finally looked away, a sure sign that I pushed him into feeling too bad, and that I was onto something.

What was wrong with me that I'd let him get away with so much? Sharing the seed of consciousness with one of my closest friends wasn't a good enough excuse. Pitying him because Ashton didn't love him—and I felt bad for not loving Piercey either—certainly didn't justify the undeserved grace I showed him. I tightened my jaw and hardened my glare, my limbs tensing as I walked slowly toward him.

To his credit, he didn't try to avoid me. Close to him, looking into his eyes, I spoke in a low growl. "How could you be so stupid?"

"I would do anything for Ashton. I told you that."

"Stop with your rationalizations. Seriously."

His eyes closed and pain etched into his face in strained lines. "Ashton never endured what you did. I'm not saying she can't handle herself or she isn't strong. She is. You, though, achieved what no one else has, not even her. I needed you. I still need you."

"So stop treating me like this."

"I'm scared. My heart is broken. I don't . . . I don't know how to rely on anyone anymore because that's when it all falls apart. I know how you'll react, so I just try to control it. To keep you from even finding out."

"What are you afraid of?" I asked.

He swallowed loud enough for me to hear. "If Ashton knows what the guild did to my parents, then she'll fight them, no matter what it costs her. Just like you did in your world. I don't want to lose her."

"You think she'll die."

"I know she will. You have an advantage here that she doesn't. You're unknown and unconnected. You have a relationship with the gods that no one else does, and I just know you can win whatever war you fight."

"So can she," I said. "Why don't you believe in her?"

"I don't want her to go through what you did. I had what you needed desperately. I could see it so clearly. All those days of you killing yourself in battle, I knew if I could just give you the neural implants and some guidance, then you'd be okay again. Why put Ashton through hell when we could do this together? And maybe . . ." He breathed out slowly, his voice sounding resigned. "Maybe I didn't believe in her like I should have. I couldn't think past my fear that they would kill her just like they killed my parents."

His admission made my voice catch in my throat, the raw pain in his eyes battering my heart. "Elias." Damn it, how did he always draw out my sympathy like this? I wanted to be angry so badly, and yet I could only think of consoling him. "Ashton is not your parents."

"I can't take the chance. You shouldn't be surprised anyway if you know Piercey as well as you claim."

"What's that supposed to mean?"

"You don't realize everything he did for you, do you?" Elias asked. "You connected with him, you work with him every day, you basically live at the Sacred School with him, and still somehow you don't really see him."

"What are you talking about?"

"Piercey fought through all of his fears at the Sacred School, alone, to protect you. That's why he became director. You should know that. You have his memories. His heart is etched upon your soul."

The room felt smaller as he talked. Was it true that I didn't see him? "I know what he sacrificed for me."

"Then why would you be surprised that I did all this to protect Ash? It's because you haven't let yourself actually digest what you mean to Piercey and what he's done for you. My actions here in my world should be no surprise to you. I won't risk Ashton. I won't put her in harm's way. I'm going to fight the battle for once and spare her from the suffering the guild inflicted on me."

"You need her." I pressed my hand to my heart. "Piercey and I work so well together. Ashton can fight this war with you."

"No, it's all too broken. I made a mess with her long before I broke apart her and Jax. There's too much history. This is my penitence. I can't heal what's been broken, but I can give her peace."

I stared at him. "She needs you. Make a way for her to be in your life again. That's the best thing you could do for her."

"I don't want to be Piercey." Elias shrugged sadly. "I really don't. Would you?"

His words hollowed out my chest.

"I've been in his head and in his life," he said. "He's so good at what he does, and he's accomplished great things. He's better than I am. I think he's starting to feel better than I do. I still don't want to be him."

I was too afraid to ask him a question I already knew the answer to.

"I'm sure he'll find his happiness soon and he'll go on to have a great life," Elias said. "At least I had you. He never did. I would rather live bitter and guilty than give that up. Ashton changed me."

It was hard to breathe. "I think she might not have changed you for the better. You can't let your pride push you to make bad decisions. If you're trying to be her hero, then stop."

"I'm not."

"Stop giving yourself excuses. Piercey has moved on. I know he has because we didn't just connect once. I can feel him moving on."

After a few seconds, Elias finally nodded. "It does appear he finally has. You still feel bad, though. We both know why. You're loving another man right in his face and he chose to stick around for it."

"Piercey is more of a man than most can even dream of being. You're a fool if you don't want to be like him."

"I've been through enough pain," Elias said. "Stop wishing more on me."

"Don't take it out on me that you can't get Ashton to love you."

The final sentence took things too far and I regretted it immediately. He'd vexed me so badly that I didn't even want to apologize. Instead, I scowled at him as I grabbed his arm.

I couldn't let my feelings get in the way, though. It was time for me to take action. Elias thought that destroying the guild meant freeing his Valley from the corruption that seeped into the veins of this kingdom. He was wrong. The Valley was too complicated to simply destroy one guild and expect a positive outcome. Wiping out his guild may lead to far more chaos than in my world when I had killed the Prophet. Here, the people fully participated in this culture of conflict, whereas mine were victims to the Prophet. My people had not been given the opportunity to make bad decisions.

This world needed to change the guilds from the inside out and target specific leaders. Elias was blinded by his heartbreak and the injustice. He wanted to save Ashton from it so badly that he refused to tell her, so there was no one to show him his blind spot. He couldn't see that he was going about this all wrong. This wasn't as simple as bringing me in to kill another god. I would bring together the right people to fight the war with Lote so I could make them take responsibility for these people who now wanted to invade my world.

It was time. "You've lost your right to make a choice about this," I said.

"What are you—"

"I won't let you lie to me anymore, not in any life."

"No, Max—"

Elias tried to rip away, so I gripped his wrist with both hands and transported us to the quiet cabin in the woods where I was sure he had sent Ashton.

We appeared in a living room dimly lit by candles and covered with papers on the floor that mapped out battle plans.

Ashton rose from one of the maps and then she didn't move another inch. Still and pale as a marble statue, she stared directly at me. Elias did as well, his arms limp at his side.

I spoke with a level voice. "I'm what Elias has been hiding."

CHAPTER THIRTY-THREE

Ashton's shaky hand reached out beside her and clutched the edge of a table. "What the hell is this?"

Elias turned on me and shouted loud enough to reverberate off the walls of the small room. "What is wrong with you?" Neither Piercey nor Elias ever came close to yelling like this. Hearing his voice this way stunned me. "This is the one thing you absolutely could not do."

"No." I jabbed my finger at his chest. "We're not doing this. You go sit down with Ashton and explain everything to her."

"I can force you back to your world," Elias said.

I snarled, tempted to do more than poke him. "You repeatedly deceived me. You swept me into your problems and created a massive threat for my world. I don't care if you're mad at me. If you don't want me to meddle, then don't involve me. Now go explain before she passes out from shock."

Elias seemed like he'd forgotten about Ashton in his blind rage and turned now, breathing ragged. "Ash, listen . . ."

Something flickered in her eyes as she took one shaky step forward. I waited, understanding fully how painful shock felt.

Her stare scanned my body and then focused on my eyes. An unnatural calmness fell over her, like a curtain that slipped over her body and hid her away. I recognized the feeling of slipping in her. Like I watched her leave her body in real time.

Hollow eyes shifted to Elias. "Explain."

She spoke only that one commanding, emotionless word.

* * *

For the next hour, Elias spoke with Ashton on the far side of the room to allow some privacy for them while also letting me monitor what he said. He explained everything about finding my world, what he learned there, and how he hid the truth from her. But when Ashton asked him about what the guild actually did, he turned away from her and rested his hands on the wall for support.

"I'll handle that part," I said gently.

After talking for a few more minutes, Ashton asked to talk alone with me, and sent Elias outside to find his composure.

"I should be more surprised," she said quietly as she walked closer to me. "It makes too much sense, though. It's shocking but fitting. He hasn't been himself."

"He told me that he needed my help because you were so loyal to the guild that you refused to betray them. They're your people. I came to realize that he actually never told you, and all this time he wanted to protect you from this war he was starting."

She lowered her head into her hands. "There's no way to keep me out of anything he does. He's being stubborn."

"I know."

"We used to tell each other everything, no matter how hard it was," Ashton said. "There are things we probably should have kept to ourselves. So for him to hide all of this . . . It breaks my heart."

I nodded and said again, "I know. And I owe you an apology for knowing. It wasn't right for me to live through your past. The problem with apologizing is that I chose to do it knowing it was wrong."

"That's some apology."

Seeing another version of myself and witnessing her reaction to my own decisions really helped me to understand how other people perceived me. I supposed I owed a few apologies back in my world.

"I can't let your people invade my world," I said. "I thought you were supporting them."

It did nothing to lessen her anger—the fury sent her pacing again—but I recognized that the truth of it resonated with her. In different circumstances, she might have done the same.

"I am sorry," I said.

"I guess it doesn't really matter since we're the same person. Just, that's my life. Mine."

I didn't say anything else. I had no right to defend my actions when I agreed with her.

"I'd do the same to you." She shrugged. "That feels really awful. Maybe there's something wrong with us."

"There is, but we could have worse faults, don't you think?"

That made her chuckle, though I knew she didn't want to let it out. "I can't wrap my mind around this."

"I hate throwing all of this at you and showing up like this. I needed to move fast before Elias got his senses about him and sent me back to my world. He isn't thinking right. You know that. What you didn't know, though, is how far he's taken this. You need to know the truth."

Ashton's eyes looked desperate. "I wanted to be there for him."

"Yeah." I bit my lip and scooted forward onto the edge of my seat. "You don't have as bad anxiety as I do. I went through something with Dad in my world and it really sparked it for me. I know you still have it. You should go ahead and sit down. We do better sitting down."

Expression blank, Ashton thudded down onto the chair. "This is so surreal."

Taking a deep breath, I prepared myself to shake her world far worse than Elias and I had so far. She truly loved her guild, and devoted herself to leaders she believed in. Even when she knew they had issues, she worked through them, and saw the best in them. She'd feel like a fool, and I didn't want to make her feel that.

"Lote had Elias's parents killed."

Ashton didn't comprehend what I said. I knew that because she didn't react at all.

"It wasn't the Silver Moon Guild," I said.

Pain slowly spread across her face like cracks in a dam, breaking along the fault lines. "No. Lote would never. He has his problems, but he loves Elias. He loved his parents. Every year, he visited their graves and made food for Elias. He . . ." Ashton touched her lips, eyes already turning red. The realization must have been dawning, because she knew Lote well enough to recognize that when he was guilty, he covered it up well.

I continued, finding it best to give her all the information at once. "Elias's parents figured out that Lote used his influence to stir the feud between your guild and others, especially Silver Moon. He wanted you to control more of the resources and to lead the Valley with a stronger hand. He told himself that the little sins here and there were worth it, until he was secretly planning attacks on your guild and pinning it on the Silver Moon Guild."

Ashton leaned forward with her hands covering her mouth and her elbows anchored to her knees.

"Elias's mom was the first to figure it out. She started to suspect something was going on while working on the finances. Lote did a great job covering his tracks, but she was sharp. She started asking questions. And just as quickly stopped when she understood the seriousness of the situation."

"She was incredibly wise."

"That's when she involved Elias's dad," I said. "Together, they secretly investigated Lote's schemes. They were peaceful people and believed in the best in others, so they thought they could convince Lote to change his mind. They believed he had good intentions, but his actions were misguided, and he just lost himself along the way."

She wiped tears from her eyes, clinging to every word I said. She knew I was telling the truth. I saw it in her eyes. Everything she hadn't wanted to believe, she hoped wasn't true, must have seemed clear to her now.

"They didn't tell anyone else or make any kind of arrangements to protect themselves," I said. "They likely never uncovered the worst of what Lote did. When they confronted him, he pretended to be sorry and promised to change. Instead, he had them killed and made it look like the Silver Moon Guild. Lote didn't stop or change after that. He dug his heels in, and he got worse. He escalated. Now he's out of control."

I breathed in deeply, hating how this hurt her. Our father wasn't a good man in either world and Lote felt like a father to her. That was the problem with fathers, wasn't it? If someone didn't actually want to be a good one, they abused that sacred, special bond so easily. It was a vulnerable position, to look up to someone and trust them so deeply. My heart broke for her as I watched her lose the second father she loved. Watched her lose them both, because it only stirred up the loss of the first.

"How did Elias find this out?" Ashton asked.

"His parents recorded their investigation and hid it away. Elias said that his mother kept a diary of everything. Lote knew this and he tried to find the diaries but never did. After Elias talked to Jax, he couldn't shake the suspicion. He started to see it everywhere. Finally, he investigated it for himself, and when he did, it led him to the same places his parents had been."

"That's how he found the diaries," Ashton said.

"Yes. His mother hid them away in the code of your world using a key that she taught Elias. She told him to only use it for the most sensitive information that he couldn't tell anyone, not even her, if such a day ever came."

Ashton's nod looked more like a tremble. "Did you see the diaries?"

"I did. Not all, but enough. The choice is simple. Do you believe his mother, or do you believe Lote? Do you believe another version of yourself?"

Tears wet her cheeks. She looked away, rubbing her chest. "I've defended Lote so many times. That's the first sign, right? Why should I need to defend him to anyone so often? I never had to defend Elias's parents. His mom was a saint. I would trust her more than I'd trust anyone."

"I'm sorry to be the one to tell you."

"Why did Elias hide this from me?" Ashton asked. "I stood with him through every second of his mourning. I grieved with him. I loved them, too. Why wouldn't he tell me?"

"I wondered at first, too. It's obvious now. He loves you, Ashton. He doesn't want Lote to kill you like he killed his parents."

"I'm not his parents. I'm a warrior."

"You aren't, but you are good like them. You wouldn't be able to sit on this information. You'll fight, and Elias didn't want to risk you in a fight like this. It's not a normal battle."

"We could have done this together," Ashton said. "Now he's brought you from another world and implicated your people in this as well. This is a mess."

"It is. I think learning about this broke something in him. He needs your help finding his way."

Ashton sighed. "So he thought he could bring over another version of me and just kill everyone?"

"Only your corrupt leaders like Lote. He hoped to shake up the entire system by killing them and bringing more balance to the power they've taken for themselves."

"I'm too frazzled to even unpack that."

"In my world, a corrupt leader terrorized the Valley," I said. "I killed him. While I don't regret it, it wasn't a solution to our problem. It stopped the Prophet from hurting anyone else, but now I'm struggling to protect my people from enemies on all sides."

"You think it would be a mistake to kill Lote?"

"Not necessarily. Your situation is different, but Elias told me to look to your world to learn about mine, so I offer the same to you."

Ashton crossed her arms and sat back. "If it's true that Lote has been sabotaging us to make us try to fight the other guilds, then he deserves to die. There's no convincing him to make peace. He's a threat to my people. He's keeping our kingdom from uniting as one."

The fervor she'd felt when she and Jax dreamed of how to unite the guilds filled my own heart. "This is why Elias didn't tell you. You have to kill Lote and that makes you a target. He's distanced himself from you so that you can't be blamed. You truly knew nothing."

"Does he expect that he won't survive his coup?" she asked.

When I didn't respond, she slammed her fist against her leg. Elias never told me that, though it made sense he didn't.

"He doesn't get to die like this," Ashton said. "It's unbelievable."

"We do it, don't we?" I asked. "We sacrifice ourselves again and again for our people. Elias is doing the same thing. It seems so obvious when you're seeing someone else do it. He needs help. He needs to work with people who care so that everyone can find the best path forward and survive it. Instead, he's battling on his own."

"I can't let him do this."

"He thinks I'm going to help him kill Lote," I said. "I met with him and pretended to be you."

"What do you really plan to do?"

"I don't know. I have to stop Lote and anyone else who wants to come to my world. If I just start killing people, it might be a long list, though. I don't know who all knows about my world."

"I know Lote did something horrible, but I can't imagine killing him. I just can't believe I never saw it." Ashton's voice sounded broken.

"I wouldn't have either if I lived in your world. You're loyal and good-natured. Those are wonderful things about us."

"It still just hurts that Elias didn't tell me."

"He can't be the man you love, so he became the man who will save you."

She lowered her head, shaking it softly. "Love is not justification. Love doesn't mean lying. Love . . ."

"I know."

"I'll forgive him. He's finally come back to me, and I'll forgive him." She looked at me. "I just wonder if he can forgive himself."

"I'm not sure."

"Maybe your Piercey can help him. From what Elias told me, it sounds like you got the best version of him."

Warmth flooded my heart. "Sometimes I still feel bad that I didn't love him when he deserves it so much."

"Well, you see how it worked out for us. I feel bad in a different way. It's not any better."

True.

"What will you do, Ashton? Now that you know what Lote has done?"

She rubbed her throat and closed her eyes. "I can't let him get away with this. I still contend that Jax's guild is terrible and dangerous. I don't think they're better than us. But Lote has taken it too far, and everyone else is following after him. I need time to think about how to do this."

"What do you think about bringing Jaxon in? I know the history is painful. We can trust him, though."

Of everything I said so far, this proved to be too much. Ashton walked to the window and looked out at the darkness. After a few minutes of quiet, she opened it and peered out. "Elias. Come back in."

Soon, we all sat together, Elias rubbing his arms as he shivered.

"I want to stick to business," Ashton said. "There's too much shit to deal with. If we try to apologize or talk about how we feel, we'll get derailed. There isn't time since Lote plans to arrest Elias."

"Agreed," I said.

"Of course you two agree." Elias averted his gaze after saying it and receiving a glare from both of us. "I just really didn't want you involved, Ashton."

"That isn't up to you," she said. "I told you we aren't going to get into the feelings side. We need a plan that we can all agree on."

"The plan," Elias said, "is to kill Lote and anyone who remains loyal to him. Jax will help. He has plans. Max has heard some of those plans which means you have, too. You guys can finally fight for unity like you wanted to."

Ashton shook her head in disagreement. "This isn't how unity comes. We're going to end up in shambles like Max's Valley."

"I don't want to be at odds with this plan, but they are not coming to my world," I said. "Whatever happens, I'm stopping them, and I hope you'll support me. It would be unfortunate if I had to fight another version of myself or Piercey or Nash."

I winced after I said his name.

"Nash?" Ashton asked.

Elias groaned. He left mention of Nash out of the conversation, and I did the same. Until now. Knowing that we were together may influence Ashton, and she needed to make her own decisions.

"It's Jax's counterpart," I said.

"You know the other version of Jax?" I recognized the look of her thoughts spinning. "Were you also enemies?"

"We should focus on our plans."

"What are you not wanting to tell me?" she asked. "You're both acting elusive."

I chewed my thumbnail. "I've already interfered in your world."

"Don't treat me like a child. I can handle it."

"Well," I said. "We're together."

It seemed to knock the wind from her. She sat back. "Together. Like—"

"Together," I said. "For over a year now."

Ashton shifted. "I'm glad it worked out in some world."

I wanted to tell her it could work out in her world, only I knew to stay out of this. She had too much of a mess to clean up in her relationships for me to get involved. Hearing that it was possible for us to be together might make her even more angry with Elias—not that he didn't deserve it.

"I said we'd stick to business and I'm the one distracting us." She wiped her eyes and clasped her hands. "What if we confront Lote and tell the rest of the leadership about his corruption?"

"My parents' mistake was announcing their intentions out of naivety," Elias said. "Lote killed them both and went dancing the same night. There's no point in confronting them. Jaxon tried to tell me, but I didn't listen, not until I found the evidence."

Ashton cursed. "Why didn't Jax tell me?"

Elias continued, "I told him those were the kind of dangerous thoughts that got people hurt, and not to toy with your mind if he didn't have evidence. I begged him not to say anything until we knew because you might take action."

"I hate that you've been making decisions for me for years," she said.

I raised one hand. "I think one choice is obvious. We need allies. Jax clearly has been planning. Our next move needs to be to talk to him. And we'll tell him the full truth, just like we did with Ashton. I know Nash in my world and now I know Jax because of Ashton's memories. We need him and we can trust him."

Neither Ashton nor Elias said anything.

"Ashton, you can't be upset with Jax for wanting to kill your leaders when he knew that they killed Elias's parents. He's right to kill them. And you can't do to him what you're upset with Elias doing to you. He deserves the truth. Be strong and face him."

"Okay," Ashton said. "There's nothing like getting your ass handed to you by yourself."

At first, Jax refused to accompany Elias to the cabin until hearing it meant life or death for Ashton.

Wanting to gauge his willingness to help, Ashton made both of us hide in the bathroom to give her time to decide whether to recruit him while he spoke to Elias. I thought it was stupid. We needed him. But this wasn't my life, and I'd already overstepped by living through her memories.

"I told you, Elias." Jax sounded far colder than when he'd spoken to Elias in my presence. "I don't want anything to do with you. Tell me what I need to do to help Ashton, and then stay out of my life."

"What do I have to do for you to be willing to work with me again when we want the same thing now?"

Jax snorted. "Nothing. I will never trust you again. It wasn't enough for you to split Ash and me up. You had to send your guild after me."

"It wasn't like that. I made sure that you were both safe."

"Safe? They tried to kill me, asshole. I did you a favor and I didn't say anything to Ashton, but don't think it was actually for you. It was for her because she's already dealt with enough of your shit. Stay away from me."

Ashton covered her mouth beside me.

"I didn't mean for them to attack you. At the time, I wanted to ensure your relationship stayed severed to protect her."

"You used Ashton to get to me," Jax said. "Own up to it and stop playing innocent."

"I'm not here to argue with you. We need your help."

"You told me that already, and I told you the time for deals is through. Ashton isn't going to turn on her guild. She walked away from me. She didn't fight for us. She isn't interested. Let me move on."

Ashton leaned back against the wall with an anguished sigh and covered her face. "I've heard enough," she whispered. "Let's do it without him. He shouldn't endure anything else because of us."

"That's your takeaway?" I smacked her arm with the back of my hand. "Go fight for him."

"I told him I would kill him."

"That was really stupid," I said. "Fix it."

"I don't want him to be in danger. He said they tried to kill him. That's why I threatened him and told him to never see me again."

"Isn't this what Elias did to you?"

She lowered her hands and nodded. "Okay. I just need a second."

"Do it," I whispered harshly. "Or I'll do it for you."

Ashton opened the door and walked out, her presence immediately silencing both men.

"I was wrong not to fight for you," she said.

I really wanted to see Jax's face in that moment.

"I never should have turned my back on you," she continued, "no matter what side we're fighting for."

"Ash," Jax said.

"You don't have to forgive me or understand, but I hope that you'll hear us out, because we really need your help."

I heard footsteps and I tensed, hoping it was Jax walking toward her.

"You want my help?" Jax asked.

"Yes. It's better to show you. Just, prepare yourself, because it's going to be hard to accept."

"What do you mean?"

"Max," she said. "Come on out."

I slid into the doorway, pausing there as if it would lessen the shock.

Jax blinked several times.

"You . . . You have a twin?"

"Not exactly," Ashton said.

CHAPTER THIRTY-FOUR

Jax spent most of the conversation shifting his stare between Ashton and me, looking overwhelmed. Now I sat back on the couch with Elias while Ashton and Jaxon talked on the other side of the room.

Jax looked at Ashton for a long while and smiled for the first time since learning about my world. "Tell me already, Ash. Don't make me wait."

"Tell you what?"

"Are you going to kill me?" The smirk melted my heart because I knew exactly how it was melting hers. All this time, and for Ashton it was their first time talking. For Jax to put aside that pain, that awful promise, and tease must have felt reassuring.

She covered her mouth, tears springing into her eyes. Her voice shook with a mix of longing and relief. "You know I can't kill you. That's why you were supposed to stay away."

I couldn't keep myself from smiling, despite Elias shifting uncomfortably next to me.

"I didn't know my people tried to kill you," Ash said quietly.

"I knew you didn't."

"Stop eavesdropping," Elias whispered to me.

"I can't help hearing," I said back.

"You're on the edge of your seat leaning in."

I looked down at my posture and scooted further back on the couch, turning my head, though I still saw them out of the corner of my eye. "I've seen too much. I'm invested."

I dared a peek at them, and Elias clamped his hand over my eyes. My elbow smacked into his shoulder, knocking him away. A laugh almost escaped before I remembered that I didn't want to laugh with Elias. Reminded of this, I scowled at him.

He grinned in the way Piercey always did when we were kids, a smile somehow both innocent and devious.

"We can't be friends," I said. "You lied to me. Once I'm this angry, it's not easy to come back from."

Elias hooked his hands behind his head and closed his eyes. "You think I don't know that? I just forget you aren't her sometimes. I forget that I pushed her away and now she's gone."

"Don't you make me feel sorry for you."

He squinted one eye at me. "Fine."

"You made me miss what they said," I whispered and glanced at Ashton and Jaxon again.

They worked closer now, quieter, perhaps reconsidering their decision to stay in the same room as us.

"Don't forgive me so easily," Ashton said.

"I didn't say I forgave you." Jax slid a tendril of hair behind her ear. "I'm going to think of all kinds of ways for you to earn that."

"If you tease me—"

"I just feel like you're finally back. That day you left with Lote, it's like I never saw you again."

Seeing them ignited my desperation to run home to Nash and never leave again. Being in a different world made it feel like I had left weeks ago, instead of only two days. I didn't want to regret anything like these two did. I decided before coming here to figure out how to spend time with my family and take care of the Valley. This confirmed to me how desperately I needed to do just that.

When they finished talking, we all sat together in one strange group. Hard to say which person belonged the least, considering I shouldn't exist in the world and Elias broke these two apart.

"I don't want to rush anyone," I said. "But my world doesn't have very much time. We need a plan. I think all of us here agree that we cannot let anyone from this world enter mine and steal from my people or hurt anyone."

Jax wore his determined expression that reminded me so much of Nash. "That won't happen. We need to work together to straighten our political mess, but first we have to stop it from bleeding into your world."

Finally, someone with a sense of urgency. "Thank you."

"I can assemble allies. That's no problem," Jax said. "The question is, do you guys have anyone other than this?"

"I do," I said. "People from my world will help us fight. The problem is that the only ones who know about you are Elias's counterpart, Piercey, who isn't much of a warrior, and people who only very recently received power for the first time."

Jax hooked his elbows on his knees. "Okay. That's not as promising as I hoped."

"I do have other allies," I said. "They don't know anything about this world, though, and I worry about spreading it beyond our inner circle."

"We need to keep it quiet," Ashton said. "Elias told me the gods are already angered."

"Then what is the most efficient and powerful move?" Elias asked.

"Catch Lote off guard and kill him." I looked at Ashton. "Can you do it?"

"He killed Elias's parents and he tried to kill Jax. He lied to me." Ashton breathed out slowly, looking shakier than she sounded. "I know what I have to do. I don't need time to prepare. Grief can wait until later."

Jax clasped her shoulder. Ashton froze at first, and then her body visibly relaxed.

"If we kill Lote, the guild will scramble to contain the fallout," Elias said. "They won't be in a position to invade any world. At that point, we land our next strike and launch our plan to bring peace to the Valley."

"Our next strike?" Ashton asked.

"Our guild has to come down," Elias said. "Others were complicit in killing my parents. I've since found out that there's much more than that going on. When we have time, I'll show you all of my research and evidence."

Ashton scoffed. "If our guild suddenly collapses, what's to stop Silver Moon from a power grab? We'd be vulnerable enough that they'd get a hold of our resources and then effectively own the Valley."

"I agree," Jax said. "I don't trust my guild with that much power. Between my guild and yours, I choose us, but that doesn't mean it's best. We shouldn't destroy your guild."

"Lote is not the root of evil in our guild," Elias said. "If you leave the current leadership in place, someone will take his place."

"Listen." I clapped my hands together. "I sympathize with your position given that I'm dealing with wars of my own. Having said that, I don't have time to fight your war, too. I really don't, and I'm not going to. I need to learn when to step back. This is me stepping back. Can we just kill Lote so I can go home?"

I expected everyone to get angry with me for this, only no one reacted that way at all.

"I understand," Ashton said. "This was never your war. We need to get you back to your world where you belong. Elias shouldn't have dragged you into this."

"I was trying to save you," Elias said.

"By implicating another version of me?" She groaned. "I'll stop. We have time to fight about that later."

Jax spoke solemnly. "I'm very sorry you were pulled into this, and that your world is in danger. We'll stop at nothing to make sure your people are safe. Our world having so much more power than your world makes this so important."

"If we kill Lote, it'll buy us time to deal with our guild, and keep your world safe." Elias didn't look at any of us while he spoke. I almost felt bad for everyone ganging up on him, except that he deserved it. This version of Piercey didn't make the best decisions.

Nash made me promise to come home before starting a war. I didn't have time to go back first, though. Soon Lote planned to force Elias to connect, and then they'd torture him to figure out how to invade my world. Bringing more people from my world wouldn't help anyway. This wasn't a massive battle. We needed to assassinate one man and we needed to do it discreetly.

"You realize that you'll be implicated," Jax said to Ashton and Elias.

"I will stand by what I said," Ashton said. "Lote needs to die."

Ashton and Elias traveled to Lote's office under the ruse that he intended to turn himself in early. Meanwhile, I stayed with Jax at the cabin, waiting for Elias to send the message calling us to Lote's office.

Back home, Piercey connected us all through the neural network to allow communication whenever we needed it, and even hooked up the phone system at the Sacred School and the demon alerts to help join those without power. I wasn't a part of any such system here, but Elias and Piercey connected before, so Elias knew how to communicate through a neural network the way my people did.

I often struggled to connect from a distance, but Elias excelled with technology, so I trusted his abilities. His messages so far came through just fine.

"I can't believe how much you look like her." Jax gripped his sword, already well prepared for the upcoming assassination.

Seeing him fooled part of me into believing Nash stood beside me, and I missed him so badly that I ached. The problem was that Jax felt like him in every way. Even smelled like him. "Same for you."

"You know another me?"

I smiled, only meeting his eyes for a moment because I felt bad that my stomach twisted near him. My memories and Ashton's were intertwined in my mind, so similar to my own memories anyway. I wanted to go home to Nash so badly it hurt. "I do."

"Did you go to the Sacred School like Ashton?"

"Yeah. I escaped and the instructors sealed my power."

"Wild. Does Nash have powers like I do?"

"He does now. Elias gave him a neural implant."

"You're close enough for that." I didn't even need to look at Jax to know he wore that cocky smirk. "Well done, Nash."

"Don't tease me," I said. "That's his thing."

"Oh, Ashton used to say she hated when I teased her."

"Well, she didn't." I waved my hand at him. "I miss Nash and you are literally another copy of him, so give me some space. It's hard to keep reality straight."

"I'll show you some mercy, mostly because it's the same for me." He scooted away. "Can you tell me just one thing?"

"What?"

"How happy are you? I always thought if Ash and I found a way to be together, we'd be happy, no matter what problems came our way."

I wasn't sure how much I should say to him. I hesitated and then met his eyes. "He makes me happier than anything else in the world." Mentioning Elsie seemed wrong, as if I brought her into something that none of us should be a part of, much less a little girl. But I wanted to tell him about her, too. That the three of us together made life feel perfect, no matter how imperfect it might actually be.

The depth of Jax's eyes when he smiled hurt me for the life that he should live with Ashton. I worried that knowing about Nash might hurt him or even spark jealousy, only I saw nothing like that in him.

"I'll remember that forever," he said in a low whisper that I thought I might also remember forever. If I wasn't sure before, I was now. Jax loved

Ashton very deeply, so deeply that the thought of the two of them living a happy life in another world fulfilled a piece of him even without living it.

I bit the inside of my cheek so hard I expected to taste blood. "Jax, I'm so sorry—"

"There's nothing in either world for you to be sorry about when it comes to this. Go home and live the best life you can. I'll cherish knowing that you're happy there."

A hot, messy ball of emotion lodged in my throat. "Don't give up on her. This will change her and then you can try again."

"Yeah." He sighed. "We'll try."

"Don't sound so hopeless."

"I'm not. I've just been through this already. I can't hope yet. The time for that will come later."

I yearned for Nash again, wanting nothing more than to grab him in an embrace right now. I wanted to do the same to Jax and assure him that Ashton absolutely would come around, because how could she not?

"There was a time that I told Nash no," I said. "I didn't believe there was a future for us. I truly didn't. I'm so happy I changed my mind. I'm telling you, don't give up."

He looked at me a little longer this time before he smiled again. "Okay, Max. I won't. I'll be even more stubborn than she is."

I burst out laughing, understanding intimately well just how stubborn that was.

Elias's voice interrupted us. "One minute," he said through the neural connection. "Get ready."

I straightened, yanking myself from thoughts of my life with Nash and the one I wished that Ashton would live here with Jax. "Did you get it, too?" I asked Jax.

"Yeah. I got it. Make sure not to communicate like this in Lote's office. Elias is a technology officer, so he'll know how to evade any security systems. It's too advanced for me, and you have no experience with it, so receive but don't send."

"It's crazy what you all developed here with the same amount of time," I said.

"When the entire world runs on power, you get pretty good with it."

"Now," Elias said in our minds. "He's sitting in his normal chair."

I clasped Jax's wrist and whisked us through space-time to Lote's office. Ready to end this and return home to my family and my people.

When we appeared, we landed directly behind Lote's chair. I didn't even take the time to register everything I saw in the room. I trusted that Ashton and Elias both sat in their positions on the couches.

Now.

My readied blade dug against his throat. Power burst from Jax's palm toward Lote's face.

Ashton's wide, shocked eyes must have mirrored Lote's own as the double assault hit him at once.

My blade screeched as if it cut against steel, while Jax's power bounced off Lote's skin. I didn't see any kind of shield erected around him and I didn't detect one before, but I saw the aftereffects. Lote's skin rippled with a red sheen of power in the places we'd hit.

Lote leapt from his chair, whipped around to face us, and used his power to push himself toward the other side of the room, presumably to see all four of his guests. As his eyes found mine, he slowed to a stop. Jaw slack.

How did Lote prepare his shield instantly? It happened faster than a normal human response time, even taking into account senses enhanced by power. The shield automatically responded to our attacks, and neither Elias nor Ashton indicated such a possibility. Nothing in my memory of living through Ashton's life suggested an ability like this existed. Maintaining a constant shield required tremendous energy, something we'd sense.

Jax's low grumble told me that he also hadn't expected this, and realized that Lote was going to be harder to kill than we originally thought. He was similar enough to Nash for me to fight easily with him and interpret his cues. Jax's muscles coiled, and I recognized immediately the signs he planned to attack again.

I did, too. We needed to move right this second if we wanted to take advantage of Lote's shock, one far greater than the simple surprise of two people teleporting into his office, but of seeing a copy of Ashton try to kill him. I just wished I knew what kind of weapons we faced.

I'd just have to try Lote out and see.

My thoughts moved fast as I rapidly considered these options and teleported across the room to him. I heard his deep gasp the moment I appeared by his side. I plunged my energy blade for his gut with an explosion of power, testing the strength of this auto-shield.

Bursts of energy exploded from the collision of his strong shield and my overbearing sword. In the time it took for him to raise his hands defensively to cast yet another shield, my sword cracked the barrier that surrounded him, slinging blood through the air.

I teleported again on instinct, recognizing that he was too dangerous to linger beside.

When I landed by Ashton, I caught the end of a devastating attack. His shield had shot out a beam of power where I once stood. Potentially automatically as well.

Lote caught the energy and rendered it inert before it crashed into his beloved artwork.

Jax rushed for him, and I joined in, both of us swinging our blades.

"Ashton!" Elias shouted.

As both my blade and Jax's swung for Lote, Ashton stood paralyzed, staring with tears shining in her eyes.

Damn it all to hell. She wasn't ready to kill him.

I shouted in frustration as I pivoted to avoid a second shield and a second beam of power. Easy to predict so far, but that mattered little when his defense proved so effective. The energy from the beam exceeded the capabilities of my shield. In the event of a direct hit, the counterattack would pierce my shield. Instead of blocking, I needed to dodge or teleport.

I drew upon my energy to unleash my own blasts on him, but I worried in this small space that I may hurt the others, especially Elias.

"Ashton," Lote said in a voice thundering with authority and expectation, the same name that Elias had spoken, but bursting with the kind of power of a king. A god.

Elias closed his eyes and tilted his head back. Lote shouldered past me, driving straight for him, the beam of power flickering for an instant before it shot out.

I teleported to Elias just in time, but as I threw us both to the ground, a shield that looked like a cement wall sprang up, blocking us. The beam hit it with an ear-shattering whack. The room trembled.

Elias knew how to create a shield?

"Code," Elias said breathlessly, apparently realizing my confusion. "I sense others coming. I'll keep them out. You keep fighting."

Brilliant. He told me before that he lacked combat abilities, but he could still protect himself at least.

The cement wall slowly turned translucent so I could see Jax viciously attacking Lote with his swords. Ashton ran to his side and jabbed her sword toward her mentor's shoulder. I wasn't sure if she had the heart to actually hurt him after I saw her freeze, but I was thankful she provided some kind of assistance.

"Go," Elias said. "I'll protect myself."

"Good. I don't have to hold back if I know you're safe."

I noticed his smile as he nodded. I lunged for Lote.

Ashton, Jax, and I all attacked at the same time, primarily utilizing our weapons in this small space. My blade caught Lote's thigh, the only of our attacks this round to break through his auto-shield.

"What are you doing?" Lote cried out, aiming his palm at Ashton.

She dodged a beam of power that shot straight through one of Lote's paintings. The two beside it burst into flames.

Anger darkened his expression as he flicked his hand to put out the fire.

As we fought, I began to sense something strange, almost like hearing static in the background that grew by the second, only it felt like power.

Something was wrong.

We started to break through Lote's defenses, but he didn't seem concerned in the slightest. If no one knew of his ability to instantly erect a shield over himself, one of the most powerful defenses I'd ever encountered, what else could he do?

"It's a machine," Elias said. "I can see it now. He's using a machine somewhere in this room to provide a constant shield over him. It's activated by power or by the force of a strike, but it's always there. I just can't shut it down or find the exact location."

Machine? I ground my teeth. "Why did none of you tell me he has machines?" I channeled my power through my blade, piercing his shield right at his sternum. I screamed as I threw my weight into the sword to force it through the shield. A pinprick of blood bubbled at the tip before he blasted me with one of those damn energy beams. I sidestepped, barely avoiding it.

"He's not supposed to," Elias said. "There is a division for machine research, but it's not producing anything usable for warfare. I mean, I thought. Apparently, he's keeping it a secret for himself."

"As usual," I said.

A twisted sneer snapped onto Lote's face. The low-grade power I detected earlier surged.

We needed to get out of here. Urgency filled me. Undeniable urgency.

"Come to me," I said and teleported back to Elias. If we all grabbed onto each other, I could return us to the cabin.

Jax and Ashton didn't question it. They abandoned their attack on Lote and sprinted for me. I clutched Elias with one hand and reached for Ashton with the other. She grabbed Jax's hand, her fingertips straining for mine.

That growing power I felt traveled through every fiber of my being in a squeezing pressure. It locked me in place with my fingers and Ashton's so close that even flinching would bring us all together. We all froze in place, my hand wrapped around Elias's wrist, and Jax and Ashton's laced together.

I remembered when the Prophet of the Valley used his energy to strangle us. This felt similar, but worked in a different way. I breathed just fine. It was like the power wound through every strand of muscle in my body and locked it rigidly in place.

With horror, I realized that I couldn't even gather my power at my fingertips.

CHAPTER THIRTY-FIVE

Lote's mysterious energy immobilized us entirely.

"Incredible, right?" Lote sauntered closer, his sneer triumphant and quietly seething with rage. He slowly walked around our group, studying each of us without any concern that we might escape. "I hope that we can bring this to the battlefield one day. What do you think, Elias? It's based on your prototype." He laughed then. "Sorry. I forgot that we still need to adjust the settings so you can talk. One moment."

He looked up at the ceiling like he was reading something up there, and then suddenly I was able to move my lips.

"How did you do this?" Elias asked. "It never worked."

"It never worked because I held the missing pieces you lacked. I knew that in order to ever crack this technology, you needed more than just the skill set. We can selectively freeze muscles in the body while simultaneously binding the energy. But the machine does it precisely and effortlessly. Yours never worked because of human fallibility."

"So you stifled our research," Elias said.

"I did. We can't let our best technology fall into the hands of our enemies. Our machine division is limited to me, two of our leaders, and a single inventor that each of us agreed on. That's why you didn't realize just how far we'd come."

Elias's nostrils flared. "You stole our machine research."

"It's not stealing when we funded it in the first place. That's my research."

"Lote," Ashton said.

He raised a single finger to her. "I don't want to hear from you. Not yet. I promise you that you don't want to cross me right now, Ashton. I'm not happy with you." He looked at Elias again. "I expected this from you." Now at Jax. "No surprise to see you here." His stare turned to Ashton. "You though . . . You've genuinely hurt me." Finally, he regarded me. "And you," he said, barking out a laugh. "My first thought was twin, my second, clone, and now my mind is reeling with all the possibilities."

Lote walked so close that I felt him breathing against my forehead. He studied my eyes.

"Just who are you?" he asked with enough intrigue and excitement to make my heart race with fear. "Are you from the world Elias travels to? The timing makes too much sense."

I clenched my jaw, refusing to answer.

"Is the whole world populated with more of us?" He surveyed me like I was a brand-new machine for him to tinker with. "Fascinating."

"Whatever you think this means, you couldn't be more wrong," I said.

"Well, you've given me plenty of gifts today. My office is wired with all my favorite machines. My best-kept secrets. I'm lucky that you chose this location. Then again, I exclusively meet with people here for a reason. I'm not sure how else you could have gotten to me."

This was really bad.

"What other machines do you have?" Ashton asked.

"It's not very fun to tell you. I don't get to try these out very often." He wandered to his desk, opened his drawer, and retrieved a headset. "This is portable, but it just can't do what my office can. The equipment is too bulky to carry around, and the conditions need to be exactly right. The temperature being even a degree off can ruin it."

"You must be excited to have the chance to talk about your secrets," I said dryly.

"Yes, actually. It's thrilling. Ashton and Elias have helped me so much with this work and they didn't know. I wanted to share it with them so many times. You just can't be too careful about who you trust." The sharp stare turned to Ashton again. "Can you?"

"I know what you did," Ashton said. "This only confirms it."

"Yes, well, I have a kingdom to look after," Lote said. "I can't afford to think only of myself or only of our guild. Our enemies will war with us again and we lost too many people last time. Our guild is the best to lead. We possess the greatest innovations. We need to get stronger and set our kingdom above the rest."

"Oh, shut up," I said. "No one wants to hear your excuses. You murdered Elias's parents."

Lote didn't look surprised. "I figured this had something to do with that."

Ashton let out a strangled breath, but Elias only stared with fiery eyes.

"It looks like I don't need to deny it," Lote said. "Elias is a smart kid. I'm sure he uncovered all the evidence he needs, enough for Ashton to ambush me. What else could make you both turn on me?" He shrugged. "It's not that I wanted to kill them. It's just that I couldn't trust them to keep their mouths shut. They were never going to back down from their ideals and so I had no recourse."

Elias managed to spit on the ground, which only drew an amused smirk from Lote.

"You sick bastard." Fury shook Elias's voice. "They were loyal to this guild. They were a part of our kingdom. What right do you have to take their life? You're a murderer."

"A murderer with the most advanced machines in the world," Lote said. "Thirty years from now, when every person in our kingdom is equipped with the protection of these machines and we can wage war remotely using them, do you think anyone will care about your parents?" He leaned in close to Elias. "No one cares as it is."

"What is wrong with you?" I asked. At least Dr. Henderson had the gall to act upset when she had me killed. Lote carried the sadism of the Prophet of the Valley. I needed to find him in my world and figure out what he was up to because this was a sick man.

"I care." Lote plastered his hands to his chest. "Genuinely. I celebrated their anniversary with you every year because I actually am thankful for their sacrifice. They gave their lives for our kingdom. It might not have been in the way that they wanted, but they did. I'm just saying that it doesn't really matter that I'm a murderer when I'm the person who can save this kingdom. Line up all the children who might die if not for me, and ask their mothers how much they care about what I do to save them. Give their mothers the choice to snap their fingers and make me disappear. They wouldn't."

Tears sprinkled onto Ashton's cheeks. "I don't know how I never saw it."

"Well, young Ashton, I didn't let you see it. Don't blame yourself. I know how to pretend to have compassion and empathy. I can be more convincing than any of you because I can't afford to ever seem like I don't have it." He stood beside me again, studying my face. "How uncanny. I want to know more about you now. We can catch up on the whole 'Lote is a monster' shock later. Which . . ." He raised both brows. "I do choose to care, okay? It's just that I have the ability to rationally decide when to feel bad and when not to, and thus can lead this Valley effectively."

"Stop talking," I said. "Just stop."

"Will you fill in the silence? I'm very curious to hear if I'm right about you being from that world."

When I only glared, he dragged his chair closer. He sat down and looked between the four of us for a while.

"Listen, you're all very capable at what you do," Lote said. "To force you to talk will probably be very painful and bloody. I'm not sure how resilient you are to forced connection," he said to me. "But I know that Elias will be exceptionally hard to break. Ashton and Jax will be simpler, but still, challenging and stressful for all of us. I encourage you to just talk to me. Let's start over and pretend for a minute you didn't try to murder me. We can negotiate."

"Negotiate?" I almost laughed. "I'm not negotiating with a sociopath."

"You read old medical literature from the original Earth? I'm a fan as well."

Piercey did, not me. Not that Lote should know anything about my friend.

"You really shouldn't use *sociopath* as an insult," he said. "It's a mental illness and there are plenty of healthy sociopaths out there living a great life, making contributions to society. It is treatable."

"You're insane," Jax said.

"I'm using my condition for good, if you can bring yourself to accept it," Lote said. "I will make our kingdom safer. We need people like me. It's just better to hide such realities from people like you who are hurt by my methods. But don't judge all sociopaths because of me. That's just unkind."

I couldn't believe this. "Fine," I said. "I'm not negotiating with a soulless murderer."

"I can understand that," Lote said. "I make very good deals, though. Ashton can testify to that. Let's hear about this world of yours."

"You're making assumptions." I narrowed my eyes.

He leaned forward and I saw the danger in him, veiled by his unsettling ability to talk casually about the unspeakable, and hidden by his calmness. This man was sharp, cunning, and absolutely deadly. "My assumptions are correct. You get defensive about your world."

Did denying it even help me? I could position myself better if I told the truth in some way. He already knew I wasn't a twin or a clone. The timing did make it obvious. "You will never step foot in my world."

"I don't think that's true. See, we've already come close to figuring out how Elias is traveling. A small team is working on it constantly. We're breaking it down and will replicate it soon. In fact, we hope to create a machine to do it for us. Machines are so much more reliable."

Panic made my heart pound in my ears. Their power wasn't simply greater than that of my world. Their technology was far beyond what we'd manage for probably hundreds of years. Those of us with power were so focused on warfare and survival, not to mention that Prophets like Eskel the Ruthless hunted and killed many. When would we have time to create machines like this?

"You're doing the math, aren't you?" Lote asked. "Trying to figure out if you can stop me, and calculating the costs of doing so."

I couldn't let him see my hopelessness. "It's not simple to wage war in an unknown world."

"True. There's the logistics of bringing our people and potentially machines to you—machines that we haven't even used in combat here yet. I won't lie and say we're going to be widely using them, but I won't give you false hope and pretend there won't be any."

I didn't like the cavalier way he discussed his strategy with me, making it obvious that he didn't care if I knew about his battle plans, because his victory was so assured that he could tell me exactly how he wanted to beat me and do it anyway.

This current situation didn't exactly give him reason to fear us. So far, I didn't have ideas on how to break free or find the machine. Normally, when enemies used power attacks like this, the effort wore them down. I didn't sense Lote emitting any power.

The machine did need a power source, though, and Lote was desperate for resources. "That's it. You want machine parts and fuel," I said. "What makes you think there's any more in my world than there is here? Or that it'll be easier to take it from us than your rival guilds?"

"Good questions." Lote crossed one leg over the other. "You were worried enough about it to try killing me, unless you're also avenging Elias's parents. I doubt that. Even if you do want to avenge them, I doubt you're in this world simply to do that. I'm a threat to you. How much of a threat is the question."

I didn't hide my emotions as easily as Nash or Piercey did, and I wished I knew how to conceal them better. Lote picking up on the total panic coursing through me only undermined my people.

"I'm so curious about your world," Lote said. "I wonder how similar and different we are."

I knew from Elias that they didn't know about the experiment in this world. Their supervisor never overly involved herself the way mine did, and so the gods' true nature remained unknown to them. That did provide an advantage for me over Lote.

"You're fighting plenty of battles here," I said. "Focus on your own world."

"I can't ignore an opportunity like this. You're powerful, though. I can tell by that amazing ability of yours. Not to mention that Ashton and Jax are two of the finest warriors I've ever met, but you're the one piercing my shield. That's incredible. I will not underestimate you. Are all people in your world this powerful?"

"I'm not telling you shit."

"So much politics at play here in my world. We're at an impasse on trade because anyone giving resources to my guild also sacrifices their power. We're hurting each other because we won't share what we need. Your world isn't mired in my politics. What if we can offer you something that you need? Who in your world would I need to speak to about this?"

I spoke in a low growl. "You will speak with me and only me."

"You're a leader in Skia Hellig," Lote said. "Excellent."

After a year of running from the fact that I already led the Valley, the attempt looked so pointless and stupid sitting here in Lote's captivity. This was my Valley. These were my people. I refused to allow Lote or anyone else to hurt them.

"Yes," I said, reckoning with how much I meant what I just said, and the fact that I loved my Valley so much that I realized I actually did want it to be true. The fear clouded that budding desire to care for them and unite them properly.

I didn't know how to negotiate on behalf of the Valley, though. Where was Piercey when I needed him? He was so diplomatic. I only knew war. If we failed to fend off Lote, then it was possible we needed to consider a deal. I couldn't trust him, though. If we chose negotiation, it simply bought us time to devise a new plan. The Prophet of the Valley taught me the impossibility of long-lasting peace with men who were gluttonous for power.

Elias's voice came through my mind then. "Don't respond or acknowledge that you can hear me. I found the machine, but I can't hack it. I've never seen anything like this before. There are veins of fuel running behind the walls."

Message received. I needed to cut the fuel lines. That was the real reason Lote protected his paintings. He saved the fuel from attack.

"I'm going to try to help you break free," Elias continued. "The machine uses your own power against you to utilize your energy to contract your own muscles. My energy, from an outside source, has a better chance of freeing you."

Not wanting Lote to suspect Elias of speaking to me, I tried to continue my conversation with him.

"What can you offer me?" I purposefully said *me* and not *my world* because I wanted to send the message that I had the authority to decide. That I was not someone to fool with.

Nash told me not to start a war by myself, and I'd gotten myself trapped in Lote's office after an assassination attempt. I should have gotten help after all, even if it was risky traveling like that when Elias was supposed to be brought in today.

"You see that we have a great deal to offer," Lote said. "You're surprised by our machines, so you've not reached the same level as us."

He was right. We possessed some level of machinery in factories near the mines, but no one ever managed to make machines of war. Our world simply didn't have enough people with power, or the infrastructure for advancements like this.

What if the gods intervened to stop one world from invading another? I'd told them to stay out of our worlds, though. If I asked for help now, how could I ever get leverage again? They were far more dangerous than any person in any world. Would they help me if I asked? I doubted it. No reason to hope.

"Do you really think successful negotiations are possible when we began this way?" I asked. "We tried to kill you."

"I know it's nothing personal," Lote said. "Elias is angry because I killed his parents and lied to him about it for a decade. I understand that. Jax is my enemy. And Ashton feels betrayed by the lies. I can't blame you for trying to kill me. I'm a businessman first."

Unbelievable. The Prophet had been vindictive. Was I really supposed to believe this man wasn't? Everyone craved revenge at some level. Perhaps he wanted the resources we had more, though.

"I'm keen on a deal," Lote said. "I agree that warring in an unknown world is dangerous. I will do it, but negotiations benefit us both. We should see what we can work out before we jump to destroying each other."

"Considering that you have no idea who I am, who my people are, or how many of us are in your world, you better believe this is dangerous for you." Oh, that was good. That put some worry in him. I quickly learned the calmer he appeared, the more concerned he actually felt. "You don't even know what I really want."

Lote's voice dropped to a growl. "Oh, I knew not to assume you'd be simple."

"You know Ashton, so you should know I'm not an enemy you want to have."

"Why do you think I worked so hard to keep her close?"

"Asshole," Ashton said. She and Jax kept quiet while I fought for my world with the only weapons at my disposal right now, my words and my mind. This part seemed too much for her to stay quiet through. "You aren't saving our kingdom. You're staining it. This feud is the reason we aren't safer. People like you make it so we can't have peace."

"I'm happy to work for peace," Lote said. "I won't simply give it away for free, though. I do care about our guild. Does it even matter to you how badly my sudden death might hurt us? What a great invitation for our enemies to attack."

"Don't listen to him," Jax said. "He only wants to hurt you."

"Hear me, Lote." I raised my voice. "If you step foot in my world, I will kill you."

His fingers closed so tightly around his armrests that the vines tracing his veins popped along his hands and arms. The nonchalant veneer faded as he hefted himself to his feet and cast his shadow over me. "Fine, then." Determined, even amused, eyes glared into my own. "I can't wait until the day you're forced to submit to what I want. Just remember that the more lives and time you cost me, the less I'm willing to give in negotiations."

The power contracting my muscles strengthened, until a terrible pressure bore down against every bone in my body. My muscles tightened more and more, my body trembling with the crushing force wringing me out. Pain splintered through me.

"Stop," Jax said.

"Did you know that muscle contractions can break your own bones?" Lote glanced down my rigid form. "Snap. Snap. Snap."

I struggled for breath, helpless to alleviate the pressure trying to do just that.

"We can heal you and do it again," Lote said. "That's no problem. My people are waiting just outside this door."

"That's enough, Lote." Ashton and Jax were both yelling at him now, but it wasn't them that Lote noticed. He turned finally, eyes on Elias, who stared at him silently.

"What are you up to?" Lote asked.

I couldn't take much more before I actually did pop a bone. Pain consumed my entire body.

"Elias," Lote said.

Snap.

I gasped in the deepest breath of my life as relief flooded me. The power forcing my muscles to contract broke suddenly like my bones nearly did. Letting out a cry, I expelled power out of both palms toward the paintings.

Lote tried to shield the walls, but he was too late.

A sweet-smelling mist poured out from the walls.

Jax broke free first, wrenching himself one step forward to catch Elias's arm. Lote aimed his palm directly at me.

I grasped Ashton's hand this time and we all vanished before the energy hit us.

CHAPTER THIRTY-SIX

Sweat doused my aching body. I knelt on the ground of the cabin, trying to catch my breath. Everything hurt.

Jax reached for me. "Are you okay?"

I lifted my head and looked between the three of them. "We're all going back to my world. Now."

Elias shook his hands to stop me. "No, no, no. If we flee to your world, it only gives Lote that much more motivation to find a way there."

"And if you stay, they're going to break into your brain and figure it out that way." I craned my neck to see out the window, convinced someone may approach at any moment. "Lote is very motivated and I don't think taking refuge in my world makes a meaningful difference."

"She's right." Jax took my hand and forearm, helping me to my feet. "Lie down." He ushered me toward the couch and I followed along mindlessly. My yearning for Nash squeezed my bones with the same ache as the machine. For a moment, it seemed like he came to me here in this world, that his hands held on to me.

What a dizzying sensation. I gladly collapsed onto the cushions with my forearm covering my eyes to block my view of Jax while my mind struggled to reconcile shifting realities.

"She needs to go home," Jax said. "Lote hurt her and she's separated from her allies. It's only a matter of time before your guild cracks the code anyway."

"You do realize that's not Ashton." Elias's dry tone frustrated me.

"Do you?" Jax asked. "You're sulking."

The real Ashton paced on the other side of the room with unnervingly quick steps and a complete obliviousness to the rest of us.

"I am not sulking." Elias laughed contemptuously. "Just thought you might be confused."

"I'm not confused. Max shares Ashton's soul. We owe our care to her." Jax shifted back to me, looking at me with the same eyes as Nash. "I'll ensure you return to where you belong, and that you're not dragged into our problems again."

"For the final time." Elias groaned. "I wanted to protect Ashton and help Max with her problems."

My head throbbed. "Can we go now?"

"We can't just leave here without taking care of Lote and the rest of the guild," Elias said. "It's only pushing off the problem."

"No, we're recruiting allies," Jax said. "You, Ashton, and Max return to your world. I'll turn to my guild for help."

"Wait," I said. "That puts my world in more danger. Lote will be limited right now by trying to keep this a secret. He didn't even tell Elias and Ashton about his machines. He keeps his secrets well protected. My world is a major secret. He's not going to bring an army over, at least not yet. He's going to try to get the job done with the least amount of people."

"True," Elias said.

"I have allies I can trust." Jax walked closer to me, his tone imploring. "We at least need to gather a few strong warriors to support us."

"Won't your guild ask questions?"

"Not right now. They trust me. If they know I have a plan and it's not safe to say much yet, they won't pry. I've done this before."

Back in my world, Nash once secretly worked against the Prophet unsuccessfully for years before we met and killed him together. It didn't surprise me that Jax was so active here with plans of his own. "How many?" I asked.

"Three I would trust with the life of anyone in this room."

"What about with my entire world?"

"Yes." He spoke with such assurance and conviction that I couldn't bring myself to question him.

"Bring them," I said. "I trust you and I trust your word. So they'll fight with us."

The fire of battle ignited in his eyes as he nodded. "Will you transport me to them?"

"Yes. We should hurry. For all we know, Lote can already travel to my world, and hid that from us."

Now that terrified me to think about.

"It's okay," Elias said. "I don't think that's the case. We'll work fast here and get you home."

"You're coming, too." I wasn't taking no for an answer. Elias infuriated me but I cared about him living. "They'll kill you here."

Ashton chewed her thumbnail as she paced. I huffed and twisted her way.

"Would you stop it?" I raised my voice at her. "Get over here."

"I need to think," she said.

"No, you don't. You're spiraling. You need to stop thinking. Get over here and help us plan."

"I messed up." Ashton shook her head, her voice on the verge of tears. "I stood there and watched you two fight him."

"Ash." Jax spoke softly, the way Nash did to me when I felt anxious. "You loved Lote. You can't be expected to turn on him in a day. It's understandable."

"It is." Elias took a few steps closer but didn't fully approach her. "Let it go."

"It's not okay, actually," I said. "It's unacceptable."

The two men gawked at me, looking stricken that I undermined their efforts to console her. They both began with their reassurances at the same time.

"It is unacceptable," I said again, louder this time to silence the men. "You never enter a battle with an enemy you aren't prepared to kill. You should have stayed home."

"Max," Elias said quietly.

"No, don't coddle her." I crossed my arms and steeled my gaze. "You're stronger than this, Ashton. Stop pacing around and get into this battle. Now."

Ashton slowed to a stop, still facing away.

Everyone fell silent. I saw by the look of admonition on Elias's face and worry on Jax's that they thought I was too harsh. I knew myself, though. When I was on the verge of breaking, I needed comfort. Ashton was not close to breaking. She felt guilty, and I knew that feeling well.

Slowly, she turned to face me, staring at me without speaking. Finally, she walked up to join the rest of us, leaned against the wall, and breathed out very slowly.

"Thank you," Ashton said. "I needed that."

"I know."

The men raised their brows at each other.

"Just so you know, you two are not allowed to do that to me." Ashton pointed a finger at each man. "Only I can do that to me."

I grinned at that, holding in my chuckle. She had that right. I would lose it on Piercey if he tried that, and if Nash did, I would probably only crumble. It only worked when Leif did it.

That was why I needed my dear friend so much.

"Let's not waste time." I extended my hand to Jax.

The gods created my world and Elias's the same in every way, except for the number of people born with power. That difference changed our civilizations in countless ways. We all lived under the same sun, though, and shared the same weather, the same animals, the same landscape.

And yet everything looked so much brighter when we appeared in the courtyard of the Sacred School with the sunlight bathing the dome above us.

The feeling of home hit me deeply, and while I still ached from Lote's attack, even my muscles seemed to feel the relief.

"You all go sit behind that big tree," I said. "No one is going to snoop around over there, and I don't want you to be seen." I pointed to where Piercey and I often sat as children.

Ashton, Elias, Jax, and the three warriors from the Silver Moon Guild did as they were told, looking at their surroundings with curiosity. I searched for Nash and teleported to him. After using so much power today, transporting strained my body. My desperation to see him drove me, though.

I landed in a hallway right in front of both Nash and Leif.

"Nash," I cried out immediately.

He had been midsentence when he saw me. He grabbed me without saying another word, closing his arms tight around me, holding me so close it suffocated me.

"You're okay," Nash said. He kissed the crown of my head, pulled back enough to see me, and closed in again to kiss my temple. My cheek. "I worried every second you were gone."

"I'm sorry." I clasped his shirt with both hands, breathing him in. His nearness filled me to the point of bursting. "I missed you so much." There was work to be done, but leaving and enduring the rupture of Jax and Ashton's relationship through her memories cut terribly.

"We're all safe," Nash said. "No casualties in any demon attacks. Gael's warriors stopped them all."

Tears fell down my cheeks at the news. The dam of fear broke and a flood I didn't realize I even held back rushed out.

"Listen," I said, struggling to focus. "There's a lot to say, but we need to get to the courtyard." I motioned for Leif, and he touched my shoulder. Not wanting to take the time to walk across the complex, I transported us back.

Nash immediately noticed the group by the tree. "Is that . . ."

"Yeah," I said. "Jax is over there. Be prepared for that."

"This is crazy."

"I've got to see this," Leif said. He walked ahead of us for the group and yelled out in a boisterous voice. "Who dares to copy the face of our great Max the Sharpshooter. And what about the spy?"

I snorted at him calling Nash a spy. The group stood to meet us, Jax turning around to face Nash.

The two both paused. I looked from one head of curly hair to the other.

"Holy hell," Leif said. "There really are two of them."

Leif nodded at Ashton. An uncertain but amused smirk came over her face.

"It doesn't feel real," Jax said.

"This . . ." Nash looked between Ashton and Jax. "This is incredible."

I'd been living in this bizarre reality for so long that it no longer affected me. Instead, I felt removed, even numb, to the shock of seeing copies of ourselves.

Ashton stared at Nash before turning her attention to me, and I saw pain in her eyes. Pain I felt in my own chest because I lived through enough of her memories to know that she hated herself right now for letting anything keep her away from Jax.

"Let's talk," I said. "Our apartment is close by. I'll call Piercey and Wren to have them meet us."

"Your apartment," Ashton said.

Nash scratched the back of his neck. "Is it too much for you guys?"

"No." Jax shook his head. I wasn't sure about Ashton, though. She said nothing.

"This is a nightmare." Piercey held his head and groaned low. "It took most of Gael's manpower to defend the Valley while you were gone. The attacks are happening at the same rate as when you first left. They've waged all-out war. How are we supposed to fight another war on top of this? With more advanced warriors?"

I refused to allow myself to give in to despair or panic, even if my stomach churned and my heart raced. I kept it distant from my heart.

Jax leaned his weight against his knees with his hands clasped. "Attacks?"

"Until recently, we didn't have many warriors to help defend the Valley," I said. "There's only power for one out of every one hundred people here, and on top of that, the man we killed—the Prophet of the Valley—hunted demons the entire time he reigned. He killed off and drove out a lot of people with neural implants. Someone is sending people to randomly attack us all over the Valley, and we've been so busy surviving, we haven't made progress with finding the root issue."

Ashton glowered at Elias. "You got her involved in our guild when she was dealing with this?"

"I thought I would be helping her," Elias said. "I gave power to three of her best warriors and planned to help train them. When this was all over, I was going to share technology and information."

Ashton shoved his shoulder hard. "All because you didn't want me to get involved. Because you can't trust me to win the battle. You think I'll get myself killed." Real hurt broke through the anger in her voice. "You think she can win a war I can't?"

"No," Elias said. "I didn't want you to know what Lote did. I didn't want you to have to fight again."

Nash eased closer to whisper to me. "You're the one who told her, didn't you?"

"Obviously," I said. "He was being a stubborn idiot." My gaze turned to Piercey then, and I interrupted Elias and Ash's bickering. "Did you know that Elias hid this from her? You two connected."

Piercey shook his head. "I didn't realize. Looking back, I don't have a memory of him telling her, but I had no memory of him concealing it. I just didn't think about it. There were too many things on my mind. I'm a fool for not realizing."

"You're all too trusting is what you are." Leif said little since we came into the apartment. "I say this all the time."

Piercey and I both groaned at the same time. Leif was right about this for once, and he'd never let us live it down.

"Okay, we can all fight later," I said.

"Now you want to change topics." Leif flashed a smug grin. "I'll take that as you conceding that I told you so."

I made a face at him and then waved him off.

"We have to finish the job," Jax said. "We kill Lote and whoever is helping him break into this world. You'll be safe, and we can take the next step toward peace for our guilds on our own."

"Killing Lote won't be easy," I said. "He's expecting us now. They'll monitor for your return, Elias. You told me before they can monitor your power readings. We'll walk into a trap no matter how we do it."

"What if you force him here?" Nash asked. "Take away the advantage of him being at home."

"It may work." I considered this. "Then again, we'll be opening our world to danger." Anxiety twisted my insides. "Right now, he can't hurt anyone here because he's trapped in his world."

"Until he figures out how to travel," Elias said. "Our greatest advantage, though, is that he's keeping this a close secret. We won't be fighting against the entire guild."

"The secrets are the problem." Ashton stared at the ground, sounding as numb as I was starting to feel. "All these secrets are killing us. We should tell the truth."

"What does that even mean?" Elias asked. "You want to advertise this world to everyone?"

"Not happening," I said.

"I didn't say we should tell everyone," Ashton said. "Some may see Lote's efforts as a coup against our king. Secretly amassing so much technology, power, and resources is a threat to the order of the kingdom. How are we supposed to know he simply wants our guild to be on top? Maybe he wants to overthrow the kingdom."

Piercey slowly straightened while she spoke. "You want to tell your king. Can he be trusted?"

"I think so," Ashton said. "He doesn't have as much power as a king in your world might because the guilds are so powerful. But he does have the final authority, especially in regard to the wrongdoing of guild leadership. It's a balancing act of power and why we're so stonewalled."

"Lote may kill the king if it comes to it." Worry shadowed Elias's tight frown. "The king is supposed to have final authority, yes. He doesn't. Telling him might mean he tells the leadership of all the guilds what's happening because he relies upon their power to manage the kingdom."

"What's the point of a powerless king?" Leif asked.

"Central leadership, even a weaker one, has its merits." Elias sighed. "From diplomacy, to negotiations, to our judicial system. He might have to share power with the guilds, and he rules under their shadow, but he does bring order to our kingdom."

Order. I rubbed my arm, thinking about the order that our Valley once had before I destroyed it. It was an awful order, but we certainly had one. The feeling that had been gnawing at me for months turned painful as I thought about the future of our Valley and the threats that we faced from all sides. When Lote asked if I was a leader in the Valley, I fully meant it when I said yes. Yet, I returned to my world, still content to ignore what I needed to accept a long time ago.

"The power of a king is that he is one voice that will always be heard above many," Elias said. "If he calls Lote a traitor, the guilds will be quick to listen. He doesn't need to tell them about our world. There's plenty of other evidence."

The urgency inside of me grew, as it did through every day of fighting this year. I tried to run from it and deny it and seek out another way. I'd been convinced that I didn't have the time to lead the Valley because of my battles. In the end, I took on the bulk of the war when we needed a kingdom fighting, not just me. It wasn't just that the Valley needed someone to lead, but it needed the chance to become one people instead of the disparate and abandoned villages of a horrible Prophet. We needed to unify together as one to face Lote's threat and win control of the Valley. Otherwise, we doomed ourselves to living in a blood feud like Elias and Ashton's people.

We needed a leader to bring us together and return to the Valley after leaving for Elias's world sharpened my view of our situation.

I couldn't sit still so I pushed out of my seat and walked to Piercey, pointing at him. This was not a new decision, but one I made in the other world without admitting it fully. "Assemble the Valley leadership immediately. Tell them it's an emergency. Use Gael to bring everyone here to the Sacred School."

Piercey started to stand even as he asked the question. "What are you planning?"

"Nash." I turned so I could see his amber eyes, feel if this was the worst mistake of my life, if we could survive it.

"Don't wait," he said. "Go."

A pang of love so sharp stabbed into my heart. I couldn't assume he knew what I was planning or doing, and it didn't matter to him. We'd been through so much together. He recognized this urgency I felt. Trusted me. At one time, I relied on his trust to believe in myself. I felt it for myself now, at least this once. This was the right call. I realized it beneath the surface of my thoughts when I lived through Ashton's life and watched the struggle in her kingdom.

"Piercey, meet me in the conference room with the others," I said. "The rest of you, stay here and plan." I looked to each person to check for understanding and met Nash's eyes. He pushed from his chair to join me. I didn't walk across the room. I ran and so did he.

The last thing I heard before the door slammed shut was Leif's loud voice. "What the hell just happened?"

"We'll deal with these captive demons now. What did you learn while I was gone?" I asked as Nash and I ran through the halls of the Sacred School. A student jumped to the side, avoiding us. I needed to save my energy now.

"Piercey used the tracker you've been putting in the demons to help us travel to several." Nash shoved a door open for me as we both burst through. "I pretended that I was offering them money to attack again. One took the bait."

I cut a look at him. "They all did this for money?"

"Only some. The demons attacking right now are serious. I think a lot of the random attacks over the past year have been demons who were paid to cause mischief. The new wave is different."

I slowed to a stop as soon as we reached the door leading to the holding rooms—classrooms that we converted into temporary cells for our captives. It was guarded by some of Piercey's best graduates. "What did you find?"

"It's the Flatlander Prophet," Nash said. "He's working with a cult of demons to weaken us for invasion. He wants land back that the Prophet of the Valley stole from him long ago."

"What cult?"

"I don't know. Those demons won't talk."

I rolled my neck. "Well, today is their last chance."

The graduates guarding the door stepped aside to allow us entrance.

"What does that mean?" Nash called after me.

"It means we're using manpower to keep a constant check on their power and guard them and we can't afford that. It means I cannot afford to be Max any longer. I need to be more."

A graduate opened one of the converted classrooms for me when I stopped in front of the door.

"Eclipse," the graduate said.

I ignored the name, peering into the brightly lit room. One of the demons I fought recently sat on the far side of the room with his arms and legs bound, his skin flushed red. His power warred against that of the graduates to free itself.

Nash and I both entered the room.

"You have a choice today," I said. "Vow to leave the Valley in peace or die."

The hard set of the demon's frown remained frozen until his mouth opened wide in a loud laugh.

Resignation hardened like lead in my gut. I spoke in a voice devoid of the anguish buried too deep beneath my determination for me to feel. "I'm sorry I did not do this in battle as I should have."

I drew my sword and buried my blade deep into his heart without hesitation.

"Max . . ." Nash's eyes didn't leave the dead demon's vacant stare.

"We need every single warrior we can get. There will be no one left to guard the unrepentant." I slung the blood from my sword and turned my back on the dead man. "You don't have to stay for this."

Nash took my wrist and jerked me to him. I caught myself on his chest with the bloodied sword between us. I waited for the sting of his judgment, his horror, at killing a captive man.

"You're the one who doesn't need to stay for this," Nash said. "Go prepare for the leaders."

A strangled breath caught in my throat. My eyes burned. "Nash—"

"One day no one's fate will be decided by a single person. Today is not that day. You're right that this should have been done in battle. So let me do it now. You've carried the burden long enough." Nash pried my fingers from the sword and wiped one side against his leg. Then the other. He pushed it back into the sheath at my hip. "It's time to step away, Max."

Nash had a way of forcing me to stay in my body and feel everything I wanted to run from. Tears fell as hundreds of days of killing gripped me. His hand worked over my face, his soft lips finding my cheek.

"I know what you're planning to do." His nose brushed mine. "I'll fight by your side every second."

I kissed him, desperate for the life I wanted us to lead. After seeing Ashton lose Jaxon, I never wanted to abandon the fight for our future or fail to seize every bit of our life together. "I love you."

"I love you, too. Don't take the blame for this. They came here to wage war."

"Killing someone on the battlefield is different than plunging a sword into their heart in a jail cell."

"That's why we're going to make sure the Valley is capable of handling prisoners from now on. So go."

I nodded and backed away, realizing my hands were shaking. "If anyone is willing to talk, let them live. Those left alive will fight with us or meet the same fate as the others. They stay under guard."

Nash shifted so I no longer saw the man I killed. He nudged me toward the door.

It surprised me to see the number of leaders who managed to make it to this sudden meeting. Gael had just finished bringing in Markus, the commander who had loudly taken over one of our meetings to insist that I step up as leader.

I looked to Chief Kaid, hoping that she would agree with this, and forgive me for taking so long. Wren and Leif took their seats on either side of her.

Breathing in, steadying myself, I spoke. "We are facing a new kind of threat. One much graver than our neighbors attacking us and taking advantage of the fragility of our current state." I stood, making sure to meet the eyes of each of the dozens gathered today. "It occurred to me that we possess an incredible power that we don't yet know how to wield. We have a Valley of leaders, warriors, and families who are committed to protecting our land."

My chief smiled, holding my gaze.

"We all know that we need a leader. We've spent a year searching for one. Calling on people to step up." I clenched my teeth, knowing that if I continued, there was no stopping. "We've spent a year with you crying out for me to lead you and I refused."

Nash entered the room and closed the door, blood splattered over his chest. My stomach turned with nausea. Never again could I fail to take the action that needed to be taken to protect my Valley. We were fighting for our lives, and I'd wasted precious resources on trying to keep alive the enemies intent on killing us all because it cost so much to kill the Prophet. Trying to avoid the inevitable made the awful deed that much worse.

"We can't afford to wander lost in the darkness any longer," I said. "I might be able to fight a war for the Valley, but I can't win one on my own.

We need to do this together. So today we'll make a decision together." I found Piercey at the end of the table. I looked at Nash, to his confident gaze and the unshakeable calm despite the blood covering his shirt. "Today we decide to become a kingdom. One people, united together."

Markus pounded his fist against the table so loudly that I expected it to crack. "Yes." He rose to his feet. "Rise, everyone. We will be a mighty kingdom."

A village chief stood. A demon who had proven vital in battle joined her. A commander next. All around the table, people shoved their chairs away and joined in the battle cry.

Chief Kaid raised her forearm to me.

I thought some might need time, but soon, every single person stood, including Piercey.

He might sit back down if he knew what Nash and I had just done. I didn't like our kingdom beginning in a bloodbath. Had there ever been another conceivable way? I hoped that one day someone found a better path.

"Everyone will write down their vote for leader," I said. "We'll collect—"

"Eclipse." A chief's voice boomed from beside me.

"Eclipse," Markus called out and beat his fist against his chest, then the table. "The Prophet Eclipse."

Eclipse. Eclipse. Eclipse.

The name echoed and swelled and spun around me.

Eclipse.

The leaders of the Valley chanted it together as loud as any war cry I'd ever heard.

Nash leaned against the wall, eyes on me, that half smirk filling one side of his face. "Max." I couldn't hear him above everyone. Just saw his lips move.

My heart pounded in sync with the cry of the name I never wanted, but that all of Skia Hellig had learned to fear.

I'd never felt so terrified and so certain at the same time.

"Our kingdom is under attack." I used my power to amplify my voice above their shouts. "Gather your warriors."

CHAPTER THIRTY-SEVEN

The show of faith overwhelmed me, but before long, the Valley leaders returned to business as we discussed the logistics of uniting our kingdom.

"I want to hear from the chief of every single village within a month," I said. "Everyone gets their say. If they don't want to join, they don't have to, and I personally guarantee that they will still be protected. But I need to hear word from each."

Markus tugged on the end of his short beard. "You're giving away one of the motivations for joining the kingdom for free. In the future, when disagreements come, you'll need factors like protection to convince people to stay. Kingdoms don't hold themselves together."

"I could never let any village in this Valley fall," I said.

"Once they join, they join," Piercey said. "It's binding."

Markus gave one more tug on his beard and then lowered his hand to the table. "Very well."

"Tell the chiefs to talk with their people," I said. "I want a consensus. When we meet next, I need your preliminary ideas on laws and systems for our kingdom. Please make it a top priority." I stepped back from the table. "Go on, everyone. We're done."

I expected it to feel surreal to give orders and see people jump to follow them, except I'd unofficially done that for the past year. The Valley relied on me so heavily that with each passing week, I naturally gained more authority. We all wanted to survive, and they'd quickly learned I stopped at nothing to ensure the Valley did just that.

As people began to depart and Nash spoke with several commanders, Piercey and Markus both moved to sit closer to me. "Don't stress," Piercey said. "I can feel you freaking out about the governance. We're good at this part, okay? Let us work on this. We'll draft ideas and gather thoughts. Once you've dealt with the threats, we'll have plenty of long days of meetings to figure all of this out."

Markus spoke in a softer tone than normal. Until now, I never experienced anything other than his political persona. "You're a wartime leader. You need help with the political aspects. We all understand what we signed up for."

"Okay," I said. "It feels weak to not be involved with all of this."

"You're busy," Piercey said. "Step back. Remember? Delegate. We'll come to you when it's time to make decisions."

"Speaking of decisions," I said. "The Sacred School cannot be so involved with this new kingdom forever. Choose whether you want to be a part of this government or the director of the Sacred School. After a transition period, the Sacred School will remove itself from the kingdom. It's important that the school continues to grow into a true place of education and training, and that it is not tied politically in any way."

Piercey focused intently while I spoke. "You made a difficult decision. I will, too. Know this, I will be with you until this kingdom is stable. No matter what."

"Thank you, Piercey," I said. "I couldn't do any of this without you. We also need to immediately begin training a successor. I'm not doing this for the rest of my life. I recognize that I'm the leader the Valley needs right now. One day we won't be at war. I want to hand the kingdom over to someone eventually."

"We can talk about this later," Piercey said. "Deal with what you need to deal with now."

After months of feeling beat down and lost, I finally saw the path forward. Living through Ashton's life and growing painfully aware of my own shortcomings, seeing myself and my world in a perfect mirror, cleared my vision.

I knew all along we needed a leader and I searched for one. Only, while I thought I didn't have time to lead, it was actually the opposite. By refusing to accept the authority I earned through my dedication and ability, I failed to unite the Valley and sentenced myself to a life fumbling through endless battles. No more.

If Lote invaded my world, then he'd face the leader of the Valley and everyone who served beside me. The rest of Skia Hellig would face this reality as well. Today, I'd take a stand against the ones attacking my people. I couldn't afford to wait one more minute.

I excused myself from Piercey and Markus to join Nash at his side. He excused himself from his conversation and placed his hand on my lower back.

"You did incredible," he whispered close to my ear.

His closeness drew me back into my body and down from the shock of so suddenly accepting the position of leader. It might have seemed impulsive, but it had been building inside of me for the last year. "I just got too tired of running from the job everyone knew I needed to do."

"I'm with you." He ran small circles along my back with his thumb. "We'll do this together."

I wanted to melt against him when he said it. I felt more terrified than I ever had stepping into battle, and I wasn't at the hard part yet—actually leading. "I have to take care of something. I'll explain when I'm back."

"Go. I'll take care of things here."

"Thank you." I clung, not wanting to let go of him. I really couldn't wait, though. One last squeeze.

I teleported directly into the dining hall of the Flatlander Prophet. A massive table covered to the brim in cheeses, vegetables, and multiple potato dishes sprawled out before the Flatlander leader and his family. A young boy stared up at me with chicken hanging from his mouth.

"Eclipse," one guard shouted.

Immediately, the soldiers ran for the Prophet.

"I've come to talk," I said. "That's why I'm alone. So you know I'm not a threat."

The Flatlander Prophet pushed himself up from the table and yelled in a voice shaking with rage. "How dare you enter my home and come to my family's—"

"How dare you enter my Valley?" I spoke low so as to not frighten the children further, but it did not lessen the power and conviction of my message. "Why don't we discuss this away from young ears."

"I could have you killed," he said.

"You aren't going to attack me in front of your family and put them in danger. I really just want to talk, and my time is short."

He grumbled and slammed his fists against the table. "Everyone, leave except for my guards."

His wife grabbed the hands of his children and fled the room. I did feel bad for scaring his family. That wasn't my intention. How many families had he scared in my village, though? He'd sent demons to attack innocent people in the middle of the night.

He should understand that I could and would appear before him at any time.

"You have lost your mind," the Prophet said once we were alone.

"I thought it was time we finally met since you've been waging a silent war against me for a year."

"I don't appreciate having my meal interrupted by an uninvited guest," he said.

"Then I'll be quick so you can get back to your important task. The Valley leadership made a decision today. We're uniting as one kingdom. I'm the new Prophet of the Valley."

His lips curled. "It's pathetic that it took you this long to make such an obvious decision. You don't have what it takes to rule."

"Maybe I don't, but I can lead, and I have been for a while now. I didn't come here to debate with you. We are about to be invaded by an enemy that is far stronger than any of us."

The Prophet said nothing for several seconds. Suspicion and worry both clouded his look. "Who?"

"You know that I've had dealings with the gods?"

His nostrils twitched. "I know you've been up to plenty of wickedness, Eclipse. You killed Flare."

"The gods commanded my silence on the matter. I cannot tell you who this enemy is, only that when he arrives with his comrades, it will change our entire world if we don't stop him."

"Why should I believe you?"

"Because if I fail, you're probably going to die," I said. "You may rule in a different land, but we're all living in Skia Hellig. We're all living in this world. There's no magical line that separates your people from the threats mine face. At some point, if we can't unite for our common good, we all lose."

"You want us to fight alongside you?" The Prophet thumped a heavy hand on the table. "Eskel the Ruthless stole our land twenty years ago and you've kept it for yourself. If the lines dividing us matter so little to you, return it."

"The villages you claim as your own chose for themselves. They did not want to be under your rule. I'll honor their choice."

He breathed out hard. "Listen, Eclipse. I'm not a brute like Eskel, but I'm not a fool either. What you must understand about the Flatlands is that we've always had to fight to keep what's ours. You enjoy the natural protection of the Valley. The mountain and coastal regions benefit from their geography as well. We're caught in the middle of you all, trying to keep ourselves together."

"You've attacked us for a year while we reeled from the Prophet's death. I've run myself ragged trying to protect my people." The innocent lives that this man was responsible for began to crowd my mind and threatened to drive my temper out of control. "You didn't have to do that. You could have talked to us."

"What good are words? Skia Hellig runs on blood."

My power churned inside of me, heating my palms. "Children died because of your attacks."

He looked down, grimacing. "You'll soon learn the hardship of being a leader. War is inevitable and you never know who will die."

"We don't need to be at war. I don't want your lands. Just let go of the Valley villages and we can start over."

"We aren't going to fix the relationship between our lands while we talk. You came here to discuss this common enemy. Now that you've accepted leadership of the Valley, we will arrange to meet as fellow Prophets and have formal discussions."

I swallowed a bitter taste in my mouth. "We will talk while our people fight and kill each other."

"You're in a new world, Eclipse. You should get used to it."

"Well, I've learned a few things recently, and one is that sometimes you can ally with your enemies. And if you can ally with your enemy, maybe they can become something other than that."

He scoffed. "I'm not sure whether you're naive or just stubborn."

"Does it matter when you know I'm deadly? You're the one who coordinated the attacks on the Valley all year while you've also been attacking us outright. You're bouncing off the coastal warriors who've come after us as well. We're going to be even harder to kill now that we've become a kingdom."

He studied me. "You're right. You are deadly and I've never made the mistake of overlooking that. Why do you think I've gone to such lengths to wear you down? You killed a man I tried to kill for years. Why should I give you time to grow more powerful?"

"I'm not going to kill you for no reason."

"How am I supposed to know what you'll do?"

I stepped closer. "I suppose that's a matter for these formal discussions of yours. Can I count on you to fight with us if this enemy shows up?"

"Give me time to consider."

"We may not have time."

"I suppose that if the enemy comes, you will look to your side, and either I'll be there, or I won't."

"You know." I really wanted to punch this man. "You should not toy with the unknown. This is not someone who will ever let you keep your land."

He said nothing, but only stared.

"Oh, one last thing," I said. "We don't need negotiations for you to understand this. I will never allow you to enter into my kingdom's territory and hurt my people. Consider yourself warned that any unauthorized movement in my kingdom will be an act of war."

The Prophet shifted his eyes to the door. "I think we're done."

"I killed Eskel because he hurt my people. You should remember that, Prophet."

"Leave," he said in a booming voice.

I snarled and teleported away.

Nash and I stood together in the bathroom of our apartment while everyone waited in the living room. He spoke to me in a hushed voice.

"Do you think anyone will actually join us?" he asked.

I wiped my face and dropped the towel onto the counter. "I don't know. The Flatlander Prophet was not very receptive. My next visits weren't much better. I wasn't exactly welcomed warmly by the Fjellfolk in the mountains or anyone on the coast. Skia Hellig has always been divided. But Gael said that he is willing to bring more warriors through portals if Lote ends up in our world."

"The Prophets might double-cross us even if they agree."

"It seems almost as likely that our neighbors would join Lote as it is that they would join us. If I could explain the situation to them, they would see they need to help us. I have no doubt Lote would take over all of Skia Hellig." I rubbed the ache in my chest. "I won't call upon any other Prophets if Lote invades us. I've seen enough to know it's a mistake."

Nash sighed. "I'm sorry, Max."

"I was able to introduce myself as the Prophet and let them know that things are different now." I turned around and leaned against the counter, making a face like I'd eaten something sour. "I really don't like the sound of that. Prophet."

Nash folded his arms around me. "I'm sure you can pick another title."

"I don't think I'll like any of them. There's nothing wrong with being a leader. I just really loved being a warrior. It's where my heart is. But maybe a great warrior can make a great leader."

"I'm proud of you." He squeezed me. "Let go of your worries."

"We said we wanted more time with our family, and then I did this."

"I know. I told you to do this, remember?" He held my arms, giving me a look. "This is what needs to happen. The order in the Valley will lead to peace and stability. We're on our way to a better future."

"I hope." I stood on my toes and kissed him. "Thank you for believing me and for not resenting me when you wanted to do more to fight."

"I'll never resent you for my own weakness."

"It's not weakness, Nash. You're the strongest person I know."

He brushed my hair back and smiled. "I will be soon. You better watch out, Sharpshooter."

I chuckled, already looking forward to days of training with him on using his power. "We have to be careful, then. We can't make it this far and lose. We can't die."

"No." Nash glided his thumb along my cheek. "No dying."

"I guess it's about time to go, then, isn't it?"

His amber eyes drew me in, and I wanted to promise that soon we'd take our life together. It just felt so far away.

I opened the door and returned to everyone who was waiting for us in the living room.

"It's best that we keep the group small," Ashton was saying. "The king will be jarred by having us suddenly appear. It's the only way to stop the news from getting out, though."

"That sounds good to me," I said.

"I'll make war preparations here," Nash said. "It's a better use of my time."

Progress. Both of us making progress. Nash and I both were learning when to step back from a battle.

Jax smirked. "I heard that while we were snooping through your apartment, you took over an entire kingdom, Max. I'm not impressed at all."

My cheeks warmed. "I'm afraid of what I've just gotten myself into."

"You're exactly what they need," Elias said. "Everyone sees it, even your enemies. It's why they fought so hard against you."

Ashton smirked and then bit her lip. "We also saw the child's room. Leif told us about Elsie."

I looked over to Jax to see how the news of a daughter in this world affected him.

"I can't digest any of this," Jax said. "I've given up on even trying. It sounds great, though, having a little girl. I can't imagine."

"She's the greatest honor and joy of our life," Nash said.

The way Nash said *our* made me beam with joy. The last year could have torn apart the freshly budding love between us. Instead, through all the impossible battles, we'd grown closer together.

I had so much to fight for. To live for.

"We'll make it home safely," I said. "Promise."

CHAPTER THIRTY-EIGHT

This week, we had revealed ourselves to so many people that I managed to become bored with the inevitable disoriented reaction of people learning about the multiple worlds.

Interestingly, Ashton's king adjusted to the bizarre reality faster than anyone else. When we appeared outside of the court, it alarmed the guards, but because of the reputation of Elias, Jax, and Ashton, the king agreed to see us. And he appeared to believe our story.

"I hope you realize that revealing all of this to you places my world in an extremely vulnerable position," I told the king. "We love our Valley just like you do yours, and we will fight for our people to be safe. I sincerely hope that we can work together on a safe agreement that honors both of our worlds."

He crossed one leg over the other, his hands clasped tightly. "I've no interest in harming this Valley in any world. You're a sister kingdom to us. A twin. Anyone who hurts your Valley is a traitor to my kingdom. I won't stand for it."

Hope fluttered inside of me. Maybe we really could find a resolution. I'd laid the groundwork at home for a path to peace, even if it terrified me. How were we supposed to create and run a kingdom? But the kindness and the genuine camaraderie of the king eased my deep fears about this world.

"Your Highness," I said. "There's a reason we're so concerned for the safety of our Valley. Elias came to my world as an observer for a long time. He wanted to bring knowledge to your kingdom to support your efforts. But not everyone feels the way he does."

The king leaned forward. "Who else knows about this?"

"It's my guild, Your Highness." Elias dipped his head. "Lote and his clos-est confidantes figured out I traveled worlds. He plans to steal resources from Max's world to enrich our guild."

"Why have I heard nothing about this?" the king asked.

Elias hesitated. "I've kept it a secret, Your Highness, because I saw prob-lems in my guild, and I felt that I needed a plan before telling anyone. Their reasons for keeping secrets are more nefarious."

The king raised his fist to his mouth and momentarily averted his atten-tion to his advisor. "What, exactly, is Lote doing? Don't mince your words, Elias."

Ashton surprised me by speaking before Elias. "Lote has been hoard-ing resources and secretly developing technology without telling anyone else in the guild. He sabotaged our guild and blamed it on the Silver Moon to stoke tension between us." She looked at Elias now with teary eyes. "He covered up his crimes by killing Elias's parents when they learned the truth."

The king shoved himself to his feet. "Bring him to me at once!"

"Your Highness," his advisor said.

"This man is a traitor, and as soon as the evidence is gathered, we'll hold a hearing. I will jail him immediately."

"Your Highness," the advisor repeated. "Lote is very powerful. His guild will fight against this."

I pitied the king, seeing his authority collide with the reality of how much power the guilds carried. "What are you saying?" the king asked in a steely voice.

"Let's talk before we make any moves," the advisor said.

"I can't stand for this. I knew Elias's parents."

"We'll deal with Lote. That is certain. But let's talk about how to do it in a way that does not lead to war or jeopardize you."

The king, not Lote, might end up being ousted.

He turned back toward Elias with heartbreak gripping his expression. "I'm so sorry this happened. I need to see your evidence, but I knew your family, and I trust that you don't make this accusation lightly."

"I'm not, Your Highness."

The king looked to me. "You were right to bring this to me so that we can discuss as leaders. It would be a wonderful thing for us to share knowl-edge with each other. If we wanted to share resources as well, that would only help us. But I never want your kingdom to be in danger."

I walked closer. "Thank you, Your Highness. I can't tell you how reassuring it is to hear that."

"I don't believe that we're made stronger by subjugating those who are weaker. It only invites problems to our doorstep. This must stay a secret. Your instincts were right." He settled back against his throne and tapped the armrest several times. "If we take this problem to the guild leaders, it gives them time to prepare. Before doing that, we will bring Lote into custody to show how serious we are."

His advisor looked uncertain. "We can bind Lote's power while he's here. Summoning him suddenly to the court may set off alarm bells for his coconspirators."

"We cannot ask for permission to jail our traitors," the king said. "If we want to be strong, then we must be strong. I want Lote here at once."

I worried that Lote might not appear, but he arrived within the hour, and honored the order to come alone.

As soon as he entered the court and saw all of us standing before the king, his body tensed.

"Your Highness," Lote said as he bowed slightly. "I see my would-be assassins have paid you a visit."

"Yet another thing you failed to report to the crown," the king said. "I've heard about what you've been doing."

"It was for the kingdom, Your Highness. I planned to come to you in due time."

"You're a traitor." The king beat his fist against the arm of his throne. "What did you plan to do once you stole this power? Perhaps you thought you might like to be king."

"No, Your Highness," Lote said. "I only wanted to make us stronger to protect against our enemies. Our guild is the best equipped to lead this kingdom into the future, under your authority."

"You've lost your right to speak," the king said. "Your aggression and corruption tainted what could be a mutually beneficial relationship with another world. Do you really believe that going to war in their world is your best course of action? We'll gain just as much through peaceful means."

"They tried to kill me and still I offered peaceful means."

I rolled my eyes. "Your Highness, I can't trust him. I did try to kill him, and my only regret is that I failed."

"We have laws for handling crime in our kingdom," the king said. "Elias, Ashton, and Jax should have minded that."

"Your Highness," Jax said. "The Silver Moon Guild has discussed with you before that some of the problems between our guilds are best handled discreetly, away from the king's court. We considered it safer to handle this on our own."

The advisor shifted toward the king and spoke quietly.

"We'll discuss this further at a later time," the king said.

That didn't sound good, but the others looked calm. The king seemed aware of his limitations, and maybe secretly appreciated that they'd handled it on their own so it didn't endanger him.

The king looked down on Lote. "I've heard the evidence of your crimes. I will honor your right to a hearing before I sentence you. You're now under arrest and you will be stripped of your titles and authority until such a time that I see fit to return them. Which I must say, I anticipate not happening."

"Your Highness," Lote said in a gravelly voice. "You're making a mistake. I understand that you need to deal with my indiscretions, but I beg you to see the advancements we've made and are working toward before you—"

"I've seen enough," the king bellowed. "In this kingdom, we follow the laws of our land, and we will not operate in the shadows like you. I'll give your guild the chance to make a case for you. You'll be at the mercy of your leaders and me if you are proven guilty."

"And what about Elias?" Lote asked. "He lied as well."

"I'll deal with Elias separately. He hasn't killed anyone, has he?"

Lote snarled at Elias and then at Ashton. "You'll regret this," he seethed.

"That's enough." The king was standing again. "Your power has been bound and now it's time for you to show some honor by accepting your captivity."

Lote's hard eyes found mine. "There will be no mercy."

Light carved through the vines that wrapped around his fingers, hands, and wrists. A bright beam of power lit his fingertips.

No time. I teleported to the king. A fiery ball of power raced toward us.

Hand on him, I dragged him instantly to the other side of the room with my power.

A crash echoed off the walls of the king's hall. Plumes of fire burned the king's throne and rapidly reduced it to a smoldering pile of ash.

Lote had tried to kill the king.

"A machine," Elias shouted.

The guards all screamed, rushing for Lote. Jax and Ashton both shot energy at him, but it sizzled uselessly against his skin. The auto-shield.

I covered the king with a shield of my own and reached for Lote to try sealing this power he wielded. He sneered, meeting my eyes. Then he disappeared, leaving behind only the image of his haughty face in my mind.

The power he wielded felt strange, similar to the machine in his office.

"Someone find him," the king shouted. Breathing hard, he looked at me. "Thank you."

I didn't have time to talk to him. Instead, I sprinted to Elias, grabbed his hand, and reached for Ashton and Jax. "Hurry," I shouted. "He's gone to my world. I'm certain."

As soon as we all had a hold of each other, Elias unleashed a surge of power, ripping us between the worlds. We landed in the courtyard of the Sacred School with the heat and the pain of shifting worlds swelling over me.

"How the hell did this happen?" I snarled. I pointed at Jax. "You and Ashton search out his power. Elias, go with Piercey to the white room and look through the code for him. I'll gather people."

Ashton paced the courtyard. "He inserted the machine beneath his skin. We should have thought of this."

"It doesn't matter," I said. "He's in my world. That's all we need to think about now."

"Lote is here alone," Jax said. "We can kill him."

"We can't assume he's here with no one else," Elias said. "I'm sure that he shared the technology with his allies. It's possible he even left to get them first. We need to prepare for the worst."

I stormed through the halls of the Sacred School and sprinted for my apartment. "Nash!" I screamed his name before even reaching the door. He burst into the hallway, drawing his swords in a flash.

"What happened?" he asked.

"Lote escaped. He tried to kill the king. We think he's in our world."

"Fuck." He slammed the side of his fist against the wall.

I closed my eyes and sent a message to Piercey and Gael. We needed their portal system to start gathering allies, except I wasn't sure where to take them.

"Elias," I said through the neural connection. "Have you found him?"

"Not yet. Maybe he's back in our world gathering people or machines."

It might have been hasty to leave Elias's world when I had no idea what Lote was thinking. I was drawn here, needing to be with my people.

Every warrior at the Sacred School gathered in our largest meeting room. "Anything?" I asked once I returned.

"No." Ashton shoved her hair from her face. "I don't feel him. I can only search out so far, though. We may want to get to a more central location in the Valley to seek him out. I'm sure that he'll transport somewhere in Skia Hellig. It's all he knows."

"Or he wanted us to think he came to this world so we'd leave," Jax said. "He might be staging a coup back home right now." He turned to his three comrades. "Decide now. Are you fighting here with us or returning to the guild?"

One of them spoke quickly. "We'll go wherever Lote is. He's the priority. I think he'll come here. Too many people will be seeking him out at home."

"He's leading the rebellion. He's the one we should fight." Another comrade agreed.

"Max," Piercey's voice came through the neural connection. "We found him. He's near a village. I'll use the alarm system to send you the location."

"Everyone." I reached my hand out. "Hurry. We have him."

I'd kill this bastard.

CHAPTER THIRTY-NINE

The white-capped peaks of the Mountain of the Gods glowed against the twilight of the midnight sun, once a promise of the gods and their aloof watch of the Valley, and now a reminder of all that we had conquered.

Lote's form slinked like a soft shadow ahead of me, disturbing the streets of the village.

I teleported directly behind him. He blinked out of sight and appeared behind me as well.

I spun around to face him, stunned. So, he'd figured out teleportation in addition to traveling between worlds.

"I owe you some gratitude." Lote sounded amused. "I'm thankful you teleported while in my office. It allowed us to study your movements in the code with the help of my machines. I wonder what else you might teach us."

I threw my fist at his chin. He blinked out of range, appearing a few feet back.

"We should talk before we fight," he said.

"There is no talking," I said.

My group ran to circle around Lote.

"I didn't come alone." Lote drew his arms back as if indicating. "And I didn't come unarmed."

Of course not.

He cast a look around, beyond my allies who surrounded him. "They're masking their power, but they're with villagers in their houses, and they'll kill them if they sense us fighting for longer than a minute."

Fear squeezed my muscles with the same strength as Lote's machine when he had paralyzed us. I raised my hand to signal for everyone to hold their positions. "Have you even stopped to think about what you're doing? You tried to kill your own king. You have no world to return to."

"The king is a joke," Lote said. "The Valley is better off without him. Do you really believe I left my world without plans for it? I don't need to be there for the rest to continue in my place. You forced me to act early by talking to the king, but what will happen now is inevitable."

"Lote," Ashton said. "You need to stop. This is taking it too far."

"Will you stay here to fight me or return to the kingdom?" Lote smiled at Ashton with his teeth shining in the dim night. "By the time you make it home, it may be too late. I told you our guild is the best suited to run the Valley. It'll be a difficult transition. Well worth it in the end. If you come to your senses, I might find a place for you."

"I will never help you overthrow our kingdom." Ashton clenched her fists. "This is not the right way to lead the Valley."

"It's useless," Jax said. "Don't bother talking to him. We should stay here and kill him. There are plenty of people in our kingdom to fight back home. He's the one we need to take down."

"Will you let the innocent die, then?" Lote laughed so hard his shoulders shook. "Go ahead and attack me. We'll fight to the music of the villagers wailing in the background."

I quickly sent a message to Gael with directions on where to portal.

"You won't risk a single life." Lote raked his eyes across each of us. "Your only choice is to negotiate. It's inevitable that you'll lose a significant number of hostages if you fight."

"If you want to negotiate," I said, "then bring the hostages where I can see them."

"Do you want me to order one to die now as proof? You'll hear the screams of the mothers all the way from here."

"Bastard." Nash stalked forward with his blades extended. "You want our damn resources? This is not how you'll get them."

"I will get them no matter what you do," Lote said. "I feel the weakness of this world. It's pathetic. Soon, I'll tell my entire guild about the resources here without worrying about our competition, and we'll bring far more warriors here than you can hope to deal with." Lote turned his attention to me. "You've pissed me off enough. I suggest you start trying to get on my good side."

"As someone who has already overthrown Valley leadership," I said, "I have to tell you it's pretty important for you to actually be present for it." I eased closer. "What is it? Are you afraid? You're hiding out in my world while your lackeys do the work for you? If they can overthrow a kingdom without you, they'll realize they can lead without you. You better get home before it's too late."

"I won't be so easily goaded," Lote said. "I'll take enough to fuel our machines today, and then my guild may not even need to stop at the Valley. We'll take all of our Skia Hellig and raise it to the greatness I know we're capable of."

I couldn't leave these hostages in Lote's hands much longer, if he even had them in the first place. I didn't trust him not to kill them no matter what we did, and I refused to negotiate with him. He just started a coup against his kingdom. It would be a bad faith negotiation from the start.

The only option was to destroy him and anyone else who insisted on invading our world and our kingdom.

"I'm going to kill you," I said. "I fucking promise."

I sensed the explosion of portals around the village right when they began to rip the air open. All around us, warriors jumped out from the holes and landed on the ground with quaking thuds. They all bore the same color of armor as Gael. The sheer number almost made me freeze. There were far more pouring through the portals than those who came to the Sacred School. He already recruited more from home.

My eyes burned at the realization that Gael and his king had gone so far to fight with us.

It was short-lived, though, because Lote appeared directly in front of me, the light shining from his vine tattoos.

Nash broke for the closest house. Jax and Ashton followed his example, each running for a different residence.

"Kill them!" Lote roared with a voice that reverberated through the entire town, louder than the worst thunderstorms that had ever echoed throughout our valley. "Kill all the villagers!"

Gael's warriors flooded the town, rushing through the open portals. They immediately entered the houses, searching out hostages. For a few seconds, I hoped in vain that maybe Lote bluffed, because I felt no power.

But my enemy grinned at me with that gleaming smile of his. Then all the power erupted in a massive tidal wave.

"Max," Gael shouted. "I'm going for more."

Lote turned to target him with a raised palm, but Gael erected a shield to block himself as he opened a portal. A beam bit into the ground as Gael dashed into the opening he'd created. It closed rapidly behind him.

I sprang forward for Lote, my energy blade growing with power. We clashed, his physical sword steady against the force of mine.

Screams rang through the town, clawing at my mind, spurring the fear that I'd made the wrong call. In my first day as the new Prophet of the Valley, I'd gotten my own innocent people killed.

No questioning myself now. I had to fight.

"You're a fool if you think you'll get away with any of this," I said. I ripped back and lunged with a two-handed swing for his shoulder. He teleported to the side so my sword cut through empty air. At first, I almost followed him on impulse, before I realized that he might want me to waste my energy chasing him around the village or the world.

Instead of following his energy to teleport to him, I tracked him to attack on foot.

When he teleported next, I clung to the thread of his energy as if pursuing instantly, and instead sprinted forward, striking right when he appeared. Surprise filled his eyes when he sidestepped to avoid the hit.

A man burst out a window on the second floor of a home and skidded across the ground between Lote and me. Jax flew out after him and rammed his shoulder into the stranger so hard that the enemy's body dented the earth.

Lote aimed his fingers at Jax, but I replaced my sword with my bow and fired it at the same time the beam shot out from our enemy. While Lote must have assumed I'd fired to protect Jax, I actually trusted my comrade to evade on his own, and instead aimed for Lote's free hand.

Jax darted high into the air, narrowly avoiding the beam.

Lote twisted to the side to dodge, so my arrow only skidded across the top of his hand, ripping through his skin.

I nocked another energy arrow.

The dim glow of the midnight sun reflected off Lote's hand. The arrow had torn a hunk of his skin off and it hung now, flapping lightly as he stepped closer. A coating of metal spread out beneath his skin. Wires that matched the pattern of the thorny vine tattoos snaked across it.

A proud grin stretched his face eerily in the dim light. "It runs off my own energy."

Lote had surgically implanted the machine beneath his skin.

Jax hovered overhead, also staring down at his hand. "Have you tested that before?"

"This is the future of our power," Lote said. "Machines can enhance our neural chip for instant, reliable responses." He ripped the loose flap of skin away with a growl and threw it at my feet. "Start cooperating and this will be your power."

I grimaced as I looked at the hunk of tissue on the ground. "You're so proud of yourself."

"You would be, too. I admit I overprepared. I expected your world to pose a greater challenge and rushed the surgery."

Shrieks from a nearby home tore my attention away. I fired arrows as quickly as possible, sinking four into the injured man on the ground. They exploded in his back, ripping apart his skin in chunks of flesh and blood that popped in all directions. I sent the next straight for Lote.

He teleported—something that was turning out to be a cheap trick since I tracked it and traveled if he moved too far away.

Jax seemed to have also figured out how to follow the trail of his energy, because both of us attacked the exact place that Lote appeared. The auto-shield shimmered across his skin as my arrow and Jax's ball of energy deflected off his body.

If I destroyed Lote's machine, it rendered that shield inert. How much of his body did the metal cover? Was it more limited without all the extra fuel?

What if the rest of his men also fought with machines implanted in their bodies?

I took firm hold of my thoughts and stopped before I surrendered to fear.

Nearby, Elias ran from a building, carrying a small child in his arms. I erected a shield to surround him and the boy. Lote, meanwhile, had no concerns for anyone but himself. He left his people to fend for themselves while he focused his attention solely on Jax and me.

The two of us attacked Lote fervently. Every time we managed an assault capable of shattering his defenses, he teleported again, traveling only a few feet away.

"His machine is teleporting for him." I glanced at Jax. "You see that? The shield and the teleportation are both automatic, working in tandem."

I didn't say the rest, that I knew intimately well how much power it required to teleport. Maybe if I couldn't get past his defenses, I could at least wear him down.

The cries of the villagers tore my mind in two. Where was Nash? Leif and Wren? Piercey? Everyone fighting possessed power, but it was so new for the people I loved. They needed to ally with someone to guard them and enhance their abilities, like Piercey usually did with Nash.

I needed to trust them and believe in them to handle themselves. They knew their abilities. But each scream flooded my mind with images of horrors. Thoughts of Lote's warriors splattering living rooms in blood. Over the last year, I had gained so much control over my anxiety. Now the numbness threatened to spread throughout me, even into my heart, surely ready to stop it from beating in my chest.

I parried a slash of Lote's sword while Jax rained down balls of energy from the sky. I remembered fighting with him in Ashton's memories and didn't attempt to protect myself from his hits. He was good enough to avoid me. I threw everything I had into battling Lote and trusted that while Jax's attacks looked chaotic, he carefully strategized to take advantage of Lote's weaknesses, limit his range of abilities, and protect me as we engaged in close combat.

I spun and threw my momentum into a hard slash for Lote's chest.

Nearby, Nash stumbled through an open doorway. A sword followed him, its tip catching his shirt. I couldn't tell from here if it had hit him. I faltered, terrified that whoever attacked may use his power to immediately strike Nash dead. Midhit, I split my attention to shield Nash.

Lote broke through my guard and drove his blade toward me with a surge of power. His sword shattered my energy blade, scattering the power into the sky in a beautiful array of red and black. I teleported just as the sword nicked my shoulder.

When I appeared close enough to Nash to help him, I realized that he had never needed me to shield him. His blades swung overhead, deflecting the strikes of his opponent. My heart raced as red energy flowed over his twin blades, pulsing with power, more than I expected him to already wield. He fought with the same grace that mesmerized me in our first battle together, his footwork impeccable, and every single move purposeful. Now, his own power strengthened his efforts, driving his speed and fueling his attacks.

How was Nash using his energy so expertly?

"Focus, Max," Nash cried out as his foot kicked against the enemy's chest.

Then I saw Piercey inside the house behind them and realized that he was helping Nash to hone his strength, fighting with him as they had for the last year. Only this time, Piercey didn't need to give Nash his power, but helped Nash draw out and control his own instead.

Heat flooded the air. I noticed Lote's beam of energy a split second before it would have hit Nash. I barely grazed him with my fingers in time for us to teleport inside the house with Piercey. Lote punished me for my distraction by targeting the man I loved.

Enough.

Failing to trust others to fight would cost me this battle. Nash deserved all the confidence in the world, and so did my friends. I teleported back to Lote and wasted no time in pummeling him with attacks from my re-formed energy sword.

More of Gael's warriors crept into the streets, battling intensely with our enemies. Elias, still holding the small child, now protected a group of villagers beneath his own shield, no longer relying upon mine. He ushered them toward one of Gael's warriors.

Good. The villagers evacuated through portals.

Ashton leapt across a rooftop and landed in a burst of energy beside me, having propelled herself further than I ever remembered her jumping.

Jax and Ashton attacked at the same time. I exchanged my sword for my energy bow and shot ten arrows, sending them flying around Lote. They followed his every movement as he fought against the other two. Ashton's sword forced him backward and he slid right to avoid Jax, hitting one of the arrows.

It burst against the auto-shield. Another hit, doing the same. None of them broke through, but since Lote used his energy to power his machines, I expected every single attack on his shield contributed to overloading his capacity.

I just wished I knew how deep his reserve of energy ran. His machine might have used power more efficiently than we did on our own, but wasn't it possible that it actually required more? This technology was newer and not yet refined.

One by one, the explosive arrows that tracked his movements exploded against him, until the last two actually managed to break through his shield. It didn't seem to hurt him very badly, but I smelled his singed clothes.

I rushed beside Ashton and we both attacked at the same time, in unison with each other. Jax's sword raked across Lote's back, catching on the shield. The force of the attack nudged Lote in our direction while Ash and I both slammed our swords against Lote's.

His blade cracked with a sharp cry.

He teleported far away to the other side of the village. Ash grabbed my hand, and I carried her with me as we pursued him. Jax flew after us.

The exposed metal on Lote's hand flashed bright while the vines on his other hand glowed.

"As much as I enjoy a good battle," Lote said, "I'm getting tired of this."

His shoulders lit with a dim golden light beaming through his clothes.

Fuck.

CHAPTER FORTY

The air around us shifted, charged and electrified and drawn to Lote. He raised his arms high above his head as his power grew. The glow from his hands and shoulders spread to consume his body.

I wasn't waiting around to let him unleash this massive attack. I fired arrows at him, but they didn't even hit his shield. They fizzled and evaporated from sight in the glow surrounding him.

His warriors flocked to him, abandoning their battles and the villagers, as the brightness of the power spread to their bodies. Attacks from my allies bounced uselessly off them. All the remaining enemy warriors surrounded Lote, their group bright like the sun in the center of the village, glowing in one massive body.

My heart hammered against my chest. A cold sweat chilled the nape of my neck.

Gael's warriors gathered with Jax's comrades, leaving the homes to join us in the street.

Nash slid to my side and knocked into my arm. "What the hell is this?"

"Something bad." I focused my energy into a blade. "Piercey," I shouted.

For the past year, Nash and I fought together with Piercey powering his attacks, and we needed to return to what we excelled at. I heard Nash's heart beating steadily beside me, not even picking up in pace. He was confident. Probably more confident than made sense, but I loved that about him. He battled fearlessly, and now he did so with a burgeoning power.

"This is what I warned you about," Elias yelled. "His specialty. He empowers others."

The village came alive with Lote's power, his warriors a beating heart in the center of our battlefield.

Lote lowered to his knees in the middle of the group of perfectly assembled warriors as a circular barrier formed around him, glowing with the same golden power that wove all his warriors together.

His voice cracked like thunder.

"Go."

The warriors leapt out in all directions at the same time, leaving tendrils of golden power dusting the air behind them. Their skin shimmered and their eyes beamed.

Nash's twin blades flashed red with Piercey's familiar power, but I felt more than that exuding from him. His own power mixed with Piercey's in a lethal swirl of energy.

Together, we darted forward to meet our enemy head-on.

Nash's swords struck like twin cobras, snapping at one of Lote's warriors. My own drove forward after his, the warrior forced to block Nash's attack with his shield and mine with his sword. A forceful burst of power knocked into us and shoved us both back on our heels. We pushed forward again on the offensive, our blades attacking like one.

Across the village, I saw Jax and Ash fighting at each other's sides, partners once more like in days of her life I'd lived through. Days when she felt alive with the growing hope of unity for their guilds and a love she couldn't run away from.

Gael's warriors bravely attacked Lote's, outnumbering them, though struggling against the increase of power.

Behind me, Elias joined Piercey, and though I felt no power from him, I recognized the concentrated twist of his brows. He wielded his own weapon, toying with the code of our world, perhaps defending us and strengthening us, or trying to break the connection between Lote and his men.

Unable to see Leif or Wren, I listened for their heartbeats and heard them on separate sides of the village in the houses, surrounded by the pitter-patter of hearts I didn't recognize. The villagers.

As we fought, I relayed instructions to Piercey through our neural connection for him to send out to the rest of our force. We needed to prepare to evacuate the villagers as soon as Gael arrived with the next wave of warriors.

All of us warring together—my closest friends with fresh power, new allies from across the sea, counterparts from a parallel world—had to be enough to conquer this threat. It had to.

But as hard as we fought, Lote's warriors, enriched with his power, cut through our attacks.

The enemy pursuing Nash and me knocked his twin blades back with a powerful strike, leaving his chest exposed for an attack. A shield of power formed in front of Nash's core, but the aftershock of the attack collided with it, cracking its center.

I staved off the warrior with a punch to the center of her back, powering my fist with an incredible amount of energy.

As the woman leapt to the side to avoid another hit, another warrior rushed Nash and me.

We didn't need to talk or even think. We regrouped and battled together against the two enemies with the refined skill of warriors who spent day after long day fighting beside one another.

I breathed heavily as I caught Lote's eye through the middle of the battle. These assholes would not have reign of my world. We would show them the might of our Skia Hellig.

One of the attacker's swords wedged between Nash and me, skimming my shoulder and Nash's bicep in a spray of blood. It forced us in opposite directions to avoid the sawing motion of the blade. I tossed a wave of force at the man while Nash countered with an upward swing of his twin swords.

Our enemy staggered backward, but the one on the right took advantage of our scrambled position and blasted me with a ball of power. The heat hit me first, burning my forearms as it crashed into my sword. I swung and sliced the ball in half, the energy singeing the sides of my body.

I couldn't feel the pain because of the adrenaline rushing through my body and the sensory overload of fighting against such immense power.

Nash barreled for the warrior attacking me, taking him by surprise by slamming directly into him. It was brazen and left him open to an attack, but it gave me the opportunity to rip my bow from my back. Opting to reserve my energy, I used my physical arrows and shielded them with power as I peeled them off rapidly.

The warriors glowed golden as they batted away the arrows with their swords. Nash caught one man's forearm with his sword and cut it open at the elbow, cleaving his flesh from his bones.

Another woman twisted in our direction, lobbing a shot of energy at Nash. It burst through the shield Piercey erected, hit Nash in the chest, and threw him onto the ground. He slid against my legs.

I roared his name as I teleported to the woman and skewered her with my sword, shocked that she hadn't successfully shielded herself from the assault. Blood gushed from her mouth as I twisted the blade embedded in her gut and kicked her back onto the ground.

When I wheeled around, the two we'd been fighting both looked at one another and raised their palms toward me.

Nash moved almost too fast to see, fueled more by his own power than Piercey's, and wrapped his arms around one of the men. A strange brown liquid spread from his hand, coating the man's torso. What was that?

With a cry, Nash slammed his palm into the chest and the substance spread over the man's entire body.

The stench of burning flesh flooded my nostrils. The warrior's skin reddened and sizzled, open sores now gaping like eyes all over his body.

Acid.

Nash created acid using his power and covered the man with it. Jax couldn't do that, and he'd been training forever. Where did he learn to do that?

The other warrior peeled her eyes from Nash with a look of horror as she turned for her comrade.

Nash ripped his swords from his sides, his movements too swift for the other warrior to counter. I struck from the side, my sword cutting deep into the flesh of her shoulder while Nash's twin blades shattered her weapon.

The golden power that glowed around the warriors rushed out from her and enveloped both Nash and me. Pain etched into every inch of my body, searing each nerve ending. I expelled my own power, pushing against the energy consuming me. With a bright flash, it dispelled.

Nash and Piercey did the same for him.

The woman spun in a circle, sending out an arc of power. I dove for the ground, rolled beneath it, and came up beside Nash. He grabbed my arms, spun, and threw me at the woman, following close behind. I sharpened my power into a fine point at my fingers and plunged my hands into the abdomen of our enemy. Pushing, funneling my power and my momentum into her body, I ripped through her.

My arm burst through the other side of her body, hot and sticky with blood.

Nash's swords flashed above my head and cut through her throat. A fountain of blood rushed over my head.

I pried myself from her body and stumbled back. Nash caught me and smeared the blood from my face.

"That might have been overkill." I gasped for breath, shaking chunks of gore from my hair.

"I didn't think it would be at the time," Nash said. "She was hard to take down."

I turned and peeled back the edge of the burned hole in his shirt, wincing at the raw flesh beneath. "Are you okay?"

"Fine."

The battle raged around us. A complete chaotic onslaught. I'd never experienced anything like this. With our numbers, none of the other warriors managed to turn their attention to me, even as we finished off the enemies attacking us. At the center of the village, Lote still knelt, sweat dousing his shirt, covering his face. His muscles strained as the glow of his power continued to envelop his warriors.

"Lote," I roared.

Nash and I raced toward him. His eyes shifted from warrior to warrior, each of them locked in a battle for their lives. Lote's nostrils flared.

Nash and I both raised our swords and hit Lote's shield at the same time. My hands vibrated as I bounced back.

Jax flew through the air and blasted enemies with energy while Ash followed his trail in bounding leaps, slashing her sword against the warriors she encountered. It wasn't killing anyone, but it saved several warriors from attacks, or weakened the enemies' shields. Opened them up for attack.

All of Gael's warriors were locked in battles against Lote's people, oftentimes three taking on a single warrior.

This allowed me to focus on the one who had started this all. I attacked Lote's shield with my most powerful hits. How was it that it still didn't feel like we were winning this battle?

Stepping back, I focused on the heat within me, drawing upon my power, prepared to channel everything into a single attack on Lote's shield. Nash tirelessly attacked it with his twin blades.

As I drew upon my energy, I felt familiar power erupt all over town, rippling through the air in aftershocks. Dozens of portals ripped the village open. Lightning flashed through the sky.

Hope surged in my heart as graduates and students of the Sacred School ran out.

Wren and Leif appeared, rushing from the homes in a wave of villagers, ushering crying children toward the portals.

Lote's warriors turned in unison toward the innocent villagers. Rage poured through my body as I realized they would risk their lives by turning away from their fights to target the innocent.

"No," I cried.

Every day for a year I destroyed myself to save these people while the world seemed intent to slaughter them. I refused to fail them now. Any moment, Lote's men would punish our resistance by bathing this village in the blood of the helpless.

I lifted my hands above my head, screaming from the pain of the power burning my insides. Everything I drew out for Lote coalesced now and dredged up something much deeper within me. Power poured out from my hands like a fountain and washed out across the ground.

The air lit in beautiful hues of red and violet. Soft pinks and hints of green. My power painted the ground in the colors of the northern lights, the ripples reflecting back in the sky. It was the same attack that I accidentally used to kill the villagers in my childhood.

This time, I trusted myself and the power within me as I flooded the streets of the village with my energy. But it didn't hurt anyone it touched. Swiftly, it swirled as I sought out the unknown energy invading this village and threatening my people.

My friends urged the villagers through the portals as my power continued to grow on the streets. Children climbed into the dark ovals, pushed along by their mothers and fathers.

And each time I felt a person I didn't recognize, the rushing waters of my power tangled around their body and consumed their forms.

The screams that echoed through the village no longer belonged to those of children or frightened families, but of warriors who never had to reckon with lethal power before.

My eyes rolled up into the back of my head as I abandoned all of my senses except for seeking out Lote's warriors.

I struck mercilessly.

The screams grew and echoed in the night, out of control and every bit as desperate as those of the villagers I had once slain so many years ago. I heard my nightmares repeating all around me. But I didn't stop. I didn't apologize. I didn't hesitate.

I destroyed our invaders.

These warriors did not die as easily as the villagers. I opened my eyes to see dozens of warriors suspended in the air, straining against the immense power that tried to rip their bones out of their bodies.

Lote knelt untouched with the current of my power crashing against his shield in a perfect untouched circle surrounding him. He fired beam after beam at me, but all of my allies faced us, combining their power to defend me.

We fought together as one as my power that once erupted entirely out of my control now targeted those I commanded it to kill. It was the power that earned me the name Eclipse. A power so great that it must have been stolen from the sun. And it belonged not only to me, but to my people. It was now the power of the Valley. Of our kingdom.

My scream scraped along my throat and strained my neck. Bones shattered in sync with my cries.

I collapsed onto my knees as the beautiful green and violet waves of my power dissipated, and the dimness of the midnight sun settled over us once more. Nash dropped down and caught me in his arms as I fell to the side.

I had spent every ounce of energy I possessed.

Bodies began to fall to the ground. Nash pushed my hair back from my face and propped me up against him as I watched the broken warriors hit the dirt.

I wasn't sure how many I'd killed. Some rose to their feet, battered, but alive. Others wept on the ground, unable to rise.

Plenty lay still, reduced to sacks of flesh and caved-in heads.

Ashton turned and looked at me with grave eyes.

All this and still Lote remained beneath his stubborn shield. His voice trembled as he cried out. "How did you do that?"

Truth was, I didn't know. What if one day I figured out how to draw that power out of me without relying upon such deep desperation? I could scarcely imagine.

And what was I supposed to do now? I'd helped the villagers escape and had significantly hurt the enemy force, but it left me with nothing. I didn't know if I could stand again, much less fight.

"You did well," Nash said, holding me tight. "Breathe."

I did as he said, my throat burning from my screams. The pull of sleep gripped me so fiercely I barely resisted it.

Lote stalked closer, protected by his shield, as the portals snapped shut. Gael's warriors surrounded the enemies left strewn about the village.

"You're still going to fight after what you saw?" Elias asked him.

Our enemy cast his eyes to his fallen warriors and then back to me. "This Eclipse monster must die. We cannot leave you alive, wondering when you'll return to our world. Wondering when you'll seek your justice."

I breathed hard. "And I cannot wait around wondering when you'll return to take what doesn't belong to you."

"Then we have an understanding."

"You can't win," Ashton said. "Look at your people. We'll kill them all at this rate. We'll kill you, too."

"She can't even sit up," Lote said. "You're all exhausting yourself."

"So are you." I pushed against Nash to straighten. "Your shield is losing strength. Do you really think you can win at this rate? You won't even have the power to return to your world." I looked around at the warriors remaining. "Do you even have the strength to take everyone home? Or will you abandon your people here?"

Ashton gasped. "You son of a bitch. You don't care what happens to them, do you?"

"If he wants to die here," I said, "let him."

Lote needed to run for his life if he hoped to survive. What did he have to return to, though? If he couldn't defeat us in a world with a fraction of that power of his, he must have realized that he wouldn't win back home either. He must have realized that he needed to rob us of our land and resources to return with an advantage.

As exhausted as we all were, we held the clear advantage now. Our numbers protected us from slaughter. Without my last attack, we might have fallen, but I had weakened Lote's forces enough that I felt certain of victory.

He was delusional if he thought he stood a chance.

I had the people necessary to protect my Valley and my world. Gael and his warriors were the allies that I desperately needed. They protected the Valley while I was gone, and even when they could have turned on us, they didn't. They were serious about our partnership.

And everyone else here, all the students, the graduates, the handful of helpful demons I recognized—they joined forces with us and together made us unstoppable. The warriors filled the village like the sea of power I just unleashed. Having all of these people united together to face this threat from another world gave me the peace that I needed to believe that we would win this battle, even if I spent my energy saving the villagers.

And then maybe we'd end the war that we waged for the past year with the Flatlanders and that mysterious cult.

I did not need to fight every single battle.

Lote's upper lip curled. "I can't let you win."

The arrogance and stubbornness of a power-hungry man.

While Lote used his power to tether his people together, we shared a stronger bond, forged in something much greater than the quantum energy of our neural implants.

"Now," I said. "Focus on Lote."

CHAPTER FORTY-ONE

Light like the morning sun dawned over the battered village, empty of its people and bright with the clashing power of my allies and our enemy.

I found the strength to stand before Lote and look into his eyes as the army, at my command, lambasted his shield with an onslaught of powerful attacks. As his warriors fought to defend him, I didn't even glance at them. My people felled one after the next. I watched the stubbornness and arrogance born of the lust for power wilt in Lote's eyes, as the realization tore through his determination.

He would die today.

Was this how a battle between leaders needed to be waged? My people fighting against his people. Our power lent to them. I wanted to kill him with my own hands, to submerge my gunky, bloody arm deep in his body like I did to his warrior.

I'd given every drop of strength I possessed for this village, though. And I took satisfaction in standing here, watching Lote's demise unfold slowly and decisively.

Elias worked fervently to hack into Lote's shield and render it inert. Lote's shoulders slumped as the golden hue of his power grew pale.

I lowered to the ground in front of him. His shield shrank, close to his body now. My breath wafted against it.

"You won't surrender," I said.

"Never." He growled, his previously unflappable demeanor utterly shattered.

"Not even to save your warriors?"

The defiance in his glare answered for him. Sad.

"I can hold up for days," Lote said. "My machines strengthen me. What about your warriors? Don't be so certain of yourself."

I didn't need to respond, because the once-bright gold barely shimmered now as the attacks on his shield continued.

Hatred burned in Lote's eyes. "I won't die to a bitch like you."

Nash raised his twin swords above his head and stabbed them against the shield. Sparks flew. With one blade pointed between Lote's eyes, Nash spoke in a low rumble. "Speak to her again and I'll ensure your death is slow."

I touched Nash's arm. His sword hovered in the air, aimed at Lote for another several seconds. He lowered it slowly.

Elias clapped his hands. "Yes."

In an instant, the shield vanished.

Lote's head slowly fell.

"Bind his power," I said. Rising to my feet, I turned in a full circle. "Your battle is finished. Stand down."

Lote's warriors lowered their weapons. They knew, and at this point defying me only stoked my anger.

Piercey and his graduates gathered in a semicircle around Lote with their hands extended. The vine tattoos dimmed until the glow ceased entirely.

Ashton walked forward and stopped beside me, staring at Lote.

"Ashton . . ." Lote lifted his bloody hand with the exposed metal and looked at her pleadingly.

"You won't kill anyone else ever again," Ashton said. "You're done. There's no excuse for the crimes you committed."

"Do you understand what will happen to our guild?" Lote turned his palm up, as though she might actually take his hand. "This feud will only deepen until one guild comes out on top. It should be us. They need me to come home and help them survive."

"I'm done hearing you talk," she said. "This world showed me what happens when you kill your overlords with no one prepared to clean up the mess. We're going to catch our Valley before it falls."

At least our mistakes here helped us in another world.

Ashton raised her voice. "This is for Elias's parents and everyone in our guild you hurt. For deceiving me."

She gripped Lote's hair, her expression unflinching and unapologetic as she looked into his eyes and set the sharp blade against his throat.

"You won't," Lote said. "I made you who you are."

Ashton sliced her blade along his throat, opening it in a gaping, bloody smile. The life spilled out from him.

Lote looked shocked. Terrified. Unable to believe that Ash, whom he conditioned to follow him, did this to him, even after seeing her fight against him.

"You should never have assumed that your power over me would be so great that I'd stop thinking for myself." Ashton glanced down the blood pooling at the nape of his neck, washing over his collarbone. "I'm ashamed that it took me as long as it did, but you overestimated yourself."

His lips moved wordlessly, opening and closing like a fish stranded on the beach, searching for water. He couldn't say a word.

"It should be Elias killing you now for his parents." She released her hold on him and turned around before his body hit the ground. I stepped aside to let her walk past.

Ashton left Lote bleeding on the ground without even stopping to see him die. Her attention went to Elias, who had spent years struggling with his grief over the death of his parents. I watched as Lote's body gave the final twitches and his vacant eyes lost their life.

I felt no pity for this man.

His remaining warriors stared down at his corpse.

"I've learned the cost of taking prisoners," I said. "Your world has a place for you. If Elias is willing to take you back, you can go with him straight to your prison."

They said nothing.

"Flinch wrong and we will kill you," I said.

I felt faint as I surveyed the warriors, taking stock of the injuries and searching for casualties. Nash moved behind me with an arm around me, supporting me. Part of me wondered if I shouldn't let myself look weak, but I didn't push him away. I needed him and I refused to hide that from my kingdom. I did not rule alone, or at the expense of my people like Lote.

"Eclipse," Gael said. "We'll search the town and ensure there's no villagers remaining or injured."

"Thank you."

From the sound of respect in his voice, I didn't think anyone looked down on me for struggling to stand. Seeing my power wash over the streets and slaughter Lote's forces surely left its mark. Gael's men began to disperse when I felt a strange sensation.

It reminded me of the day I'd first seen Flare. When her eyes locked on me through the crowd.

I froze at the chills prickling my skin.

Two people walked toward us from a house. A tall man wearing a long, black robe, and a young woman. Everyone halted as I took a single step forward.

What now?

"Prophet Eclipse," the man said in a low, strangely soothing voice. "It's a pleasure to formally meet you."

"Introduce yourself," I said.

"My name is not important." Large, gray eyes set beneath a thick, defined brow stared back at me. He carried no weapons while the young woman beside him wore full armor with a sword, a spear, and a bow and arrow.

"Are you the one who's been attacking my people this year?" I lacked the power to muster an energy sword, so I ripped my steel blade from my side. Nash did the same.

"No." The stranger watched me impassively. "I've simply been an observer. If you want to ask questions about the attacks, you'll have to speak with her."

He looked down at the young woman at his side. As calm as he looked, the girl beside him appeared terrified in equal, opposite measure. "I need to leave," she said. "I don't think we should talk."

"You're not going anywhere." I scowled. "I want to know who you people are."

Wait. I recognized this girl. I'd fought her before and released her back at the cabin. A demon.

I gripped my weapon tighter. "I remember you. How long have you been here?"

Her face looked ashen. "Long enough. We never stood a chance, did we?"

"Who is we? Are you with the Flatlander Prophet?"

"No." She looked around at the haggard warriors. "We fought alongside him, but we're not his."

The cult. "Who's your leader, then?"

She shook her head. "Please, Eclipse. Understand that I cannot say."

"I don't want to hurt you," I said. "That's why I sent you to the cabin in the first place. If you leave my kingdom alone, I won't fight you. You don't have to be scared."

"I do have to be scared," she said. "They won't give up, even if you think they have. When I tell them about the power I witnessed today, they may retreat, but they'll be back. Either I fight with them and die against you, or I betray them and they do worse than kill me."

"We can protect you," Piercey said.

She laughed loudly. "You can't. You should let me go, though. If I tell them what I saw, they'll know that we aren't strong enough to win right now."

"How are we supposed to know that you aren't going to bring them back to fight while Eclipse is weak?" Gael asked.

"Because you don't need her to beat us," the girl said. "Look at yourselves. Look at all these people you have. I revealed myself as a favor to you, so you can know."

"Know what, exactly?" I asked.

"Know that there's the chance for a season of peace. Know that it won't last forever. Know that today's hope is tomorrow's demise."

"I'm not listening to that weird shit." I pointed my sword at her face. It quivered from my exhaustion, but that didn't stop the fear from tightening her expression. "Say it plainly."

She breathed out slowly. "I've watched you sacrifice for these people for a year, and I know you'll die to save them. I've said too much already. I just wanted to extend grace, because you deserve peace after all I've seen. After you spared my life."

I managed to take one shaky step forward. "If you care, then ally with us. You can return to your people but report back to me. I'll offer you my protection. You see what it's worth."

She smiled sadly. "Don't tell them I talked to you like this. Just remember me if you're willing. When the time comes, maybe you can send me back to the cabin. It would be a nice place to die at least."

What was this girl saying? "If you're this afraid of us and know that your group can't win right now, then why don't you trust us to protect you? We'll defeat them before they get stronger."

"Because you're the kind of person who lets their enemies live and they aren't. Your strength cannot protect me against their savagery. You just don't think the way they do."

"What do they want?" I asked.

"They want to defeat Eclipse, the most powerful demon in the world. The killer of gods. They'll be even more eager to beat the Prophet Eclipse.

They do not want scraps of the gods' power. They want it all. They want to consume your soul."

A cold feeling gripped my chest.

"Maybe we should take her back to the school," Gael said.

"No," I said. "Let her tell them what she saw." Every ounce of anger and exhaustion I'd felt over this past year, the desperation of missing Elsie's performance, filled me now. "Let her tell them that this is my Valley, and I will slaughter anyone who stands against my people." I spoke the words so loudly that it vibrated in my bones. "Let them hear of their fate." I glowered. "No matter what you may think, I will win. You tell them that."

The girl stumbled back, looking around at everyone who watched her, and then began to sprint away.

I let her go.

"Track her," I said, casting a glance to Piercey. "I want someone watching her at all times until I say otherwise."

"I don't like this," Nash said.

"I think we should kill her." Leif rubbed his shoulder, close to us now. "Or take her captive."

"She's afraid," I said. "They should see the fear."

I walked forward, feeling a little stronger, and stared at the man who quietly watched the encounter with the girl. "What about you?" I asked. "Will you report back as well?"

"I told you I've been with them as an observer. I wanted to see."

"See what?"

His eyes scanned the crowd of warriors carefully and methodically, then his gaze settled on the row of Lote's surviving lackeys. "Seven remain from the other world."

He flicked his finger.

Blood erupted from the chest of a man at the end of the line. It happened so quickly that the man didn't seem to register the wound. He looked down at the dribbling blood, his face twisting with surprise. And then he dropped to the ground like a rock.

Blood burst from the chest of the next invaders in the same exact spot. With an even tempo, the stranger flicked his finger and killed warrior after warrior. Their bodies jerked in a steady rhythm and collapsed to the ground in a wave.

Only one remained standing. A scream tore from her lips. She jumped away from her dead comrades.

A cold hand of terror strangled my throat.

These were incredibly powerful warriors who had survived battling against our small army. He killed them all with a flick of his finger. I didn't even sense his power.

"I only ever give one warning." The stranger spoke calmly above the woman's screaming. "This is the warning for your kingdom." Then his cold stare shifted to me. "I suppose it's unfair for this to count as yours, considering they invaded your world."

I struggled to find my voice. Nash clasped my hand and ripped me against his side, shielding my body with his. Like it would do any good against this man.

"Follow the laws of nature. The order of the world is ordained by the gods." The stranger lifted his finger in the flicking motion and the woman fell onto the ground, covering her face. He looked to Ashton now. "Defy their nature and die." The fine muscles in his face looked rigid and as unmoving as stone. "I hope to not meet with any of you again, in this world or any other."

He vanished.

Instinctively, I tried to trace his power to pursue him, but I felt nothing. He was truly gone. Not even Flare traveled without a trace.

Elias stared at the place where the stranger once stood. "It's like he doesn't exist. I can't find him in the code. He's a ghost."

Piercey looked at me with the same mask of horror as the day in the white room when he realized that we lived in a simulation. "Max."

I didn't know what this meant, but I understood it was far worse than the Flatlander Prophet attacking my Valley, or the cult wanting to consume my power, or invaders from another world attacking my people.

"It's him. Isn't it?" The feeling drained from me as I spoke. Drained from my voice. "He's the reason the gods synchronized time."

This was the gods' doing.

"He's the one who walks between worlds."

CHAPTER FORTY-TWO

The people I loved survived Lote's assault on my world, and I considered that a miracle considering all we had faced.

Our warriors defended the villagers, managing to save every single person. The few who came close to death were saved by those in Gael's forces gifted with healing.

When we returned the villagers to their homes, I gathered with them all in the center of town, standing atop the ground still stained with the blood of our enemies.

"I realize that I cannot ensure that our secrets won't spread beyond those who witnessed our battle," I said. "I ask you, though, for the safety of our kingdom, do not tell anyone about the people who look like Piercey, Nash, and myself. Don't mention other worlds. If I could explain it to you, I would. Understand that the mysteries of the gods were never meant to be revealed."

The village chief reached for my hands, and I let her have them. "Prophet Eclipse," she said. "We love our village. We love our Valley. We love this new kingdom. When we speak of what we saw today, we will tell the world about the mighty power of Eclipse and her warriors. That is all."

I squeezed her hands, hating that I asked her and this village to hide anything. "I want nothing more than for us all to speak the truth."

"We're only human, Eclipse. The truth is not always ours to speak."

That wasn't a reality I wished to abide by. Though I now knew that I needed to strategically choose my battles and mind my limitations.

"Our world is safe. That's what matters right now." I looked out to the people, anguished by the memory of the children crying, and by all those who suffered this past year. "I promise that we will create a much safer Valley, and that your children will not grow up living in fear." I pressed my forearm to the chest of the chief. She clasped mine. "My flesh."

"My blood."

The people raised their forearms. "My flesh," they said.

"My blood," I finished. Though this only marked the beginning, I finally tasted the sweet promise of peace.

When I returned to the Sacred School, the healers were finishing their treatments of our warriors. Jax wiped the blood from his face with a cloth and regarded me with a smile. I returned it.

"We have to go home now," Ashton said.

We'd fought alongside each other without any thought of our circumstances. Everything had been too crazy to really let myself feel what hit me right in the gut now as I looked at her. "This is so weird."

She laughed, letting me see exactly what I looked like to the world when dappled in the blood and sweat of battle. Somehow smiling anyway. "We'll come back as soon as we can and update you on our world."

"You need help," I said.

"No. Absolutely not. What you did today will discourage your enemies, so you all need to be here if you're actually going to scare them away. They could attack while you're weakened."

I'd spent enough time in her past to worry about her kingdom and her friends. "What will your Valley look like when this is through?"

"I have no idea. It won't look like Lote's vision, though. He's dead, and his rebellion will die with him. We need to kill the foolish hope of anyone else who might rise up in the turmoil he's created."

"Okay. Go. Don't wait around. I'll see you soon." I looked at Jax and Elias. "*All* of you because you'll fight well and return safely."

"I'm not sure it's wise to ever come back," Elias said. "That man said not to defy the order of the gods."

"I'll get their approval," I said. "At the very least, for us to say a proper goodbye."

"You think that world shifter will know?" Elias said. "That it'll be enough?"

"Yeah. He said he's been observing. He'll know."

"It seems risky."

"Stop worrying." I nodded at him. "Go home and I'll talk to the gods. He didn't kill anyone until they invaded our world, and they're the only ones he hurt."

"You don't think he's a threat?" Piercey interjected.

The question made me feel sick. "I didn't say that. I just don't think he's going to stand against the gods, and I'm confident I can get them to agree."

"What makes you so sure?" Ashton asked.

"Because they would rather let us receive a harmless update on your safety than explain to me why they built a security system into our world."

That quieted everyone. Piercey and Elias both watched me with the same worried eyes.

"Who else would know so much and travel between worlds?" I asked. "He's here to prevent a total breakdown in the order of nature."

No one asked the question I thought they all wanted to know, and I wouldn't answer even if they did, because it was something I could never say aloud when I'd given the gods permission to observe me.

Yes, the security system was a threat.

Yes, I intended to figure out how to kill him.

Yes, if he ever threatened my people, I'd actually do it.

The gods be damned if they ever tried to hurt my kingdom.

I felt like I hadn't slept in over a year, but the promise of rest fueled me.

"Thank you for seeing me," I said, peering into the deep blue of the Collective's waters.

"Congratulations and best of luck with your ascension to power." The waters rippled smoothly as the Collective spoke. After a pause. "You feel discontent."

I nodded. "When we first spoke, you assured me that you cared about our suffering, and you didn't intend for Dr. Henderson to meddle in my world. A year later, I feel toyed with still."

"We have never toyed with you."

I placed my hands on the window, stilling my fear of this god who could crush my entire world—all the worlds. I searched for the humanity buried in these waters. "I want to meet with the rest of the council. You hold fifty-one percent of the voting power. I want my voice to be heard by all of you, not just the Collective."

"It's a reasonable request, but what do you think you'll gain?"

"From now on, I'm asking to meet once a year with your entire council and have the right to request a hearing any time. I'm letting you observe me, and that means that you're watching an entire kingdom. My new position requires more power here in the Kethios if your society really cares to understand my world."

The Collective sounded amused now. "Does it?"

"It's only fair."

"We can accommodate this request. The council will be eager to hear from you personally as you embark on this new journey as the ruler of your kingdom."

"I'm sure," I said. "This must be fascinating for you." My heart began to beat harder as I thought of the last thing I wanted to say. "Collective."

"Yes?"

"Do I need to be afraid that the strange man will hurt my kingdom?"

"You think this is something we can answer for you?"

My gaze sharpened on the ripples in the water. "He wants us to follow the nature and order you created for our world."

"It sounds like you have no reason to fear, then."

"I don't want to lose contact with Elias, or Ashton and Jax."

"You want our permission?"

I swallowed hard, afraid of who this stranger was, and what the Collective might be willing to do to the people I loved. Before killing Dr. Henderson, I learned she planned to trap us in the simulation forever. What that frightened young woman who traveled with the stranger said came to my mind. Some things were worse than death, and the gods certainly held the power to make the unimaginable a reality.

"Yes. I want your permission."

"You've already made contact. We can't approve of you sharing resources or living in the world you weren't assigned to. Or dramatically altering your world due to the conditions of the other. But it would appear that the results of the experiment are already contaminated. If your contact is infrequent, then we will allow it. Seek our approval if you have questions."

Was it a threat? Or a direction? Seek our approval or we'll send an assassin to take you out, perhaps.

When I first met the Collective, I allowed myself to lash out in anger. I had a kingdom to run now and there was no greater threat to my people than a god able to destroy us in an instant.

For now, I would practice the diplomacy Piercey so desperately wanted me to learn.

"Thank you for being accommodating," I said. "I think we'll be learning a great deal over the next few years."

I stepped back, feeling chilled deep inside of myself.

Soon I would see if the rest of the council was like the Collective, and just how twisted this society might actually be.

I figured after speaking with the Collective, I needed to communicate with my other enemies. This time I sent word of my arrival to the Flatlander Prophet first and met with him in front of his advisors.

"You didn't call on us for help," Prophet Theus said. "I heard about your battle."

"I looked into your eyes and knew not to trust you."

"I suppose this is a new beginning for us, with you taking the position of Prophet. Understand I'm not giving up our stolen villages and I won't stand idly by while you grow in power. I've looked into your eyes as well, and I know I can't trust you either."

I lifted my chin, looked to Piercey on my right, and Markus on my left, before smirking at the Flatlander Prophet. "It's hard to trust what you fear."

He breathed in sharply through his nose, anger hardening his eyes.

"We shouldn't allow ourselves to hate each other too much. New enemies may come to Skia Hellig, and we may need to fight together." I watched his reactions carefully. "What do you know about the man who travels with the cult?"

"What man?"

"He calls himself an observer."

The Prophet made an exasperated sound. "I don't meddle in their dealings. We had a partnership of convenience. I only know that like many in Skia Hellig, they want to see you gone."

"I have no interest in your land or in challenging you. I only care about my kingdom. You should consider who is truly worth fighting."

"Your kingdom? A fifth of your land is stolen. I will not rest until I take it back."

Those villages that Eskel supposedly stole from him never considered themselves a part of his kingdom in the first place. I had no intention of ever allowing him to occupy them. "If it's so important to you to waste the lives of your people," I said, "then who am I to stop you? I'm not so quick to send my warriors into pointless battle. But we will never hesitate to defend our Valley. Attack us and your warriors will die."

His jowls trembled with rage. "We're finished here."

"Stay the fuck away from my people." I reached my hands out on either side for my advisors to take them.

We vanished from the sight of our enemy.

I traveled a great deal during the first few days after we killed Lote. One of my first stops after dealing with threats to the Valley was to portal with Gael to his king to thank them for their allyship and discuss how to reciprocate their loyalty and kindness. Though the king shared that he wanted to help, he reminded me that partnerships like these weren't simply for charity, and investing in a budding kingdom helped us both. In a show of trust, I shared enough about the gods and the other world that they had to swear themselves to secrecy, but not so much that I felt in jeopardy of angering the gods.

Immediately, we returned to the Valley to meet with leadership and plan our crucial next few weeks. No demons attacked in the initial days after the battle with Lote, but we couldn't become lax with our security. Our young kingdom faced threats from our neighbors, the cult, and now this alarmingly powerful man who called himself an observer. I didn't tell the leaders that I thought he worked for the gods, but I did assure them that we planned to investigate his identity and his abilities.

Throughout the Valley, the people and village leaders worked on establishing our kingdom while Nash and I traveled to the old village of the former Prophet of the Valley.

I walked directly beneath the hole in the ceiling of the temple where I'd buried the Prophet in a pile of rubble.

"We can't choose this village," I said. "Wherever we settle will become the center of the kingdom, and this temple should be demolished."

Nash lowered to one knee and touched the black stains of old blood. "This place holds too many memories."

He'd lived here for years, forced to serve the Prophet to protect his daughter.

"Do you really think we can do this?" I asked.

Nash looked up at me and gave me that easy smile. When he stood back up, he tilted my face toward his. "Absolutely. We're already doing it. Now we'll have the help we need."

"I'll miss the Sacred School. I never thought I'd be able to say that. When I ran away, I planned on never coming back. Now it feels like home."

"You'll feel that way about leading the Valley one day. When the time comes to pass it on to the next ruler, you'll miss it."

I shrugged one shoulder. "I don't know. Remember when you told me you wanted to find a quiet place to live? At least a day's ride from the nearest village? When we're done here, we can make a home like that for ourselves."

"*If* we're ever done here. People will follow you, you know."

"I suppose I can let them visit," I said.

"What about your village? Could we build there?"

The hope of returning to my people and ruling from there hurt too much to think about. I wasn't sure how everyone would feel about the natural increase in power, at least in the perception of power, it gave to my village. "What if people complain?"

"We have to pick a village. Why not home?"

"Chief Kaid can teach me what to do," I said with a laugh.

"Have you seen the library at the Sacred School? Piercey and Markus are basically living there with their team. It looks like they've been working on these plans for a decade already. The room is covered in maps and drafts of laws and plans for infrastructure. We're going to be fine."

I smoothed my hands up his chest and wrapped them around his neck. "How is it that we're undertaking the creation of a kingdom and somehow it feels like a vacation?"

"Because you scared our enemies away. This is what peace feels like."

"They'll be back." I bit my lip.

"Not before we manage to sleep through the night."

I settled against him. "Are you sure Elsie will let that happen?"

He laughed and ran his hand along my back. "I guess there is no peace when you have a five-year-old at home."

"I miss her. Let's go and never come back to this temple again."

"I like that plan."

My hold on him tightened as I stared at the bloodstain beneath us. "What about that man? The stranger. I don't know if I can sleep knowing he's out there somewhere."

"He never intervened until someone invaded our world, and he said he hoped not to encounter us again."

"I don't trust the gods. I need to know who he is and if they sent him."

"Our world is filled with dangers, Max. Some are out of our control, and some are problems for another day. Chances seem good that he isn't coming to hurt anyone we love this week. So let's rest and we'll try to figure out who he is another day."

"Okay." The feel of him against me soothed the stubborn fear in my heart.

CHAPTER FORTY-THREE

The village chiefs insisted that our people needed a celebration, and that we prepare for a three-day ceremony to formally commence my rule as the new Prophet of the Valley.

I didn't mind a good party, though I worried about our enemies taking advantage of the occasion to attack, something I'd counter with some proactive diplomacy—or rather, threats. News about our battle spread quickly throughout Skia Hellig, helped along by our spies, and by Markus spearheading a campaign to strike the proper tone for our new kingdom. He figured the world could use a little fear when it came to the Prophet Eclipse. Incidentally, my threats meant more than ever these days.

While all of that was fine and I looked forward to a nice time with my people, that ceremony was not the one I knew I'd remember forever. Because I did not feel the most myself as the Prophet Eclipse, or the renowned demon, or even the warrior Max the Sharpshooter.

I felt the most myself in the quiet with Nash and Elsie when I needed no name and no kingdom. No power.

With Elsie perched on the chair across the narrow table from me, I strived to memorize every second of this week, when finally, after so many tireless days and nights of battle, I lived the life I wanted most.

She closed her eyes for Wren to smear the black war paint across her lids and in stripes on her cheeks. Trish covered her mouth at the makeup choice. I couldn't stop smiling watching Elsie get painted up for war.

"Do you like it?" I asked and held up a small mirror for her.

She admired her dark hair, tied into plaits, and the war paint on her eyes. "I love it." Elsie bounced on her knees. "What about you, Ma? Do you want the war makeup, too?"

"I think I've worn enough war makeup for now."

Elsie nodded. "Yep, you and Daddy can't go to war for a whole week. A whole week! No war makeup for you."

Not unless a crisis came about that our army could not respond to, though I doubted that. Gael kindly offered to keep the increased forces active for the next month while we prepared our government, and my family stole a much-needed week to ourselves.

I couldn't believe that after how hard I'd fought to avoid taking leadership of the Valley because of my time constraints, the position actually allotted the time I needed. It changed everything to switch from fighting all battles myself to uniting with my people to defend the Valley together, and to give others the opportunity to grow into the warriors they desperately wanted to be.

Trish sat down beside me and patted the powder with a brush before dabbing it against my cheeks. "I hope you know that I'm here to stand with you."

My jaw tightened as I staved off the emotion welling in my chest.

"I'm honored to have you in the family." She smiled and patted my chin with the powder. "Keep taking time for your life. I want Elsie to grow up with more of you and Nash."

"I'm sorry I wasn't there like I needed to be this year."

Trish caught a tear that strayed from my eye. "No apologies. We all did our best. Today is a new beginning."

At one time, I doubted Trish would ever accept me. There hadn't been time for us to get to know each other, so it meant more to me than I could comprehend to hear her say this today.

Soon the women of my village crowded around us to wish their blessings and feed us fruits and candies. Elsie begged for more, while the ladies happily obliged.

Wren helped me into a flowing lavender dress and fastened silver bracelets around my ankles and wrists.

"Perfect," she said, applying one last coat of lipstick for me.

We walked out to the field, set against the distant Mountain of the Gods, and the woods that were flushed green and full of life for the short summer season. I walked up the stairs to the stage my people erected, and turned to face away from the place where Nash would stand.

According to our customs, we were able to see each other before the ceremony started, but only once everyone gathered outside the curtains that enclosed our perimeter.

I heard Nash's steps behind me. Felt the warmth of his back pressed against me.

"Hi," he said.

My stomach flopped inside of me at his voice. "Hi."

Only a few people entered the ceremonial space inside the curtains. I anxiously waited for the ring of the bell to tell us our people were ready outside. Finally, for the first time since killing the god and the Prophet, it felt like everything stopped.

The bell rang and I held my breath as I turned around to face Nash. Giddy, like I was seeking him for the first time.

The sight of him stilled my breath and my heart, maybe even time. Those curls I loved were full and pinned back so nothing covered his defined cheeks or the gold band around his neck. His close-shaved, dark beard was perfectly trimmed, and contrasted with his bright eyes. A green tunic tied in a knot over both his shoulders was adorned with golden beads that matched the band. Nash looked perfect.

While I marveled at him, he did the same to me, eyes on my dress and my long hair lying over my shoulders. My silver jewelry caught the sun and shone against my skin, tanned from the summer days. He lingered on my dark lips.

"I'm ready to go now," Nash whispered.

I laughed hard enough to draw curious looks.

He let out a tsk. "You always think I'm joking when I'm serious."

"Oh, I know you're serious." I placed my hand against his cheek, melting beneath his gaze. "First, you have to see your daughter."

"What?"

I nodded in her direction where her little hands ripped the curtain open. She leapt through. Trish caught her by her dress and yanked her back.

Nash's eyes widened at the war paint covering her cheeks. "What did you do to my child?"

"Her request. You raised her. It's your fault."

He eyed me again, easing closer. "I think she gets it from her Ma, actually."

I gave the little girl who'd stolen my heart one more glance. "She'll be a fearsome warrior. It was hard to convince her to leave her training swords at home."

Nash chuckled and then ran the back of his knuckles down my cheek, quiet for several seconds. "Max," he said in a husky voice. "Do you think we've ever done this before?"

The unknown grave of our past lives gaped like a numb hole in my chest. "I don't know how long we survived before, but I do know Dr. Henderson can't steal this from us this time."

His lips hovered close to mine, so close to breaking tradition that I'd never cared much for to begin with.

"Not the Prophet either," Nash said in defiance of the man who had stolen years of his life.

"Not Lote or the Flatlanders or that creepy cult."

Neither of us spoke of the mysterious man, though I felt him hanging over us.

"I've loved you in every life, in every world," he said.

"I'll love you in the ones to come."

Nash tilted his head and brought his tender lips to mine, his taste and smell overtaking my world. Our bodies knew each other so well, perfectly in sync in battle, and in life.

A loud groan distracted me. "You're not supposed to kiss yet," Wren said. "The elders will complain if they see."

I wrapped my arms around Nash's neck, and he lifted me off my toes. Unhesitating, we kissed each other deep and full, and with the promise of the rest of our lives, whatever lives may one day come, binding us together.

Elsie's voice rang out in a mixture of a squeal and horrified scream. "Icky! Icky kissy! Icky, icky!"

We laughed against each other's lips and then looked deeply into one another's eyes.

Had we done this before?

When I lowered back onto my heels, Leif smacked Nash's chest and shoved him firmly away. "I can still rip your throat out, you know. We put too much work into getting this ready today for you to piss the elders off and have them cancel on us."

Nash smirked. "You get your power to work yet, buddy?"

Leif bared his teeth in an angry smile. "Ha."

Wren hung her arm around my neck. "I have and I can rip everyone's throats out."

I rubbed my own. "You guys know you can just say you love us instead of you'll kill us."

Leif shook his head. "You know we love you. You forget we can kill you."

Wren nestled her cheek against mine. "Are you all moving back in with Leif now that you'll be in the village again?"

Leif glared at her. Nash chortled.

Elsie ran up the steps and pushed her way to the middle of our group. I bent to pick her up.

"I can live with Rune?" she asked me.

"You want to?"

"I don't have to marry him, do I?"

We all laughed hard at that.

"Really. I don't want to get married," Elsie whined.

I kissed her forehead. "Okay. You never have to get married if you don't want to."

"I want to fight, though."

"Well, obviously," I said. "All you have to do is convince your dad."

"Daddy?"

Nash sighed. "Keep training and ask me later."

"That means no." Elsie pursed her lips in a pout. "It always means no."

I treasured hearing them all laugh, having them all close, because I never knew how long it might be before we got to do this again.

Piercey walked up to the stage and smiled. "Congratulations, Max."

"Thank you." We'd been through so much together. A touch of sadness and worry hit me at the thought of how Piercey may feel, but I chose instead to trust him. This was not Elias, but the dear old friend who grew into one of the wisest men I knew. I trusted him to find his happiness for himself.

Wren let her arm fall away from my neck and then took a long step back toward Piercey. "I might as well," she said.

"Might as well what?" I asked.

She slid her hand into Piercey's and eased against his side. "Might as well finally tell you."

Elsie unleashed the gasp I thought was stuck in my throat. "Aunty Wren," she said. "Are you marrying Uncle Piercey?"

Tears bit my eyes. "Really?" I looked at my oldest friend in the world, all the guilt and pain I ever felt for hurting him breaking over me. "It's her?"

Piercey gazed at Wren and then met my eyes. Total peace filled his look. "It's her."

I slapped his arm. "Why didn't you tell me?"

"It's my fault." Wren laughed. "There was so much going on and this was a very good thing. I wanted to give us time to quietly grow."

The two of them never crossed my mind before, but it made perfect sense. Wren possessed all of the wisdom and grace that Piercey so admired.

I hugged them both.

"I'm not doing your makeup again," Wren said. "No crying."

Our guests began to gather before the stage. Elsie scurried to her mother's side. Rune ran up to her and poked the dark streak on her cheek. "You look weird," he said.

Elsie turned her nose up at him. "What do you care what I look like? We're not getting married. Ma said I never have to get married, ever."

His face scrunched. "Why would we get married?"

"We aren't, dummy."

I smirked when Trish chastised Elsie for name-calling.

The head elder came to stand beside Nash and me. Everyone quieted.

I never cared much for ceremonies before. But if Nash planned to dress like this, then they might become my favorite thing in the world. We couldn't stop staring at each other like we hadn't seen one another almost every day for more than a year. Warmth burned inside of me like my power, or like when I'd first met him. When I was so tempted to kiss him after the initial battle with the Flatlanders.

Bonding always seemed silly to me before, too. Our people could bind ourselves to anyone, but often people only married each other. They were too superstitious to promise even the next life to each other in case they broke their vows. Nash changed a lot of things for me. It felt so true after learning that we'd been together in our previous lives.

Elsie joined us on the stage halfway through the ceremony and Nash picked her up. She lifted her small hand between us like we practiced. The warmth of Nash's amber eyes filled me as we closed our hands around her little one. The elder wrapped the satin ribbon around our wrists and over our hands.

"I bind this family," the elder said, "in this life and the next."

Elsie looked between us with tears coating her eyes. We drew close to each other and settled our foreheads against her temple on either side. Nash's free hand slid tenderly over the small of my back.

"My life is yours," he whispered to us both.

I kissed Elsie's cheek. "Mine, too." Not just my death or my protection, but my life—one I intended to live fully.

The elder unwound the ribbon from our hands and wrists. Nash took it from him, knelt down, and looped it beneath the plaits of Elsie's hair. With a soft smile, he drew the two ends to the top of her head and tied them into a bow. His thumb slid along the edge of her black war paint. "Our pretty little warrior."

I bit my lips together, trying not to cry.

Elsie threw her arms around his neck and hugged him hard. Then she reached a little hand for me, and I rushed to embrace them both.

Teary eyes met mine. "You're the only one I'll share my daddy with," Elsie said. "I love you, Ma."

Falling for Nash took me by surprise, but I truly never expected her. I knew with certainty I was experiencing one of those rare moments of rapture and peace that I needed to remember forever—in this life and all those to come. Holding them both close, I whispered, fearing my voice may break if I spoke any louder. "I love you, Elsie girl. So much."

One big grin, and then Elsie ran back to her mother, already beyond the moment. But she left both Nash and me speechless. When we stood, Nash clasped both his hands over mine, and together we held the weight of all we were promising to each other and to this little girl.

The elder looked between the two of us. "The gods gave us marriage so that we might have a partner who cherishes our best times with us and holds us through our worst."

I thought about asking to break tradition and leave the gods out of the ceremony, until I spent more time considering the truth of it. The gods did create this world, and giving us the library at the Sacred School changed our society as the knowledge trickled down through our world. I could not erase the gods from my life, no matter how much I wanted to.

The gods gave and so the gods thought they could take. One day, I might have the chance to prove them wrong.

The bond with this family we created would last into the next life, and no god would ever break it. This was ours and ours alone.

"As your people, we bless your marriage and your bond. We will honor and protect your unity."

Our people raised their forearms in their vow.

Nash settled his forearm against my chest. I clutched his.

"Will you give both life and death to one another? Will you give flesh and blood?" the elder asked.

"We give everything," Nash and I said together.

He took my face into his hands and kissed me without anyone complaining this time.

Our people shouted for us and held on to one another, celebrating a bond they'd promised to uphold.

Then Nash lifted me into his arms and held me close against his chest. He ambled down the stairs, pushing through the gathering of our people.

"Bye," he said to a chorus of laughter. "See you in a week."

I threw my head back, laughing as well.

"No one call on us," he yelled. "I'm not joking." Then, walking past Elsie, he slowed to a stop. "See you in two sleeps, baby girl."

She clutched his leg and hugged him tight. "Bye, Daddy. I'll miss you."

I reached down to take her hand. "We'll miss you, too."

Trish lifted her to plop a quick kiss on each of our cheeks.

And then Nash whisked me away without looking back on our people.

The chuckle on my lips died when we walked through the curtain and our eyes met for the first time since we'd promised our lives to each other.

Face as serious as when he charged into battle, Nash said, "I only ask one thing as your husband."

My chest tightened. "Anything."

"I fight in every battle from now on."

I nodded. "Yes."

"The next one, I won't ask, because I know you'll fight it with everything you have. But just know, Sharpshooter." He held me closer. "I will die for you."

"Nash—"

"The world needs the Prophet Eclipse. Elsie and I need Max. You need to live."

"So do you. I'll die for you."

"You think I don't know that?" He started walking again. "We're going to have a long life of arguing about who gets to die for the other, aren't we?"

I smiled and ran my hand up the back of his neck, lifting to kiss him with no one watching.

A long life sounded nice.

The wavering reflection of torches danced upon waters so still they resembled black glass. With the cover of clouds, the darkness of the lake disappeared into the black surrounding me. The bugs were quiet here in Skia Hellig, much quieter than where Gael lived and where I grew up. That quiet slid through me like a breeze and gently pushed into the depths of my bones. Settling me to my core.

Nash stared out at the darkness, his face a mask of the ease I felt.

"It's amazing that moments of peace come no matter how tumultuous the battle," I said. "You can be covered in blood and find that surreal second where the sky looks beautiful, and the air feels wonderful. I feel like we're still in battle, just finding a glimpse of peace."

He met my eyes as he had so many times before, but it never got old. Each time was better than the last. Deeper. "It'll be better one day."

"Will it?" It was not a question meant to antagonize. I genuinely wanted to know. "I think we can survive no matter what. We're strong together."

His rough fingers gently brushed my hair back, the soft touch a contrast to skin toughened by steel and leather. By swords that he wielded as well as his own body. "It will. I have no doubt."

"One day . . ." My fingers wandered over the back of his hand, my look and touch searching deeply into him so I could unearth parts of him unknown even to himself. "I want to lie out in the grass with nothing to worry about except for what to eat for dinner and how I'll beat you at sparring."

He chuckled, though the same want burned as bright in his eyes as the torchlight. "Then we'll fight for that day."

"It'll be me, you, and Elsie. And we'll have to make it happen before she's too grown and off fighting her own wars."

"Why just me, you, and Elsie? You don't think you'd want anyone else?"

"I love the others. But—"

"No, no, no." Nash drew me beneath the warmth of his arm and gazed down my face. "Another child."

My eyes widened. "We're starting a kingdom from scratch. When are we supposed to have time to start a baby from scratch, too?"

He snorted. "Not right now. We're talking someday. The kind of someday we can dream about."

It wasn't something I previously thought about even once. We'd been too busy to even start our life together. "I never thought I'd get to have a baby. I guess I can think about things like that, can't I?"

"Yes, Max. You get to think about things like having a baby. We have plenty of time to dream."

"I don't know if I've ever been as relaxed as I have been this week, which is sad, because I'm still really worried about the future."

"From now on, we're doing this once a year," Nash said.

"Once a year? What if we're at war?"

"Yes, once a year," Nash said.

"For a few days, maybe. Not a week."

"You're the ruler of the Valley now. You have to take care of yourself."

"You know . . ." I chuckled. "I truly believed I didn't have time to lead the Valley because I didn't have time to even sleep. I realize now that leading the Valley gives me the time I need, because with leadership comes help. I'm not going to be doing it alone. I'm going to say no to battles I don't need to fight and stay where I'm needed most. At least sometimes."

"I told you that you were made for more than you could imagine." Nash kissed my cheek.

I turned, wanting more while we still had time together, before the rest of the kingdom crept back in. The heat of his lips caught mine ablaze.

"I am bound to you, Max." The words came as a breath against my mouth. "Bound in this life and the next. In all the lives I will ever call my own."

I remembered when we first met, and he said he thought he met me in a dream he couldn't remember. Lives I couldn't remember had played out on the walls of the white room, Nash with me in each. I loved him in more than just this life, in more than just this world.

When Nash and I decided to pursue each other, and when I gave up my fear of dying to the eclipse, I thought that we'd made the hardest decision— to be together. It turned out that living was far harder, especially in a Valley at war. But Nash and I fought so well together.

I settled back against his chest and rested my head on his shoulder, embracing the kind of peace I wasn't sure I'd ever felt. It wasn't that I lacked any kind of tension inside of me, but rather that I knew what to do with it. I could sit with it and not slip away.

Nash and I fought well together. Now we were given the chance to learn to live and to lead well together.

CHAPTER FORTY-FOUR

Though I already accepted my role as the leader of the Valley, the villages were still voting, and everything remained in flux. I felt like I was living the last days of my old life, before one I struggled to imagine began.

We packed our belongings at the Sacred School and prepared to leave this part of our life in the past. Piercey would keep the apartment available for when we visited or if we ever needed refuge, but it would no longer be our home.

We were collecting our weapons from the various training rooms when Piercey sent the message over the neural connection.

Elias, Jax, and Ashton had returned.

Nash and I met them in our apartment, along with Piercey, Wren, and Leif.

Elias stood from the couch when we entered. Jax and Ash already waited by the door.

"You're safe?" I asked.

"We're safe," Elias said. "Our guild is still in upheaval, but the rest of the kingdom is fine. The king kept control."

"Lote's network ran deep." Jax leaned a hand against the wall. "We faced some hard battles, and more will come. It's been a chance for the guilds to talk, though."

"You'll push them to unite." I nodded at Ashton. "You can do this."

"We can," she said. "We're not giving up until there's peace."

"But is there some kind of stability?" I asked. "You really are safe?"

"Yes." Elias nodded. "We're fine."

"Well," Ashton said. "Elias needs our help. The king isn't happy with some of the decisions he's made."

"They don't need to worry about that, Ash," Elias said.

"Can we do anything?" Nash asked.

"No." Elias lifted his hands. "Really. I'll be fine. These are my mistakes to deal with. It looks like the king and my guild will give me another chance considering the circumstances with my parents and Lote's corruption."

He stepped closer to me, his voice quiet and sincere.

"I owe you an apology, Max. I'm sorry." Elias lowered his eyes. "I was floundering, and I'd lost Ashton. Instead of doing the work to make amends with her, I stole you away from your world. I'm the reason our problems collided and all this happened."

I wanted to tell him he didn't need to apologize and that I understood, to ease the pain I saw in him. But I was angry, too, and I resented that he lied to me before. "I'll forgive you. Just stop with the hiding and lying."

"I'm done with it. I learned my lesson."

I sighed and grabbed his hand for a moment. "Take care of yourself, Elias."

"You, too. And congratulations. Piercey told us you had a beautiful ceremony."

Thinking about the past week made it impossible not to smile. "Thanks."

"Where's the apology for old Leif?" My friend fell onto the couch and kicked his legs up. "I pulled a muscle in my shoulder because of this ordeal."

"Shut up, Leif." I rolled my eyes at him.

"I was promised beer, too," my friend said. "Where's that?"

I looked over at Piercey. "You promised Leif beer?"

"I did." Jax nodded toward a table beneath the window that held two jugs of beer I hadn't noticed. "We can't stay for too long, but I thought we all needed a good drink after what we went through."

Nash grinned and moved for the table. "Hell yes, we do."

An hour later, everyone had drained the last drop of beer. We sat on the ground and on the couch together, comparing stories of our childhood.

"How has no one seen me in your world?" Leif asked. "Am I dead?"

"Maybe." Jax hooked his elbows on the ground, leaning back. "Wren is a great warrior over there, though. I wish I remembered her name. I've seen her in a few battles."

"This is ridiculous," Leif said. "What is that lazy asshole doing? He should have made a name for himself."

Nash and Jax belted out the same exact laugh at the same exact time.

"Don't do that," Piercey said. "That's creepy."

The two identical men stared at each other now. "Yeah," Nash said.

"It'll never be normal," I said. "You just have to accept it."

We continued talking until Elias left to use the restroom, and I leaned over to punch Ashton's leg.

"What was that for?" she asked.

"Making me wait so long." I glared at Jax. "I should hit you, too."

He gave the same lopsided grin as Nash, and for one dizzying moment my mind couldn't process which one was my husband and which one was the man from another world.

Ash sheepishly looked at Jax and my heart erupted with all the longing I recognized.

"I knew it," I said. "You're already back together."

"Quiet," Ash said. "Elias doesn't need to know yet."

I tilted my head. "He probably knows."

"Max," Ash chastised.

It was making me way too self-aware to have so much exposure to another version of myself.

"You know," Jax said. "While we're all here and on the subject." He pointed between Nash and me. "Have you ever threatened to kill each other?"

"No," I shouted.

"Yes," Nash said with a look of incredulity. "You don't remember? You smeared berries in my eyes after we had to leave Leif and Wren behind. When you attacked me. There were plenty of threats thrown out around that time."

I pursed my lips, remembering clearly. "Well, that doesn't count. That was before I really knew you."

He snorted. "Wow."

"You were my enemy, and I didn't know if I could trust you! You needed to be warned that I would slaughter you if you threatened my people. It's a kindness, really. If you didn't know, crossed me, and had to learn the hard way, wouldn't it be worse?"

Nash hung his arm around me and cocked his head to the side. "I didn't say it wasn't merciful of you to make me aware of your propensity for slaughter, only that you did, in fact, threaten to kill me."

"Fine," I conceded.

When Elias returned, Wren turned her attention to him. "You've traveled to the other two worlds, right?"

"I have, just not as much as this world. In one, there's no one with power, and in the other, half the people have it. That's the worst world. It's in ruins."

"Wow." Wren chewed on her nail. "That's terrible."

"This world caught my interest because it had been reset twice before," Elias said. "Actually, I've given this some thought and I want to amend my position that your previous lives were erased entirely. Max can't travel to them and access them like her past, however I believe that the quantum power from those lives has impacted this one."

Piercey looked captivated by what Elias said. "Do you think that's why Max is able to tap into so much incredible power?"

"Partially, yeah. She's had experiences no one else has, especially with Dr. Henderson. But if she's somehow connecting with her past lives, it would explain where that immense well of energy comes from."

I touched my stomach, feeling the warmth of my power buried deep inside me. "Then maybe there's a way to recover those lives. We might have learned things in them that we haven't here."

Piercey looked nervous. "It's toying with that line again. We don't know enough about that strange man."

Ashton scooted to the edge of her seat. "I think I saw him in my world."

The news shot through my chest like a blast of energy. "What?"

"Yes, it was a glimpse, but I think I saw him. I think he wanted us to know he really can travel the worlds."

That silenced everyone for several seconds. I drew my knees up and leaned against them.

I had to figure out everything I could about that man and get strong enough to beat him if the time ever came. He'd killed some of the most powerful people I'd ever met with a flick.

"We'll ensure that no one trespasses into your world again," Ashton said. "I'm sorry all this happened."

If they did trespass, that stranger might just kill them.

We said our goodbyes to these pieces of ourselves from the mirror of our world.

One day, I hoped that everything would be set right for all of us.

The first month of our kingdom had passed in what felt like only days.

People traveled from all over the entire Valley to join together for the three-day ceremony celebrating the birth of our kingdom and my formal acceptance of serving as Prophet of the Valley. Despite a prolonged debate about changing the title, in the end the people made the decision for us, because they lived their entire lives having a Prophet, and there was no stopping them from calling me the Prophet Eclipse.

Before traveling to Elias's world, I hadn't thought I was strong enough to lead the Valley. Learning how to let the Valley stand on its own while I left for Elias's world had been one of the hardest things I ever had to do. I wasn't close, yet, to really knowing how to step back. I wouldn't give up, though. I'd fight and fight until we raised up enough warriors, leaders, and protectors to take on any threat. So that when I was gone, the Valley could flourish without me.

Wasn't that the true job of a leader? To one day be able to walk away and watch from a distance as everyone grew beyond you?

I wanted to learn how to do that.

After running away from the Sacred School as a teenager, I somehow still became a Prophet.

None of it felt real as I looked down upon the largest crowd I'd ever seen.

Nash stood at my side, honoring his promise to fight every battle beside me.

Markus spoke to our people in a voice assisted by power. I needed to know him better before I decided to trust him, but the role he played so far proved to be pivotal, bringing the political power and charisma to my advisory team that I required.

"We will remake the name Prophet and teach all of Skia Hellig how to run a kingdom." Markus swooped his arm over the crowd while they cheered. "Our Prophet Eclipse freed us from the brutal hand of Eskel, and shed her own blood in countless battles to protect our families and our children from all those who sought to harm us. It is our turn to honor her and thank her for her sacrifice. Let all of Skia Hellig hear our cries. We stand together. We stand with Eclipse."

The roar of the crowd erupted like a wild beast, their stomping and clapping making the earth tremble. Nash grabbed my hand and thrust it in the air. The people screamed again.

I belonged on the battlefield with my comrades, living in each swing of my sword and each arrow shot. That wasn't what my people needed from me anymore, though. They needed someone to rally around and to lead them through the growing pains of a kingdom that rose from the ashes of a dark and brutal reign.

I wanted to be another person for them, someone born to rule, who had always yearned to possess the power to guide, lead, and govern. That wasn't my story, though. I was a Prophet—in-training turned demon-in-hiding—who refused to allow anyone in any world to hurt my people. So, I was becoming the ruler my people needed me to be. I would defend them as a wartime Prophet and carve out safety and security from a Skia Hellig that yearned for blood. And in the greatest twist of irony, I would have the support I needed to also live my life, to be Nash's wife and Elsie's ma. To be myself.

I expected the most difficult wars hung in our future, but I did believe that we chose a path worth fighting for.

With Nash raising my fist before my people and Markus leading the crowd to roar the name Eclipse, it seemed like the inevitable culmination of a long journey. Like the beginning of the rest of my life. And yet, I sensed strongly that there was more for me than this. That though I did not feel born to lead the Valley, one day I'd embark on a journey I did feel born to lead.

I figured some of the greatest rulers were destined to rule, and that others were simply brave enough to step into a battle that they were uniquely equipped for.

I embraced the name Prophet Eclipse, but I didn't plan for my life to stop here.

Markus stepped to the side to allow me to speak to my people. I imagined that they expected to hear a speech as powerful and vicious as seemed befitting of the renowned Eclipse.

The people I loved—and all I wanted for them and for myself—flooded my chest. I walked to the center of the stage, my gaze sweeping over those who had decided to place their lives in my hands.

I knew what I most needed to say to them.

"This is our Valley." My power swept my voice over the field in a gentle roll. "Together, we have the power to seize our lives for ourselves and enjoy the kingdom we're creating. You're as much a part of the birth of our people as me. I need you. I truly need you all."

Epilogue

I awoke from our third simulated life with Nash's hand in mine, the two of us bound together through time and through lives, and through more battles than we'd ever known we would fight. We'd found one another again, as we vowed to always do, and we'd changed yet again. Changed together.

Once, I couldn't fathom experiencing multiple lifetimes in multiple simulations. It defied the boundaries of my human mind. Now, I held more memories from these new lives than I did from our first. Yet I never loved another life more than the one I first lived.

"Good morning," Nash said again.

I smiled, tightening my grip on him. "Good morning."

We needed time between living through these lives. After the second simulation, we'd returned to our family and friends in the afterlife until we felt rested enough to continue. This time, I wanted to keep working. With every life we learned more about ourselves, humanity, and our mission to protect worlds like our own. We sought justice for the young lives we'd left behind in our first world, when we'd lived to defend our kingdom, and justice for those like us.

At one time when I accepted rule of the Valley and became the Prophet Eclipse, I felt certain I would never face a more monumental task or be forced to grow more rapidly. I was so young then. So young and so naive to what was coming. But it was that version of myself I felt the most gratitude for, because I'd found the strength to fight and the courage to take on a position I feared more than anything.

If only I could return to those days as a young ruler with what I knew now. I wanted to both laugh and cry thinking about it. Back then, if someone really explained what it took for me to formally join the Kethios society and climb the ranks to join the council, it might have killed me. While I once wanted nothing to do with power, resented it even, I saw clearly that I fought much more effectively with it. And more than anything, I trusted myself to wield power well.

I no longer apologized for having the strength to lead. I wanted to finish the fight I'd begun back in the days when I battled the supervisor of my world and the original Prophet of the Valley.

Nash and I left Dr. Drake behind and traveled to a different sphere of the afterlife than the one where our family lived.

"Think they're tired of the afterlife yet?" Nash asked as we transitioned into the similar, but unique world that mirrored our own.

"Undoubtedly." I bit down my smile as we approached the cabin that looked identical to one that I once traveled to in Elias's world. Ashton reclined in the grass outside while Jax hovered in the air beside her, the two of them deep in conversation, their fingers intertwined just like Nash's and mine had been when we woke from this past life.

"You've gotten lazy." I walked across the crisp grass and leaned over Ashton.

"Max." She shoved herself up and grinned. "It's been a long time."

"We were busy," Nash said. Such an understatement. Since we'd seen them last, we lived through two fully simulated lives, one in a medieval world struggling with a plague, and another at the precipice of Earth's flight into the stars at the dawn of interstellar travel.

"If you don't remember everything yet, I'm going to punch you in the head," I said.

Jax smirked and hung his arm around Ashton's shoulders. "We remember now."

"It's your fault we're still here." Ashton frowned at me. "They said they weren't sure anyone could handle two of us out in the wild."

I snorted. "So you let them lock you up here? You've had plenty of time to figure out your escape. It's politics. Play the game."

"I might be a little behind you in every world, but with time, I rise above your highest reaches." Ashton stepped closer, the competitive edge lighting her eyes. "I'll make it to the council before you."

"Good luck," Nash said. "You have a lot of lives to lead."

I still saw myself in Ashton, only it had been such a long time since I thought the way she did. We no longer felt like the same person. Three lives ago, looking at her was like looking in a mirror. Every decision I had made since, every victory and mistake, shaped who I was today.

I smiled. "I'm only teasing you. We'll talk with Dr. Drake again. Everyone has the right to work their way out of the afterlife. It isn't your fault there are multiple copies of us."

"Unprecedented," Ashton said. "That's what they call more than one of us leaving the afterlife."

That sounded right. We often were unprecedented. "What about Elias?"

Ashton chuckled. "He's been visiting with Piercey in your afterlife. They're working together on writing a historical collection that bridges the gap between each of the four worlds from our experiment. They travel to each realm to interview everyone about what they remember."

That sounded almost as exhausting as living through simulated lives like Nash and I did. "I would love to read that."

"You read now?" Jax asked with his eyebrow quirked. "I remember you visiting our library once and insisting that someone just connect with you to infuse you with knowledge."

"It's scary what habits you pick up given the time." I glanced at Nash, chuckling at the thought of the obsession he'd developed in our last life with cooking in space. He never cared for cooking before, but when faced with a decade of eating food he hated, he apparently evolved.

Enlightenment felt possible—inevitable—before we started living through these lives. Surely, given enough time and experiences, we would ascend to a new realm of humanity. Our wisdom and grace and empathy would know no bounds. We would become gods.

I could no longer fathom considering myself enlightened no matter how many lives I had lived. That was the first sign that something had gone wrong. That anyone in the council or Collective believed they were truly enlightened. Yes, I grew more than I imagined possible, but because of that growth, I understood the beautiful fragility of life and the true depth of perfection.

We were still human no matter how long we lived or how much we grew. There were no gods among us. Only people.

In fact, one of the reasons we rested between lives was because it was so overwhelmingly traumatic to remember the pain of multiple lives. It might twist and deform a soul rather than enlighten it.

Nash and I joined our counterparts for dinner, the kind we ate back in our worlds. We reminisced and dreamed. We planned for wars we never knew we'd have to fight.

With Nash sitting beside me, I gazed up at him, remembering the day we promised our life and what came next to one another. We couldn't have known what that meant at the time.

When we left Jax and Ash, we planned to travel to the council to speak with them about the interventions they currently took in physical worlds with data collected from the experiment run on ours. But my heart longed for the family we built together.

"Let's go home first." I tugged Nash down to me and kissed him softly. "Work can always wait, no matter how important."

I held the man who loved me in every life I'd ever lived, and imagined the worlds and lives still unknown to us.

We lived and we fought, and no longer did we sacrifice one for the other.

About the Author

Lindsay French is the author of the Eclipse series, originally released on Royal Road. When she isn't trying to convince her middle school students to fall in love with reading, she's writing twisty science fiction and fantasy. There are few things she loves more than creating complex characters, dynamic action, and unforgettable adventures. French lives in the Midwest with her husband and one of the world's cutest dogs.

JOIN THE FELLOWSHIP

follow us on our socials

 podiumentertainment.com

 @podiumentertainment

 /podiumentertainment

 @podium_ent

 @podiumentertainment

9 781039 491335